THE ROAD TO CANTOR

The Maiyochi Chronicles
Book Three

PHILLIP L. JOHNSON

Black Rose Writing | Texas

ISBN: 978-1-68513-291-0
PUBLISHED BY BLACK ROSE WRITING
www.blackrosewriting.com

Printed in the United States of America
Suggested Retail Price (SRP) $23.95

The Maiyochi Chronicles: The Road to Cantor is printed in Book Antiqua

*As a planet-friendly publisher, Black Rose Writing does its best to eliminate unnecessary waste to reduce paper usage and energy costs, while never compromising the reading experience. As a result, the final word count vs. page count may not meet common expectations.

THE ROAD TO CANTOR

The Maiyochi Chronicles
Book Three

PROLOGUE

Were someone to ask, he would say the unchanging view was the worst part.

He was lying on his back staring up at the ceiling; of that he was sure. How long had he been this way? There was no way for him to know.

Since regaining consciousness, he had been unable to move. Not his head, not an arm, not a finger. Not even his eyes, which were locked in a fixed stare that only revealed a gray ceiling barely brought into focus by the dim light filtering in from the edges of his awareness. His breathing, one of only two things besides the ceiling of which he was aware, was rhythmic and smooth, unchanging even in the time that panic at his helpless state had temporarily engulfed him.

The panic had now passed, leaving him with the same unaltered view and no way to judge something as basic and vital as the passing of time. Thank God his eyes could still blink, though even this was beyond his conscious control. Blinking was the second of two things, besides the ceiling, that he was aware of, and he was thankful for it.

I mean, how bad would it be if, on top of everything else, I had to lie here looking at that unchanging view with dry eyes?

He had jokes.

In his current situation, that had to be counted as a positive. The fact that he could produce even bleak humor meant that he was not yet insane, right? Of course it did. He wasn't insane. Not yet. But he was no fool, and he could imagine insanity on the horizon if his circumstances didn't soon change for the better.

Soon.

A relative term that brings us back to 'time', he thought.

Time was a concept that he continued to have difficulty with. How long had it been since his eyes opened? Had a minute passed? Of course it had. Had an hour? He couldn't be sure.

He was surprised at his present state of calm, given the dire circumstances of his awakening. In order to maintain this calm, he felt he should keep his mind occupied as much as possible. And so, he did the only thing available to him to do: he counted.

He counted his breaths.

He counted his blinks.

He counted his breaths between blinks and his blinks between breaths.

After he had tired of this exercise, he had no idea if it had consumed hours or just minutes.

He remained calm, but he was slowly reaching a point where he thought he could feel the dread at the edges of his mind. Its advance would be slow but persistent, and he feared it would overwhelm him at some point.

That's when the insanity would begin, he thought.

Had it already begun? Am I emersed in it now? How can I know…how can I be sure? And what if…

Suddenly he heard a sound. It was a loud metallic sound, metal against metal, as in a latch being freed. And there was an ever so slight increase in the dim light that came from somewhere on the periphery of his sight. It came from somewhere to his left, the same direction as the sound. And then, as if a switch were flipped, the light increased all about him and the gray ceiling turned a stunning white. Finally, he heard a voice.

"Nurse Brown! Come quick! His eyes are open!"

CHAPTER 1

Those first words had set off a frenzy of activity. The medical professionals - doctors, nurses, techs, and orderlies - had been buzzing around Raymond all morning. He was sure it was morning, since he had heard a nurse say that Dr. Osborne was due to arrive at 7:00am, "about another 15 minutes".

He had been given a thorough 'once-over' by the time the good doctor arrived. His sheets were changed and he had been given a sponge bath. His waste bag was emptied and all the various catheters, tubes, and monitor lines were checked, cleaned, and secured. His vitals were checked, and his records updated from the night before.

Dr. Osborne arrived right on time, as usual.

Keith Osborne was a tall, lean man, somewhere in the neighborhood of his mid-to-late fifties, with his still dark hair showing not a hint of grey, but sporting a small comb-over in the front to disguise the onset of male pattern baldness. By nature, he was not a 'people person' and his gaunt features, devoid of facial hair, appeared locked into a permanent scowl even when he was in a good mood, which was fairly regularly.

He was the lead physician on Raymond's case, having preformed the initial evaluation and the surgical procedure to ease the pressure from a slow growing epidural hematoma thought to have been caused by severe trauma above the brain stem. The trauma, and the aggressive treatment required to address it, caused swelling and edema of the brainstem that had left Raymond comatose for almost three weeks.

Compared to the nursing staff, Dr. Osborne's time with him was brief. His only physical contact was limited to checking for dilation of his pupils, checking his reflexes, and recording his response, or lack thereof, to stimulation of the extremities. Following the brief examination, the Dr. spent a great deal of time out of Ray's very limited field of vision, reading the logs and the updated reports, and conversing with the nurses about his case as if he were not in the room.

"I'm still not convinced this doesn't represent a persistent vegetative state," he heard Dr. Osborne say. "Dilation of the pupils is not definitive by any standard, and his lack of physical response to outside stimuli cannot be discounted simply because of what could be interpreted as a reflexive neuropathic response. It's been three weeks with no appreciable improvement. He still requires intubation for respiration, a PEG tube for nutrition and, by all indications, cannot respond to any stimulation of the senses. I believe we are reaching the point where we have exhausted our options. We have done all we can do for him. It may be time to alert his family. Someone could have to make a decision."

After Dr. Osborne had gone, Ray replayed in his mind much of what he had heard. Two phrases particularly stood out: "persistent vegetative state" and "lack of physical response to outside stimuli". He wasn't a medical professional, but he knew what was meant by these words. They meant he had lost all voluntary mental functioning and, by extension, all cognitive function, and that he lacked the ability to recognize and interact with his environment.

At least that's what he *thought* they meant.

But he *knew* what they implied.

Together, those phrases worked to close the door on any hope that had accompanied the discovery that his eyes had opened. They transported him to a place beyond saving; a place whose inhabitants simply waited for a death that was inevitable and, to the thinking of some, had already occurred.

The only problem was those words implied a reality *that was not true.*

He could feel, hear, and smell...everything.

He was completely aware of everything that his senses were positioned to experience.

He could smell the coffee that had spilled on the smock of the nurse who bathed him that morning, the cigarettes on the breath of Dr. Osborne, and the antiseptics in constant use about his room. He could hear every sound within his room, and many of those outside, including the casual and offhanded discussions of his condition and possible fate. He could feel the cold that seemed to be the go-to temperature setting in every hospital he had ever visited and, even though he could not express it, he appreciated the warmth that came when the nurse was considerate enough to pull an extra blanket up to his neck and tuck him in. In his prone position his eyes remained fixed on the ceiling above but, when his head was elevated or he was turned in his bed, he was able to take in the details of his surroundings, including the relative attractiveness of his caregivers.

He took this as a sure sign that he was far from death's door.

He was alive, with full cognitive and sensory awareness but, without the ability to manipulate any voluntary muscles, he was powerless to convince the medical staff of this fact.

By mid-morning his room had cleared, and he was again left with only his thoughts and his view of the ceiling tile immediately above him. He used this time to reexamine everything he could recall about his morning.

He now surmised that he had awakened from a coma sometime in the night or early morning. Again, there was no way to tell how much time had passed from the time he regained consciousness to the entry of the first nurse. He recalled Dr.

Osborne saying he had been three weeks in their care. Three weeks…

…since the river!

The canoe trip down the DeFrance River with Frank, Doug, and Wendell!

That damned Wendell! He had taken the lead down the river and led them straight to the place they had planned to avoid … the whitewater.

Now the memories came flooding back.

He remembered the warm relaxation of drifting down the DeFrance with his friends in late summer and watching helplessly as it turned into a terror ride through churning rapids and past jagged rocks. He remembered the canoe had cracked and was taking on water. He was trying to maneuver it through a dangerous patch… Doug was in there with him… there had been churning rapids and rocks… great boulders and jagged outcroppings… there was an impact and…

Now he was here, apparently in a hospital ICU, fighting for his life. Fighting for some way to let them know that he still had a life and was not yet ready to give up on it.

But these memories were troubling.

He didn't remember being rescued from the river or how he ended up here, but he had other memories, or so he thought. There were things he felt he should be aware of… other memories… that he couldn't quite get a handle on right now. Memories he couldn't quite access. They are there, he knew, but they seemed to be locked away, just beyond his reach.

****

Raymond spent most of the rest of the day struggling against his own mind, trying desperately to grab hold of memories that remained just out of his grasp. His caregivers performed their appointed duties, and were in and out of his room at regular intervals to ensure his needs were being met, but these brief minutes of human interaction did nothing to quell the frustration that sprang from his internal struggle.

If anything, they heightened it.

They heightened the frustration he felt due to his inability to move, to speak, to respond to the presence of others and convince them he was awake... that he was here. And now, after the shock of awakening in this physical state, to find that his mind was playing tricks on him, too? It was quickly becoming too much to deal with.

What was it he couldn't recall? Why couldn't he seem to remember?

He wondered why he was so obsessed with capturing what almost certainly were wisps of delirium... pieces of dreams spawned by a mind either crippled due to trauma or altered due to medication. He figured they had been formed while he was completely unconscious, so they couldn't be real memories, or even important imaginings. Yet there was a part of him that believed that these memories were of vital importance... a part that would not allow him rest until they were recovered.

He was immersed in his struggle to recall when he heard the now familiar sound of the latch releasing and the door opening. Because of his condition, caregivers were expected on a more-or-less regular basis. Someone entering the room was no distraction to his current state of concentration. However, the words that followed were.

"Hey man, they told me your eyes were open."

These words were spoken softly, soothingly, even as the door was gently closed. They were spoken by Douglas McKinley. Dr. Douglas McKinley, or 'Doug' as he had been known since they were eight years old, and these words definitely got his attention.

Of course, there was no way for Doug to know this as he approached the bed of his lifelong friend, still as unmoving, and apparently unfeeling, as on Doug's many previous visits to his hospital room. Moving closer to the bed, Doug checked the monitors, the connections, and the tubes, before leaning in to examine Ray's open yet motionless eyes, all the while keeping up a running monolog as much for his own sake as possibly for Ray's.

"I was excited when they told me," Doug said. "This is the best sign you've given us in the three weeks you've been up here. Actually, it's the only sign you've given us," he said while continuing his quick examination.

Ray caught short glimpses of Doug's face as he leaned in during his examination of Ray's eyes. It was on the periphery of his vision and, being unable to move his eyes or change his straight-ahead focus, it was akin to seeing an apparition that was there, and then not there. Still, the joy and excitement he felt at seeing and hearing his friend was palpable to him, and caused a brief increase in his heart rate; an increase that registered on the monitor and was noticed by Doug. He paused in his monolog to look to the monitor, look to Ray, then back to the monitor and again back to Ray. Then he continued speaking.

"Do you know me… did you just recognize me…?" he asked rhetorically, wonder and excitement in his own eyes.

Douglas started to alert the on-duty nurse, but hesitated. He moved his face more-or-less directly into the path of Ray's vision and alternated glances from Ray's face to the monitor.

Nothing.

No movement or recognition in Ray's face. No change in the monitor's readings.

"That must have been my imagination," Douglas said, disappointment evident in his voice. "Man, it's a different feeling when you have a relationship with a patient."

He pulled a chair closer so that he could talk to Ray in more intimate tones… talking to his friend… talking to himself.

"I guess that's why they discourage us from treating our friends and loved ones. You know, I had to beg Dr. Osborne just to let me sit in with you daily. I had to promise not to bother the nurses, or to attempt anything that could be interpreted as 'treatment'."

He briefly smiled as he made air quotes, but the strain and disappointment was heavy in his voice as he continued talking.

"Ray, I hope you can hear me… and understand me. I hope you're fighting as hard as I imagine you are. You gotta be 'cause, at this point, there's not much else to be done by the staff. It's up to you man… it's all up to you. I'll be here for you… every day… and I'll keep talking. Use my voice, man… use It! Grab hold of my voice and use it like a rope to pull yourself back…"

Dr. Douglas McKinley was long gone. Only his good friend Doug was in the room with him now. Making an effort to calm his voice, and wiping away the moistness that had begun in his eyes, Doug continued.

"Frank has Bruin," he said, the thought of Ray's big Doberman bringing a smile to his face. "I would have taken him, but we both know I wouldn't have the time to care for him properly. Plus, my apartment complex isn't pet friendly. Grace wasn't too hot on the idea at first, but Frank always loved him, and I hear he gets along well with their yorkie."

"Frank's been up here a couple of times, but it's hard on him. He's a lot more sensitive than he lets on. He wasn't quite ready to see you like this or to give you encouragement. I suggested, for your good and for his, that he step back… at least until you show some improvement."

"Wendell's a mess," Doug continued. "He blames himself."

Doug paused here as if considering his next words.

"I know I shouldn't say it, but he's right. We blame him too. He's keeping a low profile. I haven't seen him since the rescue. He answered his phone once, but went to pieces right away, crying and slobbering and saying how sorry he was. I tried to talk to him but in the middle of it he hung up. He hasn't answered his phone since."

"Your mom and dad were here, too," Doug continued, "for the first three or four days after your surgery. They took off from work for that whole week. There wasn't anything they could do. They kept hoping you would wake up and come off the respirator. Once we'd gotten the inflammation under control, your EEG continued to confirm normal brain activity," Doug said, reverting briefly back to his medical persona, "but you never came around. You just never came around and…"

Raymond heard a hushed sob, and then silence. After a while he heard two sniffs and what he guessed was tissue being pulled from a dispenser.

After wiping his eyes and blowing his nose, Doug regained his composure and continued.

"Dr. Osborne sent them home after the first week. There really was nothing they could do for you here, and every day seemed more painful for them than the last. He tried to comfort them… the man has got a lousy bedside manner… but he wasn't sugar coating your chances for them either."

Now Ray felt the sheets stir, as Doug searched for, and then grasped, his hand.

"Prove that bastard wrong, Ray!" Doug spoke in a whisper, an intense and passionate whisper. "Show him that medicine isn't like math, where the same numbers always add up to the same result. It's about more than the numbers, more than the diagnosis. It's about hope and faith. It's about you; your strength and your will to fight… your will to live!"

The room fell silent as Doug continued to squeeze Ray's hand. Ray felt the warmth and pressure of that grip, and wished he could return it. He also felt the desperate strength that Doug seemed to be trying to send from his own body into that of his friend.

In that moment Raymond was thankful. Thankful that his friend had apparently been there from the beginning and that, through his communication, he continued to give Raymond reasons to struggle… reasons to fight for his life.

Eventually Ray felt the intensity of the grip diminish and, finally, Doug released his hand, rearranged the bedding, and stood.

"Keep fighting, Ray," Doug said. "I'll see you tomorrow."

CHAPTER 2

Over the next several days there were some wonderful occurrences regarding Ray's condition. The first of them happened two days after Ray regained consciousness and was noticed by the afternoon nursing shift.

Beginning her shift in her customary fashion, by briefly looking in on all her patients, a nurse causally cracked Ray's door for a quick peek inside. To her surprise, her patient was doing his damndest to see who had opened his door. Still unable to move his limbs or neck, he did this by moving his eyes as far to the left as he possibly could.

This set off another round of excitement as all the nurses on the floor, even those on their way out following the end of their shift, rushed in to see for themselves that the poor young man in room 427 was now moving his eyes on his own! The nurses were soon followed by the physician who was on-call for Raymond's case, Dr. Osborne being long gone by this time, and by Doug. Doug had left word with the nurse's station that he be alerted if there was any change, good or bad, in his friend's condition.

The on-call physician, Dr. Tete - known as 'Dr. Head' when she was not around - was an older physician, short of physical stature but with the knowledge, experience, and steely gaze that guaranteed her voice was heard whenever she spoke. She had been a fixture at several hospitals before moving here to be closer to her grandchildren.

Dr. Tete had seen much in her years of practice. She would tell you that she had witnessed miracles, and her experiences made her far less inclined to make definitive pronouncements on a patient's diagnosis without all possible information in hand.

She ran a series of tests, beginning with an examination of Raymond's eyes; testing which revealed that he could now not only move his eyes, but could blink on demand.

Whatever caused this sudden improvement in the patient's condition could not yet be explained, but was greeted as wonderful news by the medical staff. Simply being able to blink on demand presented a baseline for communication that could now be used in other types of testing, the results of which could only be guessed at before. First, it was established that Raymond had control of his faculties, hearing and understand what was being said around him. Then a rudimentary sign language was established, with Raymond blinking in response to direct questions. As a single blink could occur reflexively, it was agreed upon that two blinks would be taken as a 'yes' and three would mean 'no'.

Doug entered the room not long after this discovery, and was surprised when Dr. Tete requested his help in administering several tests of Raymond's tactile response. He assumed she was aware of the restrictions placed on him by Dr. Osborne as a condition of his continued presence. She was, yet she still asked for his help and he readily agreed, applying the shaky reasoning that 'testing' and 'treatment' were two entirely different things.

Together the two doctors worked quickly and efficiently and, after completing an documenting a series of tests, Dr. Tete asked Doug to join her in the small conference room usually used for discussions with family members. Taking a seat next to Doug, rather than across the table from him, the no-nonsense physician began.

"I am aware of the constraints Dr. Osborne has put in place as a condition of your maintaining such a high degree of contact with your friend," Dr. Tete began.

"Yet you still allowed me to take part in his testing," Doug replied.

"It is *because* he is your lifelong friend that I allowed it," she said. "I trust that in a non-critical situation, your medical training would not be compromised by your feelings of friendship, and I was hoping your more intimate knowledge of the patient would lead you to notice things... quirks... deficiencies... little things that may have escaped my eyes. What say you?"

Doug hesitated before responding, mentally reviewing his observations during the testing.

"If" Doug began, "you're requesting my opinion on his cognitive functioning, such that can be assumed from a limited test and response template, I can say that I found his cooperation and responses to be normal for what I have come to expect of him. From a temporal standpoint, his functioning was within expectations and his responses appeared certain, with no appreciable hesitation. Overall, I would say that he performed satisfactorily for what we were asking of him, so I really can't speak to any observed cognitive deficiencies."

Dr. Tete smiled at Doug's decision to limit his response to one expected of a detached physician.

"What of the results?" she asked.

Now she saw a different look come to Douglas's eyes, a look best described as guarded excitement, as he considered the results of their testing in a manner much more expressive and engaged than the typical diagnostic physician.

"If I can be allowed to step out of my professional detachment," he paused theatrically before continuing, "I can state that the events of this afternoon have left me feeling damn near giddy! To have regained this degree of bodily control... a small degree in relative terms, but substantial in how it will impact his future treatment, and in the optimism it will generate toward his prospects for a greater recovery…," Doug looked into the elder Drs. eyes, "I can't lie, I wanted to shout hallelujah in there!"

Dr. Tete smiled at the emotions at play across Doug's face, then leaned forward in her chair as she reached out to squeeze his hand before she spoke.

"Every now and then," she said, "something happens that makes you glad you entered a profession so rife with tragedy, heartache, and loss."

Doug returned her squeeze, a sense of reassurance and camaraderie passing between them before she released his hand and leaned back in her seat.

"Of course, Dr. Osborne will go over our notes and, in consultation with myself, attempt to make heads or tails out of our findings. I have an idea of a possible diagnosis, nothing definitive yet but, after more research, I should feel more confident in at least indicating a possible direction for his future treatment, and his prospects."

"Is it anything you feel you can share with me now?" probed Doug.

"And tempt the legendary ire of Dr. Osborne by discussing a diagnosis with a physician not officially attached to the case *before* discussing it with him?" she asked, a contrived look of anxiety on her face. "Sacrilege!"

****

The next morning brought a new feeling of hope and excitement, with Doug fairly vaulting from his bed in anticipation. He knew that, per Dr. Tete, she and Dr. Osborne would meet to go over the newest developments in Raymond's case this morning, probably coming together on a definitive diagnosis and, possibly, a new direction in his treatment. Doug planned to take full advantage of the situation.

Regardless of the diagnosis, he already had a plan that he felt would benefit Ray while allowing him to participate more directly, if only on a limited basis. Arriving early for his usual shift, he sought to clear his mind and narrow his focus to his duties, leaving his thoughts and concerns about Ray for a time when they could be of some benefit, not a distraction.

He had arrived at the hospital, coffee in hand, about 6:10am and settled down into his tiny office. He referred to it as his 'closet', as it was probably referred to by many of the fledgling physicians who began their careers in this same space. Around about 7:30, he was surprised when Dr. Osborne, followed closely by Dr. Tete, appeared at his door.

The office, if it could be called such, consisted of a wraparound desk that took up nearly all available space. There was just enough room for a chair immediately inside the door which, when in use, placed the door to his back. There wasn't room for anyone else to enter, and Doug had to swivel his chair around to face Dr. Osborne who, while standing in the doorway, was right on top of him.

"Good morning, Dr. McKinley," smiled the senior physician, gloating at the cramped quarters to which his subordinate was cursed, or so Doug imagined.

Barely containing his surprise at the morning visit, Doug managed to stammer a response.

"Good morning, Dr. Osborne, Dr. He... Dr. Tete."

Dr. Tete smiled and nodded her 'good morning', not acknowledging Doug's slip or whether she had heard it.

"I've been brought up to speed about the new developments in the case of Mr. Covington," Dr. Osborne continued. "Dr. Tete thought it might be beneficial if someone with baseline knowledge of him, his personality, his character and quirks, were able to evaluate him and what progress he makes on a regular basis. She thinks that, since you have already been sitting with him every evening, you can continue to observe him while working ostensibly on his communication skills."

Doug gave a quick glance to Dr. Tete, who stood behind Dr. Osborne smiling and nodding in agreement, before replying.

"Of course, Dr. Osborne," he said. "I'd be glad to be of assistance on Ray's case in any way that I can."

Dr. Osborne could not contain the small frown that followed Doug's 'familiar' reference to his patient, but quickly recovered and continued.

"I'm sure you are aware of the necessary and appropriate level of professional detachment expected in this instance," he said. "And any involvement with Mr. Covington will be in addition to, and not at the expense of, your usual daily responsibilities."

"That's understood, sir," Douglas replied. "Thank you for the opportunity. And thank you for the recommendation, Dr. Tete."

"One more thing, Dr. McKinley," Dr. Osborne said. "These are not to be simply social visits. I will expect extensive notes on any activities in which you engage with Mr. Covington, his responses, and any inference you think can be taken from them."

"Absolutely sir," said Doug. "I will be professional."

After a quick nod of his head in acknowledgement, Dr. Osborne turned and made his way down the hall toward his own office.

Dr. Tete followed him with her eyes for a moment before turning back to speak with Doug but, before she could open her mouth, Doug spoke up.

"I really want to thank you, Dr. Tete," he said. "I know Dr. Osborne would have never considered allowing my interaction on this case without your prodding."

"Prodding is hardly the word for it," Dr. Tete replied sternly. Then she smiled. "I know how much he means to you and, contrary to other opinions, I think your familiarity with the patient will be a benefit, not a detriment."

"I certainly won't let you down, Dr.," Doug replied. Then he continued. "Uh, about your thoughts on a diagnosis…"

Dr. Tete's features took on a new level of seriousness before she spoke.

"There is nothing definitive yet," she said, "but the tentative diagnosis is of a little-known condition referred to as 'Locked-in syndrome'."

"I've heard of it," said Doug, "but I haven't done much reading up on it."

"Not much is known about it," replied Dr. Tete. "We will be flying by the seat or our pants on this one… which is why your participation, and your notes, will be of such importance. Once Dr. Osborne was convinced that a diagnosis of 'locked-in' was worth considering, it was an easy sell to bring you onto the case.

"I'll expect a treatment/therapeutic plan on my desk by this afternoon," she finished, as she turned and started down the hall.

"Yes Mam!" Doug replied to the retreating figure, already wondering how he would possibly be able to focus on his daily duties now.

CHAPTER 3

Ray awoke from his drug-induced sleep feeling like hell.

He hated the fact that he needed medication for rest but, ever since regaining consciousness from his injury and surgery, he had such a difficult time getting to sleep that the medical staff thought best to induce it through injections administered intravenously. This was sleep only in the most technical sense of the word. It never lasted more than three or four hours and Raymond never seemed to awaken feeling refreshed. Most troubling to him was that he did not have dreams, or any type of awareness, during the times he was supposed to be asleep. It was more like being heavily sedated than induced to actual sleep.

The lack of dreams was also troubling for another reason. Ray felt very strongly that his best chance for accessing those memories that appeared to be locked away from him was through his subconscious mind… through his dreams. He had nothing concrete to base this on, just a strong feeling that seemed to grow stronger with every wasted period of sedated sleep.

Not wanting to focus completely on the negative, Raymond tried to brighten his mood by thinking about his latest blessing; he could now direct his vision and blink at will! This happened after waking up the evening of the day before. He was sure of the timing now because he could focus his vision to his right and see the large clock on the wall with twenty-four numbers, indicating military time and date.

Being able to move his eyes, and blink at will, seemed like such insignificant things… until he was unable to do them. But when unable, they take on an importance difficult to explain to someone who has never been deprived of such basic control over their body. And now, after just over forty-eight hours had passed since he regained the ability, he was already taking for granted what was old and had become new again. If he could, he would be smiling at the irony of it all.

Surprisingly, he was at peace with his current situation. Though not able to move his limbs, manipulate his facial features, or breathe independently, he still wasn't feeling the dread he imagined as part and parcel of the experience for anyone in his current position.

What if nothing else changed? What if he was never again able to do so many of the most basic functions of living that everyone else took for granted? Not complicated functions like walking, eating, or basic hygiene, but simply being able to move an arm, a hand, a finger… or being able to speak; to simply communicate with his fellow human beings. Didn't that scare him? Shouldn't he be filled with dread and questions about his future? And if not, why not? Had he already reached a point of 'acceptance', completely bypassing the first four stages of grief?

He had lots of questions, and not many answers.

Raymond's thoughts were interrupted by the sound of the door opening, and he forced his vision to the left as much as possible to see who was there. Expecting one of the nurses or orderlies, he was happy to see Doug's curly-haired head peep through the door, glance his way, then retreat. Before the door closed, he heard Doug say, "He's awake now. Go ahead and take care of him. I'll be back in about thirty minutes."

The latch clicked and Raymond knew that, in the next few minutes, the care team would enter. He should expect to be poked, prodded, turned, flipped, probed, cleaned, and spoken to like an idiot... or an infant... or a puppy.

Just be gentle this time, he thought.

****

Doug waited patiently as the care team bustled out the door, making room for him to enter and have one-on-one time with his newest patient.

"He's all yours now, Dr. McKinley," the last nurse through the door smiled. Her name was Nurse Rhudine Brown, a short, slightly plump, middle-aged woman with the rosy cheeks of a Norman Rockwell painting. Good natured, she seemed to always have a smile and a kind word for him no matter when their paths crossed.

The first thing Doug noticed when he entered was that Ray's eyes were alive... dancing all over the place as if trying to look at everything at once.

"Now you're just showing off," Doug said, closing the door gently behind him.

He approached the bed with a big smile on his face, the sound of his voice having caused Raymond to focus his eyes in his direction. Stopping at the bedside, Doug continued to smile down on Raymond without making a sound. It was a smile that Raymond had seen before; a big, cheese-eating grin that told him Doug was exceedingly pleased with something. Having no choice, Ray waited patiently until Doug chose to reveal the source of his delight.

"Ray," Doug began, "today we begin a new chapter in your treatment. Despite the previous reservations of Dr. Osborne, he has seen fit to officially attach me to your team." Doug paused after this pronouncement, as if he expected Ray to shout with joy, then he caught himself and continued.

"The first thing I want to do, bud, is establish more complex communication between us. This is now possible due to your newly acquired ability to blink. Sounds kind'a crazy, huh? Well, it's just that simple."

With that, Doug lifted his leather satchel onto the edge of the bed, reached in, and produced what appeared to be a wheel. It was about a foot in diameter, with a small window near what looked to be the top edge. Presently, the window framed a field of white, leaving a question as to its function. The wheel was set upon a wire frame resembling an easel. There was an electrical wire coming from the rear of the contraption, leading to a controller that presently hung from the right front leg of the easel. Doug extended the legs on the easel and placed it in the bed with Ray, the two front legs on either side of his upper thighs, and the single rear leg placed in the space between his knees. Once he had this tri-pod design balanced, he used the punch pad on the bed rail to raise the head of the bed until Ray was in a semi-reclining position. After removing a pen and paper from the satchel, and laying the satchel flat to provide a writing surface, he took the remote from the leg of the easel and again faced Raymond with that big cheese-eating grin.

"Ray," Doug said, "I don't know what you call this thing or what it was originally used for, but it's perfect for the use we're about to put it to."

With that, Doug pressed the button atop the remote with his left thumb and looked to the wheel. Raymond, following Doug's eyes, also looked to the wheel and saw movement inside the window at its top. The movement soon turned into the letter 'A', followed by the letter 'B' and then 'C', and it was apparent that the letters of the alphabet were being displayed in the window. As the letters continued to display, Doug explained how they would use the wheel.

"We are going to use this to communicate. Using the system we already have, two blinks for 'yes' and three for 'no', I'll turn the wheel and you'll choose letters to spell out what you want to say. I'll be writing down the letters you choose until we have a coherent message. In the interest of time, we will keep your messages short; as few words as possible to convey the thought. And since I know you could never spell worth a damn," Doug joked, "you can feel free to spell phonetically when needed."

"Understand?" Doug asked.

Raymond replied with two blinks, and away they went!

****

As Dr. Douglas McKinley made his way home through the glaring headlights of the evening traffic, he found it difficult to keep his eyes from watering again. The first words Raymond had spelled out were 'thank you'. Then he turned his eyes to Doug as tears began to roll down his cheeks. The hospital room had been silent as the two friends locked eyes with one another and simply wept.

Now in the middle of traffic, remembering that moment, Doug again felt tears rolling down his cheeks.

****

Doug and Ray continued to work on communication daily, with good results. When she was apprised of the apparatus and these results, Dr. Tete beamed! She immediately asked for a demonstration, which both Doug and Ray were glad to give.

Doug began by spelling out his thanks to the Dr. for her "compassion and dedication," and then Dr. Tete began a series of test, many of the same already administered but now with more specific feedback provided by the patient. Upon finishing the testing, Dr. Tete asked Raymond how he was being treated and if there was anything he would like to comment on. With the help of the wheel, Raymond spelled out his one major concern, after which Dr. Tete thanked him for his cooperation, receiving his "you're welcome" with genuine gladness.

After Doug had removed the wheel, and Raymond was again resting peacefully, she pulled Doug into the small conference room.

"Dr. McKinley," she started, "I must again commend you on your ingenuity and resourcefulness. By establishing communication between caregiver and patient, you have potentially increased the efficiency and effectiveness of his treatment by leaps and bounds!"

"Thank you, Dr. Tete," Doug replied. "It really wasn't all that brilliant. I'm sure it's been done before."

"Learn to accept your accolades, young man," Dr. Tete said in as stern a voice as she could muster. "You will find that they don't come nearly as often, or with as much sincerity, as you would like."

"Yes Mam," a properly chastised Doug replied.

Dr. Tete continued.

"Today you have helped me to reach a conclusion regarding a definitive diagnosis. I plan to report to Dr. Osborne that this patient represents our first documented case of locked-in syndrome."

"I've done some reading up on that since you first mentioned it, what little I could find," Doug said. "There's not much literature out there on the subject. What I have found describes it as complete paralysis of all voluntary muscles of the body, but with full cognitive and sensory awareness. There is no definitive explanation of its onset, and it's usually fatal within four months after the patient awakens from a comatose state."

"Then you realize how difficult a case this could be for all concerned," replied Dr. Tete. "While there have been cases where the patient regains almost one-hundred percent of their lost motor function, those cases are most rare."

She reached out for Douglas's arm and, grasping it with surprising strength, compelled him to meet her gaze.

"This patient is your friend," she said, "and now you may be his best chance to come through this alive and with some degree of function. You, above all of us, must maintain a positive outlook, and convince him to do the same. He must never abandon hope. You mustn't let him."

Doug understood.

He understood the gravity of the diagnosis and the slim chance for a positive outcome. Although he could not fathom the strength Raymond would eventually need to persevere, he was committed to helping him find that strength in whatever way he could, and in whatever form that strength took.

Dr. Tete saw the resolve in Doug's eyes and nodded her head in recognition.

"We've got a lot of work ahead of us, Dr.," she said. "I know we'll do our best."

As she turned to leave the conference room, Doug had a quick question.

"What about his treatment request?"

"I'll inform the nursing staff that we will attempt a trial of non-induced sleep," replied Dr. Tete. "We'll give his body a chance to acclimate, of course, but we may have to go back to administering medication if we notice any decline in his physical or cognitive health."

****

Raymond was never truly refreshed from the brief lapses of consciousness caused by his medication. Still, real sleep continued to elude him for the rest of the day. His nurses, always expecting to find him at rest, began to worry when his eyes remained open and alert deep into the night, following them about the room as best they could while they performed their duties. When at the changing of the A.M. shift, Raymond still had not slept, the head nurse picked up the phone intending to place a call to Dr. Tete for authorization to induce sleep once again. That call was never placed as, before she could finish dialing, Doug came walking down the hall toward the room of his lifelong friend.

"Dr. McKinley, you're just in time," said the nurse as she replaced the receiver atop the cradle. "I was placing a call to Dr. Tete for authorization to induce sleep in Mr. Covington. He's been awake for almost twenty-four hours."

"I'll check in on him," replied Doug as he reached for the door. "We're trying to allow him to achieve sleep naturally. It's per his request."

Doug entered the room warily, instantly on the lookout for anything that may speak to an urgent need for sleep in his friend. What he saw was the picture Ray always presented. Stretched out on the bed in a semi-reclining position, his sheets securely tucked in around him, Ray looked to be serene and at peace. Anyone unfamiliar with his situation would easily conclude that nothing could be amiss. Doug had to remind himself that, despite how he felt, Ray could demonstrate little else. As Doug stepped closer, he noted a slight redness in Ray's eyes. Whether this was the result of a lack of sleep, or for some other reason, he could not be sure.

He was happy to see that Ray no longer required the respirator for breathing. Dr. .Osborne had decided on a provisional removal after it was noted that Ray was gaining additional muscular control. This was first noted by slight movements in the upper facial muscles around the eyebrows. The tube probably could have been removed earlier, but to err on the side of caution is one of the cardinal rules of medicine.

Doug could see that Ray's respiration was steady and strong, and a quick check of his pulse showed him to be calm and relaxed. But Doug wasn't completely sold. In some undefined way, Ray did appear to be showing a need for sleep. Or maybe what he thought he saw resulted from his *looking* for symptoms of lack of sleep. He decided that on the way out he would advise the nurse to give Ray a few more hours to find his own way before requesting approval for the medication to induce rest.

This opinion was confirmed when Doug approached the bed and asked Ray if he was up for some conversation. Although even Dr. Osborne had commented on the benefits of the enhanced communication, the equipment set up and the laborious process of spelling out every word made it long and tedious. It could take up to thirty seconds just to insert one letter. Expressing a truly complex thought could turn into an ordeal.

When Ray blinked three times, showing a lack of interest in attempting a conversation, Doug was not really surprised. In a way, he was almost relieved. Today he would be content to sit with his friend and provide a companionship that needed no words. His presence would be communication enough.

He had been sitting with Ray for about twenty minutes and his own eyes were developing a heaviness that spoke to the stress and strain of long days at work. Catching himself just as he began to nod, he cast a sheepish glance toward Ray who he was, after all, supposed to be keeping tabs on. The sight he beheld brought a wry smile to his lips. Apparently, the two had been in an unnoticed race to la-la land. Ray's eyes were now closed, with his breathing deep and even. Doug eased himself out of the too-comfortable chair and silently made his way to the door. There he paused to cast one more glance at his friend who was finally sleeping without inducement.

Careful to open the door with a minimum of noise, Doug let himself out.

CHAPTER 4

Ray slept for over eighteen hours.

At one point, the nursing staff had gone from worrying he would not achieve sleep, to worrying he might not wake up. Even when he began to show signs of waking, they were only a transition into alternating periods of drowsiness and sleep that continued over the next several hours, without an instance where he was fully alert.

During this period Doug dropped in on him many times, twice conducting examinations to ensure that all was still well with "sleeping beauty". The last such check was done towards the end of his shift on the following day. At that point, having satisfied himself that Ray's prolonged period of sleep was just that, he made his way home without guilt or concern.

Now, well past the end of his first shift since Ray had awakened from natural sleep, Doug found himself sitting alone in one of the small break rooms, his mind lost in turmoil.

Before him on the table was the notebook he used to record and decipher Raymond's messages. It documented everything Ray had shared since they had come up with their novel means of communication. The last conversation recorded on these pages, completed about an hour ago, was the reason Doug was sitting here alone, wrestling with the many thoughts in his head, and trying to understand how all of this applies to Ray's now questionable condition.

Once again, he opened the notebook to the place where he had begun writing this afternoon. Once again, he considered simply tearing these pages from the notebook and discarding them. Otherwise, eyes other than his might access the conversation and reach their own conclusions about the mental stability of his friend.

Doug had come into the hospital this morning rearing to go.

He knew Ray would have gotten all of the pent-up tension from lack of sleep out of his system by now and, sure enough, when he entered the room, the look in Ray's eyes told Doug that he wanted to communicate. Eagerly, Doug pulled the electronic alphabet wheel from the case and set it up on the bed in front of Ray. Then he began the process of rotating the letters so that Ray could spell out the words he wanted to communicate, but the words that followed were not light, easy, or comforting. The words he recorded placed Doug into such a state of concern that even now, hours later, he had yet to regain his composure or to fully make sense out of the message on the paper.

"I not crazy," began the message.

Coming from someone else, this alone would raise questions about the mental acuity of the writer but, early in this process Doug had suggested, and Ray had agreed, that he would speak in an abbreviated language; spelling phonetically in most cases, and using just enough proper sentence structure to get the thought across. This greatly reduced the time it took to construct a sentence, and led to easier communication.

The message continued as Doug had translated it: "I recall life after river. No dream. No drug vision. Real memory."

As was their practice, Doug would separate the jumble of letters into what he believed represented the coherent message, then show it to Ray who would blink 'yes' or 'no', approving or disapproving the result. Once a message had been agreed upon, Doug could then ask a series of 'yes' or 'no' questions if needed to further clarify the thoughts behind the words.

Having separated the letters into the message on the sheet, he held up the result so that Ray could read it.

"Is this what you meant to say?" Doug asked the standard first question.

Two blinks for 'yes'.

Doug then re-read what he had recorded, trying to imagine what Ray meant to convey. After a moment he asked another question.

"I was told that, when Frank and Dell managed to pull us from the water, we were both unconscious. Can you really recall the rescue?"

Three blinks for 'no'.

Doug was confused by this response, and knew he would have to revise his thinking; asking better questions to fully understand what Ray was saying.

"You remember life after the accident on the river," he asked, "right?"

Two blinks.

"But you don't remember the rescue?" he continued.

Three blinks.

"You *do* remember the rescue?" Doug asked, still a little confused.

Three blinks.

"Ok, I've got it now. You don't remember the rescue, right?"

Two blinks.

"But you remember life after the accident on the river..." Doug was now speaking aloud to himself, trying to imagine what message Ray was trying to convey.

"We were pulled from the river unconscious... I was fully resuscitated on the bank... you had the head injury, remaining unconscious through emergency surgery, and for almost three weeks afterwards..."

"You've lost me Ray," he finally concluded. "What 'life after the accident' do you remember?"

Doug looked at Ray as if he expected him to speak an explanation. Catching himself, and cursing his insensitivity, he began paging though the letters, allowing Ray to choose while he dutifully recorded.

"Woods forever... No city. No people. Hanshee..."

This message was just as confusing as the first. Doug again showed Ray what he had written, confirming this is what he meant to say.

"There *are* a lot of woods down by the river... and we *were* out of the city..." Doug again said aloud, attempting to decipher the latest message. "But what does 'Hanshee' mean?" he asked Raymond.

At first Ray just stared at Doug, offering no response. Then he slowly closed his eyes, and Doug knew this meant two things. First, it meant Ray was becoming frustrated with not being able to get his message across. Second, it meant he wanted to use the wheel. This time Doug suspected it would be for a longer and more detailed message.

Doug understood, and he sympathized.

It had to be hard to have all these words in your head and not be able to make yourself understood. At times like these, he knew that his patience was essential to Ray keeping a good attitude. Once more, he settled down to record the letters Ray chose.

****

It took over two hours for Ray to spell out what he wanted to say, with Doug staying well past the end of his shift to get a complete message. Doug took the letters and made words, then took the words and made sentences. Along the way, they discovered other little tricks to enhance the communication process, like adding limited punctuation. He read and reread what he had before showing it to Ray for his approval. Ray read it.

Two blinks.

The resulting paragraph read like this:

"Hanshee is a man, a warrior. He pulled me from the river. Nursed me to health. There was no city, only woods. He led me through the woods for many days. He fed me. He taught me many things to survive. He led me to a middle ages city. I was attacked and he defended me. Saved my life many times. We captured. Taken to great city. Still middle ages. Met many people. Many things happened. Hanshee saved my life many times. I was hurt there, woke up here. No dreams. No hallucinations. Real memories. Really happened. Not dreams. Memories. Trust me. I am not insane."

After securing Ray's approval, Doug reread the paragraph again, but he didn't know where to begin in understanding what he read.

Oh, it's easily explainable, considering the medications, the surgery, and difficult recovery. When you think about all the medicine Ray was on, from pain killers, to stimulants, to medicine to stabilize his cardiovascular, pulmonary and renal systems, to anesthesia, and coming off of the depressants that helped him sleep, and all this in addition to whatever changes were wrought by the head trauma. There is no telling where his mind was for the past three weeks, or where it is at present.

Doug again showed the paragraph to Ray.

"So, this is what you are saying happened to you after the accident at the river?" Doug asked, his tone making it obvious that he was having none of it.

Ray's read his friend's tone and gave two defiant blinks. *'Yes!'*

Then he slowly closed his eyes, again requesting the spelling wheel.

"If only I could talk," was the message Doug deciphered, and he watched as tears of frustration traced their way from the corners of Ray's eyes down his cheeks, and onto the pillow that gently cradled his head.

****

Doug closed the tablet, sat back in his chair, and tried to consider everything he had just read, along with everything he knew about his friend.

The fact that Ray was probably one of the most stable and rational people he knew played heavily into his consideration. The problem was that a traumatic brain injury can alter even the most stable of personalities. He wanted to extend to his friend the benefit of the doubt, but what doubt was there to extend? The places he said he had been, and the experiences he claimed to have had after the accident on the DeFrance River... it is impossible for them to have occurred.

He had to face the fact that his friend was most likely severely delusional and needed extensive testing and treatment. He should submit a written report to Dr. Osborne and Dr. Tete so they could be made aware and begin whatever processes were needed to accommodate Ray's altered mental state.

There was only one problem: Doug could not yet bring himself to report what their communication had revealed.

Doug had already completed a detailed report on every aspect of Ray's condition that he thought was relevant, including the upgrades in their communication procedures. He had included nothing that would hint at the contents of their most recent conversation and, though he knew it violated medical protocol, he had no intention of allowing it to become a part of Ray's chart.

'*But why not?*' he kept asking himself. '*Aren't you denying him the help he needs to cope with his new situation?*'

Sure he was, and it was difficult to scrape together any good feelings about what he was doing. But he knew he would probably feel worse if he subjected his friend to the kind of future that would accompany alerting his primary physicians to his current state of mind.

Doug continued to consider his position for the next hour, fluctuating between exposing the new communications and continuing to keep them secret, both for the good of Ray. He finally decided that he would have to better understand what his friend was saying before he could justify any decision to expose him. He would continue to talk to Ray about this, for the next few weeks at least, and see how he felt after coming to a better understanding.

Hell, best case scenario… Ray snaps out of it on his own. End of problem.

CHAPTER 5

The following day was a Saturday, and the first day since he returned to work that Doug did not spend time with his friend. But Ray was never far from his mind, and Doug's constant musings over the situation kept leading him to one basic conclusion; in order to fully help his friend, he had to attempt to fully understand his friend. This meant that, having made the decision that he would keep their conversations about Ray's *recollections* after the accident under wraps, he must now approach him with a fully open mind. He would extend the benefit of the doubt, taking in everything Ray had to communicate about this *life* as it was conveyed, as if it really happened. In this way, he could extend to his friend the sympathy that he deserved, allowing him to feel more at ease and, hopefully, open up more. Doug hoped he might even learn something that could prove to be the key to helping Ray overcome the delusion and come back to reality.

Though this was his one weekend a month off from work, he made a trip up to the hospital late Sunday morning, just to sit with Ray.

Doug always kept the alphabet wheel and notebook with him, so he had no fear of Ray sharing with anyone else what he knew. Still, he was wary as he passed the nurses' station and exchanged pleasantries with the staff currently on duty. Any second he expected one of them to pull him aside to talk about the strange thoughts running through the mind of the patient in room 427. This brought a small smile to Doug's lips. He knew there was no basis for his apprehension. It was only his fear talking.

As he closed in on the door to Ray's room, he heard a sound that made his heart leap into his throat.

"Dr. McKinley! I'm so glad you came in this morning. I need to discuss something concerning Mr. Covington before you see him. Do you have a minute?"

It was Nurse Brown, and she was uncharacteristically somber as she approached Doug, who was now struggling mightily to hide his rising anxiety.

"Good morning, Nurse Brown," Doug said in as cheerful and even a tone as he could muster. "Is there something wrong with Mr. Covington?"

"Nothing wrong," replied Nurse Brown, "but I did want to inform you of an unapproved change in the patient's routine. You see, I noticed while making my late morning rounds this morning… I noticed the patient gathering saliva and attempting to swallow. Well, I took it upon myself to elevate his bed and offer him some water…just enough to wet his mouth. He was able to take it through a straw and swallow! And afterward, he moved his lips as if trying to speak! There was no sound, but I believe he was trying to thank me."

Doug stood there with a stunned look on his face, his mind racing with all the implications of her simple confession.

"I've documented his chart accordingly," Nurse Brown continued, "but I thought I would give you a 'heads up' before you went in to see him… are you alright Dr. McKinley?"

"I'm fine!" Doug said, a little too eagerly, "…just fine. Has anyone been in to see him since?"

"No, Dr.," replied Nurse Brown. "This was a few hours ago. I completed a check and took care of his needs at that time. He was resting peacefully when I stepped out."

Doug hoped the relief he was feeling was not visible on his face.

"Ok. Thanks for the heads up, Nurse Brown," he smiled, before reaching for the doorknob and easing into the dimly lit room.

Ray lay in a semi-reclined position, eyes closed, apparently asleep. Doug watched him closely as he quietly made his way to the other side of the bed and the comfortable chair that was provided whenever a patient was known to have family and friends prone to extended visits. Easing himself down into the chair, he tried to find relaxation while digesting the news just presented to him.

Too much, too soon, was his conclusion to himself.

Before this moment, he could not have imagined a scenario where he wouldn't be happy about Ray possibly regaining the ability to speak. Now he thought this could not have happened at a worse time.

Sitting there beside his friend, thinking about the recent complications that had arisen, Doug never noticed that Ray had opened his eyes and was trying to see who was sitting in the chair to his right. Eventually Doug looked up and saw Ray, having given up on identifying his visitor, staring at the ceiling. Doug repositioned the chair to allow Ray an unconstrained view of him before reseating himself. There the two of them remained in silence.

It was obvious that Doug was uncomfortable. He didn't quite know how to broach the subject he was there to talk about. The longer he waited, the more awkward the silence became. Finally, he decided that the only way to do it, was to do it.

"Ray," Doug began, "I've given a lot of thought to what was said Friday... what you told me about your memories of your time after the accident. You have to understand... it's difficult for me to believe... to wrap my mind around what you told me. You see, it's just not possible for you to have had *real* experiences while I was watching you lie here in this bed, comatose. But I've been thinking, and maybe I need to slow down in my judgment with this and try to fully understand what you are telling me, or what you mean when you say you remember another life and all these people and experiences."

Doug knew he was rambling but could not seem to control himself. He paused, took a deep breath, and finished:

"Look, man, what I'm trying to say is that I'm your friend... have been all my life, it seems... and I'm not gonna desert you when you need me most. I'm not gonna dismiss what you told me out of hand. I'm here today to listen and understand. Hell, for all I know, everything you told me is true and really did happen to you. I mean, you have the memories, right?"

Doug had been staring into the distance while trying to find the words and, now that he had finished, he sought Ray's eyes with his own. Ray stared up at him, his brow slightly furrowed and his eyes moist. His lips moved... just a little... prompting Doug to rise from the chair and lean forward to place his ear close to Raymond's mouth. He held his breath so as not to drown out the smallest of sounds, and strained to catch any words that might possibly make it past those slightly moving lips.

There... a sound! Ray was trying to say something! Doug moved his head closer, so that his ear was almost touching Ray's mouth, and listened.

"...you know... how... crazy... you sound..."

Doug snatched his head back and looked at Raymond's face. Maybe it was his imagination, but he thought he could see it... right there in Ray's eyes. He was laughing! Not 'ha-ha' laughing, but laughing on the inside!

Doug started to chuckle too, hesitantly at first, but with more abandon as he became surer that his friend had just turned the tables on him! He allowed himself to fall back into the chair as he enjoyed a small but genuine laugh that served to release much of the tension that he had imposed on himself, and this situation, since the revelations of two days past. After a minute, finished laughing but still smiling, Doug again looked his friend in the eyes.

"That was a good one," Doug said, shaking his head once more. Then he locked eyes with Raymond. "But is it still true? Do you really believe everything you told me on Friday?"

Two blinks.

"Damn," Douglas said with a smile, again shaking his head. "Okay, we've got all day. I've got the wheel right here," he lifted the satchel, "and you can even whisper... a little bit. Tell me everything."

****

Most of their communication was still done with the alphabet wheel but, interspersed with whispering and blinking, Ray was able to communicate a surprising amount to Doug during the rest of the day. When he finally left the hospital, around nine-thirty that night, Doug was exhausted and Ray was sound asleep.

He had a lot to think about, he mused as he made his way home through the light Sunday night traffic. As he drove, his mind returned to one thing Ray had communicated to convey the depth of his belief in his memories.

"Those... things... those... memories...," Ray had struggled to whisper as he could only make faint sounds as he naturally exhaled, "...realer... than what... we do... now."

****

Ray continued to relate his experiences to Doug for the next few days, usually when Doug came by in the evenings after his shift had ended. For his part, Doug remained open and nonjudgmental, only speaking to get clarification or to help Ray move forward with his narrative. In this way, he learned a surprising amount in a relatively short period.

Every now and then, when the opportunity presented itself, Doug would take Ray back to a statement made hours, sometimes days, earlier. This was done ostensibly to allow Doug to get his bearings, but Doug always used these opportunities as a barometer of Ray's mindset while telling his tale. Checking his notes against Ray's narrative, he found that his friend was always consistent in his narrative, relating the same experience in the same way each time, and correcting Doug when he tried to confuse him by mangling the names or confusing the timelines, circumstances, and experiences.

By Thursday evening, when Doug drove his car from the parking garage, he was almost convinced that Ray had actually lived these experiences, or sincerely believed he had.

Friday morning began with Doug sitting in conference with Drs. Osborne and Tete. He gave an oral report on Raymond's current condition, noted his recent improvement, and passed on his recommendations for Raymond's continuing treatment. It was a detailed report, echoing all that was in the written report that had been given to each Dr., while exploring some issues in greater depth.

What was not mentioned… not in the written or verbal reports… was Raymond's continued insistence that he had lived another life while comatose.

Doug knew the implications of withholding this information. If he were to come forward now, having sat on it for this long, he could open up himself, and the hospital, to ethics charges that could potentially cost millions of dollars, and place his future as a physician in jeopardy.

"No, Dr. Osborne," Doug replied to a question about the pace of Raymond's improvement. "His last breakthrough occurred last Sunday morning when he displayed the previously undocumented ability to move his lips, however slightly, and communicate in limited whispers. I say limited due to his being constrained by the pattern of his breathing. He still displays no control over any voluntary muscles below the neck, and only very limited control of some facial muscles. When he whispers, it is in concert with normal exhalation. Along with his extremely limited ability to use his mouth, lips, and tongue to form the precise sounds needed for speech, it is clear that the alphabet wheel is still our best means of precise and efficient communication with Mr. Covington."

"His limited voluntary muscle control," Doug continued, "allows him full range of motion in his eyes, facial expressions limited to a slight manipulation of his brow, and extremely limited verbal communication and voluntary manipulation of the esophagus. There is zero cervical range of motion, and certainly none below the cervical level. This has been his condition for the last five days; his longest documented stretch of stability since he regained consciousness. Any speculation on when or if he will exhibit improvement in his speech, or control over his voluntary musculature, is just that... speculation."

More questions were asked, and answered, before Doug was dismissed by Dr. Osborne, who was to consult with Dr. Tete on Mr. Covington's future at the facility.

On his way back to Ray's bedside, Doug considered the current situation.

He was confident that his presentation was convincing, and that there would be no issue concerning the content of the sessions he and Ray shared. Considering all his responsibilities at the hospital, he was somewhat surprised that the possibility of Ray's stories getting out was his major concern. Neither would tell, of that he was now sure. As a further precaution, he had taken to leaving the bulk of his notes at home so that no one would accidentally come across them and learn of the things Ray claimed to have experienced.

As he entered the quiet confines of Ray's private room, his thoughts turned from protecting Ray, and himself, from too much scrutiny, to concern over Ray's condition and prognosis. He was concerned that, after a limited but steady course of improvement since awakening, Ray had shown no additional signs of progress for the past six days. This could represent a plateau in the course of his condition or could even be the precursor to a downward trend. It was too early to form any conclusions but, for a friend, it was never too early to worry.

Ray was sitting up when Doug entered, as if awaiting the placement of the alphabet wheel and the resumption of their string of conversations about his memories. He must have somehow indicated to the nurse that he wanted to be positioned this way, probably with a whisper, Doug thought. Doug smiled at the sight of his friend. Ray followed Doug with his eyes as he crossed the foot of the bed and came up on Ray's right side.

"Doing good today, are we?" asked Doug. Raymond responded with two blinks, causing Doug to smile as he commenced setting up the alphabet wheel. Once it was situated, he removed a pen and pad from the leather case, and turned his attention to Ray, who continued to eye him expectantly. Sensing his friend's impatience, Doug triggered the wheel and began recording Ray's first statement. Just a couple of minutes later he sat back in the reclining chair and stared at the message on his note pad.

"*I leaving soon,*" was what he read.

Doug held the message up to Ray and asked if it was correct. Two blinks.

Doug's head reeled with confusion. He had no idea what Ray meant by this. Deciding to humor him to see where Ray would take this, he teasingly asked him, "So, where are you off to?"

"*Other life,*" was Ray's reply.

Several moments of silence followed Doug's reading of this message. When he did speak, it was with no less confusion than he had felt before.

"Where is this coming from?" he asked in exasperation, looking to Ray as if expecting a verbal explanation.

Doug continued to turn Ray's statement around in his mind, not knowing how he should respond. Finally, he refocused on Ray, who had been waiting patiently for his attention, and remembered his friend's limitations. Taking the remote in his left hand, and his pencil in his right, Doug settled down to record the letters Ray would choose.

"Okay," he said. "I'm ready."

CHAPTER 6

It took the rest of the day for Doug to get a cohesive message from Ray concerning that last statement.

This was a normal workday for Doug so he had to snatch time with Ray in between his regular rounds and duties. Sometimes he would be free for fifteen or twenty minutes, but Ray would be occupied. The nurses still had to turn him, change his waste bags, clean him up, change his sheets, and provide all the general care that an invalid patient required. Still the two of them managed to make progress through the day with lunch, and breaks, and down time. Even so, the evening shift of nurses found Dr. McKinley hunkered down with his friend, turning the wheel, and meticulously recording its messages. Periodically Doug would rise from his seat to hover over Ray, placing his ear as close as possible to Ray's mouth to not miss any crumb of sound that might come forth.

So it was that, after the stop and go messaging of earlier in the day, and the steady march of their later session, Doug finally had Ray's 'statement'. The actual words were a fragmented jumble of thoughts, but Doug added the needed letters, words, and punctuation to clean it up beyond his normal editing. After reading it, Ray approved.

The finished statement read as follows:

"When I was allowed natural sleep, I found memories I had only felt were there before. These were not dreams or hallucinations, but real memories... of things that actually happened. Every night I was presented a clearer and more detailed picture of those months with Hanshee, and I tried to relay these memories to you. Even through your doubt, you allowed me to tell my truth.

Thank you.

Since that first night of finding my memories, I have felt something pulling at me. Every night it has grown stronger. Now it is so strong that I feel it pulling at me even when I'm awake. At first, I didn't know what it was. Maybe I didn't want to know what it was. It was weak, and I could ignore it. Now it is strong, and there is no ignoring it, or denying what it wants. It is pulling me back to that other life I've been telling you about.

I could go sci-fi, and speculate on the why and how, but the truth is I don't know. Is it another world or another time? How did I end up there? Did my mind leave this body for another? Or was it my soul that switched places? How? I don't know the answers to any of these questions. I don't know how I know it is real, but I know.

I am being pulled back.

At first, I fought it. I have decided not to fight anymore."

After piecing the messaging together, and getting Raymond's approval of its content, Doug was overwhelmed. He felt compelled to understand what was happening in Raymond's head; to throw his friend a lifeline to haul him back from the apparent insanity consuming him.

"Ray, I know you believe these things are real, and that they really happened to you," Doug said, "but you gotta know that we're in the real world now. No matter how strongly you feel these things right now... at this moment... they are all in your head. This feeling of being drawn back to this life you may or may not have known... for all we know, it could be your unconscious mind giving up, and drawing you toward your death! Man… you've got to fight this! Why won't you fight it?"

Another days-long bout with the alphabet wheel, and more whispering, brought forth this reply:

"At first that life was terrifying beyond description. Nothing was like I knew it. It was foreign and strange. It was lonely, and hard, and savage, and brutal, and it always remained so. You couldn't imagine. But after a while, when the terror went from constantly staring me in my face, to sometimes living in the background, there were moments of peace, and laughter, and happiness. The terror was always there. Every moment I was there, I would have given anything to be back here… in the world that I knew, living the life that I knew."

"Now I am."

"Look at me."

"I lie in a bed, unable to move, unable to talk, unable to do anything that amounts to living any kind of life. And do you know what I spend my time thinking about?… what I daydream about?… what sends my spirit soaring? Not anything I ever did in this life. I spend my time rehashing, reliving, and longing for the life I led for those seven or eight months, more so than the twenty-six years of life that came before."

"When I was there, I had the feeling of being linked to something unknown but important. Hanshee endured the trials and tests, and left his home to travel for almost two years. He was searching for something to aid his people. He found me, and he is sure that I am what he searched so long to find. I believe I was needed there. I am needed there."

"First, I remembered the fear and uncertainty, the terror, the savagery, and the brutality. But now I also remember the excitement, the challenges, and the thrill of meeting and overcoming them. The places I went, and the things I saw. The things I was learning, and was learning to do. And the promise of more sights and sounds, more challenges, more excitement."

"It is not death calling me. It is life… but not like I know life here. There were times when it was so intense… but the dangers all around

us made the smallest of victories a great reward. And every reward seemed so much sweeter there."

"You ask how I could give up the life I have here for that life? How could I not?"

****

It was well after midnight on Sunday morning when Doug finally got home. Still, he crawled into bed with the many notes he had taken from his sessions with Ray over the past three weeks. He read and reread them, attempting to understand what madness had taken over his lifelong friend. They didn't sound like dreams. Reading them, it really felt like Ray was telling about events, not random wisps of thought with no pattern or logic.

Doug's head was swimming in confusion. He didn't know if he was reading to convince himself that Ray was crazy, or that Ray was making sense. On its surface, the whole idea was both impossible and insane. But that's if he looked at it from his own perspective.

What about Ray's point of view?

His last message laid out a pretty convincing argument. If everything he confided is absolutely real to him, why wouldn't he trade a bedridden life as a quadriplegic - or as is typical with locked-in syndrome, death in a matter of months - for a life of excitement and adventure?

Wouldn't you? Doug asked himself.

And if this 'other life' is not real, but his belief in it makes Ray happy? Doug thought.

Would he take away the only happiness Ray has found... might ever find... since the accident? Why? What purpose does it serve to bludgeon him with a cold reality that holds almost zero hope of any joy?

These thoughts and questions weighed heavily on Doug's mind, even as exhaustion was dragging him closer to sleep.

One of his last cogent thoughts was that he would find it hard to live with being the one to wrestle even the tiniest shred of happiness from the grasp of his friend. Instead, he would embrace the narrative just as Ray had shared it with him. It would still be between them alone, and Doug would support his friend to the end in hopes that the end, whatever it may be, would be a peaceful one for Raymond.

I'm in, he thought, as he drifted off to sleep.

****

The next day, at his first opportunity, Doug told Ray about his late-night decision.

"I read and reread everything you've told me, Doug said quietly, "and it just doesn't read like a dream or hallucination. It reads just like you say, like you lived it."

"One of the things I learned in med school is that, as a doctor, I can tell you I see no reason for your pain. What I can't tell you is that you are not in pain. Well, I can't tell you what happened in your head; what you've experienced. I can only say that I don't have an explanation for it. But if you say it's real, then I'm right there with you."

He took Ray's hand in a gesture of solidarity.

"What do you need from me?" he asked Ray expectantly, then caught himself and reached for the alphabet wheel.

"Your support," was the message that Ray's recorded.

"OK," Doug said, as he put away the wheel and his notes. "I'll be in and out all day today, as usual. I'll definitely be back on my lunch break, and I might just have a surprise for you."

He winked at Ray before heading out the door to begin his daily duties.

After the door closed behind Doug, Ray lay alone in his room, closer to being at peace with his condition than at any other time. He couldn't say why but, hearing from Doug that he now stood squarely in his corner, meant much more to him than he would have previously thought. Was it a validation of his sanity, maybe?

Having all these memories flooding back into his head almost every night, he wasn't absolutely convinced he was sane when they started. He still had questions of his own. How could he not? But the pull he felt was so strong, and so different from anything he had ever felt, that he knew something momentous and life-changing was on the horizon. And he knew it was all tied to those memories of a life that logic and common sense told him could not possibly be real, but that he felt... no... he knew... was indeed real.

Logic and reason are in a constant battle with intuition and the unexplained. Raymond thought he felt a smile moving slowly across his face as words from the Bible... from First Corinthians 13:12... sprang from nowhere into his mind and then faded slowly away; *'For now we see through a glass darkly...'*

****

Doug stepped off the elevator onto the fourth floor with Frank in tow, and the two of them started down the hall toward room 427.

"Believe me," Doug said, "he'll be surprised and happy to see you, but don't expect to see it in his face. He's still mostly paralyzed, and can't show much of anything resembling emotion. Look in his eyes. Sometimes it feels like you can read him... his emotions, in his eyes."

Suddenly finding himself walking alone, Doug turned to find Frank standing three paces behind him, staring into space with a troubled look on his face.

"Frank..." said Doug, as he slowly approached his friend.

"Hold on," said Frank, as he fought to regain his composure. "I'll be alright. It's just..." he dropped his head, shaking it back and forth as the water welled up in his eyes.

"I know this is hard for you," said Doug, trying to fill in for the lack of words from Frank. "But you *need* to see him, too. It'll be good for you. You need to know that Ray is still Ray."

Doug placed a comforting hand on Franks shoulder.

"He's still the guy we all know and love. He's got some challenges ahead of him, and knowing we're still there for him, regardless of his circumstances, is going to help him cope. It's going to help *us* cope, too."

Frank nodded his head, periodically sniffling as he fought to control the tears now running down his face.

He had dreaded the idea of seeing Ray in his current condition. Being a sensitive guy, he knew he would have difficulty holding it together. He had reasoned that it would be bad for Ray to see him go to pieces at the sight of his friend. Doug had been working on him for a while now, and he had finally screwed up the courage to pay Ray a visit.

"You're right, Doug... I know you're right," Frank managed to get out. "He needs this... and *I* need it too."

This thought seemed to calm Frank down, and there was a momentary silence as he wiped his face with a fist-full of tissue Doug handed him.

"I'm ok now," Frank finally said.

"Are you sure," Doug asked, scanning Frank for more signs of stress.

"Yeah, I'm sure," Frank replied. "I think I got it all out that time," he said with a small chuckle. "Let's go see my-man."

They made their way down the hall and past the nurses' station, quickly reaching Ray's door. Not wanting to leave any additional time for drama, Doug opened the door immediately, then stood aside and allowed Frank to step into the soft light of the private room. He quietly closed the door before joining Frank at the bedside of their friend.

Ray had his eyes closed and appeared to be sleeping peacefully.

But there was something wrong with this picture... maybe not wrong... but definitely different. Raymond lay peacefully in his bed, eyes closed, chest rising and falling rhythmically, and with the corners of his mouth lifted into the tiniest of smiles.

CHAPTER 7

The cold air from outside crept along the polished stones and plush carpets of the floor, eventually meeting warm air from the fireplace. The two swirled and mingled, becoming one and making the large room more bearable, at least for one of its occupants.

He lay on a low bed, protected from the icy cold outside by a covering of fine sheets and rich blankets, though the perspiration heavy on his brow would lead one to believe he was far from comfortable. Maybe this was due to the constant roar of two fireplaces which the servants had stoked prior to taking their leave.

The other, upon entering the room, had removed his heavy winter robe to reveal a physique clad minimally in a loincloth of soft leather and nothing else. Still, the sweat glistened off the hard muscle and taut skin, marked with the occasional scar, making up his lean and athletic frame.

It was he who had cracked the portal to the balcony to let a cooling breeze enter and offset the heat thrown off by the twin fires. It was he who, even now, was replacing the heavy blankets covering the other with lighter sheets that were no less rich. Having already mopped the brow of the other, he was now prepared to settle back, allowing the mingling of the air from within and without to bring the room to a more tolerable temperature.

Sitting cross-legged on the thick rug that lay beside the bed, he watched, as he watched every night. He watched the others breathing, steady and strong this night. He watched for changes in his facial expression which would tell of discomfort, even though the other was unconscious. He watched for movement, the tossing and turning that had recently begun, alerting him that the strong potions needed to heal such a grievous injury had done their job, and the other might soon be ready to rise from his sick bed.

Careful to move only his eyes, he glanced to his left, toward the thin sliver of opened door that led out onto the balcony from which came the cool air. Then, leaning to his right, he filled a small, long handled pot with water and placed it at the edge of the hot coals of the fireplace to reach a boil.

As he continued to sit, he took note of the temperature slowly falling. He no longer saw perspiration on the brow of the other and noted with some satisfaction the light tossing, signaling increasing strength as the effects of the medicines slowly wore off.

With a nod of satisfaction, he wound the brow cloth around the handle of the pot. The water had begun to boil, and he gripped the long handle tightly before rising effortlessly from his seated position. Carefully carrying the boiling water in front of him, he turned toward the larger fireplace, on the opposite wall, and the second bed near the far end of the large room.

As he passed the slightly opened balcony door, he delighted in the crisp coolness of the air seeping in. He would ordinarily spend a portion of his evenings outside on the balcony. The confines of rooms, even large ones constructed of hewn stones, had always felt unnatural to him. He considered this as he took a second step past the door and then, with the speed of a cat, pivoted toward the open portal and let fly with the steaming contents of the pot, straight into the face of he who had chosen that exact moment to charge through!

The boiling water caught him completely off guard, stopping him in his tracks and halting, before it could begin, the downward thrust of the dagger that had been poised to plunge into the unprotected neck of his would-be victim. The shock of the fierce heat on his face, and in his eyes, caused a quick inhalation, soon to be followed by a scream of pure agony but for the speed of he who wielded the pot. Throwing the water, gripping the knife arm, and clutching the throat appeared to be all one motion. So swift was he that the water from the pot almost scalded his hand where he grasped the intruder's neck. But the heat did nothing to loosen his grip, and the scream of pain the intruder was poised to let fly was strangled in place.

Quickly dragging him further into the room, he slammed the back of the intruder's head into the heavy mantle of the large fireplace with enough force to render him senseless. Then he twisted the knife arm until he heard, and felt, something tear, and saw the knife fall free. A quarter turn to his right and he drove his left foot into the outside of the intruder's right knee, watching as the joint assumed a grotesque angle, tearing tendons, ligaments, and more. Releasing the arm, he watched the intruder collapse to the floor.

Crouching down, he scanned through the dim fireplace light for a glimmer of the blade just dropped but, before he could find it, his eyes caught more movement from the balcony. A second intruder was moving low and quick through the open door, his long dagger held in a sword grip. Rising quickly from his crouch, Hanshee turned and sprang forward in time to meet this new threat.

Blocking the first thrust, which was aimed at his torso, Hanshee took a shallow cut to his left arm before locking his hand around the wrist of the knife hand. This second assailant held Hanshee's right wrist in a similar grip and they remained frozen for an instant, separated only by the fallen body of the first assailant that lay between them.

His adversary was slightly smaller and lighter than he, but with more strength than would be thought for his size. After first meeting the intruder with equal strength, Hanshee allowed himself to be pushed back. This forced his attacker to sacrifice his balance as he stepped over his comrade. As soon as he felt the shift in balance, Hanshee pulled the attacker toward him, while lunging forward and driving the crown of his head into the center of the attacker's face! He felt the nose explode... felt the blood splatter... and felt his attacker's strength momentarily fail. In that instant he again pulled his attacker forward and again moved in to meet his momentum, this time with a hard knee driven up into the solar plexus. As the attacker slumped, Hanshee repeated this move again, this time driving the knee into his attacker's chin, and watched as his eyes rolled back into his head. Then he quickly pried the blade from his assailant's hand, sinking it between his ribs and deep into his chest.

Still clutching the second intruder close, Hanshee pivoted to his left just in time to avoid the blade of a third intruder, one he had seen coming as he was prying loose the blade of the second. This pivot kept the body of the second intruder between them and caused the trust from the blade of the third to sink into the back of the second. The blade was thrust with such force that it completely penetrated the body, protruding from the front of the upper torso and sending a half inch of iron into Hanshee's own body just below his right rib cage.

Feeling the tip of the blade pierce his own flesh, Hanshee pushed the now twice stabbed intruder into his brethren, separating himself from the two as his right hand instinctively went to his abdomen to test the severity of his injury. All the while he kept his eyes locked on the two before him and saw the shock on the face of the third assailant as he realized he had sent a killing blow into the back of his accomplice.

Releasing his grip on the knife, the third assailant saw the body of his comrade fold toward the floor. He then raised his eyes to Hanshee and there the two stood, in the flickering light of the fireplace, eyes locked onto one another.

Having taken in much with his first glance, Hanshee had noted the hilt of the longsword that protruded behind the third assailant's right ear. But, knowing it was there, he was still astonished by the speed at which it was brought into play. The draw and strike were one motion, and had he not taken a step back and stumbled on the pot that had held the boiling water, Hanshee's torso may have been laid open. As it were, he recovered in time to see his remaining assailant step over the corpse of his downed comrade as he drew back is sword to launch a powerful two-handed blow.

As Hanshee had stumbled, his hand found a stool which he had used to brace upon and keep his balance. Now, as he saw the flash of the blade being drawn back, he raised the stool before him to catch the downstroke. So swift and strong was the blow that it penetrated two thirds the way through the seat of the stool, lodging in the thick hardwood.

Seizing his chance, Hanshee pushed forward, driving his attacker back, dislodging the sword from his grip and tripping him over the body of his stricken brethren. Casting the stool aside and following the swordsman to the floor, Hanshee sought a grip that would give him an advantage. But his opponent was almost as quick as he. They thrashed and struggled on the carpet, now soaked with blood, each trying to gain an advantage and put an end to the battle.

As he struggled, Hanshee's mind wandered of its own accord, speculating that a fourth assailant could be entering the balcony door at his exposed back. Twisting his body to the side as a precaution, he unwittingly granted his assailant enough momentum to continue the motion and Hanshee now found himself struggling from below his adversary.

The sweat and blood made it difficult to gain a tight grip, and his opponent managed to free his right arm and reach out, returning with the blade dropped by the first assailant. Hanshee fought to reestablishing his grip, and then struggled to control the knife hand. It was a losing battle with only one hand on the slippery wrist, and he finally had to bring both hands to bear just to hold the blade at bay. Even this two-handed grip was failing, and the tip of the knife was now poised inches above his chest, his assailant straining with all he was worth to force it home. Hanshee worked equally hard to stop the downward momentum, even as he felt his grip on the wet flesh of his attacker slowly slipping.

The battle for his life became a surreal experience and Hanshee's mind seemed to detach from his circumstances. Without fear or regret he concluded that his attacker's strength, weight, and leverage, would soon win out.

Then a shudder was felt through both combatants as sharp iron met soft flesh. Hanshee looked into the eyes of his assailant, perhaps to witness the moment of satisfaction taken by another at his death. But there was no satisfaction reflected in eyes now gone wide in shock.

There was instead a question… and the furrowing of the brow, perhaps signifying a struggle within… a struggle to maintain control… a control that seemed to be slipping away…

As he witnessed his assailants' changing expressions with detached curiosity, Hanshee felt the pressure against his tired arms fading. He saw his assailants' eyes go wide again, this time with surprise, as he felt the strength seep from his arms and saw the knife fall from his grip. Still aimed toward the center of Hanshee's chest, the knife fell the short distance tip first, shallowly penetrating the skin of his chest. There it stood upright, frozen for a moment, before beginning a slow fall to the side, like the fall of a tall tree after the last blow of the woodsman's axe.

Hanshee watched the blade as it fell away from him and then returned his gaze to his assailant. Still atop him, but now with no strength to bring to bear, he had become something to be pushed aside.

Hanshee did just that.

And as the quickly weakening body, wet with sweat and blood, slid from atop him and onto the knife that had moments ago been poised above his chest, Hanshee released a sigh of relief at the image that greeted him.

There stood Raymond, fresh from his sickbed, his body still weak, his expression asking the questions his lips could not yet form, and with a knife hastily pulled from the body of the second assailant clutched in his right hand.

****

Ray had already been on the verge of consciousness when he was awakened by the noise of the conflict.

Struggling to make sense of what his eyes and ears told him, wondering if it were a dream, he watched impotently as Hanshee fought for his life. One attacker was down and Hanshee seemed in the process of dispatching the second when, out of nowhere, a third attacker appeared. The images became confusing to Ray, but by now he was sure this was real. He struggled to rise from his bed even as he saw the two combatants go to the floor in a tangle of limbs.

Ray had been unconscious and unmoving for so long that he had to focus just to get his arms and legs to cooperate. By the time he had managed to gain a seat on the edge of the bed, then push his way to a standing position, it appeared the fight would soon end, and not for the best.

Forcing his legs forward, he staggered toward the combatants, the stranger atop Hanshee blocking his view of his friend. He hoped he was not too late as he instinctively reached for the hilt of the knife protruding from the back of the dead man laying at the feet of the two who were locked in a life-or-death struggle. Coming up behind Hanshee's assailant, Ray acted without hesitation, plunging the blade into his exposed back. Luckily, the blade found a path between two ribs and sank deep. Ray, still functioning on automatic, pulled the blade free and plunged it in again, this time vigorously moving it about before pulling it free. As he gathered himself to strike yet a third time, he saw Hanshee heave his bloody and nearly limp attacker to the side and look up into his face.

Seeing Hanshee alive, Ray felt something release in his body and he dropped to his knees, then to all fours, where he heaved the meager contents of his stomach into the blood that was already soaking into the ornate carpets. Then he felt himself being lifted, his feet shuffling, as he was helped back to his bed.

After getting Ray seated on the edge of the bed, Hanshee found his pouch. He pulled out a small leather bag tightly tied with a leather strip around a wooden stopper. He untied the pouch and opened it to reveal a fine white powder, a pinch of which he placed beneath Ray's tongue. Then he helped Ray into a reclining position before securely retying the bag. Replacing it in the pouch, he first closed and secured the door to the balcony, then returned to sit cross legged before Ray's bed to wait.

He did not wait long.

"WHAT THE...!," Ray suddenly sat bolt upright in the bed, mouth agape, wild eyes darting around the room only dimly lit by the two fireplaces and a thin beam of moonlight piercing through the covering of an upper window. A sheen of perspiration covered his face and his hands clutched handfuls of his covers in a white-knuckle grip. His head thrashed back and forth, only coming to rest after he caught sight of Hanshee.

Hanshee rose to a kneeling position and leaned forward to look more deeply into Ray's eyes. Satisfied with what he saw, he stood and walked over to the table, returning moments later with a goblet filled with cool water which he handed to Ray.

"Drink," he commanded, and watched as Ray first took a sip and then turned the cup up until no water remained.

Hanshee nodded, took the goblet from Ray, and brought it back to him refilled.

"Sip this time," he said. "And stay seated until I return."

Before Ray could find words to question, Hanshee had snatched up his harness, on which hung his knife and longsword, and disappeared through the balcony door.

The minutes passed as Ray waited for Hanshee to return. He had so many questions about what had just happened; questions about himself and what he had awoken to.

He also had much to tell Hanshee.

He now had a better understanding of what had happened to him on the DeFrance River so long ago. Not a complete understanding, just better. He still didn't know where he was, how he got here, or why he came to be here. What he did know was that, even while he was here, he was somewhere else. He was back in his world, stretched out in a hospital bed, paralyzed almost head to toe and unable to do much more than faintly whisper one poorly formed word at a time.

He thought about this while he waited for Hanshee to return. Even with his most recent experiences, there were lots of questions still unanswered, both in this world and in his own.

Thoughts of his paralysis made him more aware of his body and he began consciously opening and closing his hands and curling his toes as he continued to think things through. When he thought about what he was doing, he smiled. Then he laughed out loud. Having just returned to this world, he had vivid memories of how helpless he had been in the hospital. It felt good to move again!

That was how Hanshee found him when he returned; like a little kid, sitting on the edge of the bed swinging his arms back and forth and alternately kicking his legs up into the air; and laughing through all the motion. He was so happy that he didn't bother to stop when he heard the balcony door open and saw Hanshee slip back into the room.

Hanshee paused in the threshold and gave Ray an unreadable look. Then he entered, pulling two bundles of furs in with him before closing the door and going to the larger of the two fireplaces to warm himself.

The sight of Hanshee at the fireplace, silent but stern of face, brought Ray out of his brief euphoria and into the present. In the flicker of the firelight, he could just make out the two bodies still laying where they had fallen on the carpeted floor, and it came back to him that he was responsible for the death of one. He knew he would grapple with this later but, for now, he needed to know what situation had led to his action.

Ray started to stand, hesitantly, and was surprised at how easy it was. Pausing for a moment beside the bed, he took a cautious step forward... then another. A moment later he found himself standing with Hanshee before the fire.

"The *tabba*, in its distilled form, can be surprisingly potent," Hanshee said, not yet looking away from the fire.

Apparently 'tabba' was the plant that produced the white powder Hanshee had placed under his tongue. Ray took this in before turning to his friend.

"What happened?" he asked.

"What do you last remember about yourself?" was Hanshee's question in reply.

Ray opened his mouth to speak but caught himself and turned this question over in his mind before responding. He remembered much, from both worlds, but he reasoned that Hanshee was referring to what he remembered about what happened here, in this place.

"I was sitting on the floor of a corridor," Ray began slowly. "I was hurt, bleeding, and had a wicked pain in my back. You were fighting the guards who were leading us to an audience with King Ammon. You were fighting... and then I passed out."

Hanshee nodded in conformation of what Ray remembered.

"It was a trap," he said. "We were attacked in the corridor, and you were struck by an arrow. Thanks be to The One that you live. I had you brought back to our quarters, where I practiced the healing arts. You have been sleeping for some time but now I see that the potions have done their work. Your body is healed."

Ray's eyes had narrowed as Hanshee told him what had happened.

"How long was I healing?" he asked. "How long was I sleeping?"

"This is the night of the fifteenth day," replied Hanshee. "The herbs are potent and healed you quickly. Still your wound was grave, and in their healing, they rendered you unconscious."

Fifteen days thought Ray. *So, there's no direct correlation between time spent there and time spent here. But I had already figured that.'*

"You awakened," continued Hanshee, "to save my life."

Hearing these words, Ray looked over Hanshee's shoulder at the carnage that remained in their quarters. He gave an involuntary shudder upon catching sight of the two dead bodies and felt a queasiness beginning in his stomach.

"What did I awaken to?" he asked cautiously, not sure if he was ready to jump back in headfirst but feeling he had no choice.

"Yet another attempt to kill the 'Harbinger', I would think," spat Hanshee. "Three approached as I kept watch on you. Were it not for your timely awakening, our journey to my homeland would have come to an end here." He paused and looked at Raymond.

"Another sign from The One that you are the reason for my journey," he said. "That you and I travel the correct path."

Ray paused to think things through.

Hanshee, a warrior of the clan of Dula, Maiyochi to his people, was sent into the world to find, and bring back, that which his people needed to stave off disaster. He had traveled for almost two years, by his reckoning, before coming upon a river, the 'river of dreams' he called it, beyond any settlements of men. There he waited for days for a revelation, and there he pulled Raymond from the waters. Half drowned and barely clinging to life, Hanshee had nursed him back with these same potions he had used to heal the arrow wound in his back. And now, after many adventures, they find themselves in the Royal House of the Citadel, in the capital city Pith, of the nation bearing the same name, a *guest* of the King and at constant risk of assassination because the priests have identified Hanshee as the 'Harbinger of the Fourth Prophesy', or so they believe.

Even though he had lived it, it was still a lot for Ray to digest.

"But you said there were three assassins," asked Ray. "I count only two bodies."

"I did not kill the first," replied Hanshee. "I had questions. The others were upon me before I could ask. While I fought, the first managed to escape. I injured him, yet he made it to the rocks, where a fourth must have waited. I followed his trail to the cliff where the three came down. He could not have climbed up without help. There was a fourth."

Hanshee motioned toward the two bundles of furs he had brought in when he returned.

"These bundles are their belongings," he said. "Robes of fur to protect them from the cold, with supplies within their folds. They were shed prior to the attack to allow free and silent movement. We will use them when we leave."

"When we leave?" asked Ray. "We're leaving?"

"The worst of winter's chill is behind us," Hanshee replied. "We have now survived four attempts on our lives. So long as we remain, the attempts will continue until we are dead. We must leave this place."

Ray was shocked and confused by Hanshee's sudden pronouncement.

"Where will we go?" he asked, his voice now apprehensive. "And when? How could we hope to get away from this place now? Where would we go?" he repeated.

"We go west," said Hanshee, "and we go this night."

"But, wha… whe…" Ray sputtered, trying to understand what was happening. "I'm an hour removed from a sick bed! You're telling me that we leave tonight? Are we ready? Am I ready? Am I strong enough? What about supplies? And how do we even get out of here, out of the Royal House?"

"We leave as did the two living assassins," replied Hanshee coolly. "We take the leavings of the dead to supply our escape, and we survive from the bounty of our Mother, as we did before our capture by the Pith."

"But am I strong enough for this?" Ray asked, almost plaintively.

"The tabba is a wondrous plant," said Hanshee. "It can replenish your strength when you think you have none. For short periods it can 'be' your strength, if it is not abused. I mixed a small portion with other healing herbs to quicken your healing. Together, they made you sleep, which is not so good a thing. You must be watched and tended by a deft hand; one who knows the herbs and the roots deeply. I am such a one. If done correctly you will sleep for many days without waking, but when you do wake, it will almost be as if you were never injured, never sick. Almost."

Ray was speechless.

He knew that in this world, Hanshee was his trusted guide. Hanshee would only advocate for what needed to be done and what was good for Ray, even above what was good for Hanshee. Even now he knew that it was fear for his safety that motivated Hanshee more than anything else. But they had been out of the woods, literally and figuratively, for some time now. Maybe he had grown too comfortable with the pampered life provided them in the Royal House and did not relish returning to a life of constant travel and living off what they could find or kill. Maybe it was his recent brush with helplessness that caused him to doubt his mental and physical readiness.

Maybe he should just put his trust in Hanshee to make things work, as he always had.

"You sound pretty sure of this," Ray finally said. "When did you decide that this was the time to leave?"

"This moment… as I returned from outside," Hanshee said, catching Ray completely off guard. "I have planned since first we stepped into the Pithian capital. As we moved around the Temple and Royal House, I took note of where things were kept. Things we would need to leave. Nothing was stolen. Instead, I remembered their location. I knew where to find what was needed when the time came. I sought out maps and charts to tell where we were and the best route to take to escape. When the king showed his maps, I would only glance at them, so as not to alert our hosts. But I would take their memory with me. Now I carry a map in my head, to be ready when the time came.

"Since we came into this place they call 'Citadel'," Hanshee continued, "my concern has been leaving here unseen. The only road out we know as a tunnel through a rock wall, well-guarded within and without.

Now he turned to Ray and held his gaze with an intensity born of conviction.

"Tonight, The One has blessed us with opportunity! Tonight, he has shown me a way other than the tunnel through the rock and blessed us with many of the supplies I would take from the Pith when the time was right. Having also blessed us with our lives this night, the message is clear; we should take this opportunity to leave this place. After Ammon learns of this," Hanshee waved his hand to encompass the death and destruction around them, "guards will surround us. We may never have this chance again."

Ray listened to all Hanshee said, his mind racing. He was trying desperately to form a counter argument that would convince his companion that staying put, for now, was the right thing to do. What he discovered was that he couldn't even formulate an argument to convince himself.

He thought back to the few times he had ignored Hanshee's advice and insisted on doing things his own way. The first time was at the river of dreams, after Hanshee had nursed him back to health. He had insisted on walking back to the city, or to a road that led to the city. How had that worked out for him? Hanshee had found him on his hands and knees, in a darkened forest that he had no clue how to cope with. Within half a day he had been reduced to a filthy, sweaty, bleeding, sobbing, broken man.

Then he had insisted on going to the first city, Aggipoor, a place Hanshee had told him held nothing for him. Though only there for two or three hours, Hanshee had saved him from assault five separate times: twice from certain death.

These thoughts tumbled through Ray's mind in moments, and in that brief time he concluded that the lesson was clear; if you would continue to survive this place, trust the man standing before you.

"Alright," Ray conceded. "What's the plan?"

CHAPTER 8

The bundles Hanshee brought from outside contained a wealth of supplies, beginning with the furs themselves.

Once untied, they revealed themselves to be thick fur cloaks with hoods, probably made with the winter skins of wolves. They were heavy enough to protect against the bitter cold but not so heavy as to prove cumbersome when traveling. Inside the unbundled fur robes were boots; sturdier than most they had seen since being captured by the Pith, with good soles that could stand up to hard ground and jagged rocks.

Hanshee had already decided they would take the leggings from the two dead assassins. They were the closest things Ray had seen to pants since arriving in this world. Made of skins sewn inside out, the leather had been worked to a suppleness that made for an easy range of motion during everyday activities. With short, soft fur on the inside, the pants - *might as well call them pants*, thought Ray - were both comfortable and warm against the bitterest cold. A short length of rope secured the waist, and the bottoms extended far enough to tuck into the tops of the boots.

One of the nicest surprises was found inside the heavy fur robes. Each robe had several folds sewn into the insides, allowing the wearer to carry many needed items on their person while keeping their hands free.

In each robe was found a pair of heavy fur mitts, as well as flint and an iron striker for sparking a flame. There was also a wetting stone for keeping the edge on a blade. Each robe contained varying amounts of dry material to use as tinder, sharp paring knives in sheaths, and several arrowheads. One robe contained several long strips of cloth and some ointments, while another contained a small package of cheese and jerky, carefully wrapped in oilskin and tied with a heavy woolen thread. In a small pocket placed to the front left-hand side, both robes contained two gold coins.

The only other thing of use found in the bundles was a light leather shoulder harness, one per bundle. From both harnesses there hung leather flasks for drinking water. One harness also had what appeared to Ray to be a 'tomahawk' in that the shaft was long and made of very solid hardwood. An examination of the head showed it was made from iron, tapered and sharpened on one side to a razors edge; thick and blunt on the other for use as a bludgeon.

Hanshee and Ray inventoried the supplies as they dressed themselves in the heavy winter clothes. Hanshee surmised that the assassins must come from higher up in the mountains as some of their clothing was similar to what he had seen among those serving the Elders of the Blue Mountain in his homeland. The Elders lived year-round at much higher elevations than those of the tribes.

They took all that they found in the bundles and Hanshee insisted that Ray take the longsword born by the third assassin, as well as the harness which was used to sheath it. They left the slender long-bladed knives for the King's men to find, as they were clearly meant as weapons of assassination, not tools.

Apparently, the assassins preferred their clothes long and loose for, though at least two of them were of smaller stature than their targets, all their clothes were of adequate length to cover Hanshee and Raymond. Even the boots were comfortable enough for each to don a pair.

After all was inventoried and the two of them were outfitted, Hanshee brought forth the cache of dried food that he had been hoarding for this occasion. It was an assortment of dried fruits and meats, with some nuts and a few hard cheeses. He carried this, along with his weapon harness and weapons and, of course, his 'magic pouch' as Ray had named the pouch which contained Hanshee's powders, potions, ointments, wetting stones, flints, coins, and who knew what else. Both carried small bundles of clothes to wear after leaving the cold weather.

After filling the water flasks and taking one more look around the large room for anything useful, Hanshee led the way out across the high balcony.

At its far end, the balcony hung twenty-five feet above the snow-covered courtyard below. Here they paused as Raymond watched Hanshee uncoil a length of rope with a piece of metal attached to one end. It had the appearance of a grappling hook, though Raymond couldn't be certain since the 'hook' was covered in leather. The purpose of the leather soon became apparent as, when Hanshee attached the hook to the balcony, it made no noise on contact with the heavy stone. After making sure the hook was secure, Hanshee threw the rope over the side. When Raymond looked over, he saw that it more than reached the ground below, with about half its length to spare. First Hanshee, to demonstrate technique, then Raymond, descended to the ground. Once there, Hanshee whipped the rope, dislodging the hook which made little noise as it fell through the snow to the hard ground. Hanshee quickly coiled the rope into a manageable bundle, and the two set off across the courtyard and into the rocks.

As they approached the rocks, Raymond could see the breaks in the ice and snow marking the passing of the assassins. It weaved in and out between the boulders for about one-hundred fifty feet, each step taking them higher than the last. The trail ended at a rock wall approximately twenty-five to thirty feet in height and as smooth as the outer walls of Stronghold. This would be an impassable barrier, except for the length of rope that Hanshee carried.

It took six tries before he lodged the treble hook onto something stout enough to give them the confidence to climb. Hanshee went first, climbing to the top quickly and with relative ease despite the weight of the additional clothing and supplies he carried. Once on the ledge, he repositioned the hook to ensure it would hold. He then signaled Ray to begin his climb. In this Ray surprised himself. Despite the injury, and the fifteen days in bed, he made the climb just slightly slower than Hanshee. Though he had considered himself extremely fit prior to his injury, he was certain the tabba had something to do with this.

There were two more ledges to reach, neither as high as the first, before they arrived at something resembling a path. Here the snow was more windblown, but still it was possible to see feint tracks left by those coming and going along the trail. They led off to the north. Hanshee bent down to examine them by what moonlight they had and, after following them for a few yards, returned to Ray.

"It is as I thought," he said. "There are two sets of tracks leading to the north, but they overlay four sets coming south. There were four assassins."

"Which way do we go?" asked Ray, hoping Hanshee would say 'south' and away from those who had sought to kill them.

"North," was Hanshee's one word reply as he stepped off in the direction the escaping assassins had taken.

Ray wanted to speak up, to say that to go the way of those who would kill them made no sense but, if he had learned anything all those months in the wilderness with Hanshee, it was not to doubt him. He would find a trail or make one, but he would get them free of these mountains and the Pith.

They followed the trail north for about an hour by Ray's reckoning. As it wound higher and higher the increased winds added a whole new element to the sub-freezing temperatures. Now the heavy hooded cloaks, which Ray had thought to be a bit much, proved their worth.

The winds made it difficult for the ice and snow to accumulate. This meant that the trail was much less slippery, and less dangerous, than they expected.

As they traveled, the path they traversed varied in width from as much as twenty feet to as little as three. Thankfully, the narrower sections were not of any real length and Raymond, who claimed not to be afraid of heights but of sudden drops, kept his eyes on the hooded cloak before him and hugged the wall as much as possible.

After about two hours they reached a point where the rocky trail seemed to split into two separate trails with the trail to the right continuing on an upward slope, and the trail on the left appearing to take a downward course toward the floor of the valley far below. Hanshee called for Ray to hold here while he investigated the lower trail and Ray was glad for the respite. Having eaten only the broth that Hanshee had been able to coax down his throat for the last fifteen days, he was feeling both hunger and weakness as the effects of the tabba began to wear off.

Standing with his back against the high rock wall, he closed his eyes and immediately felt himself succumbing to the weariness. He knew that, given the chance, he could lie down in the folds of his cloak and, in no time at all, fall asleep.

'No,' he thought. 'Now is not the time,' and he quickly opened his eyes and tried to shake off the lethargy fast developing in his mind and body.

From his position on the high ledge, the valley known as Stronghold stretched out before him. Having begun behind and above the Royal House, they had passed above the walls of the

Citadel and he now stared down onto the city proper. The various lantern lights, along with windows illuminated by roaring fireplaces, caused the expanse below to resemble the night sky above. He looked off to his left in an attempt to find the Royal House and knew he had found it when he spied a tall building with an inordinate number of fires burning for this time of night.

The Royal House never sleeps, he thought to himself, just as Hanshee was making his way back up the lower trail towards his position at the fork.

"The lower trail ends at a very long drop," Hanshee said, "We go upward."

Turning on the snow swept ledge, Hanshee continued to lead Ray north along the upper path. Another hour passed, Ray thought, then two, and he found himself so tired that when Hanshee came to a halt in front of him, Ray walked into his back. The warrior seemed not to mind as he remained motionless, focused on something up ahead. After a while, he carefully lowered himself into a crouch, reaching a hand back to Ray's shoulder and encouraging him to do the same. Once settled, he turned to face Ray.

"Stay here," Hanshee said. "Do not move. I will return soon."

Before Ray could find the strength to voice a question, Hanshee had disappeared into the night.

Ray took this opportunity to adjust his position, fully sitting, with his back to the wall and his legs stretched out in front of him. Closing his eyes, he repeatedly filled his lungs with the cold mountain air. In this position, he was less vulnerable to the icy winds. Although he felt the chill, he was amazed at how warm his boots, pants, and hooded fur cloak kept him. He supposed that their constant movement also factored into why his body had yet to succumb to the sub-freezing temperatures. But now, he thought as he pulled his heavy fur more tightly around him, it was his weariness that took the edge off of the severe cold, and he felt himself drifting off to sleep within moments of Hanshee leaving.

He was awakened by a strong grip on his shoulder shaking him vigorously. Even so, he was too tired to be startled, and slowly opened his eyes to see Hanshee again crouched beside him. Ray had no idea how long he had been sleeping. The wind seemed to have picked up and Hanshee leaned in close to his ear to be heard.

"There is a fire up ahead," Hanshee said. "I was not sure of the distance, so I went alone to see. It is farther away than I first thought, and I never reached it. I found another trail. It leads to the other side of these peaks and then to the south. It is the way we must go."

Ray was still trying to clear his head of sleep, so didn't fully understand all that Hanshee said. Focusing on what he did understand, he asked, "A fire… who made a fire up here?"

"The assassins," Hanshee said. "We will not confront them. The trail to the south forks off well before we approach them."

"We should build a fire," Ray heard himself say, truly feeling the cold for the first time since their escape began.

"With what?" Hanshee asked. "In a place such as this, fuel for a fire must be carried. We carry none. Also, a fire could be seen by those up ahead and those down below." Hanshee let his arm sweep out to encompass the valley spread out below them. "Only when we reach the eastern face will we build a fire, if fuel is found."

With that, he reached into his pouch for the bag containing the distilled powder of the tabba.

"Open," he commanded, and placed a pinch under Raymond's tongue to dissolve.

Even having experienced it before, the burst of energy that hit Ray took him completely by surprise! His body jerked as if it had been struck a physical blow, his heart throbbed in his chest, and his eyelids sprang open in a wide-eyed stare. He rocked once, and then turned to Hanshee, who was ready with a water bag before his face.

"Drink," he said, and Ray took several deep gulps of the cold water before Hanshee pulled it away while continuing to watch him. After a few minutes Ray felt his pulse slow down and his face relax. A few more minutes and a satisfied Hanshee stood and stretched out his hand to help Raymond to his feet.

"It's like powdered adrenaline," Ray commented absently as he steadied himself, but Hanshee heard him even above the winds.

"I know not this 'adrinen'," he said, "but be on guard. This time it will not last as it did before. You must tell me the moment you feel yourself weakening."

"I will," Ray promised, as Hanshee continued to watch how he spoke and how he stood. Finally, with a nod of satisfaction, he turned and again led Ray forward.

As they approached what appeared to be a fork in the trail, Ray could see the slight glimmer of a fire between the rocks far ahead. He paused to see what he could make out before following Hanshee as he took the right fork, moving away from the distant light.

The fork veered abruptly to the right, then downhill and southward toward the eastern face of the peaks they now traversed. Hanshee started down this trail without hesitation, having already traveled down much of its length while Ray slept.

Ahead, silhouetted against the night sky, stood two towering peaks; the little light cast from the moon was almost nonexistent between them. After a short pause to give his eyes time to adjust, Hanshee led Ray into the darkness. The wind was not as fierce here and Ray marveled at the relative silence that allowed him to hear Hanshee's every careful footfall on the loose rocks that covered its surface.

They followed this narrow passage between peaks for about another hour before coming to an opening. Ray was starting to feel exhaustion again and he alerted Hanshee, who had been anticipating this.

"We will rest here for a time," said Hanshee, indicating a patch of level rock about twenty feet short of where they would exit the space between the peaks.

He helped Ray ease into a sitting position, making sure his fur was free to be wrapped around him for warmth. Then he reached to the harness Ray wore and untied his water flask. Ray was fine with Hanshee doing this for him. Whereas the first experience with coming down from the effects of the tabba was a gradual descent, this time was like a sudden fall. He was grateful for Hanshee, who handed him his flask before offering him the store of nuts, dried meat, dried fruit, and cheese.

"Eat your fill," were Hanshee's words to him and he would have, had his arms not been so weary that, after chewing through three mouthfuls, he found himself unable to reach for more. Sleep was upon him in no time at all.

CHAPTER 9

Long before they reached the barren peaks that led to their destination, each had gathered a bundle of wood which they carried on their backs. The first night, half a bundle was burned. The other half was left to be used on their return. This was repeated the second and third nights. The afternoon of the fourth day brought them into position, where they waited for the setting sun to provide the darkness required to complete their task.

Mem had been unusually quiet as he made his preparations, putting a razors edge on his longsword as much to keep busy as anything. Though it went with him everywhere, he had no plans for its use this night. The longsword was a weapon that required a certain amount of space to be wielded efficiently. It had been decided that this kill would be done with the long slim knives their people had perfected for delivering a quick death from close quarters. It was this instrument to which he now applied the wetting stone. With long smooth strokes he ensured that, when the time came, his blade would perform its function without fail.

The twins were not as sedate and introspective as their older brother. Just past their eighteenth year, and bursting with the nervous energy born of the opportunity to partake in such an important mission, it was all they could seem to do to maintain their position of cover on the high ledge. Their constant movement, whispering, and giggling, was a reminder of their youth and inexperience and it grated on their older siblings.

Nola, especially, took exception to their frivolity and disrespect on the eve of a killing such as this. She found herself constantly glaring at her younger brothers, who would quiet down under her icy stare, but only for a moment. Soon they would be whispering and giggling anew, as they cut their eyes in her direction.

Nola also looked to Mem, questioning why he allowed his two younger siblings to behave in such a way. Seenio certainly would not. The Beast would demand a period of silent meditation prior to a killing of this magnitude; a killing *inside* the Royal House, on the direct order of the Lord High Priest himself! A certain respect was required when undertaking such a task. Mem should know this, Nola thought, and exert the authority Seenio had bestowed upon him by allowing him to lead a mission of such importance.

Nola had not agreed with the choice.

She had hidden her surprise when her father had chosen to delegate this killing to another, even though the 'other' was his first-born son. It had been many years since the High Seat had called upon its servants, and she had thought that the head of the Masscus Clan and Guild of Assassins would personally see that naught went awry. But Seenio had made his choice and the word of The Beast was law within 'Strongholds Crown', the name by which the northern mountains were known. Even as the eldest, she dared not raise a question to the word of Seenio, unless at Seenio's request.

Nola's position was undefined. She was the first born of the House of The Beast but, as a female, could not be given the same status of a first-born male. As far as she knew, there was still no precedent for *that*. Her future should have been in the pastures with the flocks, or in the fields teasing the sparse crops from the rocky soil of the mountain meadows. Or given to the priests of the lowlands to be dedicated to the Temple, in service to The One Spirit through servitude to the Lord High Priest.

But she had managed to avoid the banal future allotted to most every other female born into the Masscus clan.

****

Seenio Masscus had been enamored of his first born and, not far removed from childhood himself, took delight in their evenings of play. As she grew, he would often place her on his knee to enjoy his stories of daring and adventure, even placing in her hand a miniature version of his own sword that he had carved from the wood of a hickory tree. He smiled when this sword became her favorite toy and laughed when the six-year-old Nola eagerly brandished it against all who would question whether a female should be brought up in this fashion; teased with the toys of men and visions of a future that could not be hers. But Seenio loved his daughter, and he indulged her childish fantasy of growing up to follow in her father's footsteps. What harm could come of it?

When it was time for her brother Mem, not quite two years her junior, to begin the training that would serve as the foundation for his future, Nola demanded that she also be allowed to train for combat, to be taught weapons and killing techniques and stealth and languages, and the code that had guided this guild of assassins for almost eight-hundred years. Seenio again indulged his eldest, casting a hard eye at any who would dare whisper of this breach of custom. She is just a girl who loves her sire and wants to play at training, he reasoned. What harm could come of it?

When the teachers, mostly his uncles, came to Seenio with reports on the progress of his offspring, they spoke hardly at all of Mem. Instead, they spoke of Nola; of her focus and dedication to learning everything put before her. They spoke of her drive, her intensity and her ferocity when putting her teaching to use as she sparred with her peers. They went so far as to compare her to The Beast himself at her age!

At first Seenio's heart swelled with pride, but then the teachers asked the crucial question; 'What shall we do with her?'

Now the dilemma that Seenio had brought upon himself, and his father's house, became apparent. The training of his ten-year-old daughter was no longer an indulgence. Her dreams of inclusion in the Guild of Assassins were no longer a childhood fantasy. Her promise and skill was evident and could no longer be ignored. Tradition dictated that she could not be allowed to continue with serious training. Seenio would have to bring this to a close.

Though it took some time, Seenio called for Nola one evening and, before her trainers and her peers, told her that the time of her indulgence was at an end. Her training must cease. It was for the good of the Guild and the future of the House of Masscus that her brothers who showed promise be prepared to one day lead the family without the distractions caused by the silly ambitions or an older sister.

As leader of the Clan and head of the Guild since the death of his father, Athel, Seenio's spoken word was considered law. Thus, the matter should have been decided.

But Seenio was unready for his now twelve-year-old daughter to question his decree, and grossly unprepared for the passion and logic of her argument.

"Has it not always been our tradition that the best lead The House," the child had asked? "Is that not how *you*, father... Seenio, 'the Beast'... rose to lead the family despite the ambitions of your three older brothers? Have we not always rewarded skill, dedication, and achievement in our choice of a leader, and is this not a wise tradition?"

Seenio had to admit that the child had learned well the lessons on tradition as well as the lessons on combat. He smiled down at his young daughter, proud of her courage, her knowledge, and her conviction, even as he knew her training was over.

"Yes," Seenio had replied. "All that you say about our tradition is true."

"And is there not a precedent for a female to be honored amongst the Guild?" she had asked.

This question set Seenio aback, for there *was* one such precedent. Once, a female had been allowed a place in the Guild of Assassins and she had flourished among them. Though she was spoken of now as if a myth, all knew that the legend of Erica was true.

Like Nola, Erica had been allowed to train with her brothers, and like Nola she had excelled in all aspects of combat and strategy. Maybe because she knew she could never match her brothers in size and strength, she worked to perfect every aspect of her combat skills. She learned all that she could about tactics and strategy.

And she learned to *read* her opponent.

It was said she had but to watch a man as he crossed a field and she could deduce his strengths and weaknesses, his dominant hand, and his taste for battle. If she once saw him fight, she would memorize his tendencies and how best to attack him, and defend against his attacks. It was said that she had an iron will that could not be cracked or dented, and that she never lost a contest of skill.

When at the end of years of extensive training, she was judged the best among all who trained, her father stepped in and stated that her entry into the Guild must be denied, as no woman had ever been admitted. It was in the heat of that denial that Erica stood and, facing her father, flatly stated that she would not be denied! On that day she renounced her womanhood and pledged to live as a man, a male member of the Guild of Assassins, from that day forward.

When Erica rose to defy her father's dictate, he then had the right to order her pitched from a height; cast from a high ledge to a certain death on the rocks below. But the Head of the Guild was so taken with her courage, her spirit, and the boldness of her pronouncement, that he ordered her father, his younger brother, to relent. He told all present that, as outrageous as it was, he would honor her declaration… and hold her to it. She would be admitted into the Guild of Assassins… as a man… and she was never to break from her self-assigned role, or she would be put to death.

Erica agreed, shortening her name to Eric and, for the remainder of her life, served first as a Reaper, then as an Elder in the Guild. Legend had it that she even took a few wives who bore children in her name. And so convincing was she, that those she claimed as sons and daughters were unaware that he whom they called their sire was not a man. There was but one injustice mandated by her condition; though she was acknowledged as the most worthy, she was never allowed to *lead* the House of Masscus.

When confronted with the story of Erica/Eric, and knowing its truth, Seenio was at first speechless. As he continued to look into the eyes of his beloved daughter, most probably the only one in the village who had the courage to confront him in such a way, he found his heart again swelling with pride, even as his features hardened to that of a statue.

The silence between them grew as Seenio's visage grew ever darker and more impassive. The others in the room, both child and adult, grew increasingly uneasy as Seenio stared cold daggers into his beloved daughter. Nola never turned from his gaze.

Finally, Seenio broke the silence.

"Your training will be permitted to continue," he had said, "as long as you continue to excel. But know this, Nola…" Seenio now raised his head to address those around him. "…know this, everyone! This child will not be coddled! None will soften their words or their blows for fear of injuring a female. None will hold back in training for fear that she is not ready, or worthy, of your best!"

Seenio turned his gaze away from those gathered around, and back to Nola.

"I will not call for you to renounce your gender, though I have no doubt that you stand ready to do so. You stand before me now brazen and bold, but *that* is a decision you are much too young to make.

But you will be held to a standard.

I see it as your choice to relinquish your role as the beloved daughter of Seenio for a new distinction. To achieve this, you will be worked as you have never been before. You will be tested and tested again. No mercy will be shown; no quarter given because you are female… or my offspring.

If, at the completion of your training, you are not broken in spirit, crippled, or dying… you will be acknowledged as Nola of Clan Masscus, First Born and Daughter of Seenio; a Reaper… in the Guild of Assassins."

Those words rang in Nola's head even today.

Never again in her training years did her father acknowledge her as a female, nor treat her differently than his sons. Some even said that he was much harder on her. When asked, Seenio would say that an extra portion is given to, and expected from, the eldest.

If asked, Nola could not swear that her training was any harder, only that her dedication, intensity, and ferocity increased. Her skills were already ahead of her peers, but puberty would soon gift them with a physical advantage. She knew most would one day be bigger and much stronger than she. She could not hope to match their strength but instead, through steady and devout training, she developed the speed, agility, and *precision* which, coupled with a natural fluidity and grace, led to a different kind of power. She had embraced the challenge of her sire until all those familiar with the Guild of Assassins, knew also the 'Daughter of the Beast'.

****

Nola was understandably proud of her accomplishments, so it was easy to understand her disappointment when Seenio had given Mem the lead on the first mission requested by this Lord High Priest. Her purpose here was to observe and support, but not to strike the killing blow.

CHAPTER 10

The four assassins had waited until well after sunset, welcoming a night of wintry beauty. The light of the stars was dimmed by a magnificent full moon just rising above the eastern peaks into a cloudless sky. The cold mountain winds swirled the snow and ice about them as they huddled beneath their heavy fur robes, biding their time, and watching for signs that most in the Royal House had settled in for the night. To move too fast was to invite detection from the Royal Guard or from the target himself. He was said to be 'as a warrior priest of old' and no slouch to be trod over lightly.

Nola found it hard to imagine a dangerous priest.

They had been given the crucial information; the location of the quarters and a description of their target. These had been confirmed several days hence when Mem and Nola had scouted the location and terrain in preparation for this mission.

The cliffs and peaks east of the Citadel had provided a natural barrier since its initial construction. It was thought that no one could enter by this route and, if entry were possible, certainly exit was not. It was this reasoning, and the centuries of history that supported it, that made this the least guarded perimeter of the entire compound.

When the third hour after sundown was struck the ropes were lowered and, first the twins, then Mem, slid down the cliff wall and took up positions among the rocks in the hills above the private cloister.

Nola had watched from the lowest of the three ledges as Darien, the younger and stealthier of the twins, made the first approach to the Royal House. He took a circular route around the perimeter of the cloister so as not to leave an obvious and direct path through the snow that still lay on the ground. He hugged the outer wall of the courtyard and the walls of the Royal House, keeping to its shadows as he approached the balcony. His grappling hook, wrapped thickly in leather and heavy cloth, made hardly a sound as it floated up and over the top rail of the balcony, finding purchase on the bottom protrusion of a thick balustrade carved from a single granite block. When he had tested and climbed the rope, and taken up position near the north door, he signaled for his brother, Lux, to approach.

Lux was to follow the path his brother had laid and, upon his signal, climb up to the balcony and position himself at the south portal, on the opposite side of the chimney. Once they had assured themselves that the target was present, and that there were no unforeseen complications, Mem was to be signaled. It was Mem who was to make first entry, probably ensuring him the honor of striking the killing blow. The three would then fade back into the darkness of the mountains, leaving a corpse that would not be discovered until well after dawn.

It was a simple but well conceived plan, and it failed miserably.

Nola suspected something was wrong when Darien, after signaling his brother, left his post at the northern door and moved to the southern door, which had been left ajar. There he began to shed his winter cloak and harness. Mem, who was waiting in the rocks at the edge of the cloister, saw this and immediately knew its meaning; his foolhardy younger brother had spied what he thought was an opportunity for himself to enter and make the kill. Instantly he left his place of hiding and rushed directly across the cloister, even as the elder twin, Lux, was climbing over the rail of the balcony. By the time Mem had reached the rope and climbed high enough to see between the balustrades, it was too late. Lux was almost shed of his own robe and harness while Darien, after first looking back with a mischievous grin, raised his blade and charged through the slightly opened door!

Nola saw Lux follow his brother shortly, while Mem clawed his way over the top rail and dashed across the balcony, shedding his robe in the process. Drawing his dagger, he too disappeared within the balcony doors, and Nola had naught to do but wait for the three to reemerge.

Her wait was not long.

Shortly after Mem disappeared from her view, an obviously injured Darien staggered from the same door and reached for his cloak even as he stumbled clumsily across the balcony and fairly launched himself over the side. He was barely able to grasp the rope with his left hand, which kept him from plummeting unhindered to the frozen courtyard below, Still, after sliding one-handed down two thirds of its length, he lost his grip and impacted the ground hard. Lying still for a moment, Darien gathered himself and half limped- half crawled across the snow-covered courtyard and into the cover of the rocks. Nola lost sight of him once he entered the rocks and allowed her gaze go back to the balcony, expecting to see her other brothers come forth. Through her interminable wait, no one else appeared.

Nola continued to scan the balcony, and the doors and windows visible to her, until she heard a signal from below. Darien had made his way through the rocks and emerged directly below her position. She scowled down at him in the darkness as he pleaded for her to throw down the rope. She wanted to delay until he explained what had happened inside, and where their brothers had gone, but she could better pry loose those answers once she had him safely up the wall and beside her.

She threw down the rope, casting expectant glances toward the balcony while waiting for Darien to tie the end around his torso. Ordinarily he would be expected to climb up under his own power which, under normal circumstances, would be easily done. Now, he was obviously injured. By the way she had seen him move, she knew it was his right arm and right leg. This meant that he would need her help to climb up and she angrily set her jaw as she bent to the task of hauling her brother, with little help from him, the twenty-five feet to the ledge on which she perched.

As Nola was pulling Darien over the edge, she caught a movement from the corner of her eye. A head had emerged from the open door, and she strained to identify its owner. After a moment, a man moved lithely through the door. Pausing briefly at the bundles of furs still on the balcony, he made his way to the grapple attached to the railing. First noting the rope dangling from the balcony to the ground, he soon spied the moon-lit tracks that led across the cloister and toward the rocks.

Nola continued looking as she pulled Darien's almost limp form away from the cliffs edge. Cloaked in the shadows of the cliffs, they were not visible to his eyes, but Nola was not one to take unneeded chances.

The man on the balcony, definitely not one of her brothers, gave a brief look back toward the still open door before going over the edge, using the rope to descend to the ground.

Seeing this, Nola quickly pulled in the rope she had thrown to Darien. Urging him as he crawled, she joined him at the very back of the ledge. There they waited in silence, their backs against the frozen rock, for what she knew would come next.

His footsteps were barely audible, even on the loose gravel that covered the ground below the ledge. She thought she heard him arrive and waited to hear his footsteps recede before she dared to move. There was a slight scraping of feet on the gravel, Nola thought, as the man examined both the ground and the cliff face. Then there was only silence, and Nola imagined him still standing at the base of the cliff, looking up to where she and Darien lay hidden. How long he stood there, she could not say, but she never heard him leave. Only the sight of him climbing the rope back up to the balcony allowed her to relax.

Now she turned to her injured brother to get answers to her questions about what happened inside.

"Where are the others!" she had asked, her voice not panicked, but concerned.

"Lux is dead," Darien said in a strained whisper. "I saw him fall. Mem was locked in battle with a man... the warrior-priest. He tore my leg... and my arm."

"You left Mem to fight alone?" Nola asked

"I was injured!" whined Darien. "I barely escaped! Mem is a great fighter. He will surely prevail."

"And yet he has not emerged," Nola stated flatly.

Darien looked up at her in pained silence and, though Nola had thought her night vision good, it was only then that she noticed the blistering skin on his face and neck. She reached out a tentative hand and he recoiled in pain as she touched him.

"I saw you enter first, against our plan," she continued. "How did he overcome you?"

The pain in Darien's voice did not recede, but was now joined by his shame.

"I had him," was his whisper. "I was at his back, and he had no blade. I had him!"

"And what happened?" Nola pressed. "How did you fail?"

"I don't know," Darien began. "I had his back and was poised to strike... and then my face was on fire! And he was upon me!"

To Nola's ear Darien's tale was incoherent, but she decided to let the matter rest for now. She knew that the other, probably the warrior-priest they were sent to kill, would return. Most likely with Citadel Guards in tow. She knew she had to get them both up the wall and back to the trail that would lead them away from this place. She would have time to question her foolish brother once they were safe.

****

Nola sat cross-legged with her back to the small fire she had built. She sat close enough to enjoy its warmth without allowing its glow to steal her eyesight in the darkness of the early morning.

Their campsite was on a wide portion of the trail, situated between two rock outcroppings that provided sufficient cover so that a small fire would not be noticed from below. They had used this campsite on their way toward their mission, and at that time had left the firewood that she now burned.

Darien, lying between the fire and the inner wall, was made quiet by the pain of his injuries and the shame of his failure.

In the light of the fire, Nola had clearly examined the peeling blistering flesh that had been his youthful face. All she could do was use what strips of cloth she had and what snow and ice she could find, to wrap his face and neck in a cold compress. This would lessen the pain. She had addressed his knee as soon as they had ascended to the cliff-top trail. She fashioned a splint, using the long handles from the hand axes they carried, which she secured above and below his right knee. This prevented any flexing of the damaged knee and, even though he still experienced great pain with every step, allowed him to limp along the trail. His right elbow was dislocated, and his right shoulder was damaged in a way she could not understand or treat. She had also applied a bandage to a gash on the back of his skull, the least of his injuries.

Darien was not fit to travel, yet she had hardly slowed the pace of their retreat. She expected pursuit and was determined not to be caught. She counted his suffering as the price he paid for his failure and, considering the price his brothers paid for his carelessness, had little pity on him.

Understanding that he had received all the help his sister was prepared to offer, Darien bore down and made every step on his own, collapsing in a heap against the wall when they arrived and not moving since. He was paying a heavy price for his rash behavior, but he was paying it well. Nola was almost proud of him for that much. It remained to be seen how Seenio would react when they reached the village. Truly, these could be among Darien's easiest days.

After building the fire and tending to Darien, Nola retraced their steps to see if they were being following. As she moved away from the fire, she felt more at ease. Darkness was indeed Nola's friend and her special talent, if she could be said to possess one, was in operating at night. She was known to see better at night than any others in her guild and was always smooth and agile as she flowed from one step to the next. In the dark, she was almost feline in her ability to move in surefooted silence.

So it was that she was there, hidden in a crevice in the rock wall, when Hanshee moved up the trail toward her fire. She had heard the slightest crunch of gravel underfoot, seen the slightest movement of a shadow among shadows, so she lay in wait to see who, and how many, followed their trail. She was prepared to spring from cover and deal with them if it came to that, but felt a palpable relief when the shadow chose the trail to his right which led back to the south. She waited a while longer and was still in place when he reappeared, taking the trail back toward the Royal House instead of proceeding toward her campfire.

Should she follow? From her place of hiding, it was difficult to see, but she thought it was but one man.

The warrior-priest? Nola mused.

If it were he, she could follow and possibly complete the task that had been so badly botched. But if it were not, then what would be gained by following one who had turned back and was no longer a threat? Ultimately, she returned to her camp and now sat looking back toward the place where she had seen the shadow move.

She replayed the events of the night again and again in her mind, merging what her eyes had told her with what her brother had revealed.

According to Darien, he had gone through the door only when he had the priests back and he was perfectly positioned for a quick kill. What her eyes told her was that Lux had followed through the same door, maybe within ten heartbeats of Darien. Mem had followed Lux after about the same amount of time, maybe a beat or two more.

She could not say exactly what happened between the walls of the chamber but, whatever she could or could not prove, it appeared this warrior-priest had been caught off guard by *three* Reapers of the Assassins Guild and, within moments, had lain low all three!

Nola thought back to the shadow. Could it have been he? If so, perhaps she had been wise not to engage.

Darien shifted in his sleep, letting loose a low moan and Nola rose from her seated position to check him. Seeing that he was still asleep, she pulled his heavy robe closer around his neck. Despite his undisciplined behavior, and all that it had cost them, she worried about him.

The relatively short trek to their current campsite had taken a heavy toll on her remaining brother in terms of pain endured and strength lost. What lay before them was a three-day journey across the rugged northeastern peaks before they once again cast eyes on their home. Darien was not up to this, she knew, but the alternative was to leave him here to die.

Nola pondered this new dilemma as she pulled her own cloak tightly around her body. To return alone, without having completed the mission, meant that she alone would have to endure the wrath of The Beast, and all that came with it. This mission was taken after the summons - the very first summons - of this particular lord high priest. Seenio had wanted so very badly to impress upon His Imminence the worth of his servants. His rage would be vast!

Nola knew that getting Darien back to the village in his condition would be a heroic feat, and be seen as such; a golden arrow in her quiver. She also knew that, with Darien standing alive before Seenio, able to answer for himself, she would no longer fear being the sole focus of his anger. But how could she insure his survival during this long and arduous trek?

She pondered this dilemma further, even as she settled in to get what sleep she could in the few remaining hours before sunrise.

CHAPTER 11

Laretha's scream cut through the morning silence of the Royal House, causing the two guards stationed outside the foyer to freeze in mid breath!

AAAAAAAAAIIIII!

Another high piercing scream, and the guards bolted through the door, quickly crossed the foyer, and burst into the Harbinger's private quarters, short swords already half drawn from their scabbards.

The first thing they noticed was Laretha standing near the foot of the bed once occupied by the injured acolyte, but now empty. She was frozen in place, her hands drawn up to her face, staring at something on the floor on the far side of the bed.

Rushing around the bed to get to the stricken servant girl, the guards caught their breaths at the sight that greeted them; scattered debris that told of a struggle and the corpses of two men, each lying in their own congealing pool of blood. Neither of the dead men appeared to be those who were quartered here, and a quick glance around confirmed that these were the only bodies to be found.

Though taken aback by the discovery, the first guard turned quickly to his companion and barked a command.

"Run and sound the alarm, man… quickly!"

As the other guard sprinted from the room to alert the Royal House, the first guard placed both hands on Laretha's shoulders in a gentle but firm grip. Startled at first, the servant girl relaxed some when she realized it was the guard touching her and allowed herself to be led toward a chair at the large table near the door. She had placed the tray carrying the warm bread, meat, cheese, and dried fruit, that was breakfast for Raymond and Hanshee, here before looking around for the two.

The guard helped her to a seat, attempting to calm her with soothing words promising nothing to fear and that all would soon be handled. He knew he lied. Even now he was steeling himself for what could be the breaking loose of all hell.

****

Jusaan was one of the first to hear of the events of the prior night.

A member of the Council of the Nine, the tall delicate priest, thin but for his sagging pot belly, had been placed in charge of ensuring the comfort of the Warrior-priest and his acolyte during their stay as guests of the Royal House. He had been given temporary quarters not far from theirs, to be in a better position to see to their needs.

He had arisen early this morning, as was his custom, and was preparing a bundle of scrolls to be returned to the Library in the Temple. Standing near his portal he heard the faint screams of Laretha and wondered had the poor girl seen one of the huge rats that sometimes infiltrate the Royal House in the winter months. He didn't give it a second thought until he heard the unmistakable sound of slapping leather and clanking armor as it moved quickly down the corridor. His curiosity piqued, he stuck his head out from his apartment door in time to see the guard who had just hurried past.

"You there... Guard!" he said in a screeching high-pitched yell. "What is all the early morning commotion about?"

"Your pardon, Lord Priest," spoke the guard, who had halted his headlong rush and now quickly approached Jusaan. "There has been turmoil in the quarters of the Harbinger! The House must be alerted!

As the guard turned again to dash down the corridor, Jusaan pulled him up once more.

"What kind of 'turmoil'?" Jusaan hurriedly asked. "Speak up, man! I am responsible for the Harbingers comfort! Tell me now!"

That is how Jusaan came to be awkwardly stumbling down the corridor behind the reluctant guard, toward the chamber now occupied by twin corpses, neither of which were those who King Ammon IV counted as the priest's personal responsibility.

The first guard looked up as the other re-entered and, knowing he could not have alerted the House so quickly, prepared to tear into him in the most vicious manner he could think of. That is when Jusaan stumbled into the room after him and the first nearly choked on the words already halfway out of his mouth.

"What the he...ahh...wuh...Milord Jusaan!," he finally exclaimed, looking back and forth from the stoic face of the guard to the Priest, who was red faced and huffing and puffing after such a short sprint down the corridor.

"Wha....what is...going on...here?! Jusaan finally managed to ask. "Where...is...the Harbinger?!"

"Milord," began the first guard, "neither he nor his acolyte are here. I sent Kale to alert the Royal Gu..."

"NO!" exclaimed Jusaan. "No one will be alerted until I see for myself what has transpired here!"

With that pronouncement, Jusaan gathered the skirts of his bed robe about him and walked around the bed to stand beside the first guard. His body convulsed and he made a slight retching noise upon almost stepping into the pool of congealed blood that framed the torso of the first corpse. Catching himself, he looked around and spied the second dead body, the stool nearly cleaved in half, and the various scattered debris that spoke of a battle within the chamber. He also noted the most important thing: no Harbinger.

"They've been taken!" Jusaan bellowed as he fell to his knees in what appeared to be anguish over the fate of the Harbinger, but was in fact the realization that his plans of power and influence were starting to unravel. Twisting his body around, he looked up into the face of the guard.

"Alert the Royal Guard, you fool!" Jusaan said. "Something must be done!"

The second guard rolled his eyes at these words, and again wheeled down the corridor toward the quarters of Commander Colevant of the Garrison of Pith, under whose control the Royal Guard had been placed. Because of the current instability caused by the presence of the Harbinger, Colevant had gone to the unusual length of taking quarters inside the Citadel and assuming personal command of the Royal Guard from its newest Captain, Hendric.

****

Commander Colevant was a lifelong soldier, the son of a soldier, who had been posted as a senior officer to the Garrison of Pith after distinguishing himself in campaigns with the first and second expeditionary forces. With his sterling reputation as a military man, and his gift for both politics and blandishments, he was soon under consideration to head the garrison; a most comfortable position he had now held for almost twenty years.

This morning Colevant was already up and about, having the tendency toward early rising brought about by a lifetime in the military. He had just finished what was for him a late breakfast, and was gearing up to make his morning rounds, when he was lifted from his thoughts by an urgent knock on his door.

The commander's eyes grew wide, and his brow deeply furrowed as the guard told him the basics of what had been discovered in the quarters of the Harbinger only moments ago. While the soldier might have thought the Commander was considering possible ways to track down and apprehend the abductors, utmost in Covenant's mind were the threats issued by his King. Threats which had prompted him to adopt a hands-on approach to the Royal Guard.

"Who else knows about this?" Colevant asked conspiratorially.

"Only myself, Calvin, and Council Priest Jusaan," said the guard. "We were assigned to guard duty outside his quarters last evening." He braced himself for the explosion of rage that he had expected from the moment he and Calvin had walked in on the carnage. Instead, he was shocked as Commander Colevant took him by the shoulders and held his eyes with his own.

"Listen very carefully," the Commander said. "Go and find Captain Hendric and Chief Advisor Cecil. Bring them to me in the quarters of the Harbinger. Tell no one else, understand?

The confused guard nodded his head in affirmation.

His immediate superior, being left out of the loop, would be furious when he found out, but Kale had performed his duty by relaying information about last night to the Commander of the Garrison of Pith himself. It was the commander who had instructed him to tell only two others. He was now in a position only Commander Colevant could absolve him from. He only hoped that Colevant remembered this when Kale's immediate superior sought his head. His salvation now lay in following the commander's orders to the letter.

After giving a hasty salute, he was off.

****

Lord Cecil was the last to arrive at the Harbingers quarters and was not surprised to see this assortment of fellows as he entered. That was because almost nothing surprised Cecil anymore.

Six and a half feet tall and well over three-hundred fifty pounds, Chief Advisor Cecil was a powerful man both physically and in terms of his role in the Royal House. But his influence did not come from his physical stature, rather from his mental acuity. None were his equal when it came to the games of intrigue that were the staple of life in the Citadel, and he needed every advantage that his knowledge and influence could bring him to manage the affairs of the realm and protect the position of his King.

Allowing his vision to sweep the room, Cecil took in all that lay before him. Jusaan was the most animated, flitting between the guards, the servant girl, and Commander Colevant, talking incessantly and appearing on the verge of hysteria. The Commander was stoic, apparently keeping his thoughts to himself until a time he deemed appropriate. The servant girl appeared to still be in shock, as did the guards, who knew that they were the first to be blamed no matter what else occurred.

And then there was Captain Hendric who, having arrived just before Cecil, was busying himself examining the quarters.

Upon Cecil's entry, Jusaan detached himself from the guards and made a bee line for the Chief Advisor.

"Lord Cecil!" the priest began from ten paces distant. "It's horrible! The Harbinger has been taken!"

Cecil lifted a meaty hand and Jusaan found himself both halted and silenced. The Chief Advisor then spoke in his most authoritative voice.

"I assume that we here are the only ones aware of this at the moment?" he asked of the guards, who nodded agreement. "Good. You two return to your posts outside the foyer and remain there. Let no one pass without my order."

"Council Priest Jusaan," Cecil used the priest's formal title in hopes of bringing some dignity back to his behavior. "Please take this servant girl into the foyer and calm her. She may be in need of your counseling at a time such as this." He waited while the guards, happy to escape blame for the time being, and Jusaan, now saddled with a look of confusion, quickly obeyed his orders.

When those he designated had left the room, Cecil gave a quick glance toward Colevant. The garrison commander returned his gaze with steely eyed resolve but remained silent. Cecil knew the fears Colevant thought to hide with his stoic demeanor. With an air of satisfaction, he turned away from the commander to begin his own appraisal of the situation.

Cecil took his time, examining every part of the large room, the two dead bodies, the debris that was strewn about, and even onto the large balcony. There he joined Hendric, who stood at the far banister, looking out over the cloister and to the rocks and cliffs beyond.

From their position at the far edge of the balcony Cecil could look down at the tracks which, though still in the morning shadow of the cliffs to the east, stood out clearly on the icy ground below. After a while he turned to Hendric, one eyebrow lifted in question. Hendric returned Cecil's questioning look with an enigmatic smile before motioning him to cast his gaze to the right and along the walls of the Royal House. Cecil did so and after a moment or two of confusion his face blossomed in awareness. He nodded his head twice before again turning to Hendric. Together, they turned and made their way back into the large room that once quartered the Harbinger of the Fourth Prophesy.

Colevant had not moved from his position beside the large table on which the breakfast tray still sat, though he had helped himself to some of the fresh bread and aged cheese. He chewed absently, feigning confidence, as he watched Lord Cecil and

Captain Hendric reenter and approach the table. Cecil took the liberty of seating himself at the head of the table opposite the breakfast tray and invited Commander Colevant and Captain Hendric to take the seats on opposite sides of him.

"Let us first attempt to reach a consensus on what we believe occurred here," began Cecil. "It appears that there was an attack on the Harbinger... the fourth such, if my memory serves me correctly."

He looked directly at Colevant as he spoke these words.

"But not from within the ranks of the Guard!" Colevant was quick to fire back. "This was not the work of one who claims loyalty to me, therefore I cannot be held responsible!"

"Loyalty is to the Throne and he who sits upon it" was Cecil's calm reply, his eyes burning into Colevant.

"Well... you know what I meant..." Colevant said, looking off to the side.

"Of course I do, Commander," replied Cecil. "After his majesties last pronouncement, I would be surprised if you didn't feel a bit... uneasy... following the events of this past evening. But we are not yet at the juncture where blame is to be apportioned. Our immediate concern is to establish exactly what transpired in and around these quarters."

Cecil directed this last to Hendric, who seemed content to let his superiors clear their chests before he attempted to speak.

"Alright then," said Colevant. "Let it be clear that, upon learning of the events of last night, I immediately ordered the guard to bring the two of you, and no one else. My expertise is as a soldier in the field. Hendric here shares my background, but also has an eye for subtleties; one of the reasons why I picked him to captain the Royal Guard. I should like to hear his assessment."

Well done, thought Hendric, a tall, strong, quick-witted soldier with a commanding presence who, though in his mid-thirties, still seemed to hold firm to the exuberance of his youth.

He wondered how much of an assessment Colevant had made prior to his arrival. *Probably none*, he thought, *which is why he has placed the weight of interpreting this situation, along with the blame for any mistakes, squarely on my shoulders.*

"This was indeed an assassination attempt," Hendric said aloud, "an astonishing one based on the evidence this room provides, and considering the previous attempts."

"Those two dead men over there," he waved casually toward the corpses still lying on the floor, "are nearly naked. Their bodies are snow white while their faces and hands are the brown of a farmer who has been busy in his fields late into the summer."

"What are you saying," interjected Colevant. "Are farmers now sent into the Royal House to kill its guests?"

"They are not farmers," said Cecil. "What crops can be tended in a place covered with ice and snow for the better part of four moons?"

Hendric smiled. He had to be careful in responding to his immediate superior and was grateful that Cecil was present to temper their interactions.

"Not farmers, no," said Hendric. "My guess would be of folk living in a place where the sun is not filtered through the branches and leaves of so many trees, but where its rays shine strong throughout the year. They are most probably high mountain folk."

"Mountain folk?" Colevant almost spit his disdain for the idea. "So now you are pulling ideas out of your arse?"

"Think about it," said Hendric. "Those dead men did not come past our guard at the foyer door, nor by those who have set a perimeter about this wing of the Royal House. They entered through the balcony doors. There are tracks in the snow and ice that circle the courtyard and follow the outer walls until they reach the balcony. Those tracks appear to begin in the rocks and brush on the far side of the courtyard and lead in only one direction; toward these quarters."

"There are other tracks," Hendric continued, "that lead straight across the courtyard and into the rocks. These tracks appear to go in both directions, however, there is more disturbance leading away from the balcony than moving toward it. The attack was launched from the cover on the other side of the courtyard and launched by those who never saw, nor were ever seen by, our guards."

Now Lord Cecil spoke up, directing a question to Hendric.

"Were there no guards in the courtyard?" he asked, already aware of the response.

"Milord," replied Hendric, "to my knowledge there have never been guards stationed in this courtyard. These are the customary quarters of the first prince to the throne. There are always considerations when dealing with royalty, one of which is privacy. The princes who lived here considered this courtyard their private domain and a sanctuary away from the pressures and the eyes of life in the Royal Court. And these high cliff walls were always considered impassable regardless of the weather. For these reasons, this courtyard has not seen a regular patrol of the Royal Guard for hundreds of years."

"But you are telling us now that this is not the case," said Colevant. "You are telling us that in the dead of winter, amongst the freezing cold and howling winds, these men managed to scale the icy cliffs, descend into this courtyard, and assassinate the Harbinger?"

"No," replied Hendric, in as delicate a voice as he could muster "That is not my contention."

"Then what are you saying, man?" said Colevant, erupting with impatience. "Out with it!

Hendric began slowly.

"The tracks that are to be observed along the outer wall tell the tale. Two men approached from that direction, scaled the balcony, and attempted to assassinate the Harbinger. The Harbinger, referred to by those who have seen him in combat as 'the Panther', has foiled every prior attempt to overpower him, and without the aid of the Guard. Last night proved no different. There," Hendric again pointed to the twin corpses, "two dead assassins lie in pools of their own blood. There is no other blood in the room."

"So, it is as the priest said?" spoke Colevant. "The Harbinger and his acolyte have been taken?"

Hendric tried hard to hold his composure, even as he saw from the corner of his eye the almost pitying expression on Lord Cecil's face.

"Commander," Hendric said, "the Harbinger and his acolyte have left of their own accord."

"That is ridiculous!" Colevant shouted, almost rising from his seat in the effort. "For what possible reason would they leave the Royal House and the protection and hospitality of the Throne?"

"Of their reasoning I can only guess," commented Hendric, still cool under the heat of his commanders aggressive questioning, "but see for yourself; the assassins did not brave the wind and cold and descend the icy peaks to go about their bloody work, clothed only in loincloths and shirts! Whatever protection they had against the cold has been stripped from them. Their blades, one still deep in the assassin's body, are all that is left of their provisions."

"Also," Hendric continued, "where are the long sword and the bow that belonged to the Harbinger? He rode in my chariot from the Ursal Mountains to the Citadel, and I can assure you he was in possession of them when we arrived. Now his weapons, along with his pouch, are nowhere to be found. If he were abducted, would the abductors also take his weapons and keepsakes?"

Cecil watched closely while Commander Colevant's expression slowly changed from confusion to clarity. Colevant's words, however, remained a step behind.

"But… why would they leave…?" he seemed to ask the air around them.

"Mayhap because they grew weary of being targeted for assassination," said Cecil impatiently.

Colevant turned his face toward Cecil, but his open mouth emitted no sound, and his eyes remained unfocused as he attempted to process the scenario that had been presented to him.

Ignoring him, Cecil turned his attention to Captain Hendric.

"Lord Captain, I agree with your conclusions," he said. "Commander Colevant and I will accompany you when you tender your explanation to the King."

Cecil smiled as he saw the satisfied expression on Hendric's face change to one of surprise.

"Speaking of which," Cecil rose from his seat as he continued, "we should already be on our way to see His Majesty."

"Before we go…" Colevant said sheepishly, "…show me these tracks."

CHAPTER 12

As the sun rose higher in the eastern sky, its rays found their way into the crevice which served as Ray's shelter since Hanshee called a halt in the early morning darkness. Now the warmth on his face, and the light on his eyes, prompted him to awaken.

After the recent time spent in what he could only describe as his 'other life', Raymond's first conscious feeling was amazement at the fact that he could actually move! He spent a few moments lifting his arms and moving his legs, wiggling his fingers and toes, and turning his head from side to side.

This is real, Ray thought. *I'm looking at myself… at my arms and hands… at my legs… I'm touching my face… I'm pinching myself… and damned if that didn't hurt! I can run my hands over my skin and feel every hair, every blemish, every old scar exactly where it should be. It's not a dream, not a hallucination. This is me and this is real; as real as anything I can ever remember experiencing!"*

Then Ray laughed.

He laughed the type of laugh you laugh, not when something is amusing, but when something just feels *too* good… just feels *too* right.

Hanshee was nowhere to be seen, and that was good because then Ray would've had to explain to his friend the joy of having something simple, something everyone takes for granted, restored to you, and how this feeling could cause springs of pure joy to well up from the depths of your very soul!

Ray soaked in the glow of these good feelings for some time but, after a while, his laughter began to tail off. Now other urgent needs began to assert themselves.

First, I need to get out of this damn sunshine!

While its warming rays brought life and comfort, they also hurt his eyes this soon after awakening. He rolled over to his left and into the shadow of the rock that formed the outer wall of his sheltering space. Then he struggled to gain his feet so that he could stagger deeper into the shadows and relieve himself.

That was difficult, Ray thought.

Then he remembered how tired he was last night on the trail, triggering more memories of his awakening in the middle of Hanshee's battle with the assassins who had somehow found a way into their quarters. He remembered Hanshee in distress and how he had acted without thought to save his friend.

In doing so, he had taken a life.

His memory moved forward, to the difficult climb up the rock face and the journey along the narrow trail at its top. It was a journey he would never have had the strength to make save for the effects of the tabba plant. The fine powder, placed under his tongue by Hanshee, had temporarily given him strength and stamina like a young bull. But Hanshee had warned that a price was to be paid for relying on the tabba, and he felt that the aches and pains in his head and body were part of that price.

Bracing himself against the rock wall, Ray made his way back to the place where he had lain for the past several hours. There he paused and looked out into the brightness of the unfiltered sunlight. Even the rays reflecting off the sheer rock walls hurt his eyes but he squinted and persevered, glancing occasionally back toward the shadows to give his vision a rest before once again looking outward. In this way, he persuaded his vision to be at peace with the sun, and eventually stepped from the shadows and into the fullness of the light.

From where he stood, more than halfway up the eastern face of the shear mountain wall, Raymond looked out onto a valley of breathtaking beauty!

What spread out before him was a vast forest of mostly deciduous trees, but with enough evergreens to provide sprinkles and patches of green even in the cold of winter. From the north ran a river that hugged the base of the cliffs far below him, before separating from the mountain and meandering off through the forest to the east-southeast. Even at this height he could see that the ice covering the northern rivers, especially at higher elevations, was breaking up in the areas of swift current. Only the slower moving waters, and those closer to the bank, still showed an icy covering that reflected the bright sunlight.

Hanshee was right. The coldest weather had passed, and winter would soon be coming to an end.

Far off in the distance, so far off that Raymond could not be fully sure, he thought this river met another flowing from the northern highlands. The two appeared to come together to create one broad river that turned slightly and continued on a southeasterly path. Further to the north, beyond the highlands, he could see the peaks of distant mountain ranges that appeared so high and so white that they must surely harbor ice and snow through every season.

The entire picture stretched out before him to the east for as far as his eyes could see and the spectacle of this primeval wilderness, made even more beautiful by the golden rays of the sun and his vantage point high above, lent an element of majesty that left him breathless.

Ray continued to take in the extraordinary view until a noise from above caught his attention. He looked up just in time to see the gravel and loose rock kicked free by Hanshee as he made his way down the face of the cliff. Ray quickly stepped aside to avoid the falling debris and only then saw the end of the rope clinging to the sheer rock wall beside him. He had been so taken with the scenery that he hadn't noticed it. Now he watched as Hanshee made his way down its length as if he had been doing this sort of thing all his life. Still five feet above the ledge where Ray stood, Hanshee released his grip and dropped deftly down beside him.

"It is good that you are awake, Way-mon," Hanshee said. "I feared the tabba had proven too much after your recent healing."

"Waking up was rough," Ray replied, "but this view is making it worthwhile."

Hanshee briefly joined Ray as he took in the forest that spread out before them.

"The beauty of Our Mother is a wonder to fill the heart," Hanshee said. "It is to be viewed with reverence. It is why my people shun the blight of cities; why we will never find understanding in those that seek to dwell within their walls."

Ray heard Hanshee's words and wondered if he too counted among those that could not *understand*. Wasn't he born and raised in a city; arguably a city much worse than the ones Hanshee had experienced? But he had also lived in the wild with Hanshee for several months. He had come to understand the bounty that nature could provide; the freedom that came with a life uncluttered.

But that life is only for those with the knowledge, the skill, and the drive to coax from nature that which was needed to survive.

Only in the presence of someone like Hanshee could someone like himself hope to experience the good and the beauty. Absent the leadership and teachings of his friend, he would have experienced only the hardship, the deprivation, the savagery, and the final judgment that nature had in store for those not attuned to her ways.

He had lived in the wild with Hanshee; was willing to do so again. But he knew, even though it lacked the modern conveniences of his *other* life, he would deeply miss the many comforts of the Royal House.

Hanshee abruptly turned from the view to cast an appraising eye at Ray.

"How do you feel?" he asked. "Have you replenished your strength? Do you feel strong enough to travel?"

Ray had never heard Hanshee repeat himself and, had he been a dog, his ears would have instantly been raised in concern. As it was, only his eyebrows went up.

"I can do what I have to," he replied, trying to project more strength than he felt. He motioned to the place high above, where the rope was anchored. "Tell me what you found up there."

Hanshee eyed him for a moment more before turning and pointing south along the base of the rock wall that they currently stood upon.

"There," he said. "Do you see where the trees begin to rise?

"Yes," said Ray, following Hanshee's eyes and pointing hand to a place on the far side of the valley where the tops of the trees seemed to be steadily climbing above those that were closer. "It looks like the ground is rising at that point."

"It is," said Hanshee, "but not as much as we need it to. This trail that we follow ends there. We would still be a great distance above the trees when it ends."

"But look above," he continued, pointing up to the ledge he had just descended from. "There is a trail that leads beyond our sight. On the far side those rocks," he pointed to the southern edge of the cliff wall, "the trail above turns inward. The land continues to rise and if we continue to follow, it may lead us from these peaks and onto the forest floor."

Ray looked down the trail they currently stood upon, then up toward the trail ledge Hanshee said could lead them down from here, measuring the distance with his eyes.

"So," he began, "we need to get up to that other trail…"

"Yes," was Hanshee's quick reply. "Do you feel up to the task?" It was a challenge as much as a question.

"I can do it," Ray said, with much more confidence than he felt.

"Then let us gather our belongings" Hanshee said, more quickly than Ray expected.

He wants to do this before I have a chance to think about it and back out, thought Ray, as he collected his cloak, unneeded in the warmth of the direct sun. He also retrieved the harness that he now wore which carried, among other things, the longblade taken from the third assassin; the one who lay dead by his hand. He tried to put that out of his head for now, knowing it would do no good to be distracted during a climb between ledges hundreds of feet in the air. But he knew he would have to deal with his new reality soon. He couldn't keep burying it in his memory the way he apparently had until just now, when he saw the sword.

Joining Hanshee on the lower ledge, he watched as his companion tested the rope that he had descended just minutes ago. Satisfied that the hook still held, Hanshee hoisted himself into the air and began climbing hand over hand. He matched each forward motion of an arm by a step with the opposite leg, which he used to keep his body clear of the rock wall. In this way, he appeared to be walking up the wall of stone. Despite the added weight of his winter gear and weapons, he climbed with ease. In no time he was pulling himself up onto the ledge forty feet above them.

My turn, Ray thought as he took hold of the rope with both hands. He tested its strength, more of a reflex than due to any concern, then leaned back and placed first one foot, then the other, on the rock wall. Balanced there, at an almost ninety-degree angle to the mountainside, he realized that what works for Hanshee does not necessarily work for him.

Starting again by standing up straight, he used both hands to pull himself as far up the rope as he could, using his feet against the rock to steady himself while he again repositioned his hands as far up the rope as he could. In this way, he made it, exhausted, to the upper ledge. He paused there for a moment, reminding himself not to look down, gathering the strength he would need to pull himself over the edge and onto secure ground. Hanshee watched him carefully during the entire process, but did not offer assistance.

Once he was lying on the ledge catching his breath, Ray asked Hanshee, "How did I do this last night?"

"It was the tabba, my friend... and I may have pulled on the rope."

Now that he was safe Ray could allow himself a chuckle, and he did, catching his breath between short spurts of laughter. When he had finally caught his breath, he rolled over to look down at the ledge he had just left.

"That's a long way down," he said, thinking aloud.

"You climbed twice as high today as you did last night," Hanshee said as he collected the rope. "And it was done without help."

"You were testing me," said Ray, as he made his way to his feet.

"Our Mother tests us daily," said Hanshee, quoting a saying of his people. "Woe be unto he who is found wanting."

Together, they started down this new cliff-trail which carried them farther south. This part of the ledge was wide enough so Raymond did not feel acrophobic as he kept pace behind Hanshee. He just stayed well away from the edge of the ledge, basically following Hanshee from right beside the wall of rock. After a while he noticed the trail begin to narrow until it reached a point where it was no wider than six or seven feet from the inner wall to the ledge. Now he was feeling some anxiety as he cast occasional glances toward the lip of the ledge, sometimes leaning farther out, just to see what he would hit if he should fall off.

After one such examination of the potential fall, Ray looked up ahead and saw that Hanshee had reached a place where he was fully facing the wall and shuffling sideways along what remained of the trail. It was no wider than two feet at this point, narrowing in some places to about eighteen inches and ending in a drop of several hundred feet to the nearest ledge below. Looking beyond Hanshee, Ray could see that this narrow part of the ledge didn't widen appreciably for about thirty to forty feet.

Upon seeing this, Ray froze.

Acrophobia is defined as an extreme or irrational fear of heights. Ray never saw anything irrational or extreme in his discomfort with places high enough for him to injure himself, or die, if he were to fall. On the contrary, he saw his concerns with falling from great heights as wholly rational and not extreme in the least.

It was because of his insistence on rational thought when faced with dilemmas such as the one presently confronting him, that he knew, with no doubt whatsoever, that he was going to turn and retrace his steps back to the Royal House, abandoning Hanshee to this ridiculous plan of escape. What did he have to fear?... more assassination attempts?... attempts that might or might not happen?

He didn't know how long he stood there, anchored to one spot, looking at the impossible trail before him but, suddenly, he heard Hanshee calling out to him. He had no idea how long Hanshee had been trying to bring him back to the here and now.

It really didn't matter.

He wasn't going to move.

But Hanshee was insistent, and his voice kept cutting through the clutter of Ray's thoughts.

"Listen to me, Way-mon. Focus on my voice," Hanshee called. "Listen to my voice my friend and do as I say. Begin where you stand and turn to face the wall. Trust in me, my friend; face the wall… yes, that is right."

Surprisingly, Ray found himself turning and facing the rock wall.

"Now," continued Hanshee, "find a place on the wall a little higher than your eyes… as high as your head… a little higher… yes, that is good. Now, spread your arms and hug he wall… and focus on that place. See a line at that place that runs across the face of the rock… Focus! Now step to your left… one step… yes… now, another… yes… focus your eyes on the wall… on the line… yes…"

Raymond found himself responding to Hanshee's voice and stepping to the left. It helped that he knew the part of the ledge where he currently stood was at least seven feet across, so it was easy to listen at this point.

"Take a step… good… take a step and focus…" Hanshee repeated. "Focus on the wall… the line straight across… focus and step… focus… step…"

For some reason, as if he were hypnotized, Ray continued to obey Hanshee's voice. He never took his eyes away from the line he imagined on the rock face. He continued to step to his left in an easy and steady fashion, not too far and not too fast. Through it all was the continuing cadence of Hanshee as he gave his instructions.

"Step… focus… step… focus… always focus on the line… and step… focus…"

When Ray heard Hanshee say, "You have done well, Waymon," it was as if fingers had snapped and he awakened from a trance, finding himself standing beside his friend on the other side, where the ledge had again widened to about five feet.

Ray looked back over the ground he had covered and was amazed. Turning to Hanshee he was almost tearful in his thanks.

"I don't know what you did just then," Ray said while shaking his head, "but, thank you… thank you, thank you! And don't *ever* ask me to do something like that again," he continued, "because I won't!"

Hanshee slapped him on the back.

"Of course not, my friend" he said, before turning and again starting down the trail leading south.

Ray looked after Hanshee, shaking his head in disbelief before falling in behind him.

****

King Ammon IV had a reaction that was quite surprising given the investment he had placed in the Harbinger of the Fourth Prophesy and the coming spring campaign.

Those present when he was informed expected not just anger, but white-hot unfettered rage of the kind only rulers can indulge in, because rulers have no one above them to hold them accountable. What they received instead was quiet composure while the king listened to the details of the previous night's events. This was followed by sharp questions about the dead assassins, the conditions inside and outside the room, and the possible whereabouts of the Harbinger and his acolyte. After listening carefully and considering all that he had heard, Ammon spoke.

"Captain Hendric," he began. "You have a sharp mind and an eye for detail. Commander Colevant was wise to promote you.

"I agree with your assessment of the assassins and of the actions of the Harbinger. It is unfortunate but understandable that, after four attempts on his life, he should question the ability of the Throne to protect him. He is most likely still within the city but gone aground to avoid further attempts. Now I ask you to take the lead in the search for him. Colevant will place the Garrison at your disposal."

The King looked to Commander Colevant, who gave a sharp nod of ascent.

"Mobilize the Garrison and the Royal Guard. Scour the city. Know that, in this matter, your calling is divine. The forces that have been set in motion by the arrival of the Harbinger are larger than King and Country. I pray that they can be harnessed, maybe temporarily redirected, until the successful completion of your search," the King concluded.

Turning away from Hendric, King Ammon then snapped, "Council Priest Jusaan!"

The priest jumped, startled to hear his name.

"Your prayers and your efforts are needed now," continued Ammon. "You were chosen by The One to bring the Harbinger before us. You speak the ancient tongue and have conversed extensively with him. You have more insight into his thinking than any other. Consult with Captain Hendric. Search the ancient texts. See if they hold a clue to this incident and his possible whereabouts."

The King then stood, signaling dismissal, and all stood with him, bowed, and filed out of the room.

All except Lord Cecil.

Cecil was chief advisor to this king, as he had been to his father before him. He had a finger on the 'royal pulse' and knew when his services were needed, even when the Throne did not. In this instance, the need for his council was crystal clear to both he and King Ammon. Once they were alone, Cecil spoke.

"You were right to praise Lord Captain Hendric, Milord," Cecil said. "He has one of the sharpest minds I have encountered in the Guard in some time. Colevant proved insightful with Hendric's promotion."

"And you have again proven your worth by arranging that which none are aware was arranged," Ammon replied.

Cecil bowed his head slightly, acknowledging that it was indeed his subtle prodding that prompted Colevant to promote Hendric. He then continued.

"Milord, if I may," he began. "I expected more passion from Milord at the news of last night's... setback. I believe that Commander Colevant was just as surprised as I, though for a different reason."

King Ammon allowed himself a smile at the thought of Colevant sitting stone faced, contemplating his fate.

"I would not have the heads of his family over something beyond his control," said the king, referring to his earlier promise of consequences should the Harbinger come to harm. "If there were evidence that the attempt on the Harbinger came from within the Guard or the Garrison, then you would have witnessed a much different temper."

"As you say, my King," replied Cecil, "but... there is something else on your mind; something that you hesitate to share with the others."

"Ever perceptive of the mood of the Throne, Chief Advisor," King Ammon said, as he walked over to a table and poured himself a goblet of wine. Only alone, or in the presence of Cecil, would his Highness indulge himself by serving his own refreshment. It was a testament to the bond they shared. But even the Chief Advisor was caught off guard by the next move of the King, as he poured a second goblet of drink which he then placed in Cecil's hand.

"Sit with me for a while, Advisor," said the king. "I have need of your ear."

"What troubles you, Milord?" Cecil asked, real concern evident in his voice.

"The brazen nature of this latest attempt on the life of the Harbinger," Ammon said flatly. "Tell me Cecil, what know you of the Assassins Guild?"

CHAPTER 13

Traversing the eastern face of these mountains was turning into slow and strenuous work, and Ray was beginning to wear down. He was thankful for the rope, which had allowed them to climb higher or lower depending on the trail they were on.

These ledges were mostly formed by great sheets of rock having fallen from the face of the mountain after many thousands of years of weather and wear. Most of the trails formed extended anywhere from a few feet to several hundred feet, but always came to abrupt ends. On two occasions they had to back track due to choosing a ledge that ended in a sheer drop to nowhere.

But Hanshee did not give up and apparently did not tire. He always found an option, if not a solution, to any obstacles they encountered, and he kept them moving ever southward.

Raymond could see that the ground was not so far below as it had once seemed. And so there was hope that all the climbing and straining, the narrow ledges and bleeding fingers and exhaustion, would soon lead to a path away from these cliffs and into the forest.

Eventually they found a flat wide ledge on which to rest and, as it was getting late in the day, Hanshee decided that this would make a good place to spend the night.

The sun had ceased to be their friend once it had passed its zenith. That is when it disappeared behind the tallest peaks and left them in the shade of the cliffs for the rest of the day. With the shade came the full force of the cold. Even the wind, which had not been a concern earlier in the day, seemed to pick up as the temperature continued to fall. Thankfully, Hanshee had spotted several bird nests - raptor nests from the size of them - during their climb. They were empty this time of year and he was able to climb to one, and to hook another with the grapple. These provided both the kindling and the wood with which to make a fire, and the two could experience much needed warmth during the coldest parts of the night.

As they sat there with the fire between them, both men were lost in their respective thoughts. Ray could not know what occupied Hanshee's mind, but he found himself pondering the life he had *escaped* just the night before.

Just over twenty-four hours ago, by his current reckoning, he was lying helpless in a hospital bed. He was paralyzed from the neck down and had extraordinarily little movement above the neck. He had been the victim of a canoeing accident, had required emergency surgery, and probably would never regain the mobility or even the full speech that could make his life at least bearable.

Doug had told him that the most likely diagnosis for his situation was *locked-in syndrome*; something he had never heard of. The way Doug had explained it, a little-known syndrome with a questionable promise for recovery. He knew his lifelong friend would do his absolute best for him; of that there was no doubt. But Raymond had been slowly coming around to the thought that maybe there was not much to be done. Maybe Doug's best was just to make him comfortable for however much time his body chose to function in the limited manner allowed by locked-in syndrome.

As he thought back to those several weeks he spent awake in the hospital - though only fifteen days here, if Hanshee was to be believed - what he found remarkable was that there had never been feelings of despair despite how gloomy his prognosis had become.

The first days of his awakening were the worst that he recalled but, even then, there was something that he could not quite grasp that prevented him from giving up or giving in. Later, after he was taken off the sedatives and allowed to find sleep naturally, his mind seemed to reach out, as if searching for an ever present something he could not identify; an itch he could not scratch. Then it connected to this place, and somehow Ray knew, almost from the beginning, that this was real.

Is that what had kept him sane? Is that why he never succumbed to depression or despair? Because he somehow knew that, regardless of how his existence there had changed, he had another life here; a life that he could fully experience?

And he knew he would be coming back?

Yes, he had known that. He had told Doug as much. Less than two days ago.

Raymond did not know how to explain this to Hanshee; didn't know if he should try. Hell, he didn't know how to explain it, period. But the truth of the matter was that he had two lives; one completely familiar, and severely depressing; the other completely foreign and, in its way, completely exhilarating! And he knew that, even while he was here lost in thought about his situation, he was there, lying in a hospital bed, most likely comatose, just as Doug told him he had been prior to awakening.

But he knew that he had been here with Hanshee.

He knew from those conversations with Doug that time seemed to pass at a different pace in each place. His three weeks lying comatose in his hospital bed there had been over seven months of fighting for survival here. About six weeks of hospital care after he awoke there had been only fifteen days of drugged recovery here.

That makes no sense, he thought. *Time can be shorter here and longer there, or longer here and shorter there, depending on… what?*

No, he was not prepared to discuss this with Hanshee. He was sure of that. Everything else was part of the big picture that he had to figure out one day. But here in this world, wherever it may be, there seemed to be no time for figuring much out. Since his arrival here, all his energies were needed to make it through to another day.

He looked across the fire at Hanshee, who was uncharacteristically lost in its depths. Ray didn't know where he was or why he was here, but Hanshee's purpose seemed clear; Hanshee was here to survive. And by doing so, he would ensure Ray's survival. Since Hanshee had found him, and saved him, they had been joined at the hip. That seemed more than coincidence but, as with most of this mystery that continued to unfold before him, Ray felt that he just was not equipped to explore it any deeper.

Maybe one day, he thought, *but not now.*

Hanshee did not seem to be worried that their fire would be spotted from the ground below. He had been searching the trees, and the air above the trees, for signs of human habitation even as they had made their way along the cliffs. He had seen no smoke trails and if someone were living down there in these temperatures, they would have had a fire. Hanshee quickly built theirs up, and then they ate more dried fruit, dried meat, and nuts.

Hanshee had warned Raymond to conserve his water as they were not sure when the opportunity to leave this dry cliff face would present itself. One or two mouths full were all that they allowed themselves this night. For the moment they were warm and comfortable, as comfortable as one could expect to be when sleeping on a bed of solid rock.

But solid rock will do just fine, thought Ray. *Solid anything is a comfort when you're several hundred feet off of the ground.*

Ray again looked at Hanshee and this time found the warrior looking back at him from across the fire.

"There is much on your mind, Way-mon," Hanshee said. "Probably much you wish to share with me."

Caught unawares, Ray was speechless.

"It can wait," Hanshee smiled. "It is time for sleep."

And that's what they did.

****

When he awoke the next morning, Raymond felt like a new man.

They had bedded down between the fire and the cliff wall, which both reflected and absorbed heat from the fire. This, along with the copious amount of wood provided by the large raptor nests, meant that they spent a relatively warm night despite the freezing winds. Now, in the morning glory of the rising sun, Ray felt rested and prepared for anything the day could throw his way.

Realizing that he was still on a ledge at least two hundred feet off the ground changed that.

Looking around, he saw that Hanshee had awakened first and apparently took the initiative to scout a path off this ledge. Either that or he had fallen during the night. Either way, he wasn't here and, after a few minutes, this started to worry Ray.

Moving out from the wall and around the remains of the fire, he dropped to his knees and crawled on his belly toward the edge of the ledge to have a look over. The tops of the trees obscured much of the ground, but what was visible did not reveal a dead Hanshee. Not that he expected it to, Ray reasoned, but it was always better to know.

What his peek over the edge did reveal was that, just as Hanshee had said, the ground was moving steadily upward toward their position on the cliff face. They had moved both up and down as they made their way southward, but their position relative to the top of the peaks had really not changed much. The ground below was on a steady incline, sometimes steep, sometimes not, but so much so that they were about two thirds closer to the ground now than when they started on this path two nights ago.

Ray edged back to his position against the wall and allowed the sun's rays to warm him while he had a little food and a few sips of water. Just as he was tying off his water bag, he was startled by the end of the rope as it slapped against the rock not three feet to his right. Ray coughed a little, the sound of the rope having made him send some of the water down the wrong tube, then he lay back so he could comfortably look up and watch Hanshee descend to the campsite. As usual, Ray could only stare in admiration.

Everything he does seems effortless, thought Ray, as Hanshee shimmied down the rope, dropping lightly beside his companion.

"Out for your morning climb, huh?" joked Ray.

Most comments like that were lost on Hanshee and this one was no exception. He never even looked at Ray as he untied his water bag and had a swallow. Then he tied it back while taking in the view from their current perch, a fine view, but not as grand as the view of the morning before.

"I have found our way from this mountain," Hanshee said when he finally turned toward Ray. "This sunset will find us asleep on firm ground, with forest about us to cut the wind."

This got Ray's attention.

"And a roaring fire fueled by plenty of wood?" he asked

"Perhaps," Hanshee said. "If we can find the proper cover, and are sure that none are about."

Raymond let his eyes wander up the cliff to the ledge that Hanshee had just descended from. He hadn't noticed it yesterday when they had decided to stay here for the night. Apparently Hanshee had.

"How far is it?" Ray asked. "About how much more climbing will we be doing?"

Hanshee pointed to the southern end of the ledge they stood upon.

"See how the cliff face disappears? he asked. "The mountain turns to the west and the trail ends. But, if we climb to the next ledge," he pointed to the ledge up above them, "it turns with the mountain."

"And then, what?" prodded Ray.

"We move from ledge to ledge down the mountain side until we are close enough to reach the ground," said Hanshee.

Ray beamed a genuine smile of happiness.

"That sounds like a plan," he said, as he began to gather up their belongings and remaining provisions.

****

By the time the sun had again passed its zenith and the high peaks again covered the pair in their shadow, Ray had a much different opinion about the 'plan'. Technically, it was as Hanshee had said; climb to the ledge above, follow it around the bend in the mountain, then move downward from ledge to ledge.

Easy!

Only it wasn't easy at all, beginning with the ledge above, which was so narrow that once Raymond had made the climb and pulled his head over its edge, his impulse was to just hang there. There was hardly any room to pull himself up onto the ledge! It was another one of those extremely narrow, extremely long ledges, much longer than the ledge he traversed the day before, and this time he felt so much fear just crouching on the ledge that he couldn't bring himself to attempt to stand. Ray crawled on his hands and knees, the entire two-foot wide, sixty-foot length of it. As before, Hanshee talked him through it as much as possible, keeping Raymond focused on moving forward and not looking over the edge.

Once they reached the end, Hanshee pointed out their next goal; a ledge much wider (thank God) but every bit of forty feet down. Beyond it Hanshee pointed out two other ledges, each lower than the previous one, making the total descent one of about one-hundred feet.

But first they had to tackle the forty-foot drop.

Hanshee was having trouble getting the hook into a stable position and did not want to risk injury to Ray, so he told him he would hold the hook while Ray climbed down. When Ray had safely reached the ledge, Hanshee would secure the hook as best he could and follow Ray down.

The hardest part was getting Ray to swing his body over the edge of a forty-foot-high drop while holding a rope attached to nothing but Hanshee, who stood on a two-foot-wide ledge smiling assurances that Ray was safe and he would not let go of the rope, nor be pulled over by the weight of his companion.

Somewhere at the beginning of his descent, Ray remembered questioning whether this was really life and whether he would not be happier back in the hospital bed. Then his thoughts ceased as he began the descent, and the next thing he remembered was touching his feet to the ledge below. He was trembling; whether from fear or relief he wasn't sure but, having that descent behind him and being on that wide solid ledge, brought relief like he imagined he never felt before.

His revelry was broken when Hanshee called down for him to take hold of the rope and pull it as tightly as he could. Raymond grabbed the rope and, leaning with his back toward the cliff wall, put all his weight on it. The grapple held and before he knew it Hanshee stood beside him, smiling, and patting him on the shoulder for a job well done.

The next two drops were shorter and from a much broader base, making them easy in comparison to the first, and Ray felt true joy when he looked over the edge and saw the tops of a small grove of evergreen trees only fifty feet below them.

"Where do we go from here?" he asked, as he watched Hanshee checking the rope for any weakness before looking for a place to anchor it.

Hanshee pointed straight down even as he was securing one of the three hooks of the grapple in a crack in the rock ledge. When he was sure it would hold, he threw the rope over the side and watched as its fifty-foot length stopped about ten feet short of the tops of the evergreens.

On hands and knees Ray joined Hanshee at the edge and saw the space between the rope and the trees. He looked up and saw Hanshee looking at him intently, a question in his eyes.

"It is the last obstacle to the earth," Hanshee said, his eyes asking if Ray had the courage to take on one last challenge.

If asked, Ray would not have been able to explain it. Maybe it was because they were so close to their goal. Maybe it was because this was, as Hanshee had said, "the last obstacle". Maybe, after all he had endured over the last two days, he was fed up with being afraid. The look in his eyes and the strength in his voice were surprising even to him.

"I'm ready," was all Ray said.

****

The drop into the trees was tricky. He couldn't drop between them. That's where the thinnest branches were found. He had to drop close to a trunk, counting on the highest, weakest branches to break his fall until he could find something sturdy enough to hold his weight, then grab hold of it. And he had to find something quick; the further he fell, the more damage he could potentially do to himself. And he couldn't drop feet first. That was a definite no-no. Once he was secure in a tree, it was only a matter of climbing from limb to limb, sometimes from limb to trunk to limb, until his feet finally touched the good earth.

Sure, he wanted to go to his knees, bend over and kiss the ground, and he would have… about an hour ago. Now he was simply happy to join Hanshee on the ground, where they picked the needles and bark out of their clothes, took their bearings, and headed south through the late winter forest.

"I hate that we had to leave the rope," said Raymond, as they walked away from the grove of evergreens. Who knows when we might need it again?

"Our needs will always be met, Way-mon," Hanshee said with quiet confidence.

Raymond thought back over all his time spent with Hanshee, from his awakening beside the river when Hanshee had saved his life, to his awakening in their quarters two nights ago when he returned the favor.

"I believe they will," he said.

CHAPTER 14

Nola was justifiably proud of herself.

She had managed to guide her remaining brother down from the treacherous eastern peaks to terrain that was much easier on his damaged leg. Unfortunately, this had placed more distance between them and their home in the northern mountains, and even traversing level ground was an ordeal that Darien could not endure for long.

This was part of the reason Nola felt proud.

She had managed to accomplish the real reason for bringing him out of the mountains; to get closer to one of the small villages that dotted these foothills.

After stashing her brother in an evergreen thicket, she had managed to steal a horse from a small farm. This was accomplished in the early morning, well before sunrise.

Due to the decrease in elevation. there was no snow on the ground surrounding the farm she had chosen, therefore, no concern about leaving obvious tracks. She had covered the hooves of the old plow horse with thick pieces of leather cut from the folds of Darien's winter robe, and she tied them on with thin leather strips obtained the same way. This helped to hide any marks the shoed horse might otherwise leave in the hard ground. Her own footprints were of no concern, as she was quite adept at hiding her movements and was certain she left none a farmer could follow.

But, for a Reaper, this resourcefulness was expected.

Often, when one of the Guild was sent to a strange place to perform a service, be it a killing, a kidnapping, a theft, an arson, or whatever, improvisation was called for. Just as they learned the many ways of taking a life, it was equally important to learn stealth... and thievery. Sometimes one had to steal whatever was needed to complete a task.

To steal a horse when a horse was needed was expected. What made Nola proud was that she had taken the horse out from under the old farmer, who had just left his barn after feeding his livestock and servicing his milk cow.

She had waited soundlessly not five feet from him, hidden in the shadow cast by a wall of the very stall in which the farmer worked. He worked under the light of a small lamp, filling a small bucket with milk for his family's morning meal, and not once did he suspect that he had more company than the beasts that surrounded him.

Nola listened while he muttered bitterly about the cold. This told her that, after filling his bucket, he would not soon be back to the barn. When he shuffled back to his small wood-framed house, she went about her business and was soon leading the horse past the shuttered farmhouse while the farmer was still noisily berating his wife for not having a fire ready for his return.

Yes, Nola felt proud. She had stolen the horse out from under the old farmer... which left no need to kill him, or any members of his family. With no sound, no tracks, and no dead, there was nothing that would lead anyone to follow her and, most importantly, nothing that would hint at the existence of the Guild.

Staying off roads that showed recent usage, and always ready to lead the horse and its injured rider into the brush at the first sign that someone approached, they had managed to travel many leagues before she felt compelled to stop for the day. Moving far off the sparsely traveled road, she found a patch of dry ground on the far side of a rise deep in the forest. This is where they made camp.

Nola made a small fire for heat, and trusted the surrounding woods to hide what little smoke it gave off. She was not concerned about the smell of smoke. In this season, as long as one was near the dwellings of men, the smell of smoke was always in the air. Here they rested and she tended to the blistered face, torn arm, and broken leg of her brother. There was plenty of time for this, and for the two of them to take their rest. Nola had decided, until they could leave the lowlands, they would travel by night and rest during the day.

Darien was exceedingly grateful to have a horse to ride, though it was awkward without a saddle. The lurching gait of the animal used for plowing and other heavy work, and his efforts to remain seated, made the ride anything but comfortable. Still, it was much better than the pain of trying to walk with the makeshift splint Nola had devised. So, Darien sat his mount, gritted his teeth, and fought through every pain in stoic silence.

With her brothers' injured condition, Nola recognized the horse as a godsend. Still, they made far less progress than they could have had Darien been healthy and they had stayed to the mountain trails. Based on their rate of travel, she calculated a destination that took just over three days to reach may take six to return from. Their people would be worried, she knew, but there was nothing to be done except keep to the steady progress they were making. They would reach home eventually.

And home would bring a reckoning for the failure she brought back with her.

****

Jusaan moved with careful steps down the corridor leading to his temporary chambers in the Royal House. He had regained his composure since the dreadful discovery of yesterday morning and his mind was again fluid with schemes.

The loss of the Harbinger meant he ran the risk of losing his relevance with King Ammon and the members of the Royal

Court. He had also been enjoying more respect from the members of the Council of The Nine due, he thought, to his being openly acknowledged as chosen by The One Spirit to present the Harbinger of the Fourth Prophesy to the people of Pith. His scheme, so hastily thrown together on one disagreeable evening in the southern forest, had been moving along so smoothly that even he was beginning to believe there was a divine plan at work.

The disappearance of the reason for his advancement could cause doubts as to his worth among those currently supporting him. This would greatly constrict his pathway to the position of Lord High Priest; the prize he had coveted even before the Harbinger was so fortuitously thrust upon him.

The remedy, He thought, was to *continue to make oneself valuable, even as the goal shifts from nurturing their guest to finding him.*

Entering his quarters, still toasty due to the efforts of his acolytes, he first secured the door, then untied his heavy winter robes and let them drop to the floor. He stepped out of them, allowing them to lie where they fell.

Giving purpose to those whose lives are currently spent in service to me, he thought smugly.

Truth be told, he often did little things here and there for the sole purpose of giving his underlings something to do. In doing so he allowed them to assuage their souls by paying a price, however small, for their coveted positions as his servants.

As he stood before the roaring fire, clad only in his undergarments and the decorative dagger marking him as a priest of The One Spirit, he let his mind wander in search of any way he could still be of service in this crisis.

Jusaan could still claim to be the person most familiar with their onetime guest. That was legitimate, as no other had spoken with him so extensively. Surely in all their conversations, some admittedly brief, he had learned a morsel of information... a tidbit of no consequence at the time... which could prove valuable in the all-out search presently underway.

This was the idea he had planted with the other members of what he secretly referred to as the 'inner circle', the core group who initiated the city-wide search for the missing warrior-priest. He was thankful to be included among them. He had no training for anything such as this yet, since they first met on morning last, his presence had been unquestioned.

If I can but prove my value now, in their greatest time of need, Jusaan thought, *I will cement in their minds my stature as a humble servant of, and blessed by, The One Spirit; the only real choice should a new Lord High Priest, for one reason or another, be required.*

He had been a mess the morning when it was first discovered the Harbinger was gone. But he had recovered. If he could but continue to keep his wits about him, maybe he could turn this tragedy into his personal triumph. To this end, he was racking his brain to remember any and everything that Hanshee had told him of himself, especially in those unguarded moments in the forest when he was but a wandering warrior-priest, before he was thrust into the chaos of life in the Citadel.

Having warmed himself sufficiently, Jusaan first thought to summon Petri from the adjoining room to fetch him some spiced wine. Seeing this as a time for contemplation, he thought better of dealing with that bumbler and poured his own, taking it with him as he reclined on a softly cushioned couch farther away from the heat of the flames.

Hanshee had presented himself as a warrior-priest in exile, forced to wander until he found penance for some unknown transgression. What he specifically sought, he did not seem to know, but once he felt himself absolved, he and his acolyte would return to his home beyond the Blue Mountains. This was the gist of his early conversations with the man.

Jusaan pondered this for a while.

Maybe this was the tidbit he sought?

At present, there were two schools of thought on the Harbingers whereabouts. Although some still theorized he was taken by his attackers and not killed on the spot, the most popular theory by far was that he and his acolyte, weary of being the target of assassins, had gone over the Citadel wall and were hiding somewhere in the city. Maybe he had already escaped the city and was hiding somewhere within the forests of Stronghold. There were more than enough wild areas in the valley to shelter even large groups of men, as the bandit gangs regularly proved.

But what if both theories were wrong?

What if he had attempted the unthinkable, daring to pass through the eastern peaks? Impossible, some said, but surely the assassins had entered the Citadel that way.

Few believed the assassins had traversed the eastern peaks. Most thought they used a previously unknown trail in the lower mountains to bypass the sentries and the wall, then came down into the courtyard in the rear of the Royal House to strike.

But the Harbinger was not of the assassins. He had proven himself to be both exceptional and resourceful. What if he *had* attempted the eastern peaks... and succeeded? Where would this put him now?

Jusaan considered and rejected the idea many times over. In the history of Pith, no one had ever traversed those peaks and lived to tell the tale. They had been studied from the ground endlessly, and all knew that the view from the other side, when in the Ninum Valley, was of a sheer cliff wall well over a thousand feet high. Only the birds dared those ledges!

But what if he *had* attempted... and succeeded?

The idea was now stuck in Jusaan's head.

If the Harbinger had succeeded, he would either make his way down into the Ninum Valley, the 'Dark Valley', an area somewhat explored but mostly avoided by the Pith, or he would head back into the southern forest, where he was found, to continue his penance and return to his people beyond the Blue Mountains.

That had to be it! thought Jusaan.

No one had yet mentioned the possibility. No one had thought to look outside Stronghold, as no one could leave Stronghold without it being known except by its northern borders, the wildest and the bitterest country, especially this time of year. He must find the courage to make this argument, and find the logic to convince Ammon of the possibility. Then, if they fail to find the Harbinger in the city, he will be seen as being a step ahead. And if the Harbinger be found *anywhere* outside Stronghold, Jusaan's status as favored by The One will be secure.

But what if he is eventually found in the city?

No matter. He must simply make this a suggestion; something to consider. If he does not come forward too boldly, his whisperings will be forgotten in the euphoria of returning the Harbinger to the Royal House.

Yes, Jusaan decided. *This will be my next plan of action; a whisper. The right words in the right ear at the right time. A gamble, to be sure, but with little on the line not already wagered, and with a tremendous payoff should I prove correct!*

Smiling in satisfaction at this new stratagem, Jusaan called for Cafran to relieve his tortured soul by seeing to his masters' bath.

CHAPTER 15

Hanshee and Ray found a good spot to make camp that night.

It was above a wash on a level outcropping of rock that was flanked on its western side by taller, broader rocks. The result was, although the surface was hard, the campsite was protected from the winds that were blowing predominantly from the west-northwest. This also made a fire easier to maintain while shielding the brightness from any eyes looking from the direction of Stronghold.

The hard surface was not a problem considering the ledges they had slept on the past two nights. The fur cloaks that shielded them from the winds and the cold of the high rock cliffs were now used as cushions to provide a little comfort for their tired bodies.

Even Hanshee was tired.

What they had accomplished in the past two days and nights was no small feat. Even augmented by the tabba, it took all of Ray's strength, endurance, and focus to traverse those cliffs. Hanshee had blazed the trail, often scouting ahead while Ray rested up, then coming back and leading him over the climbs he had already made. In effect, making the same climbs as Ray, but doing it twice and while carrying more gear.

So, they took great delight in resting this night.

They had refilled their water bags from a spring that was still surrounded by the partially melted ice accumulation of the night before. Once the fire was built and enough wood gathered to see them through the night, Hanshee settled in, and Ray did the same. Hanshee broke out the dried meat, fruit, nuts and cheese, a kind of ancient 'trail mix' by Ray's thinking, and they ate what remained rather than having Hanshee forage for winter roots or hunting. They slept soundly as they lay between their fire and the rocks, giving nary a thought to the prospects of rolling over and falling hundreds of feet to their deaths.

They had bedded down just after sunset and Ray slept until almost full sunrise. This was an uncharacteristically long time for him, but easily explained since he was not yet completely recovered from the ordeal of his injury and the turmoil that greeted him upon awaking. There was no attempt to awaken as a warrior this morning, and he groggily pushed himself up to a sitting position with his back against the rock and the remains of the fire before him. As usual, Hanshee was nowhere to be seen. He had probably awakened while the winter forest was still pitch black and used the time to reconnoiter while Ray slept. Ray knew he would be back soon.

As if reading his thoughts, Hanshee appeared from around the southern end of the rocks. He silently took a place beside the fire, to which he added a few smaller pieces of wood. He then used a longer piece to prod the still glowing embers until they set the small pieces to blaze. After adding a few larger pieces to the newly rekindled fire, he squatted to warm his face and hands in its restored glow. A quick glance at Ray told him his companion was not yet ready to go and, having pushed Ray hard for the past two days, he felt it important that he get adequate rest to be prepared for the journey ahead.

There would be no powdered tabba today. Hanshee knew well how quickly one could become dependent on the stimulant, and even now he watched Raymond closely for any sign that he had overused the potent extract.

Sitting quietly by the warmth of the rebuilt fire, Ray had time to reflect on the last two days and three nights; especially the first night after he awakened from the long sleep Hanshee had induced to heal him.

The first thing he had done was take a life. He had done it instinctively, because Hanshee was in dire need. He did not *decide* to do it, but neither did he hesitate. He did what had to be done and, in doing so, saved the life of the man to whom he owed his life many times over.

But in doing, so he had crossed a line he thought he would never cross and now had to deal with the consequences to his psyche. He had to rethink who he was and what he was willing to do to survive this strange and terrible land.

A part of him prayed for forgiveness, from God and from himself. He had now seen enough of this place to understand that life could be extremely cheap here. As he and Hanshee made their way through this world, he would most likely be faced with this dilemma again at some point. He prayed that, no matter how many times it be required, it never be done cavalierly; that he never become comfortable with the things he may have to do to survive.

Ray stole a quick glance at Hanshee and found the young warrior studying him. For some reason, he had a hard time meeting Hanshee's eyes and instead shifted his gaze, refocusing on the mysteries of the fire. Still, he continued to feel the weight of the warriors' stare and, after a while, he felt almost compelled to speak to Hanshee about the burden he was carrying on his soul.

"The first time..." Ray searched for the right words, "...the first time you..."

"Took a life?" Hanshee finished the sentence for him.

"Yes," Ray responded almost too quickly, taking a sheepish glance at his companion, and then waiting expectantly for Hanshee to continue.

Hanshee also looked into the depths of the fire while he allowed his mind to search for the words he knew Ray needed to hear.

"I was raised a warrior," he began, "in a great and proud clan, Clan Dula. As a boy I was trained in the ways and weaponry of the hunt. It was then I was taught that to kill is necessary and should be done without hesitation, but with respect for your quarry. When I reached the time of my change, lessons of the hunt turned to lessons of war. In war you must kill or be killed. In that moment there is no time for respect, and no time for remorse. A warrior does what must be done."

Now he lifted his eyes from the fire and looked to Ray.

"But only when it *must* be done." he said. "A warrior strives never to slay in hatred, or malice... or delight."

Hanshee paused again, still searching for a way to reach out to, and reassure, Ray.

"When a young warrior first takes the life of an enemy of his people," Hanshee continued, "he must look into the eyes of the older and more seasoned among his kin. All among his brethren must be faced. All must look into his spirit. There may be pride in victory, but there can be no joy in the taking of life. If it is found that one enjoys the killing of men...has become soulless...his brethren must turn their backs on him. He cannot remain a warrior, for that one becomes a danger to his own and not just the enemy."

"In taking the assassins life, you did what had to be done. And truly, I rejoice that your actions now sit heavily upon you. You are *not* soulless, Way-mon."

"Neither are you, Hanshee," Ray said. "When we were back in that first city, Aggipoor, you did what had to be done and I called you a killer... a butcher... only in my mind, but I thought it nonetheless. You told me then that my ways were not the ways of this place, and you were right. In my ignorance I condemned you, even though you only acted to save a life... my life. Having spent more time with you, and glimpsed your spirit, I now count myself wiser and I would apologize to you for those thoughts."

"With time should come wisdom," said Hanshee. "Only a fool fails to gain wisdom over time."

Ray let these words sink in for a while, then raised his head toward Hanshee with a quizzical look.

"But the soldier you fought on the dry lakebed, on the day after we were capture by the Pith? The way you fought him… you took your time. You punished him."

Hanshee stirred the coals of the fire before answering Ray.

"Though you *try* never to kill with hatred or malice," Hanshee began, "there are still many reasons to kill. For our protection, surrounded in a camp by soldiers who saw in us enemies, a message needed to be sent. The challenge he presented, as it was laid down by his commander, was a chance to send that message. I fought him, and killed him in the manner that I did, for that reason."

Hanshee turned from the fire to seek Ray's eyes once more.

"But that one *needed* killing, Way-mon… as justice for those he took pleasure in slaying… and because he had shown himself to have no soul."

****

It was midmorning before they broke camp and headed south through the late winter forest. Much of the snow had melted and the pair took pains not to walk through what was left so as not to leave obvious signs of their passing. There were pine and cedar trees interspersed among an abundance of tall skeletal hardwoods. Though bare, the trees and brush were crowded close enough together in some places so that visibility was limited to not much more than a couple hundred feet.

Their plan, as laid out by Hanshee, was to get far enough south to be clear of Stronghold Road, which ran alongside the high cliffs and led to the gates of Stronghold. This would help them avoid the military patrols and any travelers it might carry. They also wanted to avoid any settlements along the Southern Road, the road they had taken by chariot on their way to Stronghold. They had to cross this road on their way to the Ursal Mountains and hoped to do so unnoticed.

Crossing a mountain range this time of year carried its own perils, and the two would have to decide if it was worth it to chance the high passes while the cold was still upon them, or hide in the forest of the eastern slopes until most of the snow had melted and the passes had cleared. Crossing the thin ice of a mountain river in late winter, or the powerful floods of the same river during the spring thaw; neither option seemed appealing.

Ray was still turning these two options over in his mind when he and Hanshee emerged from the forest and stood above a small valley. They looked down on a large fenced-in pasture where several cows, and a few horses, were foraging for the few strands of dead grass revealed by the melting snow. In the distance, they could see a corral attached to a large barn surrounded by several wagons, and a chariot with one side held high by the single wheel that remained attached. About fifty paces from the barn stood an old wood framed house with smoke coming from two of the four stone chimneys.

Keeping to the trees above the pasture, Hanshee and Raymond made their way along its eastern edge, moving ever closer to the buildings on the far end. Hanshee kept his eyes peeled for any movement coming from the barn or the house, and for some time all seemed quiet. Then Hanshee froze in his tracks, extending an arm backward and placing his palm in Ray's chest, thus stopping him too. Though caught off guard, Ray trusted his friend enough to not only stop all movement, but also hold his tongue. Looking straight ahead at Hanshee, he noted the direction of his gaze. Slowly he allowed his eyes, then his head, to turn in the same direction.

They were now almost clear of the pasture and had an unobstructed view of the barn and the house. From about four-hundred feet away, Ray watched as a small dark-haired boy came from the barn carrying a sack. He walked to the pasture gate and climbed up its side, balancing himself with his feet on the middle board and his thighs leaning against the top. Hooking his sack onto a nail to hold it in place, he brought both hands to his mouth and let loose a piercing whistle that carried the length of the small valley. This caused every horse in the pasture to raise its head and look over to the barn. As they recognized the boy, each began to make its way toward the gate.

"I know where we are," Ray whispered to Hanshee, recognizing the stable where the palace guard who brought them to Stronghold had stopped for fresh horses. Hanshee only nodded, having recognized the stable not long after they stumbled upon it.

As they continued to watch, the old man who ran the stable shuffled out onto the porch of the house and yelled in the direction of the boy. Although they couldn't hear his words, they could tell by his high pitched and screeching tone that he was still as disagreeable and bullying as the first time they saw him.

The boy looked back at him briefly before the first of the horses trotted up. Reaching into the sack, he extended his arm, and the animal took something from his outstretched hand. He offered the same to the next arriving horse, passing out two or three more before all had made it across the pasture to the gate. Then he jumped down and swung the gate open. After the last horse had filed through, he turned and led them into the barn.

A few horses were acting a bit skittish, probably due to the continued screeching of the old man. Ray managed to catch a few words... something about leaving the gate open. The boy looked back at the open gate and noted that all the horses were following him, and all the cattle had their heads down eating grass at the far side of the pasture. He continued into the barn with all eight horses following behind. The old man was right on their heels, entering the barn not long after the last horse.

Bidding Ray to quickly follow, Hanshee erupted into motion.

Sprinting between the trees and around the pasture, the pair emerged from the woods on the opposite side of the coral that attached to the rear of the barn. From here they slowed their approach and carefully skirted the corral fence until they stood beside the barn, about midway between the front and back. The sounds of the old man verbally berating the boy came clearly through the walls, prompting Ray to wonder why they had ventured this close.

"...and get that damn load of feed over to that cow trough before I take a strop to your hide!" the old man could be heard saying.

Ray looked at Hanshee's face, trying to judge if the old man's harsh treatment of the child was having the same effect on Hanshee as it was on him. Aside from a hardening of his jawline, there was nothing in Hanshee's expression indicating annoyance with the abuse the child endured.

Creeping forward to the corner of the barn, they peered around just as a heavy wheelbarrow came into view. Behind it was the boy, pushing for all he was worth. From this closer vantage point, he looked more fragile than Raymond remembered.

Raymond and Hanshee continued to watch his progress as the boy tried to muscle the heavily laden wheelbarrow toward the trough that was used to feed the cattle. About halfway to the trough the wheel rolled upon a stone, causing the wheelbarrow to tilt and the load to shift. The boy fought it with all his strength but could not keep the wheelbarrow upright. It fell to the side, taking the boy with it and spilling a good portion of the feed onto the dust of the yard.

No sooner had he struck the earth than the boy was looking back over his shoulder into the barn. As if on cue, the old man sprinted from the open doors with more speed than one would have thought him capable. He was cursing a storm and had a wide leather strap raised above his head, ready to descend has soon as he came within reach of the boy. Not content to wait on his punishment, the boy worked his way from under the overturned wheelbarrow and, without looking back, began a sprint toward the house.

As the boy dashed by on his left, the old man swung the strap as hard as his momentum would allow. The heavy leather caught the boy on his left shoulder, the blow landing hard enough to knock him to the ground. Without uttering a sound, the boy sprang back to his feet and again made his way toward the house. Ray noticed he was hobbling now and thought he could see blood on the child's left knee, running down his leg.

The old man's momentum had carried him all the way to the wheelbarrow, even as he had brought his strap down on the running boy. Bracing himself against it, he pushed off and, with blood in his eyes, continued his pursuit of the child who was running as best he could toward the house.

Making his way to the front of the house, the child jumped over the large rocks that formed a pathway to the steps. Hindered by his injured leg, he tripped, falling face down onto the path just as the old man appeared to be gaining on him. The fear in his eyes was palpable as the boy look back at his crazed pursuer, pushed himself off the ground, and half sprinted half hobbled up the seven steps leading to the narrow porch.

Reaching the door, the boy grabbed for the handle and heaved with all his might, but the door didn't move! Again and again he tried, but his efforts were in vain as the old man had set the high latch before following him into the barn.

The old stable master cackled in triumph as he saw the predicament of the boy and forced his old legs to move even faster as he neared the steps. The boy continued his futile attempts at the door until he heard the old man's boots on the first step, then he slumped to the dusty floor of the porch and curled into a ball to await a punishment that was never far away, and always seemed impossible to escape.

The old man stopped two steps short of the porch, his chest heaving with his exertion. He stood there, slightly bent over, laughing his cackling laugh as he fought to catch his breath. Then he drew back the strap and brought it crashing down on the child's back.

One… two… three… after which, Hanshee could take no more and sprinted from his place of cover by the barn toward the house and the old man.

Hanshee was yelling for the old man to still his hand but, not well versed in the Pithian tongue, his words went unrecognized. What did not go unrecognized was the tone in which they were yelled. Hearing this caused the old man to stop in mid stroke and spin halfway around to see who this newcomer was who was yelling in his yard. His eyes grew big as he saw the form of Hanshee, made larger from the clothes and the cloak that he wore, barreling toward him, a similarly dressed Ray on his heels. Startled, he twisted his body upon the narrow step to turn and face the oncoming men.

At this moment, for reasons unknown even to him, the boy lashed out with his right leg, kicking the old man behind his knee. The knee buckled, causing him to lose the precarious balance he enjoyed on the fifth step. The boy had never struck back at the old man before… had never dreamed of such a thing… and could only watch as his tormenter tumbled from his perch, down the steps, and into the dust of the walk, striking headfirst against one of the heavy stones at the bottom.

Ray was right behind Hanshee and neither saw the man so much as twitch after striking his head. As he and the boy looked on, Hanshee reached the Stable Masters side, bent to check for breath… then for a pulse… before standing and saying to Ray what he already knew to be true.

"The old man is dead."

Ray looked upon the dead body with mixed feelings.

All he had known of this old man was his cruelty and greed. He had a young boy… a child… under his thumb and he worked him hard and without pity. And when the child displeased him, he was beaten. Not so badly that he could not work, but Ray had seen the look in the eyes of the fleeing child, and he knew that this was not the first time he had run from the old man. This was not the first time he had failed to escape and, in failing, curled himself into a ball and surrendered to the torment that his young life had become.

Having witnessed firsthand the nature of this beast, and the pain that he caused to the innocent and defenseless, Ray should have been happy to see him fallen. At the least, he should have been indifferent to his demise. But this was not the case. Even after all he had seen of the violence and brutality, all the selfishness and cruelty, he still found himself shaken by the old man's death.

"Tell the boy," Hanshee said to Ray, "then let us move on from this place."

The sound of Hanshee's voice roused Ray from his thoughts. Hanshee had picked up some of the Pithian tongue during the months they had spent at the Temple and the Royal House. He had a good way to go, but now could piece together some of what was said in his presence. Still, he was limited in what he could speak. Obviously, he lacked the words, and the manner to deal with the child at a time such as this.

Slowly Ray turned toward the boy with a look of sadness on his face and saw him still lying prone on the wooden planks of the small front porch, looking up at Ray with large questioning eyes.

Ray glanced quickly down at the unmoving form of the old man, then met the boy's gaze and spoke.

"He is dead."

At these words, the child completely broke down, bawling loudly as the tears streamed down his face.

Ray had only seen the old man torment the child and, though not expecting shouts of glee, was taken aback by this amount of sympathy by the tortured, for the torturer.

Hanshee, too, seemed bewildered at the depth of the hurt evident in the child's sobs. They served as anchors around his feet, leaving him unable to take even one step away from the scene that was before him. The two of them stood there looking at the child and the ground until, after a time, the intensity of the crying seemed to abate. Soon the boy was simply sniffling and both Ray and Hanshee released sighs of relief.

"Who else lives here?" Ray asked the boy when, he thought he had recovered enough to respond.

The boy shook his head between sniffles.

"No one else? Where are your mother and father?"

"I don't know," said the boy.

Ray turned to Hanshee, mouth agape, but nothing coming out. Hanshee returned his look but had nothing to contribute.

"They live in Cantor," the boy said, and Ray whipped his head around to look at the child.

"How did you come to be here?" he asked.

"My father gave me to a seller," the boy answered, "to pay what he owed. The seller gave me to Chezza for a horse. His horse went lame, and he needed a new one."

Ray turned this information over in his mind.

"This is Chezza," he said, pointing down at the fallen old man. It was a statement, but a question too, and the boy nodded his head in agreement.

Ray again turned toward Hanshee as he searched for the words for his next question, but Hanshee remained silent, not sure of what had been said.

"You have no one here with you?" Ray asked, turning again to the child. "Where will you go?"

The boy looked up sheepishly at Ray, then at Hanshee, then back at Ray before responding in a tiny voice.

"Can I go with you?" he asked.

"No child," Ray quickly replied, "I do not think so. You see, we are traveling far, far to the west." Ray pointed west for emphasis.

"To Cantor?" the child said, with hope and excitement in his voice.

"Yes… to Cantor…" Ray was looking from the boy to Hanshee and back, "…but not just to Cantor. We will go beyond Cantor and…"

"Are you walking to Cantor?" The child asked, as his watery gaze moved beyond Raymond and into the stable yard.

"Uh… yes…" Ray replied as he turned about, taken aback by the questioning and wondering what the child was looking at.

"That would take a long time" the child said. "Chezza has horses. We could ride to Cantor. It won't take as long."

With his head already slightly befuddled by the accidental death of the stable master and the ensuing predicament, the last utterances of the child served to snap Ray's mind into focus. If they used horses, they could travel much faster through the mountain passes, maybe cutting their travel time in half. He was preparing to tell Hanshee what the child said when the boy spoke up again.

"We could take the Stronghold Road to Cantor and be there in nine days," the boy said.

Ray again spun in the boy's direction.

"Nine days," Ray asked of the boy, "from here to Cantor? How do you know?

"I went to Cantor with Chezza," the boy replied. "He goes to trade for new horses two times a year; after the thaw and before the first snow. It takes us nine days to get to the horse markets near the capital. It takes longer to get back because we have to manage the new horses."

Raymond let this new information simmer for a moment before saying, largely to himself, "But we've never ridden horses..."

"I can teach you!" the boy spoke up excitedly. "And I can care for the horses... all the way there! We have horses, and saddles, and bridles, and blankets and feed... anything a horse needs! And old Chezza won't care."

The boy looked down at the dead body of the old man as he said this last.

What is your name boy? Ray asked. What are you called?

"Kellen" the boy replied with a smile as he realized he would indeed be traveling west with these two strange men.

****

It had taken Raymond a while, but he finally convinced Hanshee of the new plan made possible by the death of the old man and the emancipation of the boy, Kellen.

Alone and over uneven terrain, Hanshee could probably match the pace of a horse and rider for a good distance. But Hanshee was not alone, Raymond had argued, and even with just the two of them, it could take months to reach the western nations by crossing the Ursal Mountains. Who knew the condition of the high passes, or whether a late freeze would delay the thaw and have them biding time in the forest of the eastern slopes until it was safe to continue. They would be crossing the territory of several of the mountain tribes and who knew what reception would await them if they were discovered. Of course, they could do it... by now Raymond believed that Hanshee could do almost anything... but the proposal of Kellen could work out much better.

They would all three ride horses.

Hanshee had never before ridden a horse, and Ray's only experience was sitting awkwardly atop a horse as it walked a well-worn riding path in the Tennessee Smoky Mountains. He remembered not being sure whether he had any effect on the animal as it stayed in line and on pace behind the other horses loaded up with tourists.

Kellen assured them that there were several very gentle horses in the barn; horses on which they could learn as they traveled. Ray and Hanshee could change their appearance somewhat... there were lots of old clothes in the farmhouse... and the three of them could take the Stronghold Road which, once past the Gates of Stronghold, was a straight path into Gunjunson, the capital of Cantor. It should be safe since no one would know them.

Those who might pursue them were looking for two inarticulate strangers to this land, traveling on foot and hiding their presence out of fear of death. With this new plan, they would present as two men traveling openly on horseback, fluent in the Pithian tongue, and accompanied by a child. Kellen would take care of the horses, the same as he did for old Chezza. And they could reach Gunjunson in just nine days. They would cross beyond the borders of Pith even sooner.

****

The sun was still slightly above the western tree line as they prepared to leave. All were on horseback, with Kellen holding the lead rope of a mule loaded down with provisions. Most were for the horses, but there were things for the three riders too.

Before leaving they had gone through both the house and the barn, searching for anything that could help them on their journey. Ray had pointed out that carrying food and water would save them the time and trouble of foraging. It would also alley suspicion since travelers were expected to pack provisions for their journey. Though he was accustomed to traveling light and living off of the land, Hanshee recognized the wisdom of this, and carried a bed roll and a large water bag attached to the small four-horned saddle upon which he cautiously sat.

After mounting his horse, Kellen's eyes suddenly went wide. Quickly, he climbed down from his saddle and ran back toward the farmhouse. Ray and Hanshee watched as the boy jumped over the still prone body of Chezza, lying exactly as he had fallen, and ran up the stairs and into the house. The pair exchanged curious glances but otherwise did not move. A minute passed and then Kellen's voice was heard calling from inside.

Recognizing the tone, if not the words, Hanshee was first off his horse. Ray was right behind him and together they vaulted the stairs and rushed inside the farmhouse. They found Kellen in what was Old Chezza's bedchamber, straining his little body as he tried desperately to pull a large chest from underneath the raised bed. After pausing to evaluate the situation, Hanshee walked over to the struggling child, eased him to the side, and easily pulled the chest out into the open.

It was a large, sturdy chest, made of wood and hardened leather and secured with heavy latches on three sides. Large iron locks were threaded through each the latches, and Raymond watched as Kellen tugged at each to no avail. As the boy sprang to his feet and attempted to run past him, Ray reached out a hand and caught him by the arm, pulling him up short.

"What's this?" Ray asked, pointing at the chest. "And where are you off to now?"

"Chezza has the key," Kellen said, as he tried to pull away from Ray and reach the fallen stable master's side.

"Hold up, son!" Ray hated to raise his voice, but this got Kellen's attention and he stopped his struggling. "Show me where it is."

He released Kellen's arm and the boy then walked through the house and out the front door. Crossing the porch, he proceeded down the steps and stood beside the old man's body.

Ray and Hanshee followed him outside where he waited expectantly for them to descend the steps. When they stood beside him, he pointed to Chezza.

"He wears the key around his neck," Kellen said.

"The boy says the Key to the chest is around the old man's neck," Ray said to Hanshee, bringing him up to speed.

Since Chezza had possessed the awareness to land face up when he died, Hanshee had only to kneel down beside him to examine his body. Hanshee did not want to disturb or change the position of the corpse. He saw Chezza's death as an accident and he wanted any who came across the scene to arrive at that conclusion. With this in mind he carefully opened the front of the stable master's coat, revealing the shirt underneath. On the left side of his neck, just above the collar, Raymond could see what appeared to be a portion of a braided leather cord. Carefully, Hanshee pulled at the cord until a key was exposed. Not wanting to move the dead man in any other way, Hanshee pulled his knife and cut the cord. He then pulled the entire thing from around Chezza's neck and passed the key to Kellen.

With the key in hand, the now beaming Kellen ran back up the steps and into the house. Ray and Hanshee followed to find him kneeling beside the large chest working on the first of the three locks. The locks were rather old, and not well oiled, so the boy found it difficult at first. After a while, his diligent efforts paid off and Ray watched expectantly as the front lock, the last to be opened, fell away.

Now the boy placed both hands on the lid and heaved upward, separating it from the chest and the contents it protected. Having put flame to a lamp, Hanshee leaned over the child's shoulders to see just what had begun the unexpected flurry of activity. He was quickly joined by Ray.

As the lid fell back, the contents of the chest were revealed. It contained an assortment of scrolls and trinkets that were strewn about haphazardly; piled atop one another in no particular order, with most appearing aged and dusty as if placed inside long ago and then forgotten. The lone exception was a second leather chest, small enough to cover one quarter of the space inside the larger chest and pushed into a rear corner.

This chest was of a height that allowed the lid of the large chest to barely close over it. The leather and wood appeared polished and well maintained compared to the other contents, which appeared to have been shoved out of the way to make space for it. There was no lock on the small latch that held down the lid, still Kellen fiddled with it for a few moments before it snapped up and allowed him to open it.

Ray's breath was sucked from his chest at the sight that greeted his eyes.

Before him sat a chest of about two and a half feet long, a foot and a half high, and of a similar width. What took Ray's breath away was that this chest was filled to the very brim with gold coins!

Ray turned to look at Hanshee, who showed no appreciable change in his demeanor, then turned once again to stare at the treasure that was displayed before them.

As the two watched, Kellen reached into the chest and grasped a single gold coin which he raised up before his eyes while bestowing upon it a smile of satisfaction. Then he closed the lid on the small chest. He was reaching to close the large lid when Ray spoke up.

"What... Wait!" Raymond said as he shot out a hand to stop the lid from closing.

Kellen was surprised and turned his face toward Ray, a question in his eyes. Ray looked from the boy to Hanshee and found a second pair of eyes staring questioningly at him. Ray continued looking back from one to the other, confusion evident on his face. Then, regaining his focus, he turned to the child.

"Kellen, where did this come from?" Raymond asked, placing his open palm atop the closed lid of the small chest.

"This is Chezza's," the boy said. "All except for this one," He showed them the coin in his grasp. "This one's mine."

This last was spoken as a solemn pronouncement and Kellen set his jaw as if preparing to defend his coin should Ray think to take it away from him.

Ray was puzzled at first, then the light came on and he remembered his first trip to this stable.

"I remember, Kellen," Ray said soothingly. "I was here and I saw when the soldier threw the coin to you. It is yours."

Now Kellen's eyes lit up in recognition, and he smiled brightly as he placed the coin into a fold of his tunic.

"I remember you... both of you," he said as he nodded toward Hanshee.

Having placed the child at ease, Ray now had more questions.

"Kellen, this looks like a lot of gold. How did Chezza come by these coins? He asked.

Now Kellen regarded Ray with questioning eyes.

"I don't know," the boy said. "It's Chezza's. It was always here."

It dawned on Ray that Chezza must have been building this treasure for many years, long before Kellen's arrival. The boy couldn't possibly know much about it.

Ray turned back to Hanshee, who had been patiently observing the conversation. Even without understanding all that was said, Hanshee still gleaned the gist of the exchange.

"Hanshee...," Ray began.

"It is too much," Hanshee stated flatly. "It is too much, too heavy, and by its very presence will invite turmoil."

"But, Hanshee," Ray protested, "do you know how much gold this is? This is a small fortune! With this much wealth we could..."

Ray's words trailed off as he tried to think of what they could actually do with this much gold. He was racking his brain trying to think of what they could use it for but nothing was coming to mind.

Hanshee saw Ray's dilemma and spoke up.

"Way-mon," he said, "In my time in the eastern lands, I have seen how gold effects men here. It is the same in the cities of the west, beyond the Blue Mountains. It is a thing that the priests of the blue mountains warned me of prior to sending me on my journey.

"I was warned that there are those who will do most anything to acquire gold, sacrificing all they claim to love, all they claim to believe, and all to which they have allegiance, in its pursuit. I have been told that men kill and die for gold; that it lays claim to their very souls, so that they cannot rest until they have possessed it. And having possessed it, they then destroy themselves in fits of decadence, or are consumed by fear of losing it, so that every waking hour is spent hiding, protecting, and defending it from imaginary thieves.

"If," Hanshee continued, "we take with us this treasure, as is your want, a portion of your thoughts will always rest beside it. It will change what you feel and what you do. It will affect your decisions. It will limit you, and so limit *us*. I cannot leave you, and if you will not leave the treasure, we will both be condemned by its presence."

Hanshee could see his words were having an effect on Ray, who was probably now wondering just how far he would go to hold on to this much gold.

"I would say to you, Way-mon, do not leave that decision for a future time," Hanshee said. "Make it now."

Hanshee was staring intently into Ray's eyes; eyes that appeared to be focused on something far away. But Hanshee knew that he was reaching his companion and so continued.

"Gold has its uses," Hanshee said. "We can take enough to help us along as needed; a few pieces for my pouch, a purse to carry inside your tunic. But we should turn our backs on the *treasure*. It is not needed. Have we not lived well without it? I fear that if you cannot leave it, then for the reasons I spoke, and for reasons unspoken, it will lead to our end."

Finished now, Hanshee waited for Ray to respond. Kellen had been staring at Hanshee, not understanding the words but caught up in the passion with which he spoke them. Now the child turned to Ray with a look of expectation on his face.

Ray looked from one face to the other, but could not focus on either. Hanshee's words were echoing in his mind and slowly pulling him toward the place he knew he needed to be.

Another moment and he found his voice.

"I don't know what came over me, Hanshee," Ray said. "I thought I was immune to feelings like that. In the world I come from, this would be an incredible treasure. In the world I come from, we could purchase many wondrous things."

Now Raymond's tone changed as he continued.

"But, in the world I come from, men are the same; eager to sell their souls for wealth, and not understanding what in life is *truly* important. I always thought I was different."

Ray gave Hanshee a sheepish look.

"I guess I am not as different as I thought," he said.

"You are stronger than you think, Way-mon," Hanshee said. "You will prove it to yourself again and again as we journey to my homeland."

"That sounds prophetic," said Ray.

After a search of Chezza's bed chamber, Hanshee found a soft leather purse with a drawstring. He gave this to Raymond, who counted out twenty of the gold pieces with which to fill it. This was no small sum though, compared to what remained, it was but a fraction of a crumb. Hanshee added ten pieces to his medicine pouch, then closed both small and large chests and pushed them back under Chezza's bed. There the treasure would sit until some other souls were unfortunate enough to find it.

It was now close to sunset and, though the shelter of the house and its provisions were tempting, it was decided that remaining overnight could lead to unneeded complications should some traveler arrive at the stable to find just the boy with two strangers and a dead stable master. So it was that the three of them made their way up the short road winding out of the little valley that sheltered the stable, and toward the Southern Road.

CHAPTER 16

Captain Ailean sat tall in his saddle, as was his custom, while leading the small group of guards east around the perimeter of the Stronghold walls. His orders from Captain Hendric were to "thoroughly search the area at the base of the walls for any sign of incursion". To him, this seemed the definition of a waste of time. There had been no 'incursion' against the Stronghold walls, from any direction, for hundreds of years. And even in centuries past, none were remotely successful.

Regardless of his personal feelings about their current assignment, his troops understood that, as with everything concerning their performance, he expected perfection. For this reason, he was careful to try to mirror that trait whenever in their presence. Therefore, he sat tall in his saddle as he guided his mount along the outer wall of Stronghold, keeping a sharp eye out for anything that appeared out of the ordinary. He was not told specifically what to look for and secretly thought this might be a test of himself and his command. This idea caused him to constantly chide his men to stay alert and to examine every inch of ground they covered.

They had been at this for several hours now, and soon would be moving to where the high peaks and shear walls of the easternmost outer walls of Stronghold began. Already he was noticing the ground beginning a descent that would eventually take them down into the Ninum Valley and the banks of the treacherous river of the same name. Not many ventured into these densely forested lands. Ailean was comforted by the fact that swiftly approaching nightfall would cut his search short well before he entered the true depths of that ancient forest.

He had just guided his mount around a tight group of fir trees and back toward the base of the wall, when he heard a call from his rear.

"Captain Ailean!"

Pulling his horse up, Ailean turned in his saddle to see what the call was about.

His patrol today included four guardsmen and himself, and he could see three of them spread out behind him to his right flank. They too had pulled their horses around to respond to the call of the fourth guardsman, who appeared to be waving them back toward the stand of trees.

Ailean wheeled his horse about and moved back through his men toward the last guardsman, who had dismounted. The others fell in behind him. The captain pulled up beside the dismounted guardsmen, looking down on him from his mounted position in stern silence.

"My pardons, Captain," the soldier began, and for some reason paused after those words.

"Well?" Ailean barked, baffled as to why this man would feel the need to waste their time this way. "Speak up man! Why did you stop?"

"Well, Captain," the anxious guardsman began, "I dismounted to pull a stone from my horses' shoe and, while bent over, I happened to glance into the thicket of trees here..."

"Go on," the captain said impatiently.

"Well," the soldier continued, "there's an awful lot of needles and small limbs amongst those trees near the wall," he pointed toward the interior of the stand of trees, "and they look fresh...to me... Captain" he finished weakly.

Cursing under his breath at the soldier's apprehension, Captain Ailean dismounted and gave a scornful glance back at the guardsman as he moved between the trees to have a look for himself. While he was thus engaged, his more resourceful men spread out to examine the area around the grove more closely.

After only a few strides into the trees the captain clearly saw why the soldier had called him back. There appeared to be an extraordinary amount of debris surrounding one tree in particular, causing the area around its base to stand out from the surrounding trees. It was something he should have noticed, but for his being on horseback and this tree being so close to the wall. Walking up to the trunk, Ailean peered upward through the low branches in hopes the tree would reveal the reason for the isolated debris at its base. To his dismay, the thick branches close to the base revealed nothing.

The captain then turned his attention back to the debris, picking up one of the larger pieces for examination. *Larger* was a stretch, as the piece he chose was a thin two-foot-long branch from the upper reaches of the sixty-foot tree. But a close look confirmed that it clearly had been broken off and had not fallen of its own accord. The break appeared fairly fresh, too.

Attempting to see past the lower limbs blocking his view, the captain tried to spy any obvious scrapes or jagged breaks that would show where some of the debris at his feet had originated. Before he could see anything noteworthy, his focus was again broken by the sound of his name being called.

Captain Ailean!

This was a different guardsman. Jared. One of his best.

"Captain, I think you might want to see this."

With another brief glance skyward, the captain made his way through the trees and back to his horse.

"Over here, Captain," Jared called out from a position about fifty or sixty feet beyond the edge of the stand and slightly back in the direction they had come.

Ailean first looked to his horse, then walked the short distance to where Jared sat mounted. Arriving beside him, the captain put fists to hips and looked up at his trusted subordinate.

"What must I see for myself?" Ailean asked.

"Up there, Captain," Jared pointed up toward the tops of the trees and awaited his captain's response.

"I don't see a damn thing, man," Captain Ailean spat.

"My pardon M'lord," Jared quickly said. "If you could back off a short way, you're not being mounted ..."

Cursing again under his breath, Ailean backed off a few more paces to attain the same angle that Jared had. Then he looked to the tree tops again.

"I still see nothing," the captain said, "but the tops of trees!"

"Look higher, Captain... on the cliff face above the trees."

The sun having passed its zenith some time ago, the east-southeast facing cliff had long since fallen into shadow. Now the dwindling light from its setting made examining a cliff face almost one hundred feet up even more difficult. Still, the captain scanned the height and thought... just maybe... there might be something ... unusual about the cliff ... there...

"Jared," Captain Ailean said, "What is that thing?"

"I'm not completely sure Captain," Jared said, "given this fading light and all... but it could be a rope."

****

Word reached Captain Hendric late that night of a possible clue in the whereabouts of the Harbinger and his acolyte but, in the black of night, there was no way to confirm or to even glimpse what it might be, even if he were there. He had to wait until morning to ride out and have a look for himself at what the messenger so breathlessly reported in the midnight hour.

Alone he saddled his horse and rode from the Citadel roughly an hour before sunrise, clearing the Southern Gate while darkness was still upon it. Riding east at an easy trot, he followed the trail that ran along the base of the outer wall and watched as the starlit sky slowly turned a mixture of gray and a light shade of blue. He was still in the shadow of the trees, caused by the slowly rising sun, when he reached the encampment of Captain Ailean, hastily thrown together as it was.

The captain had thought the find of the previous evening so unusual that he had decided to spend the night here and get a more definitive glimpse in the morning light. He had sent a man back to give a preliminary report to Captain Hendric, but expected the captain to wait until Ailean could make a formal report before venturing out himself. In no scenario that he could have constructed did he envision Hendric riding into his camp just as the sun rose.

"Hail the morning, Captain!"

Ailean gave the customary greeting as he watched Hendric pull his horse up outside the circle of three bedrolls that surrounded the fire; an as yet untended morning fire of little more than burning embers, with nothing upon it.

Hendric shook his head in mock sympathy.

"Hail the morning, Captain," Hendric replied as he dismounted. "That is the lowliest fire I've seen in a while. Have you no morning meat or hot broth for a cold and tired comrade?"

"Had I the makings of such, I'd probably be hiding it for myself," Ailean joked.

"Then it is fortunate for your men that I am more generous than you," Hendric smiled as he reached into a saddle bag. "Here," He threw a bundle to one of the other guardsmen. "There's bacon, biscuits, and the makings for strong tea. You do have water, and a pot to boil it in, don't you?"

Ailean laughed.

"And *that* is why you are a newly minted captain commanding the elite Citadel Guard, while I remain stuck at the

Southern Gate," Aileen said, before turning to the man who caught the bundle. "Get that meal to cooking, Gusten," he said. "Join us Jared, and show Captain Hendric what you found dangling in the twilight."

While Gusten stoked the morning fire, Jared led the way to a position about sixty feet away, just beyond the horses. There he stopped and appeared to be looking up into the uppermost branches of the trees.

Hendric scanned Jared with a furrowed brow, wondering if he had some type of morning sickness. Turning to Ailean, he saw that he was also scanning the treetops high above their position. Finally, he turned his gaze to the trees.

"Just what are we looking for, Ailean?" Hendric asked. "It's the wrong season for nesting, so no eggs with your meat today."

Ailean chuckled as the usually stoic Jared spoke up.

"My pardon, Captain Hendric," Jared said, "but we're looking at the rocks up above the treetops."

Hendric adjusted his gaze from the trees to the shear stone wall that towered high above them. The rising sun had not yet cleared the trees to the east and the effect was one of dazzlingly bright sunlight at the uppermost portions of the cliffs, abruptly dropping into shadow about fifty feet above the treetops. This made for tricky viewing for the naked eye.

"There it is, Captain Ailean," Jared finally called out, pointing to a spot on the cliff. "Above the top of the tallest tree," he said, "where the sunlight meets the shadow."

Ailean adjusted his gaze to the spot Jared indicated and was rewarded.

"There, Hendric," Ailean said as he pointed to the spot, "just above the shadow, right up there."

Hendric tried to follow the outstretched arm and pointing index finger until he thought he had the right spot. There was a line that was different from the other faults and cracks that were present in the wall of rock. From what he could see, it was not as jagged… not jagged at all, really. It seemed to run straight down the wall, for a distance incalculable from where they stood, before disappearing into the shadow above the trees.

"Is it that straight crack?" Hendric asked

"That is not a crack, Captain," Jared said. "Keep looking,"

Hendric did keep looking. He looked until he was close to losing his patience. Then he noticed it; a slight movement of the 'crack'.

"Did it just move?" Hendric asked, not fully trusting his eyes.

"The wind blew it," Ailean said. "It's a rope."

Hendric continued to stare up at the rope for a few moments longer, before turning to Gusten.

"Hurry with that meal, Guardsman!" he shouted. We should be sitting a saddle before the sun clears the trees!

CHAPTER 17

It was around midday when Hendric made his report to what Jusaan privately thought of as the inner circle, consisting of the council priest, Commander Colevant of the City Garrison, Lord Chief Advisor Cecil, and His Highness King Ammon IV.

"… and after apparently scaling the eastern peaks the entire width of the Ninum Valley, they dropped a rope to a place just above the treetops and launched themselves into the trees! They then climbed down a tree and disappeared into the southeastern forest."

King Ammon and Lord Cecil exchanged incredulous looks before again focusing on Captain Hendric.

"Upon arriving back at the Southern Gate," Hendric continued, "I instructed Captain Ailean to dispatch his best trackers to scour the area surrounding that particular stand of trees and find a trail. They will wait for us there this evening."

"Us?" Chief Advisor Cecil interjected.

"With his Majesties permission," Hendric nodded toward King Ammon, "I will put together a pursuit force to find the Harbinger and return him to the safety of the Citadel and the Royal House."

This was the pronouncement of a logical and rational plan, the utterance of which sent the minds of all within the room reeling with thoughts on how best to construct and control the 'pursuit force'.

Lord Cecil was the first to speak.

"If I may, Your Highness," Cecil nodded to King Ammon and received a nod of permission in return, "I congratulate you, Council Priest Jusaan. Your insights have proven most valuable in identifying the direction in which the Harbinger has chosen to flee."

It took all the discipline Jusaan possessed to tamp down his pride.

"It was nothing, Lord Cecil," the priest humbly replied. "I am just happy to have been of assistance."

"Assistance, seemingly inspired from On High!" bellowed King Ammon. "Surely you have been chosen by The One to facilitate the coming of the Fourth Prophesy!"

The King raised his goblet and all present joined him in salute.

Jusaan's chest was near to bursting now.

Once he had regained his composure, his reading of the situation had been crystal clear! His vision flawless! All had transpired according to his plan and now he was again a valued and revered figure in both the Temple and the Royal House. It occurred to him that he just may be 'Chosen of The One'.

"How much thought have you given to the composition of your pursuit force, Hendric?"

It was the voice of Commander Colevant. As the Commander of the City Garrison, which included the Citadel Guard, he was the immediate superior of Captain Hendric. It was his intention to have a significant say in who was, and was not, included in this pursuit force.

"I have some thoughts on what kind of men will be needed," Hendric gave a quick glance to Cecil as he responded.

"I have some suggestions along that line," said Colevant. "I would consult with you after this meeting."

Colevant then paused.

"This matter has remained… private, Captain?"

"Only those directly involved in the search have any idea of the situation," said Hendric, "and their knowledge was, by necessity, limited."

"Which means that, despite our best efforts," Cecil said to all assembled, "this is most likely no longer a secret."

Cecil now turned to address Hendric.

"I, too, would consult with you before you take up your pursuit, Captain" the Chief Advisor said.

"As you wish, Lord Cecil, Commander Colevant," Hendric said, bowing to both.

'And may The One Spirit grant me strength,' Hendric silently prayed.

****

"Captain Hendric!"

The call came from the corridor behind him.

Not long having left the meeting of the 'inner circle', Hendric was considering possible recruits for his pursuit force, and was in no mood for idle chatter or distractions. Curious as to who would be chasing him at a time like this, he was mildly surprised when he turned to find Commander Galin, of the First Expeditionary Legion, striding purposefully down the hallway toward him.

Instantly Hendric was on his guard.

"Congratulations are in order, it seems," Galin said as he came up alongside Hendric. "A messenger in my camp not so long ago, and now the Captain of the Citadel Guard!"

Hendric nodded his head in modest acknowledgment.

"How goes the training of your new Legion?" he asked of Galin. "Well, if you have the time to roam the halls of the Royal House, no?"

"My officers are more than capable of following a training plan without my presence, Captain," Galin chuckled. "If they could not, they would not be officers in the First Legion. Still, I plan to rejoin them this very day but thought it prudent to speak with you before I leave."

"How can I be of assistance to the First Legion, Commander?" Hendric asked warily.

"Captain," Galin began, "the Royal House holds few secrets from me. I am fully aware of the current... *crises*, and have sought you out to offer my assistance."

"I'm not sure to what you refer," said Hendric, still unsure how much Galin knew, or of his position in this particular matter.

"The Harbinger, Captain...," Galin said, "the Harbinger."

A slow smile spread across Hendric's face.

"I had to be sure," he said.

"You did as I would have," Galin smiled in return before pressing on. "I have detached a squad of my best, led by my very best sergeant; Sergeant Lucius. His knowledge of the lands beyond Stronghold is second only to mine, and not even I know the Southern Forests better."

"I know of Lucius," Hendric stated. "It was his squad who first captured the Harbinger. And without bloodshed," he added.

"That he did," said Galin, before adding, "however, should bloodshed ever be required, there are few men I would rather have at my side."

"Your offer is generous, Commander," said Hendric. "Though I'll not be in need of a full squad, I would be happy to have Sergeant Lucius as a member of whatever force I assemble."

Hendric knew he could not respond to Commander Galin's offer with an outright refusal. By accepting Lucius and rejecting the entire squad, he had made the best bargain available to him under the circumstances. He also knew that Galin was correct; though he will surely be the eyes and ears of Galin, Lucius would prove a valuable member of the pursuit squad in any number of ways.

Galin gave a slight smile as he nodded his head to Hendric.

"I'll give the order then," he said. "Sergeant Lucius shall be ready within the hour. Good luck, Captain."

With that, Galin spun on his heels and headed back down the corridor, leaving Hendric to stare at his back and wonder just how he had known... within the hour... of plans just recently formulated and expressed to the King.

As he retreated, Galin could feel the eyes of Hendric on his back.

He had taken a huge chance in approaching the captain this way, but it could not be helped. He had little time in which to act, and it was imperative that he have an element within the pursuit force.

Galin smiled to himself as he recalled how he had manipulated his junior officer. He knew that his offer of the squad would be refused, just as he knew Hendric would feel that a complete refusal would be akin to an insult to his superior officer.

Rank has its privileges.

Attaching Lucius to the force was ever Galin's main goal. But though Lucius be a particularly resourceful operative, he alone would be hard pressed to do what must be done.

Not to worry. Galin knew that his reach was long throughout every branch of the military of Pith. He would find a way to provide Lucius with the assistance he would need to put an end to this 'Fourth Prophesy' madness.

****

It was about two hours before sunset when Hendric led his small unit through the tunnel in the rock wall that was the South Gate. Throwing a salute to Ailean and his men, who stood in crisp formation as they passed, he turned his mount eastward toward the Ninum Valley and the two trackers that were waiting for them there.

His pursuit force presently numbered seven: himself, Sergeant Lucius, and three very capable soldiers from the City Garrison who had transferred there after extensive duty with the Second Expeditionary Legion and bore the recommendation of Commander Colevant. Hendric had also been saddled with a young priest, though a fairly hearty priest, he must admit. The priest... Petri was his name... would be invaluable for communication with the Harbinger whenever he was found. Hendric understood the necessity of a priest and was happy that Jusaan deemed himself too frail to endure the rigors of the pursuit. Of course, this had been a disappointment to His Majesty.

The seventh member of the small force was Jared, a sharp and capable soldier who Ailean was loath to lose, even temporarily.

All seven were mounted, and leading two spare mounts, as well as two mules loaded with supplies calculated to outfit a force of eleven for an extended journey into the wilderness. The trackers would, of course, be joining the pursuit force. The Harbinger and his acolyte would round out the anticipated eleven whenever they are found.

If all proceeded smoothly, the band would reach the camp of the trackers just before sunset, enough time for Hendric to assess their progress in determining in which direction they would proceed in the morning.

Though it was unknown just how much of a lead the Harbinger had, Hendric was sure they could locate two strangers afoot in the Southern Forest in a matter of days. The heavily laden mules were simply a precaution.

As the band made their way east along the Stronghold wall, Hendric thought back to his brief meeting with Lord Cecil.

"Through four assassination attempts, we are no closer to identifying the person, or persons, responsible for our current situation," Cecil had said.

"Pardon my questioning, Lord Cecil," Hendric had said, "but what you count as the first two attempts; the poisoning of the serving wench and the encounter in the training yard; could just as well have been an accident and a misunderstanding, could they not?"

Cecil smiled at the question.

"You are very correct Hendric," the Chief Advisor said, "which, as I'm sure you see, only serves to obscure the picture and make the whole of the matter that much more difficult to solve."

Hendric nodded in understanding, digesting this bit of wisdom in silence.

"We will continue to do all that we can from the confines of the Royal House," Cecil continued. "But through the course of your pursuit, you must remain ever on your guard. There may very well be spies among your group; harmless ones placed there to keep their masters informed, and those intent on finishing what was begun here in the Citadel. Choose your forces well Hendric, but understand that even well thought out choices will be no guarantee."

Hendric was aware of the wisdom in that warning and the burden it placed on his shoulders. He must at once invest a degree of trust in these men, comrades in arms for the present, while at the same time trusting no one. It promised to be a fine and stressful line that he had set for himself to walk.

CHAPTER 18

As Hendric and his party made their way toward the campsite of the trackers, Ray, Hanshee, and young Kellen were preparing for their first night on the Stronghold Road.

They had moved off of the main road and into a stand of white pines to make camp. The location gave them a degree of privacy while still being close enough to the road to hear the passing of travelers in the night. Kellen had tied the horses off a little downwind of the camp after first watering them at a small stream that ran parallel to the road for a good way. There were signs of previous travelers using this location, including a shallow fire pit with the remnants of a long dead fire. It was atop this that they built their own small blaze.

Stumbling upon the stables, and the resulting change of plans, was why they had gotten such a late start that first day. This was one reason for the minimal progress they had made down the Stronghold Road. The other reason was that neither Hanshee nor Raymond had experience on horseback. Kellen endeavored to provide a crash course in horsemanship prior to leaving the stables but he was a child, used to getting instructions and not giving them.

After leading three of the gentlest horses from the barn, Kellen had gone about attaching the bridles and wrestling the saddles onto the backs of the horses. Ray noticed that Kellen, being a slightly built lad of no more than nine or ten winters, was having a time lifting the saddles into place. He stepped forward to lend a hand and thus had his first lesson on saddle placement and cinching. Hanshee watched very closely and was ready to emulate what he had seen when it was his turn.

With the saddles attached and the cinches tightened, Kellen stared expectantly at Ray and Hanshee. Ray was first to catch the drift of this, walking confidently up to Kellen and taking the reins of the horse from his outstretched hand. Hanshee was quick to follow, taking the other proffered reins, but still looking with apprehension toward the horse.

Ray looked back over his shoulder and saw Kellen give Hanshee the reins, before the young boy again focused on him, waiting for him to mount the horse. Taking a deep breath, he placed his left hand on one of the front horns of the small saddle, his right hand on its rear, and his left foot in the stirrup. He had always been told you mount a horse from the animals left side. This supposedly had something to do with not sitting on your sword. Not truly understanding the reason, Ray thought it best to bow to tradition and had no trouble swinging his right leg up and over the animals back as he eased into the saddle.

'That was easy,' he thought, before looking back to check Hanshee's progress.

Hanshee had studied every movement Ray had taken in mounting his horse and expertly mimicked him.

Satisfied that the two strangers could sit a horse, Kellen walked over to his own mount. After hoisting himself aboard, he expertly guided her toward the other two. Both men studied carefully how the young boy sat the horse and held the reins, though they could not quite tell by what means Kellen guided the horse so precisely. They saw that Kellen held the reins in his hands and his hands stayed atop the front horns of the saddle, still the horse turned left, right, and even in a complete circle before moving in a quick trot to take a position beside the horses of the two men.

Both Ray and Hanshee knew that, for a novice, a horse was nothing to play with. After a moment, Hanshee spoke up.

"Way-mon, ask him to teach you how to command the horse," Hanshee said. "You then teach me and we will be on our way. We need only ride slowly for now. We will continue to learn as we ride."

'Makes sense,' thought Ray as he turned to Kellen and spoke.

"Kellen, we need to be away from this place, but Hanshee and I do not know how to ride. We will learn much on our journey, I'm sure, but now we need to be able to walk, turn, and stop our horses. Can you teach me this?"

Kellen gave Raymond a huge smile.

"It's easy!" he said, and it was.

****

After the quick riding lesson, Kellen had shown them how to prepare for a trip, tying only their bedroll and water bag to their saddles and the remainder of their supplies to the mule that Kellen would lead. Although Hanshee was unaccustomed to carrying so much, he understood the importance of looking the part of ordinary travelers bound for Cantor. Besides the supplies for the horses, they carried food and water for themselves, an assortment of tools, a large tarp for shelter from the rain or snow, and a pole and some ropes with which to pitch it, if needed.

When all was completed, Kellen released the remaining horses from the barn into the pasture while Hanshee and Raymond filled the feeding troughs with hay and grain. After the water trough was filled, and after the incident with the chest of gold, the trio had departed the stable with just a couple of hours of daylight left.

Raymond had given a quick glance back at the body of Chezza, still unmoved from where he had fallen, before turning to look at Kellen. He found the boy's eyes facing forward as he guided his horse and the mule up the narrow road that led from the small valley of the stable toward the Southern Road.

They had made good progress in the time they had left. Raymond had grown accustomed to riding, albeit at a walk, and maneuvered his mount to the front, thinking it would appear strange if the two were being led by a child holding the lead rope of a mule. This way he would also be in a good position to address fellow travelers that they came into contact with on the road. Fortunately, there had been none.

****

All these memories ran through Raymond's mind as he lay beside the small fire Hanshee had built for the three of them. This had been yet another eventful day, as had been every moment since he had arisen from his sick bed three nights ago.

This brought back thoughts of his time before awakening and what he had learned, or thought he had learned. There were so many things about his situation that he still did not understand and he felt he needed to find those answers before he could explain to Hanshee what he had experienced. He wanted to know the where's and how's as well as the reasons behind it all so that he could come to terms with his plight. Maybe then he would feel comfortable pouring it all out to his friend.

What he thought he knew was that he existed in two realities. Having now experienced both, he honestly could not say if one was more real than the other. He, or his five senses, seemed to experience both exactly as they were meant to. To further test this, he reached out and gathered a pinch of dirt, rubbing it between his thumb and forefinger until none remained. The sensations were as real here as any he remembered from twenty-six years in his other life.

Though he had settled on the two existences theory, he had very little else that he could apply to it. He had no idea where they were in relation to each other, whatever that meant, or how he moved from one to the other.

Maybe it's the near-death aspect of it, Ray thought. *The river almost killed me there and I wake up here. An arrow in the back nearly kills me here and I wake up there.*

But if that were the case, what had brought him back here? Was he nearing death in his other existence? And what if he died there...or died here? Then what?

Having thought himself into an enigma, Ray stared at the stars and wondered if he would ever understand where he was, why he was here, and how he arrived here. He was still wondering when sleep overtook him.

CHAPTER 19

Jared led Captain Hendric and the men through the darkness toward the camp established near the stand of trees above which the rope had been discovered. As they drew nearer, the light of a fire could be seen between the breaks in the mostly barren winter growth. A few hundred feet from the fire Jared pulled up on his reins, bringing the band to a halt, and called out to those up ahead. Hearing a welcoming reply, they dismounted and walked their horses the short distance to where the trackers had their own horses tied, then joined them around the fire.

Having served with them under Captain Ailean, Jared introduced Hendric to the two trackers. Ishmed and Fevor both had the same lean and hard look about them and quite similar facial features as well. This came to make sense to Hendric when he found that they were actually brothers, though with different fathers.

Ishmed, called 'Ish' was a full-blooded tribesman whose people inhabited the lower slopes of the eastern Ursals. When one day his father failed to return from the hunt, he and his mother were taken in by a relative of his tribe. This was their custom, to provide shelter and sustenance for those in need until the spring.

In the spring time the different tribes would congregate to celebrate the passing of winter. At these gatherings the older members came mostly for the selling and bartering, to see old friends, and to pass on news and stories accumulated since the last gathering. The younger members saw this as an opportunity to meet their peers from other tribes, forming friendships and sometimes finding mates.

Ishmed's mother was a bit old for the young males of the other tribes, and the fact that she already carried a child on her hip meant that she would probably be among the last considered by a young warrior seeking a bride.

She did, however, catch one eye.

He was a Pithian settler who, with permission from the tribe, had a small farm in a nearby river valley. Having been raised in and around the territory claimed by the tribe, he had come to know and enjoy many of their ways. He had been to many a Spring Gathering and had received their welcome to trade and celebrate with them. This particular time his bartering skills paid off handsomely and he returned to his farm with a new wife and son. The following winter his new bride gave birth to Fevor.

The two brothers were among the best woodsmen in the southern forest and had attached themselves to Captain Ailean's command as independent hunters. Later, they chose to don the mantle of the Citadel Garrison to which the protection of the South Gate had been entrusted. Still in their early twenties and extremely fit, the brothers preferred to track on foot, allowing others to lead their horse until its speed became necessary.

After the introductions, Hendric and the new arrivals settled around the fire for an evening meal postponed until now. When this was finished, Ish and Fevor came forward to report what they had found the previous day.

"We started back in the stand of trees, over near the rock wall," Ish said. As was the custom of the mountain tribes, the eldest took the lead. "I could tell which tree they came down from the sticks and needles at the base, but the only tracks we could find were from Captain Ailean and his party."

"We've been seeing them for the better part of two seasons," Fevor chimed in, "so they were easy to mark."

"Starting from the trees," Ish continued, "we worked the whole area, but the first party and their horses covered up or scratched out anything that was there to find."

"Did you find a trail?" asked Hendric pointedly, not interested in an extended report of the difficulty of their search.

"Once we took to the woods, Captain," Ish responded, pointing away from the sheer cliffs. "It wasn't much, but we think we found something. How many were there?"

Hendric had been expecting this question.

All who were involved, save those of the 'inner circle', had been given less than complete details concerning what was going on. There were many reasons for this.

The general population of Pith knew nothing of a "Warrior-Priest of Old: Harbinger of the Fourth Prophesy". Even the Citadel Guard, responsible for their safety, knew Hanshee only as 'the Panther' and a guest of the Royal House. The armies of Pith, newly reconfigured under the command of Galin and deeply involved in training during the cold of winter, had no real idea of what they were training for. Only the King and his advisors, the military leaders that comprised the Council of Seven, and the High Priest and his Council of the Nine, were aware of the true identity of their guest. They were the few who were aware that the fledgling Empire of Pith was on the brink of changes that may well rock the very foundations of the Eastern Nations. Knowledge such as this was not to be bandied about carelessly or shared with those unequipped to comprehend all of its implications.

For these reasons, the explanation for the current activities centered on a daredevil escapee from the prison, or maybe a Cantorese spy who had fled after his identity had been discovered. Better this than to throw the nation into a panic fueled by their militaristic religious beliefs.

All this being the case, Hendric's answer to Ishmed's question was, by necessity, another question.

"How many marks did you find," Hendric asked the tracker.

"Two, we think," said Ish, as he studied Hendric's expression for clues as to what he expected to hear.

Hendric was hardly a stoic, and it was instantly clear to Ish that the captain had heard the answer he was looking for.

"You've done well, I think," said Hendric. How far out did you find them and what direction did they take?"

"Well," began Ishmed, "we found the first mark 'bout a rock's throw past the heavy brush to the south. We had to walk circles for most of the day just to find that. We found the second mark farther south, toward sundown. That's when we noticed there might be two of 'em."

"Whoever they are," said Fevor, "they walk the forest like spirits."

Ishmed nodded vigorously in agreement.

Hendric let his gaze move from the face of one brother to the other and back again.

"You *can* track them, can you not?" he asked.

At this question, Ishmed drew himself up to his full height, half a head shorter than his captain and, looking him squarely in the eye, said without the slightest hint of humor, "If it's passed within the hour, I can track a fish through water."

Hendric burst into laughter, knowing that he was truly among one of his kind; a soldier. No other men could boast of the impossible so boldly.

"Then we will rest well tonight," Hendric said, amidst the last chuckling of his mirth, "and tomorrow, I shall have no worry should their spore lead to the shores of the inland sea!"

****

The next morning proved more challenging than the boldness of Ishmed had promised. After breaking camp, the brothers led the pursuit party to the second of the two marks they had found the day before. Here they all dismounted and the party settled in to let the trackers do what they were best at.

Hendric watched in silence as the brothers scoured the immediate area for more sign of the passing of two men on foot. Their efforts could be seen in the practiced way they made semi-circles through the forest, bearing in a southern direction. Every now and then one would call to the other to come and inspect what he had found but they seemed never to agree on whether the sign be from a man, an animal, or simply an effect of nature.

It was almost two hours after halting that one of the brothers returned to the group having apparently reached some sort of conclusion.

"We found their mark, Captain," Ish said. "By this one, and the other two, they're steady moving south. We think we can move a little quicker now. Fev has gone up ahead to try to establish a trail. You men can follow me."

With that, Ishmed mounted his horse and led the party through the trees and brush in a generally southerly direction. They passed the place where the brothers had found another mark which Ish pointed out to them, then moved further on for about another hour before coming upon Fevor. He was hunched down, hovering over something that had captured his concentration. He stood up when he heard the horses coming through the brush and, when he was sure they had seen him, waved them forward and moved further south himself. In this way, the party made their way through the southern forest for most of the day before coming upon the first campsite nestled among the rocks.

Captain Hendric was frustrated by the lack of speed of the pursuit party. He calculated the distance and guessed that it had taken them more than twice the time to cover the same ground as those who they pursued. Having resolved to increase their pace, he dismounted and pulled the brothers aside while the others tended their horses.

"While we tarry, these men pull farther and farther ahead," Hendric said in a harsh whisper. "At this pace they will be well clear of Pithian lands before we have a chance to glimpse them."

"We know it's been slow, Captain," Ishmed said. "We're tracking the wind through a pine forest and it can't be helped. But Fev has a good bead on their spore now. We think we can find their mark easier now since we've been on it for a couple days. The pace should pick up tomorrow."

"How can I be sure of that?" said Hendric.

"Well, Captain," Ish replied, "we have about two hours of sun left and this is as good a place to camp as we're likely to find. The men can break down here and me and Fev can continue on this trail with what light is left. We'll be back in sometime after dark and tomorrow we should have this thing worked out. Once we can track 'em from horseback, we'll have 'em."

Though still skeptical, Hendric saw no other path to take for the moment. Reluctantly he ordered the men to make camp for the night then turned and looked after the brothers as they disappeared into the woods to the south.

"Captain?"

Hendric whirled about to find Lucius, who had eased up beside him as he looked after the trackers.

"Lucius," Hendric said in acknowledgement, his frustration with the current situation evident in his voice as he continued to stare after the brothers.

"Captain," Lucius spoke, "this pursuit seems to be developing a bit slowly." This caused Hendric to turn and face the sergeant.

"Just saying, Captain," Lucius quickly added with a slight bow of his head.

Hendric saw this and caught himself, allowing his irritation to dissipate before he responded.

"Truly, this is not the beginning that I anticipated," Hendric replied.

The pair stood silently for a moment, both looking to the place where the trackers had last been visible before disappearing into the distant woods. Presently, Hendric turned back to Lucius with a question.

"Were you not he who first captured the Harbinger, Sergeant?" Hendric asked, correctly assuming that Galin had informed his man of the nature of the mission.

Lucius smiled.

"That I was, Captain, though the truth be that it was but good fortune…or the will of The One."

Lucius looked to Hendric and saw the captain eyeing him with an expectant look, so he continued.

"The… mapping expedition…had made camp in a slight depression below a ridge. With Commander Galin's permission, I had taken a few of the best archers into the woods on the other side, to hunt game with the little light we had left. It wasn't long before we came upon a game trail. We set up on the incline above it, about a hundred paces apart, and settled down to watch for deer or boar."

Seeing that his tale held Hendric's attention, Lucius concluded.

"We never heard them coming, Captain. They were just…there," Lucius said. "When we fired our first arrow, the acolyte panicked, turned, and ran. We brought him up short with another arrow but, truthfully, the sign he left in that short run was the only sign they left on that trail."

"So," Hendric said absently, "he has always moved through the forest like a cat. Perhaps 'Panther' is a fitting name for him after all. This panther, and his cub, may be difficult to catch twice."

"The men haven't noticed yet, Captain," said Lucius.

"Huh? …what?" Hendric was brought back to the present.

"I said the men haven't noticed, M'lord," Lucius repeated. "Under Commander Galin, I keep a close eye on the men... to gage their mood. I have other responsibilities, too."

'I bet you do,' thought Hendric as he again eyed the shorter sergeant with curiosity before responding brusquely, "Do you have a point, Sergeant?"

"Just that this pursuit might take longer than any of these men think," Lucius said. "Slow tracking for days on end can make for bored soldiers. That can lead to surly men looking to break their boredom, and *that*," he paused for emphasis, "leads to a breakdown of discipline."

Hendric smiled to himself.

"Why don't you help this mission the way you help your Commander, Lucius." Hendric said. "Take charge of the men. Maintain discipline. Keep their minds occupied. And report any and everything to me."

"Yes, Captain," said Lucius. "It will be as you command."

With that, the sergeant moved off toward the men, who were occupied with setting up the night's camp.

Hendric looked after Lucius as he moved toward the men. *'Was that all about a grasp for authority?'* he thought.

No. Lucius did not strike him as so superficial a soldier. Hendric believed the sergeant was truly concerned about moral on what could be a long and difficult chase. If the first two days were an indication, Lucius was probably correct,

'This is not a good start,' Hendric thought to himself, the weight of his mission now beginning to impose itself on his mind. Though it was never spoken, Hendric knew that to return without the Harbinger was unthinkable. Again, he looked back to his men and supplies.

'Whatever comes... whatever the cost,' he thought, *'my mission is to hold these men together and recapture the Harbinger. I will be satisfied with nothing less.'*

****

As promised, things appeared to move a little more quickly the next morning. Having followed the trail for two days now, the brothers were well versed in what to look for and had settled into a rhythm of sorts. They were still moving much slower than Hendric would have liked, but this could not be helped as the sign was still too vague for the trackers to follow by horseback.

It was an hour or two after the midday when the pursuit party reached the northern boundary of the small valley encompassing the stables and the pasture adjacent to it. They watched for a time from the concealment of the forest and saw no human activity. There were horses and a few cattle and sheep in the pasture, and what looked to be a flock of birds in the yard in front of the old farm house.

"Are those vultures?"

The question arose from Maleek, one of the soldiers recommended by Commander Colevant, and at its utterance all eyes strained for a better view at the black birds that were in a group, close to what appeared to be the entrance to the house.

Still uncertain, but with a growing feeling of dread, Hendric gave his orders.

"Lucius, take Maleek, Felton, and Tomar and circle to the west. Start near the Southern Road and work down toward the house. Stay to the brush and off of the road. You others, come with me."

Followed by Jared, the young priest Petri, and the two trackers, Hendric led the way around the eastern border of the pasture, careful to stay to the woods as he approached the stables. Fevor moved up beside him to survey the ground and noted with satisfaction that they still followed the path of their quarry.

Pulling up at the tree line that was the eastern border of the stable yard, they waited until they caught sight of Lucius and his patrol moving in from the west. They were parallel to the narrow road and moving down toward the farm house. After waving a piece of scarlet cloth to get their attention, Hendric signaled them to halt. He then allowed the trackers to descend to the dust of the stable yard.

The brothers moved into the yard side by side, taking their time and never seeming to lift their eyes from the ground. After a while, Ish nudged his brother and pointed to the ground off to his left. Fever nodded and Ish broke off in that direction, moving toward the corral which extended behind and beside the barn. He briefly ducked inside the barn, before rejoining his brother just as he was approaching the birds that were milling around in front of the farmhouse steps.

From his vantage point in the tree line, Hendric could clearly see the birds were vultures. The only remaining question was, on what were they feeding.

The trackers walked upright now, confident in what their observations had found. The birds became more agitated as the pair approached and finally scattered into the air, some traveling only a few feet before again alighting and waiting for this intrusion on their meal to come to an end.

Both brothers now stood before the farm house stairs, looking down at what, from a distance, appeared to be a mass of red colored clothing. They then made their way out into the yard directly before the house. Working their way through the dust, the brothers eventually moved all the way across the yard and up onto the road beside Lucius. At this point Ishmed separated from his brother and trotted back to Hendric on the far side of the stable yard.

"The pair we pursue came through here," Ishmed said. "Their tracks are everywhere. So are two other sets of tracks, one large and one small."

"What were the birds feasting on," asked Hendric

"What's left of a man," said Ishmed. "He looks fresh."

Hendric stared at the tracker for a moment, then started down the short slope from the woods to the stable yard. He had noted the doors of the barn had been closed before Ishmed opened them to check inside. Now he looked to the troughs near the pasture fence and saw that all were at least half filled with hay or oats.

He continued on toward the house, stopping before what was once a man but now a corpse. It was only half covered by clothing; most having been torn away by the birds. The body was torn open from the sternum to just above the groin, exposing the most tender morsels. Hendric recognized the eyeless face as that of Chezza, the stable master.

As he stared down at the grisly scene before him, Hendric was joined by Lucius, whose group had started down into the stable yard from the opposite direction.

"He's not too long dead," said Lucius as he inspected the remains. "Do you suppose the Panther killed him?"

"That is unlikely," said Hendric. "See there? That stone beside his head? If you look closely, you will probably find a gray hair or two on that sharp corner. It looks to me like he fell and struck his head. The blow probably killed him."

"If not, then we'll never know otherwise, eh Captain?" Lucius replied.

Hendric stepped away without comment, motioning the trackers toward him while the others gathered around the corpse.

"What else did you find?" Hendric asked of Ishmed, when he had the brothers alone.

"Well, there's many tracks here," Ishmed began, "it being a stable and all, but the freshest are the ones we followed from the forest. They end over by that hitching post," he motioned toward a rail set up opposite the porch. "After that there's only the track of four horses making their way up the road there," he motioned to the road leading away from the stables, "and out toward the south road."

"And how fresh do you think these tracks are?" asked Hendric

Ishmed turned a questioning glance to his brother.

"About as old as that corpse, I'd say," said Fevor.

"That's about right," Ishmed agreed. "Probably a day; no more than two."

Hendric had seen enough corpses to know that what the trackers said about its age was true. If the horses left here about the same time, and the Harbinger was now on horseback, then they were falling further behind in their pursuit even as they stood here and spoke.

"There's one good to take from this," said Fevor, and both Hendric and his brother Ishmed turned to him with looks of curious annoyance.

Guessing that he had probably said the wrong thing at the wrong time, Fevor ducked his head slightly, as if to evade a blow, before he continued.

"Them horses," he said, "are easy to track."

Expecting to hear something ridiculous, this utterance actually brought a smile to Hendric's lips, and he soon found himself barking orders with barely concealed excitement.

"Jared! Lucius! Search the house and the barn for anything we could put to use. Maleek! Felton! Get that corpse in the ground behind the barn! Tomar! Get some of that hay and grain into the horses. Not too much! Then water them well. We leave within the hour!"

Turning to the trackers, Hendric again spoke. "Fevor, get on that trail and follow it as far as you can. Stay on it! We will be along shortly with your horse."

Hendric watched Fevor trot up the road, then turned and surveyed the yard. All the men seemed to be in motion save for Petri, whom most believed to be useless for anything short of his purpose for being here; to speak with the Harbinger if, and when, he was found.

As Hendric watched, Petri turned and made his way toward the house, presumably to help the others search for useful items. He took great pains to avoid the corpse of Chezza, even while not looking directly at it. Hendric continued to watch Petri as he climbed the stairs and disappeared into the house, then turned back to Ishmed and again spoke.

"Ish, check the horses in the pasture," he said. "Cut out any that look superior to ours and we will make a trade." Hendric looked back toward the remains lying beside the steps. "I doubt the stable master will mind."

A short time later, the men were preparing to mount up. Two horses had been exchanged and a search of both the barn and the farmhouse had yielded at least another load of food for both the men and their horses that could be carried along should they find another pack animal. Luckily there was no shortage of animals at the now masterless stable. A horse suitable for carrying another load was soon found and loaded with the extra goods.

The only other things worth taking were a few bags of wine. Hendric's first instinct was to leave these where they were found. The last thing he needed was a patrol consumed by drunken boredom. But their quarry was now on horseback and, though moving more swiftly, was much more easily tracked. The Pithian military boasted some of the finest horsemen in the east. He was more than sure that his band could ride down the Harbinger and his acolyte, no matter who rode with them. From the footprints found in the stable yard, Ishmed thought one of the other horses carried a child. This made sense to Hendric, who remembered the bright young lad who had thwarted the stable master's plan to switch his horses when last he visited this yard.

Hendric decided to hold on to the wine. Once the mission of recapturing the Harbinger was achieved, a celebratory drink might do the men some good.

As he was securing the four leather wine bags to his mount, he was startled by a cry from inside the farm house.

"Captain!... Captain!"

Quickly looking about, Hendric took stock of his men. All seemed present accept...

"Captain!"

The cry came from outside now and Hendric looked to the house to find the young priest Petri standing just outside the open doorway, calling to him.

"What is it, Priest?" Hendric shouted toward the obviously agitated young cleric.

"Captain! You must come and see what I have found!" the priest said almost breathlessly.

Now the attention all present was riveted on the priest, with some beginning to move toward the farm house, their curiosity fully piqued.

Hendric tied the last knot before pacing deliberately toward the door that had already seen three men, besides the priest, pass through to the inside.

Stepping over the stained ground where the stable master had lain, Hendric took the steps two-at-a-time and entered the dim stillness of the main room. Spying a light from the room beyond, he passed through that doorway to find the priest and three others bent over a chest. Feeling the rest of his command pressing through the door behind him, he bent forward to see what had so flustered the priest and found himself frozen to the floor, the breath almost forcibly sucked from his chest.

Before him...before them all...lay an open chest containing another smaller chest, the smaller of the two completely filled with gold coins!

The others now crowded around to see what they could. After several astonished gasps, the room fell silent.

"Touch nothing!" Hendric barked to all, shattering the silence and placing every man on his guard. He spoke around a mouth suddenly gone dry at the sight of so much wealth in front of them all, its owner obviously unable to claim it. Working his mouth to produce what saliva he could, he continued.

"Jared and Lucius! Close that chest and get it out into the daylight, now!"

Jared and Lucius had to push others aside in order to get to the chest but, once there, were quick to follow Hendric's orders, struggling to carry the heavy gold-filled box out into the very center of the stable yard. Once it was set down the others quickly gathered around it, though none dared lift the lid to again reveal the contents.

Hendric's mind was reeling. His first orders had been reflexive; an attempt to gain control of a situation that could have quickly and easily gotten out of hand. He had known instinctively what the contents of that chest represented to men such as these.

His men were solders of the Pith, born to aggression, trained to kill, and never likely to again set eyes on the amount of wealth now available to them if they lived ten lifetimes. Hendric knew what effect gold had on men and he could only trust that these men had also been engrained with a love for The Throne and a respect for command. He now had to count on these to cement his control of the situation.

Aggressively pushing his way through the circle of men, Hendric placed one booted foot atop the closed chest and then searched out the eyes of every man present. What he saw was a mixture of every emotion that could serve to twist a man's soul.

In some there was still astonishment at their find and joy in their good fortune. There was apprehension as they considered just what would be done with the treasure now before them, and lust at the thought that they might possibly gain a share. Hendric saw jealousy as some thought of having to share this treasure with the men around them, many of whom they considered lesser than themselves. There was greed as thoughts of sharing a portion became dreams of taking the lions share, or maybe taking it all. And then there was the heat… borne of the fire and fury that rises up in a man's soul as he braces himself for violence, preparing to fight and kill his comrades in order to claim the riches contained in the chest.

Hendric looked to each man and saw all these emotions to one degree or another. He realized what this new found treasure represented; the challenge to discipline and to his authority that it posed.

Knowing these things only served to fuel Hendric's determination. He would hold this band together. He would retake the Harbinger and return him to the Citadel. He would do his duty, and it would start right here, right now.

Hendric continued to look from man to man and, when he was sure that only he had their attention, he spoke.

"We ride this day," Hendric began, "for King Ammon IV and for the Empire of Pith. As your Captain, I now claim this treasure for both King and Empire!"

Hendric saw the change in some eyes. A fire now burning hotter… born of dreams of wealth suddenly within their grasp and now snatched away…a fire, born of a greed unquenched, blazed behind some eyes. In response Hendric allowed his right hand to move, slowly and deliberately, to the hilt of his sword as he stared every man of them down. In their current state of madness, some considered drawing iron on their captain. Hendric saw it. And then he saw the thoughts dissipate as the madness slowly receded and the eyes returned to normal, or as close to normal as they could in the presence of such temptation.

Seeing this, Hendric relaxed his grip on the sword hilt.

"Now we *know* that Chezza's death was no murder," he said to the gathered men. "A murderer would have searched the house and none could have left such a treasure behind."

"We can't leave it behind either, eh Captain?"

It was Felton who spoke; probably the first Hendric had heard him speak since he attached to the squad. Hendric met his gaze and could see that there still lurked something behind the man's eyes.

Though Felton gave voice to the query, others waited anxiously for their captain's response. Hendric paused for a moment before responding, considering his next words. He knew that, for any number of reasons, what Felton asked could not be done.

"We have a duty…" Hendric began, "…a mission to accomplish. To carry this treasure would not only slow our pursuit, but would ensure that our minds and our hearts would stray from that duty."

"I'll stay here and guard it, Captain. The rest of you can catch up to the escapees and I'll be here with it when you get back."

This was Maleek, and all could hear the hollowness of his words.

"We'll not take this treasure with us, nor will we leave someone behind," Hendric said, all eyes glued to his imposing frame. "But I will tell you what I *will* do…what your King will do… for all of you here with me now."

Hendric paused and scanned the group, all anxious to hear his next words.

"We…all of us…will bury this treasure nearby. We will hide it well. And when we complete our mission, we will all together come back to this place. We will retrieve the gold and I will see that each man receives an equal share."

"Two gold coins apiece?" Felton said scornfully, more of a statement than a question, and immediately there began a buzzing of dissatisfaction among the group.

"I will disperse it all! Hendric bellowed, and the men fell silent. "We will divide it evenly among us! Every Coin! But only *after* we have completed our given duty!"

Hendric looked upon them again and saw that, although silent, some were still not satisfied.

"And if there be a man among you," Hendric continued, "who feels he cannot fulfill his duty to King and Empire with this much treasure weighing on his mind, let him come forth now," Hendric drew his sword with a loud 'sshhwinnng!', "and I promise his share will be divided equally among those that remain."

Tense silence now gripped the circle of men surrounding the chest full of gold coins.

"I'll follow you, Captain," said Lucius, who was to Hendric's rear and had kept his eyes steadily on those who had dared to question his captain.

"As will I," said Jared stepping beside Hendric, his sword hand filled with his hilt and his eyes staring intensely at Maleek.

"I'll not challenge your authority, Captain," Maleek quickly spoke up, both hands raised and his voice now dripping with humility. "I don't know why they look to me," he said as he shifted his gaze between Lucius and Jared.

Felton saw the direction this had quickly taken and suddenly found himself fascinated by the tops of his dusty boots.

"It's agreed then," said Hendric looking from man to man until all had nodded ascent. "And if it is agreed" he continued, "then before your brethren... your comrades in arms... I will have the oath of each and every man here that you will abide by this agreement and my orders, or submit to my blade."

Beginning with Lucius, every man bent a knee to give his oath.

CHAPTER 20

Ray, Hanshee and Kellen had now spent five nights on the road. They had traveled beyond the valley of Stronghold, bypassing the turn north that would have led to its legendary gates two days prior. Though still within the borders of Pith, they now traveled what was known as the Road to Cantor. This road took them in a westerly direction while working its way down from the higher elevations upon which Stronghold sat.

They had passed a few travelers on their journey and it was easy to pick up the local custom of a raised sword hand and words spoken briefly in greeting. Raymond was up to this, and ensured that they said and did nothing that would cause them to stand out. The travelers they met had no idea who the Harbinger was, much less that he was missing, so no undue scrutiny was directed their way.

But no matter how many meetings passed uneventfully, Hanshee remained on edge.

He was not accustomed to traveling the wide-open roads of the city dwellers and much preferred the cover and comfort provided by the forest. It had briefly snowed the night before, probably one of the last snows of the season at this elevation, and Ray often looked back to see Hanshee examining the tracks they left as they passed. Luckily it had been a light snow and even now there were patches of road showing through due to the melting of the slight accumulation.

Still Hanshee felt uneasy and his unease was transmitted to his companions. If Hanshee and Ray had been experienced riders, the three of them could have pushed their mounts to a faster pace. Though more comfortable in the saddle now than when they first sat their horses, they were still far from being accomplished horsemen.

They continued along at a fairly steady pace, alternating their speed so as not to tire their horses or unduly tax their novice riders.

After several hours in the saddle, they would dismount and walk the animals for a distance. This was on the advice of Kellen, and Ray had at first thought it strange.

Raymond had never seen any of his western heroes relinquish the saddle as they crossed the open plains. But he had also seen them run their horses at full gallop over miles and miles of open country, with no apparent ill effects on the animal, and he knew that was a myth. Rather than lean on his own understanding, gleaned from fictional heroes on screens both big and small, he wisely decided to listen to the young teacher riding beside him in all things concerning a horse.

It was along about mid-morning when they approached a ravine that looked to span about three-hundred feet from one side to the other. Connecting the sides was a rope bridge. About four feet wide and constructed with some of the thickest rope that Raymond had ever seen, the bridge showed obvious use but still looked extremely sturdy.

For men maybe…or for smaller animals; dogs, or even sheep if you blindfolded them before leading them across one at a time.

But this bridge was definitely not made for horses.

Kellen had dismounted, signaling that it was now time to walk their mounts, and Ray and Hanshee gladly complied, each wanting to see the ravine up close.

Hanshee walked to the very edge and leaned over to examine the depth. Ray almost screamed when he saw this. Even after his adventures on the eastern cliffs of Stronghold, his fear of heights somehow remained. He watched hesitantly as Hanshee walked over to the rope bridge and vigorously tested its strength, walking out a way and trying to shake the hand ropes to make the bridge unstable. Hanshee came back obviously impressed with the craftsmanship and safety. Taking the reins of his horse, He prepared to lead him across the rope bridge, but was stopped by Kellen's small hand tugging on his forearm.

"We can't take the horses across, Hanshee," Kellen said. "They won't go. If you try to force them, they might panic and jump the rope, or knock you off."

Having been immersed now in the Pithian tongue for several months, Hanshee understood the gist of what the lad said. Still, he turned to Ray for a word-for-word translation.

Raymond was happy to oblige.

"Ask him how we are to cross with the horses," was Hanshee's response to Ray. Again, Ray obliged and listened as Kellen explained that they would now travel north along the ravine for a day. There was a place there where the ravine narrowed to a distance over which a sturdy wooden bridge had been built. Horses and wagons could cross there.

Ray explained all to Hanshee, who thought this detour to be much to slow, especially considering the possibility of pursuit somewhere behind them.

At Hanshee's request, Ray pressed the child, who then spoke of an alternate way.

Just south of the rope bridge was a narrow path that wound its way down into the ravine. Until the two bridges had been built, the path was the only way from one side to the other and was usually used only by those on foot. It could be treacherous, and few were known to have made the attempt to lead horses along its length. Kellen said that Chezza had only used this path once, when he was late on the way to Cantor to buy new horses.

He would never use the path on the return journey for fear of losing a newly purchased horse.

Kellen had been with him then and had used it once more when leading two horses and a mule while Chezza had waited on the other side. Saddled horses could make the journey but could not be ridden. Pack animals must be unpacked before they could be led down this path and up the other side. According to Kellen the journey would take about half a day.

After hearing this, Hanshee walked the ravine south of the bridge as Kellen had indicated. He followed the edge as it curved and dipped until, rounding a stand of trees, he came to the mouth of the path that led downward toward the bottom of the ravine. A moment later Ray was beside him and together they looked down the narrow path that disappeared behind the tall brush growing beside the trail within about fifty feet of where they stood. No other parts of the path were visible from the rim of the ravine.

Having now seen that there was a path, Hanshee immediately devised a plan.

"Kellen," Raymond began explaining to the boy what Hanshee wanted, "could you tie the horses together and lead them down into the ravine and up the other side? Hanshee and I will cross the bridge and wait for you there," Ray pointed to the far side of the ravine.

Kellen tilted his head as he considered whether he was up to this. Then he looked at the horses. Lastly, he looked to Hanshee and smiled as he nodded his head.

Hanshee and Ray took a water bag and a small amount of food from the backs of their horses, then watched as Kellen tied the animals in such a way as to lead them single file.

Before Kellen started, Hanshee and Ray led the mule over to the rope bridge and unpacked it so they could carry the bundles across. Kellen smiled at them as he tied the mule on behind the last horse. Then he sounded a gentle cluck and tugged on the reins of the lead horse. Slowly the animals came to understand what was required of them and soon Kellen was leading them toward the path that would take them down into the ravine.

Hanshee led the way across the bridge, carrying a bundle with one hand as he slid the other hand along one of the two ropes that ran between waist and shoulder high along both sides. Feeling his old apprehension, Raymond held back and watched Hanshee's progress. When he saw how easily Hanshee was crossing the span he lifted a bundle, put on his brave face, and stepped out before he had a chance to give it more thought.

Ray found the bridge to be solid and sturdy, the ropes having been drawn to a high degree of tension. He wondered how this was accomplished as he stared straight ahead and made his way across. Almost before he realized it, he was on the other side.

This side of the ravine was a large, bare, almost circular clearing, over one-hundred feet in diameter. On the far side was a large oak, its limbs spreading wide, giving much needed shade in the summer to travelers waiting their turn to cross the bridge. Beyond the oak, on its northern side, was the continuation of the road that led to Cantor.

On the south side of the clearing, and near the ravine, was the path from which Kellen and the horses would eventually emerge. It wound around a formation of boulders, one the size of a small house, that bordered the west side of the path. A line of smaller boulders ran alongside the lip of the ravine, extending a little farther toward the bridge than the larger, house sized boulder. Ray walked over to examine the path and saw that it wound in and out among rock formations for as far down its length as he could see.

On either side of the road, and behind the old oak, the brush was thick and mostly green. This was due to a large dense growth of evergreen shrubs amongst the deciduous trees that had long ago shed their leaves for winter. This is where Hanshee bid Raymond to bring the bundles. He and Hanshee made one more trip across the bridge and back and, having crossed the ravine three times, Raymond now felt that he could relax.

Hanshee had ideas of his own.

First, he bade Ray to help him move the provisions carried across the ravine to a place of hiding. Then Hanshee removed his bow and quiver of arrows from one bundle and moved carefully through the brush surrounding the large oak until he found a place that provided a modicum of comfort and concealment, while allowing him a view of the clearing, the bridge beyond, and the other side of the ravine. Hanshee then carefully strung the bow, a short, re-curved, horn bow, the very one that he had taken from the pig farmer in Aggipoor, and bid Ray to settle down in the brush beside him to await Kellen's arrival.

Once settled, Ray turned to his friend.

"Hanshee," Ray asked. "Do you know something that I don't?"

"It is a feeling," Hanshee replied in a whisper, "that I have had since last evening. It may be nothing, but one should never be unprepared."

As Ray watched, Hanshee adjusted his position until he had an unencumbered view through the brush to the rope bridge. Then he settled in and became completely quiet…completely still, the bow and a single notched arrow resting on his lap as he sat cross legged in the brush. Ray could never seem to get comfortable sitting that way so he stretched his body out a few feet behind Hanshee, having first removed his robe and spread it on the ground. There he found a relatively unencumbered view, though from a lower vantage point. With the understanding that, for the next several hours it was important that he remain still and quiet, Ray settled in to wait for Kellen and the horses.

CHAPTER 21

For the first two thirds of its length the Masscus Road climbed, dipped and curled through and around all obstacles as it wound its way north. It followed the path of least resistance through the foothills that marked the northern edges of the great valley called Stronghold. It was only the final third of its length that was relatively flat and straight, running east to west. It followed a slight but constant incline, with much of the vegetation cleared from its boundaries. This meant that, though the settlement was remote and the terrain unforgiving, no one approached unseen. There would be no surprises.

The people of the settlement subsisted largely by farming and herding sheep, and were renowned for producing the finest wool to be found anywhere in the known world. The high ranges surrounding the settlement encouraged the growth of a type of wool that was unusually dense and rich.

It was the children who were usually tasked with tending the herds. They were not yet strong or durable enough for the hard work of a mountain farm, but they had been taught to draw a bow or load a sling in defense of the flocks. It was because of their positions in the pastures overlooking the road that they were usually the first to know of visitors.

So it was today.

The children watching the flocks had also been watching something on the Masscus road for some time now. At first it was a tiny speck that barely moved in the direction of the settlement. It took some time before that speck was close enough to make out the figure of a man leading a horse. It wasn't until some had left the flocks and wandered closer to the road that the man was recognizable as a woman. The horse remained a horse.

As the woman made progress more and more people noticed, some even coming all the way to the road for a better look. Only then did they notice that the horse bore a rider.

The rider wasn't noticed immediately because he wasn't sitting as a normal rider would. Instead, he was hunched forward, his upper torso nearly flat against the neck of the huge farm horse. Powerless to keep his position on his own, he was tied down with ropes and leather that kept him from sliding off.

As the woman crested the last rise, the lodge came into view. It was the central building in the settlement, where the people gathered for both celebrations and tragedies. It was second in size only to the great barn that served to house the most valuable of the animals during the harshest winter weather.

The building itself was constructed mostly from large timbers, but was built atop a huge semi-flat granite outcropping. The eastern portion of the outcropping had been worked with hammer and chisel into stairs leading up to the large double doors that served as the entrance to the great hall.

The great hall could be a raucous place after the fall harvest. The whole of the settlement would try to squeeze together inside and large fires would be lit. Some were for warmth but most were for the roasting of freshly slaughtered meat, the baking of breads, the cooking of spicy stews, and the warming of the spiced wine and mead. That the cook fires also served to warm the gathering was secondary.

From her position still some distance away, the traveler could see the people who lined the broad avenue leading up to the wide granite stairs that lay before the lodge. Most were her relatives in one way or another.

Although their ancestors carried many bloodlines, almost everyone of importance in the village was in some way connected to the Masscus clan. The Masscus are the "ruling family" of the high mountain folk, all of which are descended from those first tribal people who were driven into the hidden valley of Stronghold some eight-hundred years prior. The people now lined up to witness the woman's approach were no exception.

In their tight-nit village, most that were of an age had been raised together, trained together, and had developed almost as siblings. The woman knew most of these people as one would know brothers and sisters, cousins, aunts and uncles, and other more distant relatives.

And they knew her as well: Nola, first born and daughter of Seenio Masscus, who was also known affectionately as sister, cousin, and niece. Most were not aware of her absence, and so were curious to see her return. Others, high ranking members of the Guild, may have had knowledge of her mission and would wonder at her return without her brothers.

As she made her way through the familiar throng, no voice was raised in greeting. She trod the street before the lodge in silence, the shod hooves of the horse making the only sounds that accompanied her solemn march toward the granite steps.

When she was roughly one-hundred feet away, she allowed her eyes to precede her up the length of those steps, on the path that she knew she would soon have to travel. Up they went, to the terrace at the very top and to the figure standing there alone. It was her father, Seenio Masscus; Patriarch of Clan Masscus, known to some as the House of The Beast, from which centuries ago had been spawned the Guild of Assassins.

Nola wordlessly passed between her people and stopped before the first step. There she stood, enshrouded by silence, knowing that she was being weighed by the crowd as well as by her sire. There was a part of this that was show, for the eyes of the many onlookers. She understood… and was prepared to play her role. She kept her eyes glued to the step before her as her father allowed the drama of the moment to build.

After a while, Seenio made his way down the steps. She knew this by the subtle change in the quiet hum emanating from the crowd. Her breath came more quickly now and she could feel a nervousness that, not long ago, she would have thought herself incapable of. She sought to calm herself with the thought that it was not her; Seenio could have this effect on anyone, even those who knew him best. It was not until his booted feet came into her view that she lifted her head and beheld his face.

Though he was patriarch of Clan Masscus, her father was still a young man. When asked, he would admit to having seen thirty-seven winters and his word could be believed, as he was not a man consumed with vanity. What lines were visible on his face stemmed from weather, work, and worry, not age. He was powerfully built, standing a little over six feet and with a broad frame that carried just over two-hundred and forty muscled pounds. His face was considered handsome, broad across the brow with high cheeks, tapering down to a strong chin just short of sharp due to the cleft that divided it. He had close cut curly hair that was a darker brown in his youth, but was now sun bleached due to a lifetime of exposure in their mountain domain. His complexion would lean toward golden even if he did not carry an almost permanent tan from that exposure.

Seenio wore a soft leather tunic, a match to his boots which had gray breaches tucked into their top. The shirt underneath his tunic was a matching grey. No weapons adorned the wide leather belt that encircled his waist. None were needed here. But even without weapons, Seenio Masscus had the look of a man intimately acquainted with violence and death.

Nola slowly raised her head until she was staring into the hard gray eyes of her father. The two stood center and apart from everyone else. No one could hear their words unless they themselves wished it.

Seenio made a point of searching beyond his daughter, before again meeting her eyes as he spoke.

"Where are your brothers?" he asked his first born.

"Before you sits Darien," Nola motioned to the bandaged figure tied onto the horse. "I fear that Mem and Lux are dead."

"You witnessed their fall?"

"No father," Nola replied. "I witnessed their entrance into the quarters of the targeted priest, in the rear of the Royal House of Pith; a place from which they never returned."

To those looking on, there was no change in Seenio's expression. Nothing in his bearing would even hint at the weight of the news he had just received. Only Nola could see the effect that having lost two of the three sons that he acknowledged had on him. It was in his eyes… the gray eyes that went wide with disbelief, but only for an instant. Then they narrowed and hardened and, a moment later, it was as if nothing had been said.

"And the target? The priest?" Seenio asked.

"He still lives," was Nola's quick reply.

Seenio looked off into the distance, nodding his head up and down as he digested this tale of failure and loss. After a moment, he turned hard eyes back to Nola.

"What of Darien," he asked, nodding toward the figure still on the horse.

"He was injured, with the return journey worsening his injuries. He has burns that have festered. He needs a healer."

Seenio pointed to a group of four men who were standing in the front of the crowd that had formed to await Nola. They came trotting over.

"Cut him down," he said to the first two while motioning toward Darien. "Take him inside to his bed." Motioning to a third man he said, "Run for the healer. Send him to Darien's quarters." To the last he said, "Take this horse to the barn. Feed and water it."

Seenio then turned again to his first born.

"Walk with me, child."

Up the stairs, across the terrace, and through the doors of the great hall they went. The massive room was cool and quiet with only a single fire trough alight at its center. They walked its length without speaking, Seenio leading the way and Nola two steps behind him and to his right. At the far end of the hall was a dais upon which sat two chairs; one for the master, the other for his woman. Seenio and Nola circled the dais and passed through a double door at the rear of the chamber.

Now they were in a wide hall that stretched before them for at least one-hundred feet. There were doors evenly spaced along the walls of both sides, and the pair walked down the hall until they came to the third door on the left. Here they came to a stop, still unspeaking, but both looking expectantly toward the door through which they had last passed. A moment later two men came through carrying Darien on a stretcher. They hurried up to Seenio and entered the room before which door he stood. Now he and Nola stepped through and watched as the men carefully moved the semi-conscious body from the stretcher to the bed. While one began undressing the injured man in preparation for an examination, the other went about lighting as many lanterns as were available, and then starting a fire in the fireplace against the outside wall.

Seeing that the men had the situation in hand, and knowing that the healer would be there soon to deal with Darien's injuries, Seenio led Nola out of the room and the remaining distance to the end of the hall. There they approached a set of heavy double doors that opened into his chamber.

Rather than a suite of rooms, Seenio claimed one long chamber that spanned the width of the building. Three fireplaces, one on the south wall, the north wall, and the west wall, ensured that the large space could be kept comfortable. There was furniture all about the chamber, with the different uses of the spaces spelled out by what type of furniture it held.

As they entered, Nola spied her mother busy preparing a meal at the northern fireplace. Looking up from her pot, she saw Nola come in behind Seenio and rushed forward to greet her daughter. Their embrace was warm, as a mothers and daughters should be, even though the daughter was a Reaper in the Guild. Still, Leisha could feel that something was amiss and she pushed her oldest child out to arm's length and looked her up and down.

"Something is wrong," the highly intuitive mother said, looking from Nola to Seenio and back again to Nola. "What is wrong child? Tell me."

"Leisha…," Seenio said in warning.

Leisha was a very handsome woman, and a match for Seenio in almost every way. This was remarkable for the fact that she was at least ten years his senior. Due to his celebrated savagery, Seenio had been rewarded with many women in his early youth. Leisha was the first to bear him a child and the first to bear him a son. Maybe it was due to his youth, but these *firsts* meant much to Seenio. Though he did not limit his encounters to one woman, only one woman held his heart.

Now Leisha turned her dark eyes to Seenio and probed him without a word.

"It is the Guild," Seenio said in answer to her unspoken question.

Leisha held his gaze for another heartbeat before she turned and slowly made her way back to her duties. The business of the Guild was only for its members, of which she most definitely was not. She knew, as the wife of its leader, of its existence. She knew her children all aspired to be amongst its number. And she knew what that could portend for a loving mother. Seenio watched her back as she walked away, knowing in the end she would show the courage that was expected from the woman of the Beast.

Seenio led Nola to the other end of the chamber, to a corner where hung every type of bladed weaponry. There he stood with his back to the room, allowing his eyes to roam the walls and pick out favorites he had used in training with his sons and his daughter.

"Tell me everything," he said to Nola, and she did.

CHAPTER 22

He didn't know how long he had been asleep, lying there wrapped in the assassin's fur robe. He just felt the gentle shaking of his body and, true to his teaching, came awake with no movement or noise. Before he had a chance to open his eyes, he felt Hanshee's breath on his ear.

"Listen," was all Hanshee said, and Ray focused his hearing as he allowed his eyes to come open.

For a while he heard nothing except his own breathing and the usual sounds of the surrounding forest. But, after a while, he heard a subtle rhythmic sound. It was both strange and familiar, and he couldn't place it at first. As silently as possible, he moved into an upright position to better see toward the ravine; the direction of the sound. As he studied the rope bridge and the road beyond, the sound slowly grew in intensity until, suddenly, Ray knew what he was hearing. A second later he saw the first of the horsemen come into view.

Watching from the safety of the brush Ray counted eleven riders, all men and all but one marked by their garb as soldiers.

After bringing their horses to a halt, two of the men dismounted and took a moment to examine the ground between themselves and the ravine. A moment later, both men made their way south, over to the path that led into the ravine. Finally, one man went back toward the man still sitting astride the lead horse. The other quickly traversed the bridge and sprinted over to where the path emerged into the clearing on the opposite side of the ravine. There he searched the ground for several feet in each direction before returning across the bridge to join the first man standing before the still seated rider. A short discussion ensued, with the two men on foot doing most of the talking while gesturing animatedly towards the path into the ravine.

I know that rider, thought Raymond, while keeping completely still and quiet, content to await the right moment to inform Hanshee of his discovery. Together, they continued to watch and wait in silence.

****

Hendric looked to the trackers who had been steady in their task of following the hoof prints of the four horses since leaving the stables. According to the two brothers, the pursuit was a mere few hours behind their quarry.

Ishmed, and his brother Fevor, had proven their worth in the last few days. Once they had locked on to the particular marks that these horses left, the speed of pursuit had increased considerably. They had found every place that the harbinger had camped along the Stronghold Road, each dead campfire a bit fresher than the last. So sure were the trackers of the spore they followed, that Hendric had allowed an increased pace, to possibly recapture the guest of the Royal House before he could cross the ravine.

There had been an unforeseen delay when they came upon two soldiers, with their mounts and equipment, waiting for the pursuit party at the fork that led to Strongholds Gate. The two had waved them down and informed Hendric that they were there by order of Commander Galin. Apparently, due to some disciplinary issue, the commander had ordered the two to the crossroads and instructed them to wait there on the chance that Captain Hendric and his squad passed that way. If Hendric came through, the two were to consider themselves fortunate and throw in with the captain and his pursuit squad. If by the fifth day Hendric's force did not pass, the two must return and endure whatever punishment Galin should decide to inflict upon them. Hendric had stumbled upon them on their second day.

This whole situation had struck Hendric as odd, and he spent a good deal of time questioning the two as to their identities, ranks, branch of service, and the reason behind their 'punishment'. It was ever near the surface of his thoughts that, whoever had orchestrated the assassination attempts in the Citadel would hardly shirk at attempting to place assassins within his ranks.

Hendric had been poised to send the two back through the Stronghold Gates to whatever punishment awaited them until Blige, the spokesman of the two, produced from the insides of his tunic a note bearing the seal of Commander Galin, confirming all that he had told Hendric. The captain had no alternative but to allow the two to fall in with his group or risk being brought to task for disobeying Galin's orders and circumventing his authority.

Now, as they sat their mounts before the rope bridge that served as the unofficial gateway into Cantorese territory, Hendric found that he had several decisions to make. He looked back at his company, especially the two newcomers, as he pondered his current situation.

The brothers were adamant that, instead of heading north towards the heavy bridge made from sturdy timbers, the horses had descended the southern path down into the Ravine. Fevor was just as adamant that, having found no matching hoof prints on the other side, the Harbingers party had yet to make their way there. Though it was the quickest way across, the path was by far the most dangerous way to get horses to the other side of this crack in the earth that lay before them. Hendric could head north to the bridge but, even moving as fast as they could reasonably push their mounts, the Harbinger would have gained a day if he were to emerge from the depths of the ravine onto the other side.

This left Hendric but one plan. He would pursue his quarry down into the ravine and up the other side. But he would also send a small force of men to the other side by way of the rope bridge. They would lie in wait for the Harbinger, who would be forced by the pursuit into their grasp.

But who should he trust to send? That was the question that plagued him as he looked over his hastily assembled squad.

All save the priest were soldiers of some degree of experience. One would think that would make the decision an easy one. But these men had been thrown together quickly, had done nothing as a group except follow a trail, and hardly held the trust of one another. Nor had they earned his trust. Was he not using the promise of the gold to hold their loyalty and compel their duty? What could he really hope to accomplish with men such as these?

If pressed, Hendric could not swear that any of these men now under his command were not assassins bent on thwarting the safe return of the Harbinger and his acolyte. The young priest was attached to the Temple. Was it not in the Temple that the first assassination attempt took place? The morning wine laced with poison, if he recalled. Exactly how a priest would be expected to attempt a killing. The priest could not be fully trusted, and in any event would be no good at containing the harbinger if he were to be sent across the bridge.

The training yard… that had been subtle. The three from the City Garrison who emerged unharmed swore that it was but a friendly challenge gone awry and not an attempt to kill the Panther. Was it really just an accident? Hendric could not say for sure but it was his way, especially in light of recent events, to project the worst of motives onto such situations. And Colevant was the Commander of the City Garrison. Three of the men who now followed him came with Commander Colevant's recommendation.

The third attempt had been the most blatant; four ex-military men, provided with the guise and equipment of the Citadel Guard and made familiar with the layout and the daily routine of the Royal House. They had been sent to lure the Harbinger from his apartments and into a seldom used part of the sanctuary. There they were to kill him and his acolyte. All four had been slain; none left alive for questioning. It had been a bold and aggressive plan, indicative of a bold and aggressive planner. Was not Galin such a man?

Hendric now looked to the men who followed him: a young priest from the Temple of The One Spirit, three soldiers handpicked by Commander Colevant, three more sent by Commander Galin. Only the three sent by Captain Aileen, Jared and the brothers Ishmed and Favor, had no connection to anyone who had access to the Citadel at the time of the assassination attempts.

But this offered no guarantees.

Though he thought Jared a fine soldier, the brothers seemed to him only trackers who would recede into the background when it was time for battle. He would not trust the three of them to contain the Panther until the others caught up to them.

All these thoughts ran through Hendric's mind in the span of a few breaths and, making his decision, he ordered Maleek, Felton, and Tomar across the rope bridge to lie in wait for the harbinger and his party. Though not trusted, these three had shown themselves the most consumed by greed and, therefore, less likely to jeopardize their claim to a portion of the treasure by disobeying his orders. They were all rough and aggressive men, capable in combat if Colevant be believed, and able to hold the Panther at bay from a distance, with arrows, if necessary. For these reasons, Hendric judged these three the best available choices for the task at hand. Also, because Hendric did not trust the way that Galin had foisted his three men upon the pursuit squad.

Leaving their saddles and bedrolls on their horses, the three took their water bags, a little food, and their weapons across the bridge to prepare for the arrival of the Harbinger. Hendric directed that their horses, along with the two pack animals, be tied behind the others, and that all should dismount so they could lead their animals onto the path that descended into the ravine.

****

Ray and Hanshee watched in silence as the three soldiers crossed the bridge and entered the clearing on the western side of the ravine. The soldiers turned and watched as their comrades and horses disappeared down the path on the far side before surveying the clearing for the best places to set up and await their quarry.

Hendric had not told them the true nature of those that they pursued, hoping that the three expected to corner two escapees from the dungeons who were now riding with a child. Still, he had warned them that these particular escapees were dangerous, and the terrain was scouted carefully in preparation for an ambush.

From this distance Ray could hear only parts of their conversation, but found himself surprised at their high spirits. He thought he heard something akin to "the easiest gold I've ever earned" uttered by one of the three. There had been low talk as the soldiers stood together, stringing their bows and preparing their arrows. The talk became louder as they separated, moving off to different areas of concealment. During this louder conversation, Ray thought he heard one of the men questioning what the "two newcomers" knew, while another assured him that "no one had told them" and "the secret was still safe".

Hanshee and Ray then watched as one soldier took up a position behind the house-sized boulder west of the trails end, while another took a position behind one of the smaller boulders situated across the path and beside the ravine. The third soldier started down the trail, apparently to hide until their quarry had passed him and then reveal himself to cut off any escape back down into the ravine.

The soldier behind the large boulder attempted to settle into a comfortable position to wait, before rising and announcing to his comrade across the path that he first had to move his bowels in order to sit still. Amid much laughter he was told to take it deep into the brush so that the stench would neither alert their quarry nor kill the horses. The large soldier had to laugh at this himself, as he lay down his bow and made his way across the clearing. Several feet into the thick brush he found a suitable place and turned to face the clearing before removing his loincloth, lifting his tunic, and squatting heavily down to do his business.

From the moment he heard his plans, Ray had not taken his eyes from the soldier, watching carefully as he entered the brush, and hoping that the man did not stumble onto their hiding place. When the soldier finally squatted, Raymond turned to Hanshee and...

What the..., Ray was perplexed. *Where is Hanshee?*

Turning back toward the squatting soldier, Ray caught sight his friend.

Moving as silently as the big cat he was called after, Hanshee had approached the spot where the soldier squatted and now arose directly behind him. He stood motionless for just a moment, then the sound of hooves on stone rang out from somewhere down the path and everything exploded into motion!

Hanshee's left hand snaked around the soldier's head and covered his mouth a split second before the blade in his right hand was thrust into the soldier's right temple. Hanshee moved his hand around quickly as if stirring the brains inside the skull, before stepping back and lowering the dead soldier slowly to the damp ground between the bushes. Even as this was taking place, a loud whisper was directed towards them.

"Felton! They come! Prepare yourself!

Now the sounds of the horses could be clearly heard, and Ray looked out toward the clearing to see the soldier on the other side of the path notch an arrow and begin to draw his bow. As Ray continued to watch, he saw the soldier release in mid draw, before he had fully raised his bow, his arrow impotently striking the base of the boulder behind which he hid. This premature release was due to the arrow Hanshee had sent into his right ear, snapping his head to the left with such force as to break his neck. Ray watched as the dead soldier's hand released the bow and his body slid noiselessly to the ground, his head lying flat against his left shoulder.

Just as the soldier's body came to rest, Kellen and the horses burst into the clearing! Kellen sat astride his horse while holding the lead rope of the other three, oblivious to what had transpired mere moments before his arrival.

Hanshee burst from the brush and sprinted toward Kellen, then past him, leaving the child the picture of bewilderment as he turned in the saddle and watched Hanshee disappear down the trail from which he had just emerged.

Ray understood what was happening and he stepped from the brush and gestured for Kellen to lead the horses over to where he stood. Kellen obeyed, still casting occasional glances over his shoulder toward the path. Ray was anxious too, but he busied himself loading the bundles onto the pack mule, then arranged himself astride his horse to be ready should a quick escape be needed.

Almost on cue, Hanshee revealed himself, sprinting up the path and snatching his bow and quiver from where he dropped it. He reached his horse and mounted with surprising ease, then spurred his animal toward the road known to lead to Gunjunson, the capital of Cantor. This move caught both Kellen and Ray by surprise, but Kellen spurred his mount also, and Ray had no choice but to do likewise in order to keep up.

The three of them moved quickly down the road, not at a gallop, but at a fast trot, maintaining that pace over a fair distance until Kellen yelled for Hanshee to slow down for fear of injuring the horses. Hanshee did not understand the words of the youth, but he knew what was being asked, and so pulled steadily back on the reins until his horse slowed to a walk, then came to a stop. Once stopped Hanshee simply dismounted, took the reins in his hand and continued down the road, leading his horse at a brisk pace. This allowed his companions to pull up alongside him before dismounting and the three of them led their lathered and heaving mounts down the road for some time.

The brisk walk was good for the horses. Their chests were no longer heaving and the lather was slowly evaporating when Ray finally asked Hanshee what had happened on the path. Hanshee simply looked at Ray, offering no explanation. His face gave away nothing and he slowly turned his eyes again to the road as they pressed on.

About an hour passed before Kellen let them know they could again mount the horses. They had stopped to water them at the bend of a small stream that ran within a few feet of the road. This must have been a popular spot as there appeared to be the remains of many campsites surrounding it. The three chose not to stay and pressed on down the road. Although Hanshee had yet to volunteer any information, Ray and Kellen could sense that this was the time to put as many miles between themselves and the ravine as they could.

The trio kept moving until well after dark. That was when Hanshee led them off of the road and among a stand of barren ash, where they made camp for the night. While Kellen tended the horses, well-worn from their day's journey and excitement, Ray finally pressed Hanshee on the goings on back at the ravine.

"I questioned the third soldier," Hanshee said to Ray.

"But…how did you… you can't speak the language of Pith!" Ray said. "How did you get him to speak to you... and so quickly?"

"I first impressed upon him that I would kill him" said Hanshee. "Then I told him that to speak was to live."

"How did you do…" Ray began to ask, only to be cut short by his companion.

"Way-mon," Hanshee spoke sternly, "it is better that you not ask for knowledge that will later trouble you."

The pair remained silent for a few moments while Ray digested this.

"Well," Ray finally said, "what did you learn?"

"Only that they pursue us, Hanshee said. "Whether to capture or to kill, I know not. But my guess, from how the soldiers dispersed themselves, is that they meant to kill."

This news left Ray silent as he realized that even their leaving the Pithian lands provided no safety from the unknown forces intent on ending their lives.

"Did he say why they sought to kill us," Ray asked. "And how they found us so quickly?" The questions were popping into his head at a furious pace.

"I am not so fluent as you in the tongue of the Pith," said Hanshee. "Why anyone wants us dead remains a mystery."

"As to how they found us so quickly," he continued, "that is no mystery. A horse leaves a sign that is easy to follow."

Ray considered this last in silence. Having lived in the forest with Hanshee, he had picked up a fair amount of woodcraft. Moving stealthily through the woods was something that

Hanshee had mastered, of which he had taught Ray a good deal. Of course, Ray had nowhere near Hanshee's ability, but even he had noticed how slight a trail they had left after descending the cliffs. Now he saw the downside of taking to horseback in an attempt to gain more speed.

"Speed is the last resort of both the hunter and the hunted," he recalled one of Hanshee's many lessons. *"Stealth is the first."*

"Hanshee," Ray began, "I…"

"It is not your fault," said Hanshee, as if reading Ray's mind. "Your thinking was sound. We still enjoy an advantage. We are now a day ahead. They will bury their dead before again taking up the pursuit. They will come for us at sunrise. We must not squander our advantage. We must become better horsemen. We must ride for the capital of Cantor, and we must ride with haste."

****

The trail into the ravine had been far more treacherous than Hendric expected. Half the way down one of the pack horses had been pressed to traverse a part of the trail that was too narrow. If not for the pack, the animal could have hugged the wall with its body as the horses wearing only a saddle had done. The bulk of the heavy pack forced the animal to walk the very edge of the trail and, once it lost its footing, the end was unavoidable. Unfortunately, this horse was the middle horse of three that were tethered together, and it took its companions with it on the long fall to the bottom.

For Hendric, who had been second guessing himself for sending the three soldiers over the rope bridge while he led the rest through the ravine, this was the inevitable conclusion of another poor decision. Not being one to dwell on mistakes, but rather to learn from them, he recognized that the source of his questionable decision making lay in his distrust of those under his command.

Once on the floor of the ravine, Hendric sent Jared and Sergel up the shallow stream running along its bottom, to find the animals and put any still alive out of their misery. They were then to salvage what they could of the supplies and follow the party up the trail on the other side. Hendric continued to lead those remaining up the far side and hope that the three he had dispatched to trap the Harbinger had done their job of holding him until the rest of the party arrived.

It was close to dusk when the party found itself traversing the last stretch of trail before it opened into the clearing, but there was more than enough light for the travelers to see the soldier up ahead. He was bracing himself against a boulder and waving them forward with what appeared to be his only good arm. His other arm hung loosely beside his body.

Tomar had managed to drag himself further up the path toward where he thought his help would be. When there were no replies to his cries for help, he made the wise decision to not attract the wrong attention and instead wait for the help that would be arriving from below.

Ishmed was leading the procession up the trail and so was the first to spot Tomar. Upon seeing him, he called out to his captain that a wounded man appeared to be waiting up ahead. Hendric handed his reins off to Fevor and quickly made his way up the trail, approaching Tomar with little in the way of sympathy or concern for his damaged body.

"Where are the others," Hendric asked impatiently while looking the injured soldier up and down.

"I'm not sure, Captain," said Tomar between gritted teeth.

"Damn!" exclaimed the captain, before waving his men forward. As they approached, he began barking out orders.

"Ish, you and your brother hurry up there and take a look around. Blige, you go with them. Lucius, you and Petri see to this soldier's injuries."

Having put things in motion, Hendric now turned back to the wounded Tomar, who awaited the attentions of Lucius and the priest.

"What happened to you?" the captain asked curtly.

"The three of us took up positions..." Tomar began, "...that is, after we seen you and the others start off down the trail on the other side. We took up positions for to ambush those that was coming. I was to let them pass then block their retreat once the others had stopped 'em. I heard 'em coming so I Arrrgh!..."

"His leg is broken, Captain," said Lucius. "It'll take a splint."

"Go on," said Hendric impatiently.

"Well...," gasped Tomar, trying to get his breath from the rough handling imposed on him by Lucius, "... see... I heard them coming... gasp... so I hid myself until I heard the horses run by... ooooh... they was runnin', Captain, so I waited for the Aaaaagh!..."

"His right arm is broken too, Captain... and he's missing some fingers on his right hand."

"Dammit, man!" Hendric exploded. "Leave him be until I can get some sense out of him!"

"Right, Captain." Lucius released Tomar's right arm which fell heavily to his side and struck the rock he leaned against, causing another scream of pain.

"Aaaaoooo! Ooh, ooh, ooh..."

Hendric stepped in and struck Tomar with the back of his hand, the blow catching the wounded soldier completely off guard and focusing all of his attention on the anger blazing in his captain's eyes.

"Finish your report, soldier!" Hendric said through clinched teeth.

Eyes large with both fear and pain, Tomar again managed to find his voice.

"They passed by and I waited for the signal from up above so for to come up and take their rear but... but I never heard no signal… and so I started around the rock I was hiding behind and something hit me so hard in the face, it blinded me! The next thing I know my arm is twisted and I felt my leg give way… (ugh)… then I was face down in the dirt, and someone was over me holding my arm."

"Who was it," Hendric asked excitedly. "Who had you down?"

"I never saw a face, Captain," Tomar responded. "He just asked me who we trailed and when I said we wasn't trailing him… and then I seen my two fingers fall right in front of my face… and then I felt the pain!"

Tomar was breathing heavily now, reliving the terror even as he tried to tell the story. Hendric gave him some time and the frightened soldier eventually regained enough of his composure to continue.

"He asked me again, kind 'a funny…like he didn't really speak Pith…and let me know he'd kill me if I lied again."

"And what did you tell him?" Hendric asked.

"I told him we was following two escapees from Pith…to bring 'em back," Tomar said, still obviously in pain.

"And that is all you said?!" Hendric bellowed, placing his face so close to Tomar's that the injured soldier had to turn his to the side before he answered.

"That's all I know, Captain!" Tomar cried. "I didn't say nothin' 'bout the gold, and I don't know nothin' else! I don't know nothin' else…" Tomar's voice trailed off into sobs of pain and fear as the captain stood and watched.

"Get him on a horse and up to the clearing," Hendric said to Lucius and Petri. "You can set his bones and treat his hand after we've made camp."

Without another word Hendric took the dangling reins of his horse, leading him the remaining distance to the clearing at the top of the path. What he found at the top was hardly a surprise, and in the dim light of dusk he bellowed is final orders of the day.

"Touch nothing!" Hendric said. "Make our camp tonight at the far end of the clearing. I want a fresh look at everything here in the mornings light."

****

The light of the next morning told the story of the afternoon before.

Maleek, who the trackers had found the last evening, still lay where he had fallen. Hendric asked again if anything had been disturbed and was greeted with emphatic shakes of their heads.

Hendric then walked across the path and behind the large boulder where the brothers said they found a bow and quiver of arrows. As he stood over the weapons, which were propped against the rock, his mind began to work out just what had transpired here.

Hendric looked back toward the body of Maleek, the arrow still protruding from his right ear. Then he looked across the clearing, toward the brush on the western side. With some confidence he walked toward the thick evergreens and, after first kneeling to examine the ground, arose and plunged into their depths. Within moments he was calling to the trackers. They entered behind him and a short while later exited with each holding the large body of Felton under the armpits. They dragged him into the clearing, laying him to rest in the dust as the others gathered around for a look.

The first thing Hendric noticed was the wound at the dead man's right temple. It stood out, marked by the blood that surrounded it and had pooled where the back of his head had lain on the forest floor. While Hendric examined the wound, one of the others pointed out that Felton was naked under his tunic, his loins completely exposed. This instantly became the object of snickering among some who surrounded Felton's corpses.

Shaking his head in disgust at their juvenile behavior, Hendric continued his examination, searching for any other wounds or signs of struggle on the corpse. Finding none, he looked back toward the brush where Felton's body had lain, and again out to where Maleek had set up his ambush.

Rising from the corpse of Felton, Hendric walked back to where Maleek lay and pulled at the arrow protruding from his skull. It came out with little difficulty, and he gave it a thorough examination. Noting Maleek's bow on the ground beside his body, Hendric bent down and retrieved the arrow laying in the dirt beside the rock where the soldier had chosen to hide. Now he walked back to Felton's bow, still propped up against the large boulder, and pulled an arrow from his quiver. Both Felton and Maleek carried arrows of similar make, and neither resembled the arrow removed from the skull of Maleek.

As Hendric had been examining the three arrows, some of the men again approached and formed a semi-circle around their captain, each wondering what he searched for. After a while, Hendric informed them of his thoughts.

"They were here the whole time," the captain said.

"They were here?" Jared asked, having just walked up when Hendric spoke and wondering what he meant.

"They were here… in this clearing… hiding in that brush over there," Hendric motioned to where Felton's body had been removed.

"When we arrived yesterday after mid-day, at least one of them was already on this side, in the brush, probably waiting for someone to bring their horses through the ravine. They were watching us," Hendric said, laying out the fruits of his investigation for all to see.

The captains' words had an obvious effect on the men, sparking concerns among them about just who it was they pursued. Hendric ignored their buzzing, stepping away from them to better focus his thoughts on the mistakes he may have made when they first arrived. He had allowed his clouded judgment to lead to the deaths of two of his command and the injury of a third, partly because he had underestimated the Harbinger.

Hendric's memory conjured up the nervous savage that had hitched a ride from the southeastern Ursals on the back of his chariot. Never would he have thought that man, covered in borrowed robes to hide his near nakedness, could wreak such havoc among the trained killers of the Pithian military. Hendric recalled the trail of dead soldiers and military trained assassins that littered the path of the Harbinger. He then added the two *true* assassins who had dared to try him in his quarters in the dead of night, and could only shake his head in wonder.

His thoughts were interrupted when he saw Lucius brake away from the gathered soldiers and approached him.

"Captain," the shorter man began, "the ground over on the northern edge looks to be clear of rocks and roots. I can get the men started on burying Felton and Maleek before we take up the trail."

Hendric nodded his consent.

As a captain, Hendric knew the importance of honoring the men who died in the line of duty. As well as providing the living a sense of closure, it served to bond them tighter together and reinforced in their minds their value to the empire. The time lost in pursuit of their quarry would be traded for increased morale.

"Tomar can ride, Captain," Lucius continued, "but not at a pace. He will slow us down considerably. Maybe he could make the ride back to Stronghold on his own, but we can't allow that."

These words hung heavy in the air and Hendric, who had been looking toward the perspective burial ground, now swung his gaze back to Lucius. He met the sergeants' unflinching eyes and felt the unasked question they contained.

Tomar could indeed be sent back and, properly splinted and bandaged, could most likely cross the bridge north of here and make it to the Gates of Stronghold on his own. It was only a journey of three nights. At another time this would be the best option by far, and Hendric would not have hesitated to give the order. But this was not another time, and there was one huge complication; the gold.

If Tomar was sent back, Hendric had no doubt he would set out for the gold at his earliest opportunity. And why wouldn't he? The chance would be there for him to take sole possession of the treasure while his comrades, the only other men who knew of it and where it lay buried, continued in their pursuit of the Harbinger.

It would take him a while.

Though he could probably make it to stronghold, he was in no condition to ride all the way to the stable off the Southern road, and definitely could not dig up and haul away a heavy chest of gold. He would have to trust others to help him - and unlikely scenario - or take enough time to heal until he could do the task alone. Both choices were risky, but preferable to squandering a once in a lifetime chance at such wealth.

And how would Hendric expect those who remained with the pursuit to react if Tomar was ordered back alone? Their every moment would be consumed with thoughts of riches promised that were now slipping through their grasp. None would believe that Tomar would not leap at the chance presented him, and none would be able to live with it. There would be desertion...or rebellion... and soon the all-important mission would be forgotten.

The scope of this dilemma was not lost on Hendric, and the obvious solution stared him in the face.

Lucius stared him in the face; a blunt but expectant stare that both begged the question and offered a solution, without a word being said.

Hendric had but to nod his head.

My god, thought the captain, at the realization of what he was considering. *Is this what we have fallen to… what I have become?*

"No," Hendric said aloud, answering the question in the gaze of his sergeant, as well as in his own heart. "No, we can't. Tomar will continue to ride with the pursuit. Make him as comfortable on horseback as you can."

Lucius bowed his head slightly, wordlessly acknowledging his captain's decision before moving off toward the men to organize the burial.

Captain Hendric stared after the receding back of his sergeant, wondering what kind of man he was, and pondering the many pitfalls of loyalty and duty.

CHAPTER 23

Reliving the details of the failed assault, the death of her brothers, and the trials of returning the injured Damien back to the village, was both physically and emotionally draining for Nola, but it was also a purge of sorts. Though she had not yet been given time to rest from her ordeal, the telling of it provided a catharsis, lifting a weight from her shoulders and relieving a portion of the stress that she carried.

To say that Nola had been surprised that there were no reprisals after the failure of her brothers to complete a slaying requested by the Lord High Priest himself, would be a vast understatement.

She had described, in the greatest detail, the events of that evening. She had answered all the questions that her descriptions had brought to her father's mind. And then she had waited for the eruption that never came. As she looked on wide eyed, Seenio absolved her from any wrongdoing, saying that she was only following his orders and that it was her brothers who proved themselves unworthy of such a trust. In Seenio's words, her brothers had found their respective punishments and she had performed well in securing an escape for herself and Darien. What blame remained now fell upon he who had been so shortsighted as to place this trust upon them.

After her father released her, the young woman sat with her mother for a time.

The situation being what it was, Nola had not mourned the loss of her siblings. She was too involved in survival and securing the life of the brother that remained. Now, as she and her mother sat, quietly holding hands and rocking back and forth, Nola allowed herself to release the pain... the guilt... the shame... that she carried for having not been there to aide her dead brothers in their time of need.

As Leisha began an ancient chant of mourning for the spirits of her sons, Nola allowed the pent-up tears to roll unchecked down her face.

****

Nola did not leave her parents quarters until late in the afternoon. It was then that she finally found time for the hot bath that she so desperately desired. A soak in the steaming water did much to relieve the tension she felt, while also spurring her realization of how truly tired she was. A bowl of stew and fresh bread followed her bath, the first hot meal she had enjoyed in over ten days. After her meal, with the full weight of her exhaustion now resting upon her, Nola found her bed.

If she had not been aware of how tired she was, her sleep revealed all. She slept all of that evening and into the night. The sunrise found Nola still asleep, and she did not leave her bed until just past the noon hour. The long hours of sleep in her soft bed had granted her a much needed rest, but also allowed her muscles, overused on her journey, to stiffen and become sore. She didn't mind. Sore muscles usually meant hard work, which meant something had been accomplished. She smiled as she sat up in her bed and stretched, happy to be back in the village and in the lodge and in her chamber. Nola's happiness was interrupted by the low rumble of her stomach once again demanding attention.

She was famished!

Looking from her window Nola guessed that the noonday meal might still be available and she quickly donned a robe and moved down the hall toward her mother's pots. As always, she was well received.

It was immediately after her meal that she was told of her father's summons. She was to prepare to accompany him into Stronghold. He did not know when they might return.

And so it was that, the day after returning from a long and arduous journey, Nola found herself again sharpening her weapons, checking her tools, preparing her bedroll, and donning the clothes that would keep her comfortable in the open weather.

Though not yet set, the sun had dipped below the high peaks to the west, casting the lodge into shadow as it did every day about this hour. It was at this time that Seenio summoned her to the rear of the lodge, where they set out to ascend the wall of rock that towered above it. Nola had done this before. She had scaled these cliffs, made easier by a series of chiseled handholds, and tread the mountain paths beyond them, on her first journey to meet with the Lord High Priest.

Now, in the gloom of a mountain sunset, she and Seenio retraced the steps that had last been taken with her brother Mem beside her. Four hours later they stood on the broad cliff above the temple retreat. Behind them the torches signaling their desire for an audience burned. Below them they took in the sight of the flickering blue flame visible on the roof of the retreat. Their audience had been granted.

Nola had known that Seenio would meet with the Lord High Priest Mayhew. Failure of the magnitude that had occurred could not be brushed off lightly. Seenio, being who he was, would need to look the priest in the eye as he confessed to his failure, even as he swore an oath to personally hunt down the warrior-priest and end him, if his death still be the wish of the Temple. Unspoken would be the pain of a father who had unknowingly sent his sons to their deaths and now felt the powerful need to atone by exacting revenge on he who was responsible for their killing and maiming.

Seenio would go after this warrior-priest in any event, Nola thought. What he sought now was the blessing of the High Priest of the Temple, behind which he could hide his own guilty obsession.

****

The three sat in the private chambers of Lord High Priest Mayhew, in the Temple retreat at the foot of Strongholds Crown, the name given the mountain range that dominated the northern border of the lush valley. Nola sat quietly while the Beast and the High Priest spoke softly, leaning forward in their chairs to provide for even greater privacy than that which the chamber already afforded.

Nola watched as Seenio and High Priest Mayhew discussed the events of the past eight days and how best to deal with the aftermath.

"I respect your desire to atone for the failure of your people by completing my order," Mayhew said, "but that may be next to impossible. I have it on the best of authorities that the heathen priest has fled west into the lands of our enemy, Cantor."

"Has his flight absolved the Temple of the need for his death?" Ask Seenio.

Mayhew regarded his roughhewn servant and co-conspirator with respect. The rugged outer shell concealed a sharp intellect whose questions were shrewdly worded and designed to cut to the heart of an issue.

"The answer to that question is yet unknown," Mayhew replied. "Certain plans put forth by The Crown may require the physical presence of this man. It would be difficult to move in the direction King Ammon has indicated if the reasoning behind such a move could be neither explained nor provided."

Seenio remained quiet but his gray eyes latched onto those of the High Priest and would not let go, compelling Mayhew to continue talking…to give him more.

"Even now," Mayhew continued, "an elite squad of hunters are in pursuit of the wandering priest and his acolyte." As he finished speaking Mayhew mentally kicked himself for having said too much.

"These hunters," Seenio asked, "they serve the Throne, do they not?"

"They do," replied Mayhew.

"And should they find the warrior-priest, they will return him to Stronghold, and to the Citadel, where the Throne can continue to use him to their ends?"

Mayhew did not need to answer this question. Seenio's point was well made.

The fact that Mayhew suspected assassins were planted within the ranks of the hunters was worth noting, but provided no guarantees that those who sought the priest's return would not prevail. And if the priest were returned to the Citadel, Mayhew's position would be as it was before, with even less of a chance of timely intervention prior to the plans of Ammon IV coming to fruition.

"I had hoped that the Guild would serve me efficiently," Mayhew said, in an attempt to reassert his dominance before acquiescing, "as it has served High Priests in the past."

Seenio allowed his eyes to drop in submission as he replied.

"The shame of our failure weighs heavy upon me, M'lord. If it be your pleasure, I will personally complete the task you have set for the Guild."

"Are you prepared this time?" Mayhew asked. "How will you know your target?"

"Nola," Seenio motioned to his daughter, "did lay eyes upon this warrior-priest. She will accompany me and mark him for me. With your blessing we will leave at sunrise."

"You have a long distance to travel to Cantor," Mayhew stated, "and if not yet captured, he may soon move on from there."

The room remained quiet while Mayhew again weighed all that had passed between the Masscus Patriarch and himself. There was no guarantee that the Harbinger would not be returned, and as long as he lived, so lived the fire in Ammon to follow the path of prophesy. Mayhew could not allow this, for down that path lay the anointing of one unworthy... unworthy to *his* position in the High Seat... and himself cast aside like so much refuse.

"Before dawn," the High Priest said, "you will find horses and supplies in the forest southwest of this estate."

CHAPTER 24

Ray, Hanshee, and Kellen were up early the next morning and the rising sun found them already moving west at a brisk pace. Ray had noticed the occasional appearance of lesser roads that merged into the Cantor Road from both the north and south. These roads appeared well worn, the fresh wagon ruts and hoof prints indicating they were recently traveled.

As the morning wore on, the trio came into contact with the occasional fellow traveler moving in both directions on the Cantor Road. Their numbers were few and not enough to confuse the trail left by their own horses, as both Ray and Hanshee had hoped.

As they moved farther down the road, Ray continuously pondered their predicament. He considered himself responsible for the ease with which the pursuit had caught up to them. He had pushed for abandoning the original plan in order to proceed on horseback. At the time the advantages seemed overwhelmingly obvious, but he had failed to consider what they were trading in a quest for less hardship and more speed. Having now given it considerable thought, he turned to the boy, Kellen, who rode beside him.

"Kellen," Ray began, "when Chezza came to Cantor, where did he get horses from?"

Kellen seemed happy whenever the grownups asked him questions. It made him feel important, so he did his best to give them his very best answers and to help them in any way he could.

"Chezza told people he was going to the Great Stable at Gunjunson. That is where the most horses are traded before the first snow and after the last," the boy replied.

It took a moment before Raymond fully understood the boy's response as something he should follow up on.

"Did he always go to Gunjunson?" Ray asked, prepared to draw out any information that the child might have, if need be.

"Sometimes," Kellen said, "but Chezza didn't like to go there. He said the horses were not good and were sold at too high a price. He said the stable masters always kept the best horses for themselves, so Chezza would go to the stables to trade. But they wouldn't always trade with him there. But sometimes they would."

Now Ray was truly interested and he hoped to get the answer he was seeking from his next question.

"So Chezza would trade at the stables before he got to Gunjunson," Raymond mused aloud. "Are any of these stables nearby?"

"Yes," said Kellen, and offered no more.

"Where are they?" asked Ray, trying to hide his impatience. "Could you take us there?"

"I can take you to one," said Kellen. "It's not too far."

Ray was really excited now but he tempered his excitement with the realization that children saw the world much differently than adults. Distance, direction, and landmarks could all prove confusing to Kellen, and Ray thought it best to remain hopeful while not really expecting the child to deliver on his promise. Still, he felt it prudent to advise Hanshee of his thoughts and his conversation with Kellen.

After Ray explained, Hanshee nodded his agreement. Now they rode on, both cautiously optimistic that Kellen could actually do what he said.

Their optimism was rewarded when, after another two hours, Kellen tugged on Ray's cloak, and pointed toward a road up ahead that lead off to the north.

"There's a stable down here," the boy said, as he guided his horse toward the narrow dirt road that was deeply scarred with wheel ruts and hoof prints.

Ray and Hanshee exchanged glances before prodding their horses to follow after the boy.

****

It seemed the sun had barely moved in the sky when the trio again emerged onto the Cantor Road riding three horses and leading a mule, each different from the animals they had possessed only a short time before. As Ray pondered what had occurred, the transaction had been surprisingly easy considering what they had asked.

The three had ridden up to the main house of the stable and been greeted by the stable master. Ray thought it must be written somewhere that stable masters had to be curmudgeonly old farts in order to even be considered for the job. In his time in this land, he had only met two, but the type appeared consistent. The difference with this one was that he seemed to love children and remembered Kellen from his previous trips here with Chezza.

The stable master, his name was Kale, smiled at Kellen, jostling the child's hair and sending him to the house to beg a piece of bread and honey from his wife. Then he turned hard eyes to Ray and Hanshee and asked their business.

Here is where it could have gotten tricky.

To say that they wanted to exchange the horses they now rode for different mounts, and offer no reason, was to invite suspicion. Luckily, before Ray could reply, Old Kale commented that he recognized two of the horses they rode. It seems he had sold them to Chezza; a deal he had later come to regret.

Apparently, Chezza was many things and many of them were bad, but he was an exceptional horse trader.

When Ray heard this, he knew there was very little leeway for lies. Thinking quickly, he fell back on the story of Hanshee being a wandering priest and himself Hanshee's faithful acolyte and interpreter. They had purchased these horses from Chezza, a claim Ray could see Kale look askance at the moment it was heard. The old man had immediately asked why a seasoned horse thief like Chezza would sell two of his finest mares to these two. It was a question that had Ray speechless for just a moment, but some instinct had prompted him to weave an explanation around Kellen.

He told Kale that the boy was very homesick; missing his family and home so much that he was of no use to Chezza. His master, Hanshee, had offered to escort the boy back to Cantor, their next destination, and deliver him to his parents. Kind hearted Chezza, grateful for his good fortune, offered to sell them his finest horses for the journey.

This lie brought a look of stern disbelief to the stable master's face, but just as he opened his mouth, probably to call Ray a liar, Kellen came bounding out of the house with bread and honey, and a huge smile. For some reason, the sight of the happy child had wiped the question right out of Kale's head. When he turned back to Ray, he only asked why they wanted to trade such fine horses away.

Ray had thought his explanation brilliant.

He told Old Kale that his master, Hanshee, was of a religious sect that practiced austerity, if not outright poverty, and thus was embarrassed as many of the travelers they passed had commented on the fine horses that they rode. He wondered if they could trade these for mounts still reliable, but not so fine as to draw attention.

At the time, Ray thought this story sounded implausible too, but the distraction of Kellen, and the thought of reclaiming two such fine mares, drove any disbelief straight out of the stable master's head. In no time at all he had instructed one of his men to bring out three new horses, much older than the prime breeding aged mares that they rode in on, and a new mule to boot. He even had his man change the saddles and equipment while he offered the two of them warm spiced wine. As they talked over the wine, Raymond learned that Kale not only liked children but also revered holy men. Add the fact that he was getting his two prime mares back and this seemed to be a good deal for all.

****

Raymond was still wondering how it had all happened so smoothly, even as he guided his new mount onto the road to Gunjunson. For whatever reason, his plan had worked and they now sat astride horses that left a mark unknown to their pursuers. Add to this the additional traffic that the road carried as they moved closer to the city, and he and Hanshee were sure that any attempt to track them as had been done in the past was doomed to failure.

Ray now felt he had redeemed himself for his earlier mistake.

****

Hendric's decision to allow Tomar to continue on with the pursuit party meant that any hope of quickly running their quarry to ground was gone.

All knew this, though none openly questioned it.

In order to compensate for slowing the party down, Hendric adopted a new strategy.

He instructed the two brothers, Ishmed and Fevor, to push on ahead, following any sign as fast as they could. If they were to stumble upon the escapee's or notice a change of direction, one was to stay with their find while the other was to hurry back to the main party and alert them. It seemed a good plan to most and prevented Hendric from imposing a death sentence on the injured Tomar.

On the second day after this strategic change, Hendric was surprised to reach the crest of a rise and spy two riders coming toward them. It appeared to be Ishmed and Fevor. Raising a clenched fist to bring the party to a halt, he waited as Ish brought his horse up alongside Hendric's own.

"Captain," the young tracker began, "we found where their marks leave the road and trail off to the north. We moved down the road toward Cantor for a ways to make sure and found no marks made by their horses. The road further on is heavily used but we know their mark and would've found it had it been made."

"Did you search to the north?" Hendric asked. "What did you find there?"

"Only a stable, Captain," Ish said. "The sign that we follow led right to it. We didn't follow them in as we thought it best to await your orders."

"You acted properly," said Hendric, as he mulled over what this could mean. He first considered that the Harbinger could even now be at the stable, but that explanation seemed much too simple. His mind naturally drifted toward the more devious, and his thought was echoed in the words spoken by Jared.

"I'd wager they've traded their horses," said the guardsman from Stronghold's south gate, "and there'll be no easy trail to follow from there."

Just two days prior, the pursuit had them trapped and the men anticipated a speedy completion of the mission, followed by the promise of riches for all. If what Jared speculated was true, and Hendric had a feeling that it was, there was no telling how long it would be before they would again find their quarry.

All eyes now turned to Hendric for a solution to their most current dilemma.

"Ishmed, do you think you and Fevor can pick out their trail as they left from the stable?" Hendric asked.

Ishmed shook his head.

"Too many sets of tracks around there, Captain, and we don't know their mark. Likely a dozen horses and mules have come and gone from that stable since they were there. There's no telling which mark would belong to them."

"We could have a word with the stable master," Sergel volunteered, smiling as he looked around for affirmation. "He could most likely be persuaded to help us find the right mark."

Hendric bristled at the threat implied in Sergel's words, but held his response to a hard stare directed at the man. This wiped the smile from the lips of Sergel and let the others know that he was in no mood for foolishness. As he was turning back to Ishmed, Lucius spoke up.

"Captain, if I may… We two are the only ones among us that know what these escapees look like," Lucius said pointedly. "They have been steady on the Cantor Road since they went to horseback, and it looks to be they are headed straight to Gunjunson."

Hendric received the point that Lucius obviously intended to make; that they two were the only ones here who knew the true identity of their quarry and why they were so highly valued. Hendric took this as a way for Lucius to emphasize that they were in this together. However, the rest of his statement was a mystery.

"They have yet to change direction," Hendric said to Lucius in agreement, "though they could at any time. Do you think this important?"

"It does give us one chance, Captain, assuming they are going to Gunjunson as that is where the road leads. I could ride ahead, maybe take Fevor with me, and get to the gates not long after they do. If we push our mounts through the night, we may even reach the gates before them. Either way, I'll keep a look out. If I should spy them, I'll stay with them and send Fevor back to lead you to us."

"And if they have already entered the gates? Hendric asked.

"I speak the Cantorese tongue," said Lucius. "If they are not to be found outside the gates, I will enter the city, after first sending Fevor back to alert you, of course."

Hendric fell silent as he considered the proposal. There was no doubt that Lucius was a resourceful and intuitive soldier; one who had shown himself willing to do what was needed given the situation. Though only briefly under Hendric's command, the sergeant had already impressed his worth upon his captain. On its face, his plan had little chance for success. Still, it was the best option currently available to them.

But could he trust Lucius?

Knowing the true nature of their quarry and this mission, Lucius would be perfectly placed if he were in league with the assassins. But this would mark him as the obvious suspect and there had been nothing obvious about any of the attempts thus far.

In Hendric's mind, issues of trust had already led to questionable decisions and unnecessary deaths. If Lucius were not to be trusted to ride ahead, Hendric himself would be the only other who could identify their quarry. But if he left his men to follow at their own pace, would there not be the temptation to forget about him and to turn back and retrieve the gold?

The more he considered it, the more he saw that this plan of Lucius' was not only the best plan available, it appeared to be the only plan available.

"Take the fresh horses," Hendric said to Lucius, referring to the two spare mounts they had brought along for when they captured the Harbinger and his acolyte. "Push them as you must, but get to the gates of Gunjunson ahead of the escapees. I do not relish a pursuit inside the capital of Cantor."

"As you order, Captain," Lucius smiled his reply as he dismounted. Fevor came forward with the two spare horses, and he and Lucius began transferring their gear from their old horses to those with fresh legs. It was not long after that the squad watched Lucius and Fevor as they disappeared around the next bend of the road, their horses moving at a steady trot that they hoped to hold for many leagues to come.

Hendric looked back to those still under his immediate command. Five of the six still appeared to be fit and in relatively good spirits, considering what they had been through the last few days. The sixth, Tomar, still managed to sit his horse despite the injuries that he carried.

With a wave of his hand, Hendric started the band forward.

CHAPTER 25

It was their third day on horseback and the late morning sun already promised warmth they were unaccustomed to in their mountain village this time of year.

Seenio led, his horse gingerly picked its way down a loose embankment and across a wash. On terrain such as this the Patriarch of the Masscus Clan simply kept his horses head pointed in the right direction, trusting the animal to navigate the difficulties of the landscape to the benefit of them both. Nola rode behind her father, her mount astutely following the footsteps of the lead horse, and giving her time to contemplate the many thoughts, words, and deeds that led the two of them to this moment.

They were traveling in a west-southwest direction, their destination a village known as Sandledge. Seenio said they should reach it well before nightfall and, once there, they would be little more than a day's ride from the Gates of Stronghold. Her father had also promised a surprise today, but had kept tightlipped about its nature.

Nola knew her father well. This promise of a surprise was out of character for the hard-as-stone Seenio Masscus she had known as she transitioned from a gangly young girl to the woman who now rode beside him. When she was a child and her father's favorite, many were the days she had spent on his knee, thoroughly entertained by his stories of adventure, his many jokes and riddles, and the occasional surprise.

That Seenio, the father of her youth, had disappeared years ago.

Nola could not pinpoint the time of his transformation. Maybe it was with the birth of the twins, bringing to four the number of children he claimed. Maybe it was the death of his father, her grandfather, Athel Masscus. Nola remembered him as a cold and distant man who often sneered at the affection Seenio openly bestowed upon his first-born daughter. Athel had perished in a fall from a high ledge, a fate not as common to mountain folk as one might believe. Seenio had barely been a man at the time, having seen only twenty-two winters, but he had been required almost immediately to fill the void left by the Patriarch of the Clan and the leader of the Guild.

Seenio had several older brothers and it made sense to assume that one of her uncle's would have assumed the leadership position. That was not the case. Because her father was a prodigy; displaying cunning, and skill well beyond his years, having a knack for languages, having developed an expertise with a variety of weapons, and possessing the physical superiority and natural ferocity that led to his nickname... nay, his title... of 'the Beast' when he was still well short of manhood, it was acknowledged by nearly all that he would one day lead the family. Although his elevation occurred much sooner than any anticipated, still his older brothers stepped aside so that their younger sibling could take hold of the mantle of leadership.

His brothers were a constant aid to him in the early years. Their greater experience and wisdom bolstered their younger sibling even as he learned by doing. Mistakes were made, but it was said that Seenio Masscus was a quick study, and the same mistake was not made twice. It was not long before the young patriarch could stand alone as head of the family, and leader of a guild known to most only in the whispers of myth and legend.

It was during these years, when the weight of so much increased responsibility had come crashing down onto his broad shoulders, that the Seenio Nola knew vanished. The childlike exuberance was gone, replaced with a hard coldness without which he probably could not have kept the reins of control at such a young age.

But now Nola thought she saw glimpses of the young Seenio in the man who rode before her.

They had left the wash behind and now crossed a small valley of tall grass. Their pace was unhurried and, for some reason, Nola felt the time was right to engage her father.

"I watched as you conferred with the Lord High Priest," she began. "He is a great and wise man, worthy of our respect and fealty."

Seenio cocked an ear toward his daughter, waiting for the 'other boot to drop' as he continued to ride.

"You also are a man worthy of respect and fealty," she continued. "I looked upon two great and worthy men."

"How great and worthy would I be," Seenio asked rhetorically, "if I continued to tolerate the insinuations of my first born and only daughter?"

Nola decided to press her luck.

"Father, it is only that I cannot see…"

"Have a care with your next words, daughter," Seenio interrupted her, the threat hanging heavy in the air.

Nola paused and took a breath, already regretting that she had embarked down this path, but now feeling the need to at least have her say.

"Father," she began again more slowly, "it is just that I know you not only as a man of action, but also as one of wisdom. You are the wisest man I know! I cannot help but wonder why you must bend a knee to *any* man…"

Nola wisely stopped before launching into the *"much less the…"* portion of her comment, guaranteed to insult the High

Priest and most likely earn her another backhand blow from her father.

"You wonder as a child...," Seenio replied, "... why her father, the greatest man she has yet to know, should bow before another."

Nola recognized both the insult and the truth in her father's words. Seenio was her hero and, though it be thought childish, she hated to see him show deference to any other man.

"Do you not know our history?" Seenio asked. "Do you not know our oaths... the very oaths you swore when you became a Reaper of the Guild?"

Now Seenio pulled his horse up and turned to face his daughter.

"Only by our relationship with the Lord High Priest, anchored by our pledge of fealty, does our family continue to exist," he said.

Nola knew these words from the lessons of her youth. By 'Lord High Priest', she knew her father spoke not of the man to whom he had spoken two nights ago, but of the title.

'T'was the Lord High Priest who came to aid our people in years long past...

The Lord High Priest who learned our ways and taught us then his own...

The Lord High Priest who granted us the land we name as ours...

The Lord High Priest who nurtured us 'til we could stand alone.'

These words were part of the pledge taken by every member of the Assassins Guild. They were part of the oath of fealty sworn by all to the Lord High Priest. It mattered not what man occupied the position at any time, for the title of 'Lord High Priest' was larger than any man who held it.

"If you would be so fortunate as to lead the clan, and the guild," Seenio said, "it would be your duty to respect and adhere to the standards that have kept us strong and free for the better part of eight-hundred years."

Seenio's words struck Nola like a blow to the chest, causing a catch in her breath. Instantly, thoughts swirled in her head.

Never had it been spoken that a woman could possibly lead the clan... that a woman could possibly lead the Guild! Seenio would never have said as much were we not well beyond the range of other ears to hear. But, what if...

Seenio watched with satisfaction his daughter's reaction to his words, as reflected in her changing expressions.

"A powerful word, 'if'..." he said as he again turned his horse west-southwest.

****

Another hour's ride and they came upon Seenio's 'surprise'.

As they crested a hill, Seenio beckoned his daughter to look to the south. There Nola saw smoke rising from the center of a small forest. As she continued to look, she noticed that the smoke quickly dissipated after rising a little higher than the tallest branches.

"Is that smoke... or... steam?" Nola asked haltingly.

"Steam," said Seenio with a smile, "from a hot spring. It provides a wonderful bath."

With that Seenio led the way down the slope toward the thick vegetation that surrounded the spring.

As they got closer Nola could see signs that animals regularly used the spring and the surrounding forest. Numerous game trails, made by deer, elk, or antelope, could be seen in the grasses leading to the forest's edge. Seenio followed one of these toward an opening in the foliage that resembled the dark entrance to a cave set in a cliff of solid green. Once they brushed past the leaves and low hanging branches, they found a surprising amount of space between the many trees. With no need to dismount, they continued on horseback until they had reached the interior and the pool from which the steam arose.

Tying their horses among the shade of the greenery, the two dismounted and emerged from the trees into a clearing covered in sand and gravel.

Seenio showed no hesitation, walking over to a tree close to the water and sinking his knife deep into the trunk. He then removed his harness on which was sheathed his sword and a variety of other blades, and hung this on the exposed hilt of the knife. What followed were his tunic and shirt, his breaches, his boots, and finally his undergarments. In no time at all he stood completely naked before his daughter.

"Father!" Nola exclaimed at the sight of her father's nakedness.

"See to yourself," Seenio said, disregarding his daughter's astonishment as he strode purposefully toward the beckoning water.

Nola continued to watch as he waded out into the steaming pool. When the water reached his hips, Seenio lowered himself into its depths until the water was just below his chin. There he stayed, looking expectantly at Nola as he enjoyed the warmth.

Nola, at first too stunned to move, finally mimicked her father, sinking a knife into a tree and hanging her harness upon it. That is where she drew the line. Tuning back to the head of Seenio that seemed to be floating atop the water, she had her say.

"Father, I will not bathe naked in the same pool as you, nor will I undress while you sit there and watch!"

Seenio face twisted in a frown and his eyes became slits as he regarded his daughter, obviously pondering what frivolity could be going through her mind. Were the two of them not Reapers, of the Guild? And is a Reaper flustered at the prospect of nakedness before brethren?

"So now," Seenio said, "after a lifetime of pursuing entry into the Guild above all else, the *Reaper* wants to be seen as a woman? HA!"

Nola's complexion went from golden to red as she pursed her lips and stared daggers at the smiling face of her father. But before she could speak, he continued.

"Calm yourself, child," Seenio teased. "I will wade further up, to the other side of that bush," he said, pointing to a large evergreen shrub that had grown out over the spring from a point that rose above the pool. "Will that be sufficient?"

Nola examined the bush that he had pointed out and, satisfied that he could not see her from behind it, vigorously nodded her head. Still, she did not move until Seenio had waded up stream and was completely hidden from sight behind it.

Feeling more secure, Nola now removed her clothes and carefully hung everything from the hilt of her knife as her father had done. The late winter/early spring air still carried some chill and her body reacted in her nakedness. Crossing her arms over her breasts, Nola turned toward the steaming waters of the hot spring.

"Are we not well and truly blessed!"

The words came from behind her and Nola spun around to see a man emerge from the brush surrounding the clearing. He was quickly followed by another, and yet another. When all was counted, four men stood gawking at the naked woman.

To her shame, Nola's reaction was not that of a Reaper.

Instinctively she reached for her tunic and pulled the garment to her breast before shouting, "Who are you? What are you doing here?!"

"Who we are is not important" said the glib man who had first spoken. "What is important is that *here we are...*" he smiled a wicked smile. "...at your pleasure."

Nola stood frozen in place. Still clutching her tunic to hide what she could of her nakedness, she surveyed the men who stood so brazenly before her.

They were young men, her age or a little older, and all appearing tall, stout and strong. Their leader was the shortest, about the same height as was Nola. Their hair was long and unkempt, as were their scraggly beards. Their clothing was both wrinkled and dirty, as if they had been sleeping outside for some time. If she had guessed they were bandits, she would have been correct.

These four had just recently turned to banditry and had been fairly successful. All who they approached had offered up their goods and coin, some with but a minimum of bloodshed. This had swelled their young egos to such an extent that they now fancied themselves as dashing and invincible highwaymen; *Lords of the forest paths*. They had taken to this particular wilderness for seclusion. It was well known that the northwest portion of Stronghold is its least populated.

Now they had stumbled upon this naked beauty standing before the hot springs! This, in their eyes, was justification for their very high opinion of themselves and their belief in their continued good fortune.

Suddenly all eyes turned from the woman, to the man who was just now wading from behind a bush. He was naked also but he made no move to cover himself, instead striding boldly through the water toward the bank and the clearing where they stood.

Nola noticed as the four turned their eyes away from her, and turned her head in time to see Seenio emerge from the spring, water dripping from his well-muscled form and death smoldering in his eyes.

"Step away from the girl and be about your business," Seenio said in a voice calculated to leave no doubt as to his meaning. "I'll not tell you twice."

"You've no need to tell us twice," the leader boldly stated. "Had you taken a friendlier tone, we might even now be on our way. Now, I think we will have our way with your woman… after we deal with you!"

As he spoke the leader reached into his tunic and slowly withdrew a blade, a move quickly mimicked by his three cohorts. Then, almost single file, they advanced on Seenio.

Seenio never broke stride and, if the bandits would have looked more carefully, they would have seen the corners of his lips turn up in the slightest of smiles.

The leader rushed forward slashing a horizontal arc toward Seenio's torso, but Seenio took a quick hop backward and bowed his body to avoid the blade. Pressing forward, the bandit slashed backhand with the same result as Seenio repeated his evasive move. Now the leader had Seenio's move pegged, and he took a giant step forward behind another forehand slash. But this time Seenio did not step backward. Instead, he crouched down as he stepped into the attack. He met the arm that brandished the blade, blocking it with his left forearm, then sliding his hand down to catch the bandit's right wrist. Now Seenio shuffled forward, swinging his right forearm into the exposed midsection of the surprised bandit, striking with such speed and power as to knock the air from his lungs, leaving him bug eyed and gasping for breath. Before the bandit could regain his breath, Seenio struck again. This time he targeted the solar plexus with the point of his right elbow, driving it with all of his strength into that nerve cluster and paralyzing a foe still fighting to catch a breath. The knife dropped from the bandits' grip as Seenio struck a third blow, again a forearm to the torso but this time thrusting forward with his legs so to put every ounce of power he possessed behind the strike. He was rewarded when he felt both ribs and cartilage give way as the bandit's body folded itself over the extended forearm.

Now Seenio stood to his full height, lifting the bandit, who was still folded on his right forearm, overhead. With a shrug of his right shoulder, he cast the limp body into the dirt behind him. But even as he did, he took another step forward, toward a second bandit who had rushed up behind the first.

Just as the body of the first bandit cleared his face, Seenio stepped out with his left foot and quickly struck with his left hand. His fingers were wide, exposing the calloused knuckle at the base of his index finger. This was what Seenio drove into the larynx of the second bandit, even before the first had hit the ground. After collapsing the bandits throat as far as he could with his blow, Seenio's fingers snapped shut around his neck like a spring-loaded trap. The second bandit, stunned by the initial blow and choked by the iron grip applied to his neck, dropped his blade in panic, and began flailing and digging at the inhumanly strong hand that held him captive.

The third bandit had come up behind the second and was now seeking a way around his stricken comrade so he could sink his knife into Seenio. But Seenio had total control of the body attached to the throat that he clutched, and moved it as if it were a puppet, keeping it between himself and the third bandit's blade. The bandit moved right, then left, then right again, but Seenio mirrored his movements with the second bandit's still struggling body.

Now frustration was plain in the eyes of the third bandit as he moved once again to his left, fully expecting Seenio to place his comrade in his way. Instead, Seenio stepped forward to meet him, catching him by surprise as he threw a vicious upward blow with the heel of his right palm. Seenio aimed at, and struck, right where the nose and upper lip almost meet. The upward momentum of the strike broke the nose and stunned the bandit. Head driven back, his body went stiff and he stood frozen in place, unable to react while Seenio sent another palm heel, more vicious than the first, to the same target.

The bandit's legs buckled and he dropped to his knees in the dirt, his upper body still stiff, his arms hanging limply at his sides, and blood pouring from the center of his face. His head was tilted backward so that the whites of his eyes, the only part visible, stared through the empty branches overhead and into the clear blue sky. Then the bandit slowly toppled backward into the sand, unconscious, his legs now bent at an awkward angle.

Seenio looked up from the mangled face of the third bandit to find the fourth.

He too had been looking down at his fallen comrade as the blood flowed rhythmically from the place on his face where a nose should have been. As Seenio continued to watch, the bandit shifted his eyes to the leader, still lying behind him. He was thrashing about in the dirt, blood seeping from his open mouth as he struggled to take a breath.

And then, the fourth bandit moved his gaze to Seenio, or more specifically to Seenio's left arm. Seenio watched in fascination as the bandits' eyes traveled the length of his arm and seemed to stop at his hand. Puzzled, Seenio followed the bandits gaze with his own eyes and was surprised to find his left hand still locked around the neck of the second bandit, who had collapsed to his knees, his body bent backwards, held up solely by the grip of Seenio's left hand. Seenio's fingers had punctured the skin of the neck and burrowed deep into the muscle and tissue. As he watched he saw blood gushing up in time to the heartbeat, filling the depressions caused by his fingers. After pooling around his hand, it flowed to the back of the neck and dripped to the ground, where it formed a growing red puddle in the sand.

As the fourth bandit continued to look on, Seenio flicked his wrist, tossing the body to the side. Once this was done, the bandit left standing had no choice but to raise his eyes to meet those of this man standing naked before him; this Beast.

The moment their eyes met, Seenio saw that there was no fight left in him.

Too bad.

Seenio took a step forward and the bandit dropped his blade and turned to run.

Too slow.

Seenio had already lunged forward and, reaching out, grabbed a handful of the bandit's long hair in his right hand. He snatched the head, jerking the bandit's neck and causing his whole body to bend backward. Even as this was happening, Seenio pivoted on the ball of left foot and sent his right foot crashing into the lower back of the bandit in a brutal side kick, releasing the hair after connecting so that the bandit was propelled forward into the dirt.

Now the bandit began tearing frantically at the sand and gravel with his hands, trying desperately to get to his feet and run for his life. He was unaware that his legs no longer worked. They remained sprawled out behind him as he continued to claw at the ground, shrieking in his confusion and futility.

Calmly, Seenio plucked the bandit's knife from where it had dropped and stepped forward until he straddled the struggling man's torso. Reaching down, he gathered a fistful of tangled dirty hair into his bloody left hand and pulled until the bandits' head was high and his neck well stretched. Then Seenio dragged the blade across the exposed neck with such force that only the bones of the spine prevented a total decapitation.

Seenio then turned to examine the other three bandits that lay in the dirt. Two were still struggling for life. Using the same blade, Seenio ended their struggles.

Through it all, Nola had not moved. Still clutching her tunic to her breast, she stared wide eyed as her father rose and faced her.

She had seen Seenio in training, sparring with one or more of the reapers in the yard beside the great hall. At those times she had marveled at the speed, power and technique he brought to combat. She had thought his fighting prowess amazing. Now she saw that same speed, power and technique, blended with a casual viciousness and brutality that, taken together, was enough to shock the senses.

She now understood why her father's moniker had been bestowed upon him. She now understood how appropriate it was.

She had witnessed her father, Seenio Masscus, transform in an instant from a man into a beast.

Now Nola watched as Seenio stood from the last throat slashing. The blood of his victims splattered his torso and legs, and still dripped from his arms and hands. She saw her father look to her and, seeing where her eyes were turned, look to himself to see what she saw.

"Damn," Seenio said as he started back toward the hot spring. "Now I must wash all over again."

CHAPTER 26

As they drew ever nearer to Gunjunson, the trio of Ray, Hanshee, and Kellen became aware of more and more traffic on the road. Some were moving away from the city, but the vast majority seemed to be traveling toward the capital.

Ray asked Kellen if it were always this way but, being a child and of limited experience, he could not say. Ray reasoned that he and Hanshee were even more limited in their experience with the cities in this place. Maybe there was nothing unusual about the numbers on the roads, but he found himself unconvinced. This level of traffic, the number of people streaming towards Gunjunson, seemed out of the ordinary.

With these numbers on the road, there were many times when the trio found themselves traveling beside others who were heading west. After the customary exchange of greetings, Ray tried to listen in on the conversations going on in their groups. From the snippets he overheard, he deduced that the large number of travelers was due to a custom imposed by The Crown on all citizens of Cantor.

In the late winter/early spring of every third year, before the customary time for tilling the soil to prepare it for planting, the heads of every household are required to come to the capital, register their families with The Crown, and pay their taxes. They would list pregnancies, births, deaths, marriages, and desertions, as well as what property was owned. They would then pay taxes based on their profession or the amount of land they farmed. The whole process sounded like a combination of a census and tax collection.

In some cases, whole families would make the pilgrimage. This was seen as necessary to allay the fears of a husband whose spouse and children would be defenseless if left home alone. In cases such as these the trip was sometimes treated as though it were a family vacation. Ray could see a sense of anticipation in the eyes of the older children, and even some of the adults, as they neared the capital city and its many wonders.

Not long after leaving the stables, Ray and Hanshee were surprised to see a group of soldiers moving up the road toward them. There were seven men at arms; their leader riding proudly at the head of the procession and wearing a metal chest plate so highly polished it shone like silver. His shin guards, forearm guards, and helmet were of a similar cast and sheen, and a short blue crest decorated the center length of his helmet. As the weather had not yet acknowledged a change of season, a long-sleeved woolen shirt of the same hue as the decorative crest was worn under his soft leather tunic for added warmth. A blue cloak topped off his attire. The leader was followed by six men who rode two by two. They were outfitted similarly to their leader, but with hardened leather in place of metal armor.

Their weapons and equipment were chosen with speed in mind.

All carried bows of medium length, and a quiver full of arrows. All rode with swords on their backs, the narrow medium length blades designed to be speedily deployed from horseback. There were also various short bladed knives, usually sheathed on their upper arms. Light bucklers, about a foot and a half in diameter, were hung from one of the rear horns of their saddles and, aside from a bedroll, water bag, and ration sack, accounted for all that the soldiers carried.

Ray watched as the citizens of Cantor reacted to the soldiers with smiles and friendly greetings. When hailed, the leader nodded his head in acknowledgement. The six riding behind him remained stoic, apparently not allowed to respond to niceties while on duty. Nevertheless, the people were happy to see that their King was concerned for their protection as they traveled with their families and their taxes to the capital.

There were many pilgrims on the roads and, if each carried payment for the Crown, the amount of coin and goods made a tempting target for bandits and highwaymen. Ray and Hanshee were to find that, during the times of pilgrimage, the soldiers of Cantor patrolled every road that brought traffic into the city.

In the late afternoon of the second day after exchanging horses, Ray, Hanshee and Kellen came to where the road emerged from a stand of pines just before plunging downhill to the flats of the plains. It was from this vantage point that they first took in the sight of Gunjunson.

Still a league and a half distant, the city walls appeared both tall and thick, leaving one with the impression that they were impossible to breach. This was why they were spoken of, by every soldier of every nation east of the Blue Towers, as 'the Massive Walls of Gunjunson'.

Ray had nothing to compare them to but his first view of the capital of Pith. That city, first seen as blackness silhouetted against the clear night sky, had left upon him its own impression of size and strength. In comparison, the city of Gunjunson looked both larger and stronger, like a giant block of solid granite that towered unconcerned above the vast plain that surrounded it.

The plains had long ago been stripped of much of their forests and, for the most part, appeared to be used for farming and grazing. Here and there one could see small communities that had sprung up around the city, probably the hubs of the farming networks or the estates of rich landowners who made their permanent residence among the towers inside the walls of the city proper. Most of the wild vegetation that remained appeared to follow the banks of streams, many of which fed into a river just west of the city walls. This river, the Manchess, flowed from the north to the south southwest. It was accompanied by its own vegetation, various trees and undergrowth that concealed its banks, and eventually disappeared into the distance.

Inside the city walls there could be seen the towers and minarets of noble houses and temples, at the center of which were even taller structures that Ray guessed comprised the Palace of the King. These buildings were much too far away for the trio to discern any details, which explained why Ray's eyes were drawn to the movement near the eastern gate of Gunjunson, and what appeared to be a community of tents that had sprung up near it.

The road that brought traffic from the north and the south, referred to as the Merchant Way, met the Cantor Road just before it reached the eastern gate of the city. It was this intersection that appeared to serve as the nucleus of the tent city. From their vantage point atop the rise, the trio could see people streaming in from all directions. To Ray it was as if looking down at a trail of ants moving off toward the raised mound of earth that was their nest.

The many small plumes of smoke rising from the tent city spoke of both comfort and commerce. Some were sure to be cook fires, while others might belong to smiths who had set up forges in order to service the many people and horses that arrived on a daily basis. But most were probably for warmth, as true spring was still at least a moon distant.

Many of the new arrivals planned to camp outside the city if they did not arrive in time to be counted that day. The more affluent would enter and take a room at a tavern but, for those less fortunate and for some just seeking the excitement of the crowd, the tent city provided all they could ask for. Ray could almost see it expanding with new arrivals as he watched.

All of this was taken in with just a moment's pause, and soon the three were heading down the road along with the growing throng closing in on Gunjunson from the east.

As the sun was beginning to dip behind the western horizon, the trio found themselves among the outer tents where another world beckoned. The sounds and smells that wafted from the interior were enough to stoke the fires of anticipation and make a trip to the city seem worthwhile, even absent an official reason.

After passing through the outer tents, those of the newly arrived trying to establish their place among many others, the trio passed into what Ray likened to a Turkish Bazaar.

Here were peddlers and small shops, usually with small offerings of foods and drink. There were others with various trinkets for sale, sprinkled around larger tents from which emanated strange but pleasing music from a variety of instruments, some unrecognizable. The sounds would drift in from the distance, growing in intensity as their source was approached, and inviting the listeners to enter a trancelike state as they were drawn in by the haunting melodies. At its peak, the music seemed to come from everywhere, flowing in and around them, the musicians themselves only partially glimpsed between the colorful costumes of twirling dancers and agile acrobats. As they continued past the tent, the music steadily diminished before merging with the next tune drifting in on the night breeze and, before they knew it, they were again amidst a swirl of activity as dancers, jugglers, and performers of all kinds took advantage of the atmosphere created by the press of wide-eyed people.

A little farther on and the bartering that was only hinted at among the music tents began in earnest. Shop keepers had set up tents, and even small wooden structures that could be quickly erected and torn down, so that almost overnight the many options of the city just inside the gates were available to any with the coin to pay or the goods to trade.

There was jewelry and decorative ornaments. There was pottery formed before your eyes and hardened in onsite kilns. Delicate carvings and large sculptures were presented, along with drawings and paintings depicting all aspects of life in Cantor. Leather goods of every sort were available. Tools and weapons could be custom made by smiths who had set up their forges and worked with any metals requested or provided.

And then there was the food!

Some of the most succulent dishes that could be imagined outside a nobleman's kitchens were available for any who had the price. Whole hogs were basted as they turned slowly on spits that also boasted goat, venison, and sides of beef. There was abundant fowl, from duck, quail, and pheasant, to geese, turkey and the ever popular chicken.

There were more exotic delicacies; fruits, nuts, and fine cheeses, and several beyond Ray's ability to recognize, which he thought was probably a good thing. There was even fish, eels, and crustaceans, some alive and in large barrels, that could be chosen, cleaned and prepared as the purchasers watched.

All of these different and varied meats, fowl, fish and crustaceans could be served any number of ways; broiled, roasted, fried, or in the case of certain fish, and animal organs, raw. And all could be served with the vegetables of one's choosing. This cornucopia of food could be washed down with wines and ales from the four corners of the nation, as well as several choice imports that were available. Liquor and brandy could also be had by those with the means.

But what set young Kellen's eyes afire, and caused his lips to smack, were the pastries.

They were made with the fresh milk of cows and goats, with plenty of rich creamy butter. They were sweetened with honey, with syrup, and with the sugar that was imported from the lands south of the Great Inland Sea. They were flavored with fruits that had been dried or preserved by the orchard masters, or spices that, like the sugar, were imported from the tropical lands by the many merchants who regularly made their way north to trade for grains, precious metals, stones, and tools and weapons from the forges of the blacksmiths of Pith.

The aroma of the tasty treats was enough to make Ray's mouth water, and even Hanshee stretched his neck to get a glimpse of the different offerings as they walked past tent after tent where the ovens were ablaze. Kellen was beside himself and he reached into the folds of his coat and pulled out his single gold piece, which he fingered as he weighed its worth against cream filled cinnamon sweet breads or pies baked with both fruits and nuts.

Ray saw this and was drawn back to his childhood, and the times he spent at carnivals, amusement parks, and state and county fairs.

Handing off the reins of all the animals to Hanshee, who had noticed Kellen eyeing the pastries, and taking Kellen by the hand, Ray walked over to a large tent that boasted a seemingly endless collection of all things sweet. Ray first asked Kellen what he liked. He then waited while the boy looked at every offering that was on display, and was relieved when the child finally settled on a choice. What Kellen chose appeared to be a heavily glazed sticky bun with dried fruit and nuts trapped in its folds. Ray nodded approval and sent Kellen back to Hanshee before beginning the negotiation.

One of the reasons Ray wanted to make a purchase was to get a feel for what a piece of gold such as he carried was worth in this world. The only other transaction he had witnessed was when Hanshee paid the bar girl in Aggipoor with a gold coin. The way she had responded told Ray that, for a coin of pure gold, he and Hanshee could have had a go at drinking the wine cellar dry. Living in the Temple and the Royal House of Pith, and having all of their needs met, meant that he had never again witnessed a monetary transaction in this world. Ray figured he could gain a little knowledge while satisfying Kellen's sweet tooth.

In the end it was all of their sweet tooth's that were satisfied, as Ray purchased the three largest sticky buns; one each for Kellen, Hanshee, and himself, as well as a fourth with which to surprise the boy later. He was not sure just what the four buns had cost him, but told himself that it was two pieces of silver. Still, he wondered if he had not been taken advantage of.

Since all he had was gold, the wily pastry seller had given him eighteen pieces of silver as change. She had tried to give him twelve but he kept his hand open, shaking it demandingly while giving her a hard stare. With a wary frown the pastry seller reluctantly added silver, one piece at a time, to his palm. When she reached eighteen pieces, she looked at him as if to ask if this were enough. When Ray closed his hand, she beamed.

Kellen also beamed when Ray handed him what, to the child, must have seemed like the largest, fattest, sticky bun in the world! After properly thanking Ray, the boy tore into his treat with gusto.

Hanshee accepted his treat with an air of caution. He first looked it over from all sides, then watched intently as Kellen ate ravenously from his. Ray looked on in fascination as Hanshee watched the child. After a moment, Hanshee turned to Ray and spoke.

Nodding his head toward Kellen, Hanshee said, "It must be delicious. It cannot be good for us."

"You sound like my mother," Ray replied before taking a huge bite from his bun.

"Your mother is wise," replied Hanshee, before taking a huge bite of his.

Kellen, his cheeks bulging from his latest bite of sticky bun, looked from one to the other and smiled.

By the time the trio had traversed the tent city and reached the eastern gate of Gunjunson, their hands and mouths were covered with the evidence of their happy crime against mothers everywhere.

The wait in line was brief, but provided time to clean their hands and faces.

Having found himself in similar situations in his travels, Hanshee took the time to study the interplay between the city guards and those who sought entrance into Gunjunson. As they had previously agreed, when it came their turn Ray used the same story he had used at the stables. When the two sentries learned that the trio was not there for "the counting", as the tax collection and census was called, they assumed a bearing that made entrance into the city appear highly questionable.

"A traveling holy man?" questioned the first of the guards. "I have never seen a traveling holy man who spurned a night under the stars for a tavern bed."

"It is for the boy," Raymond said, recovering quickly." He is sickly and my master thought it prudent that he have a hot broth before a warm fire and a bed off of the ground, if only for this night."

The guards looked quizzically at both Hanshee and Kellen, taking in their dusty appearance as well as their tired and aged horses.

"He would tell you himself," Ray continued, "but he comes from a land far to the west and does not speak your tongue."

"And can you afford hot broth and a bed?" the other guard asked haughtily.

This question caught Ray off guard. Of course, they had money, but he could hardly flash it before the guards. A holy man traveling with a bag of gold would probably call forth all manner of unwanted attention.

It was then that Hanshee stepped forward, a placid smile on his face as he steadily bowed and muttered words that Raymond had never heard, and were probably gibberish.

Hanshee cautiously approached the guards, who continued to watch him warily. The lead guard actually placed his hand on the hilt of his short sword. Hanshee pressed forward, continuing to bow and mutter as he reached for the free left hand of the guard, taking it into his own and then bending his head to kiss its back. As he did this the expression on the guard's face changed and, once freed from Hanshee's grip, he chanced a quick glance down at his hand as Hanshee continued to make motions over and around his head. When finished, Hanshee reached for the hand of the second guard, who looked nervously toward his fellow. The first guard gave a quick nod of his head and the second then extended his hand, allowing Hanshee to go through the same routine, ending with the motions above and around his head. Afterward Hanshee continued bowing, smiling, and muttering as he stepped back beside Ray.

Now the first guard looked to his partner and cleared his throat before he spoke.

"Express to your master our thanks for his... blessing." he said to Ray, before adding curtly, "You may pass. Next!"

As they hurriedly passed through the towering gate, Raymond looked at Hanshee with an expression every bit as questioning as the guards they had just encountered. Once out of earshot he spoke.

"What was that about," he asked. "...some kind of blessing?

"The very best of blessings" Hanshee said, "offered with a piece of silver for each palm."

"You have silver?" A surprised Raymond asked.

In reply Hanshee patted the place under his robe where his pouch rested.

"The magic pouch supplies our every need," joked Ray in an exaggeratedly solemn voice. Then he asked Hanshee a more serious question.

"When we were in Aggipoor," Ray began, "and you gave the barmaid a coin, why gold instead of silver if you had both?"

Hanshee's response was quick and succinct.

"At that time a coin was a coin," he said.

"'A coin was a coin'?" Ray repeated. "What does that mean?"

"My tribe and my clan live on the western slopes of the Blue Mountains." Hanshee explained. "Our brethren from the plains have dealings with the western civilized nations and therefore know of coins. Clan Dula has no use for coins."

"Well," said Ray, "you seem to be learning fast."

"I am Maiyochi," Hanshee replied.

Still just a stone's throw from the gate, Ray, Hanshee and Kellen continued to make their way into the depths of Gunjunson, never suspecting that unseen eyes had noticed the arrival from the east of two men of dark complexion traveling with a child, and even now followed their every move.

Though having passed through the tent city and reached the capital of Gunjunson, Ray and Hanshee were still mindful of the squad of pursuers that had been on their trail since their escape from Stronghold. They had decided that it would be safer to try to lose their pursuit in the crowded city, and slip out later to return young Kellen to his home in the south of Cantor. What they searched for now was a tavern, though not the gaudy sort just inside the city gates that called to all visitors upon their arrival. They sought a tavern away from the bustle of the crowds; some place quiet and subdued where they could take their rest and not draw any attention.

As they made their way through the city, they could not help but notice its layout.

Gunjunson seemed to have been constructed on a pattern of ever larger circles. Not far from the outer defensive walls was a much smaller inner wall that seemed to form the boundary between different districts if not different populations.

Passing through the city gates first brought one face to face with its protectors; the City Garrison. Next was the many governmental offices and dignitaries which one might have to encounter when entering a seat of power. Beyond these lay what was best considered an 'entertainment district' where the larger and more prestigious taverns, boarding houses, and brothels, were set up. Alongside were several merchant shops, strategically located to service these establishments and the many visitors to the city that they would attract.

If they turned left or right, further away from the gates but within the same circular district, they would find less and less gaudy accommodations until they entered the slums, occupied by those whose toil formed the foundation of the taverns and brothels and boardinghouses, and without whom none would exist.

This pattern remained constant as traveler passed from one district and through its delineating wall to the next. The only consistent prosperity was strung out along the main roads that connected the gates with the inner circles of the city. That is where the wealth and nobility were concentrated, living in close proximity to the seat of ultimate power…The Crown.

It was inside the third circle that Raymond and Hanshee found what they were looking for.

It was an older building, but not ancient. The sign above the door marked it as the Golden Lantern. In years past it had been a bawdy house known for the most comely and willing ladies in Gunjunson. But that was when it sat only a stone's throw from the outer walls. As the city grew outward, and larger and more elaborate brothels and bawdy houses positioned themselves to draw in the first through the gates, the Golden Lantern embraced its fate and became a simple tavern, where the locals joined with the few visitors who relished a more subdued setting amid the old timers and their stories of its glory days. They would gather in its main room on cold nights, enjoying warm bread and hot stew, good drinks, laughter and camaraderie. There were never any great numbers, but the fare had been hearty and the atmosphere genuine.

Now, even those days were in the distant past, and the Golden Lantern was a sturdy, quiet, never crowded inn, perfect for those seeking rest from heavy labors and arduous travels, or sanctuary from the turmoil of an otherwise crowded and bawdy city.

This fit the trio perfectly.

Feeling a new level of confidence since his haggling at the pastry tent, Raymond left Hanshee and Kellen outside with the horses as he entered the double doors located beneath the hanging sign.

The interior was darker than he expected, but he had no problem winding his way between the few tables, most of which were uninhabited. As he moved further into the room, he could not help but notice the enticing aroma that wafted throughout. Stew. He hoped it was a beef stew, but he would settle for a 'meat' stew. If it tasted as good as it smelled he would have no problem getting it down, especially after the appetite he had built up while moving among the many offerings in the tent city.

Ray made his way to the bar, tended by an old man who he thought certainly must have seen the glory days of the Golden Lantern and could probably spin a yarn or two if prompted.

"Drink?" the old man asked in a pleasant enough voice.

He was short and slightly bent, though he moved with a vigor that belied his age. The top of his clean head shone brightly in the lamp light, with the wispy gray hair above his ears running down into bushy pork chop sideburns that framed a long narrow nose and wide smiling mouth. He wore a long-sleeved tunic that appeared neat and clean, even this late in his workday.

"A room," Ray replied, "large enough for three if you please."

The old man's eyes grew large and he first looked behind Ray for the rest of his party before meeting his gaze.

"You're here for the counting?" the old man asked. "Don't get many families in this part of the city anymore. Most from the countryside prefer the excitement of the tents. Those with coin prefer the bawdy houses right inside the gates. You have coin?"

"I have coin," Ray smiled. "What do you charge for a room?"

"I can put you up for two silvers a head for a night," the old man said as he shifted from bartender to proprietor. "There are stables in the back if you have horses. That will cost you one silver per animal, but there's fresh hay and I have a man back there to brush 'em down and feed and water 'em."

The old proprietor watched closely as Ray counted out ten pieces of silver, retied his purse and began to place it back inside the folds of his robe. He paused with his hand still in the fold.

"How is the stew," he asked, and the old man smiled a surprisingly toothy smile.

"It's my stew," the proprietor said proudly, "my recipe, and it's better than any you'll find among the tents, that's for certain."

Ray was about to ask what it contained but thought better of it, not wanting to risk insulting the old bartender/ proprietor/ cook.

"It's fresh," the old man continued. "I just paid for a freshly butchered ox quarter this morning. I get it from my wife's brother at a good price. He's a butcher, with a shop down by the wall, and he stocks up for the counting. He's got more meat now than he knows what to do with!" the proprietor said with a chuckle.

"Then I'll have three bowls of stew and watered wine for three," said Ray.

"That will cost one more silver a head," said the old man and Ray eagerly dug out three more pieces of silver which he laid on the bar before him.

"You take your animals around to the back," smiled the old man as he raked the thirteen silver coins into his hand, "and by the time you come back in, I'll have your stew and wine ready at that table over near the fire. While you eat, I'll have a room readied for you."

Ray thanked him and made his way out the front door well pleased with himself. He found Hanshee and Kellen where he left them and, after informing them of the accommodations he made, took the lead in guiding the horses around the back of the tavern. The old man was waiting for them on the side of the building, pointing the way to the stalls before disappearing back into a side door.

After guiding the animals into the stalls, the trio went about unloading, now an efficient process thanks to the tutelage of Kellen. Once the saddles, blankets, and bridles were removed and set aside, the three made way for the stableman who was to take over the care of the horses for the night. They gathered all the gear that they would keep with them and carried it into the tavern through the same side door used by the old proprietor.

As they entered Ray again found the pleasing aroma of the stew, and he turned to smile and nod at Hanshee and Kellen. The old proprietor was standing by a table near the fire that had been set with napkins, spoons, and three large bowls of steaming stew. There was a goblet beside each bowl and a vessel of watered wine, the sides of which were beginning to show the condensation that occurs when trapped between the heat without and the cold within.

"There's a basin in the corner for washing, should you desire that before you eat," said the old man. "And I'll be out directly with bread that is just now leaving the oven."

Ray and Kellen beamed, and even the usually stoic Hanshee nodded his approval as the aroma of the stew swirled about their heads.

The trio washed their hands, arms, and faces, the two men standing over Kellen to ensure that he did a good job, then took their seats and dug into the thick meaty stew. It was delicious and, before they knew it, Hanshee and Raymond were sopping the remaining gravy from their empty bowls with the remnants of the bread.

Sitting back from his bowl with a sigh of contentment, Hanshee raised his head to Ray and spoke the first words from any of them since sitting down to eat.

"T'was a meal for a warrior," he said with a look of satisfaction on his face. "It will wash away our fatigue, replenish our strength, and prepare us for the rigors that lie ahead."

"That sounds a bit dramatic," Ray said with a chuckle, not knowing if what he meant translated well to Hanshee's language.

"It is a saying among the Dula," Hanshee explained, "a high complement, bestowed upon those who have fed you properly and thus earned your gratitude."

"Then I agree… this *was* a meal for a warrior," Ray said, "but you're still angry about that sticky bun" he teased.

At the mention of the sweetbread, Hanshee smiled a huge smile before quickly assuming a look of solemn contemplation.

"Not the bread of a warrior," Hanshee said with mock gravity, and both men threw back their heads and laughed.

Kellen briefly looked up from his bowl of stew but, understanding neither the words nor the laughter, was quickly drawn back to his meal, content that the cause of their mirth was no concern of his.

CHAPTER 27

The sun had set and the moon had risen when Seenio and Nola finally rode into Sandledge. They entered from the east, guiding their horses slowly down the quiet side streets toward the center of the village.

Sandledge had gotten its start as a crossroads situated favorably between the Stronghold Gates and the westernmost foothills of the northern mountain range now known as Strongholds Crown. It was in these foothills that the first of the rich ore deposits, for which Pith had become renowned, were discovered.

For centuries Pithian society was centered at The Gates, the only place in the surrounding walls of stronghold that was the least bit vulnerable. The entire Pithian military was headquartered there, as was the Royal Family and the Temple of The One Spirit. The craftsmen of the nation were located there, as were most of its forges and all of its smelts. The flow of traffic from the mines to these smelts and back to the mines gave rise to several villages and rest stops along what was then called The Mining Way.

But as often happens, the years pass and with them comes change.

Pithian royalty decided to build a whole new city on the far side of the valley fortress, taking with them the centers of government and Pithian culture. This had been a huge undertaking, demanding a great deal of what workforce there was in the still fledgling nation. The workers who were centered at and near The Gates moved east, taking their families with them. This prompted those who made their living supplying goods and services to the workers to follow. In the end, a mass migration occurred and soon seventy percent of the population resided in and around the newly constructed Capital, situated in the southeastern corner of Stronghold. The bulk of the military continued to reside at and around The Gates, for obvious reasons.

This shifting of the population had the effect of decimating dozens of villages that had dotted the southwestern and western landscape of Stronghold. Whole towns disappeared within a few seasons, with only their skeletons left standing where communities of people had once flourished. Nature had its way and, over the course of decades and centuries, even the scars of these towns had been wiped away as the land was reclaimed and returned to an almost pristine state. There were few rural communities that managed to survive the migration; fewer still that managed to thrive.

Because the mines continued to supply ore of excellent quality, and military smelts and forges were always busy making more tools and weapons, the Mining Way continued as an artery of commerce. Because Sandledge was ideally situated halfway between destinations that would otherwise require a two-day journey, the town continued to have relevance as a rest stop for the traffic moving both north and south.

As Seenio and Nola continued into town, they noted only a couple of ore wagons visible, and almost no one on the streets. They rode in relative silence, save for the distant pinging of a blacksmiths hammer as it worked to shape hot metal.

Emerging from between two buildings into the town square, the pair rode toward the only inn that the town had.

The huge building, known as the Cock and Stagg, faced eastward and dominated the main square. It provided almost all the rooms needed to accommodate the varied characters involved in the commerce of the mines during the busy season. When it was full, it seemed the nights would go on forever, leaving the miners, traders and wagon drivers exhausted from drinking, gambling, fighting, and cavorting. Many a sleep deprived traveler struggled to find their way down the road in the morning.

On nights like tonight, when the Mining Way, and therefore the Inn, was empty, the town closed early and late arrivals were treated only to the shadows of past gaiety and good times.

Seenio continued in the direction of the Cock and Stagg, with Nola close behind. Reaching the inn, he did not stop but continued past it, toward the pinging still emanating from the blacksmiths shop. Nola looked to the Inn as they passed, but kept her silence and continued to follow Seenio as he reined in before an ancient wooden structure that was open on three sides.

Reining in beside her father, Nola could just make out the source of the hammering that came from the rear of the shop. The blacksmith had paused to insert the cooling metal back into the forge, and was now working the bellows. The hot coals glowed bright red as sparks rose and scattered in the rush of air.

While his hands were occupied with heating the iron and pumping the bellows, the smithy cast a glance toward the new arrivals. He could not see them clearly as his view was partially blocked by the many tools, chains, and bars of raw metals hanging from the beams and posts that supported the roof. Still, he saw enough to send a shout their way.

"The shop is closed! Come back tomorrow!"

Seenio continued to sit his horse, as if he had not heard a word from the gruff farrier. Nola unquestioningly followed her father's lead.

The smithy continued working his bellows, occasionally withdrawing the metal bar to check its color, while casting irritated glances toward the horses that had yet to move on. A few more pulls on the bellows, another look at the metal, and he dropped both, hefted a hammer, and stalked from behind the hanging tangle of metal to confront whoever this was that thought to ignore his commands in *his* shop.

As soon as the blacksmith had moved past the hanging debris, and could clearly see who he addressed, his eyes went wide and his feet froze to the ground. His hammer, brandished as a threat to encourage these latecomers to be on their way, now hung limply at his side.

Nola could now get a good look at the blacksmith, some of whose features seemed to aptly describe smithies everywhere.

Though not as tall as one might expect, maybe a few inches shorter than her own height of close to six feet, the man had the stout frame and large muscles that came from working the forges and shaping the metal day in and day out. He appeared as wide as he was tall, with his large belly the only hint of fat to be seen. It was hidden under the heavy leather apron that stopped just past the tops of his boots and protected him from the hazards of his profession. His face was round, with a full beard, and from his head hung long brown hair streaked with grey, tied back and hanging between his shoulder blades. His huge arms were bare and ended in a pair of heavy gloves, worn as protection against the heat and flames.

Seenio had yet to move, placidly sitting his horse and allowing a small smile to play on his lips as he looked down at the astonished blacksmith.

"Please... come down from your horse... both of you... I have some wine in the back," the smithy said, finally finding his voice as he motioned to the rear of his workspace. He tore his eyes from Seenio only to briefly include Nola, and then his focus moved back to the Beast as he dismounted.

Seenio waited until Nola tied her mount to the post and had joined him before leading her toward the still stunned blacksmith.

"This way..." the farrier said, motioning with his gloved hand as he turned and headed toward the rear wall of his smithy shack. Once there, he went about clearing a space, moving blankets, aprons, buckets of coal, and tools, so that Seenio and Nola could sit. Then he reached up to where a leather wine bag was hanging from a wall peg set at bout the height of a tall man. Holding the spout about five inches from his open mouth with one hand, the smithy raised the bag and squeezed with the other. A burgundy stream of liquid caught the light of the lanterns as it arched through the air and into the blacksmith's mouth. He took a good mouthful before lowering the bag, swallowing, and passing it to Seenio as he smacked his lips in satisfaction. Seenio mirrored his movements and then passed the bag to Nola. After Nola drank, she passed the wine back to the smithy who again turned it up, this time taking in what seemed to be twice as much before lowering it with a satisfied sigh.

Now he focused on Seenio, who still regarded him with a half-smile, and spoke.

"I never expected to see you again," the blacksmith said.

"And why not, Suleski?" asked Seenio with apparent amusement.

"Well... uh...," Suleski the blacksmith stammered, as he looked from Seenio to Nola and back, "when last you were here... uh... surely you recall..."

"And so, you thought that I would never return?" Seenio interrupted. "Or is it that you *hoped* not to see me again?"

"I... well... I mean," Suleski seemed unable to form a complete thought, but then he stopped trying and instead raised the wine bag again, this time wrapping his lips around the spout and draining several swallows before bringing it back down. This seemed to finally give him the fortitude to speak his mind.

"When you left Sandledge, there were seven ore wagons left driverless." Suleski said. "Seven bloody heads were found perched, one apiece, atop the driver's benches of the wagons; wagons that no one would dare drive for several days! New drivers had to be brought in from the mines just to return the ore! Shipments were delayed, agreements were forfeit... and I'm told a small fortune changed hands when the owner of the smelt had to sell because of his shortage of coin."

"And why do you tell me this," asked Seenio, still visibly amused.

"Because the next morning a grapple was discovered on the roof of the inn," Suleski said. "I saw it. Although I said I did not recognize it, it was the same grapple you had me make for you... the same grapple for which you paid ten silver coin."

"I remember your work as exceptional," Seenio smiled. "Well worth ten coin."

"And there was something else," the blacksmith continued. "When I came to my forges the next day, there was a purse... hanging from that very peg," he said, pointing to the peg that had held the wine bag, "with seven gold coins inside."

"Apparently I was your good luck charm," laughed Seenio. "I would think you would welcome one who brought such fortune to your doorstep."

Suleski guzzled more wine before remembering to again offer the bag to Seenio, who waved it off.

"I told myself," Suleski the blacksmith said, "there was no proof the man I made the grapple for had beheaded those drivers." He looked sheepishly to Seenio as he said this, hoping to see something in his expression that would allow the farrier to continue in his naivety.

Seenio smiled broadly. "And there you have it" he said. "No poof at all," effectively bringing to an end any more conversation about his last visit. "But since that time," he continued, "I have discovered that you, Suleski, have become trusted in certain circles… for information."

Of course, Seenio was correct.

He knew this because, after he had compromised the blacksmith on his visit many years prior, he had sent an agent, one of many who unknowingly worked for the Guild, to cultivate the blacksmith. Suleski was a drinker and a talker, and he often held court with many people of different persuasions in this small but important village. Seenio had found his information, acquired through intermediaries, valuable in the past. He was here this night to utilize the smithy in person.

Suleski stood silently as he considered what this man, whose name he had never learned and so had always thought of as 'the deadly stranger', had said. It was not long after the stranger's first and last bloody visit that another man had approached Suleski. The man had known things… but had promised that his knowledge would remain secret if a few favors were granted. Since that time, Suleski the blacksmith had taken up a second craft. He now dealt in information, gathering all that he could from those who passed through Sandledge. He never knew what was valuable, and many times had been asked about things that had no meaning to him. For this reason, he gathered all the information that he could, on any subject that he could get a man to talk about.

Suleski did not know that he was now a cog in a vast network of spies and operatives that had, for centuries, been cultivated by the Guild of Assassins. Most of these 'cogs' knew very little beyond their own sphere of influence, were unaware that they were only one of many, and had no idea who they ultimately served. What was important was that the guild had ways of finding them when their services were needed. These men and women had been of tremendous assistance over the centuries, in ways of which they had no clue.

"I have been known to pass information," said Suleski carefully.

"Then maybe you can tell me," Seenio said, "who I must contact in the city of Gunjunson. Someone like yourself, who keeps an ear to the ground and his mouth closed... until the right question is asked by the right man."

The smithy again fell into silence as he considered the man before him and the information he sought.

Finally, having reached a conclusion, Suleski removed his heavy gloves and dipped his left hand into a wide mouthed urn filled with some kind of lubricant. Lifting the hand from the urn and shaking off the excess, he went to work removing a heavy ring from the middle finger of the hand. This was not an easy task and, to Seenio and Nola, was quite painful just to watch. At last, with a great gnashing of teeth and a mighty tug, the ring came free, with only a little blood visible on the oily finger. Suleski took a rag and thoroughly cleaned all lubricant and blood from the ornament before passing it to Seenio. It was heavy; a solid gold ring with a curious design worked into its face.

"This ring was crafted from one of the seven gold pieces that you... that was left to me that night," Suleski said. "You must pass through the east gate of Gunjunson. You must then turn south and follow the road until you come to an inn called the Milkmaid's Rest. You will know it by its banner, which bears the painted carving of a serving wench with abundant... uh... charms," he said, while glancing tentatively toward Nola. "If this ring be seen on your hand there, you will be approached by a man known simply as 'Wiley'. He is one such as you seek."

CHAPTER 28

After young Kellen had finished his bowl of stew, half a goblet of watered wine, and the surprise of a second sticky bun produced from the folds of Ray's robe, he was filled near to overflowing. It had been a long day…a long several days, as they had been rising early and traveling late in order to stay ahead of their pursuit. Now the boy, who had been exhausted before the heavy meal, could barely keep his eyes open at the table. Ray had to steer his steps as the old proprietor led them up the two flights to their room.

The third floor had a look about it as if it were seldom used, and this made sense, as the Golden Lantern did not do much in the way of boarding in this day and time. The smaller rooms on the second floor were all that were needed to accommodate the few who chose to stay a night or two at the old inn. The stairs leading to the top floor, as well as the floorboards in the hallway, creaked and groaned with the weight of the travelers. It was a burden they had become unaccustomed to in the many years they had been out of regular use. Nevertheless, they held as the proprietor, lantern on high, led the trio up the final stairs and then back down the hall a short distance to the second of three doors to their right. The key tuned smoothly in the lock, and the door swung open on hinges that had just that night seen oil for the first time in many seasons.

The room was large, containing three beds, a sturdy table with four chairs, a large chest, and a separate table upon which sat a large bowl, a larger urn, and several cloths. At the far end of the room was a stone fireplace, complete with an oaken mantle and a wide stone ledge upon which was stacked enough wood for several days and nights. A small fire had already been tended, needing only to be fed additional logs during the night for the room to take on the warm cozy feel of the great room it was built to mimic.

As the old proprietor went about lighting the various lamps, Ray looked to assess the accommodations and what one could expect in Cantor for two silver pieces per night. It was clear that much work had been done to make the room presentable while they unloaded the horses and sat down to eat. The furniture had been dusted and the wooden planks of the floors swept. Fresh rugs were laid, one before the fireplace and one beside each of the three beds. Fresh linens had been placed upon the beds and the table even had a clean fresh cloth draped over it. Still, the room held the musty smell of one long unused, abandoned to the dust and mice for many years until suddenly called into service by the three visitors.

"I hope the room is to your liking kind sirs," the proprietor said as he lit the last of the available lamps. "If not, you just call for me and I'll make sure all your needs are met."

"Who should we call for?" Ray asked, having not asked his name when they had first spoken.

"Oh, I'm Jedidiah, but there's no need to be formal. Just call for Ole Jed, everybody else does." The proprietor said this with all the warmth that a purse full of silver tends to bring out in a business man. "I'll send a girl up with more fresh water directly."

Jed closed the door softly, the freshly oiled and worked hinges making hardly any sound, and left the three to make themselves comfortable for the night. This was no problem for

Kellen, who stumbled over to the smallest of the beds, climbed under the sheets, and was snoring in the space of ten heartbeats. Hanshee and Ray watched him and, once he was secure under the sheets, Hanshee walked over to one of the two south-facing windows in the room. Mimicking Hanshee, Raymond walked over to the other and pulled the curtain back, releasing a swirling cloud of dust directly into his face.

"They missed a spot," he said, waving his hand before his face as he stepped through the dust cloud to see out of the window.

The clouds that now covered the moon meant that there was little contrast between shadow and light. At first glance all was darkness. As their eyes adjusted to the night, they could make out the roof of the stable several feet below the outer window sill. It sloped upward, away from the inn, until reaching its peak, the crest of which hid the far side from their eyes. Beyond the stable roof they could see the tops of other buildings, none much higher than the inn. Also becoming visible as their eyes acclimated to the darkness, was the soft glow of the many fires set against the cold that emanated from the many windows and yards around them.

Turning away from the window, Ray made his way over to the fireplace. A small pot of spiced wine had been set beside the fire to warm, a pleasantry provided by Ole Jeb for no additional coin. Ray smiled as he poured himself a small amount which he now sipped as he stood before the warmth of the fire. He was about to call out to Hanshee, who still stood beside the open window, when his voice was stilled by the sound of the creaking of floorboards in the hall outside of their room.

Ray cast a questioning look to Hanshee, who returned his glance before quickly focusing on the door, his right hand having moved to the hilt of the sword that was ever present behind his right shoulder. Ray refocused on the door as another creak told of advancing footsteps. After a moment or two of silence, there was a sharp knock on the door followed by the voice of Ole Jed.

"I beg your pardon, sirs," the old man spoke.

Ray again looked to Hanshee who, with a nod of his head, gave Ray leave to answer the summons. Still, Ray approached the door cautiously, his earlier experiences in this world having now bred an automatic suspicion of anything unexpected and unfamiliar. Arriving at the door, Ray spoke the name of the proprietor.

"Ole Jed?"

"Yes, milord," the old man said. "It's only me."

Hearing this, Ray still assumed a position behind the door as he cracked it just enough to see who was there.

"There is trouble with one of your horses," the old man said, the anxiety on his face clearly visible to Ray in the dim light flowing from the room. "Could you come down to the stable and see about it?"

The request had the sound of a plea to it, which Ray found a little strange. Still, it could not be ignored. He looked to Hanshee and then to Kellen, who was into a deep, deep sleep. Normally the boy would be the one to check on the horses. All that Ray and Hanshee knew of them had been taught them by Kellen on the journey between the South Road stables of Pith and the Cantorese capital of Gunjunson. But waking the boy now would be heartless and probably fruitless as he had succumbed completely to his exhaustion.

"I will come," Ray said before turning to Hanshee and repeating what had been said in a language he would understand.

"I will accompany you," Hanshee said flatly, and it occurred to Ray that he had only been out of the presence of Hanshee a handful of times since his arrival in this land.

Both men still wore their heavy robes so they had only to secure the door behind them and follow Jed down the stairs.

Once on the first floor, Ole Jed led the way down the short hallway to the side door that would bring them closest to the stables. Upon reaching the door, the innkeeper held it open for his guests, allowing first Ray, then Hanshee, to step past him and out into the small circle of light that was thrown off by the single lamp hanging by the door.

Without warning Ray was stopped in his tracks by Hanshee as the warrior darted in front of him and assumed a defensive crouch. Hanshee's left hand found the hilt of his knife, even as his right hand gripped the hilt of his sword.

Only then did Ray notice movement at the edge of the darkness. As he peered into the gloom, a semicircle of hooded figures stepped forward, making their presence known on the periphery of the light. Raymond looked to his left and to his right, seeing that the figures had surrounded them from one wall of the inn to the other. Casting a quick glance behind, Ray noted that the innkeeper had not followed them through the door, but had made way for two more cloaked and hooded figures now standing shoulder to shoulder and barring reentry into the inn.

Everyone now stood frozen in their respective spots. Hanshee had yet to draw his weapons but his stance reminded Ray of nothing so much as a serpent coiled to strike. Ray knew from past observation that those deadly blades could be freed, and blood spurting, in the blink of an eye.

Finally, a voice called out from the center of the semicircle as one of the hooded figures stepped forward.

"Acolyte, it is known that you speak our tongue. Tell your master that there will be no need for his weapons this night."

As the speaker stepped forward, he swept back the deep hood that had concealed his visage, revealing the square jawed face of a man, most probably a physically powerful man from the thickness of the neck that flowed into large shoulders barely concealed by the cloak that covered them.

Ray opened his mouth to translate for Hanshee what the speaker had said and noted that, even before he began, Hanshee had relaxed his posture as he appraised the still cloaked man standing before him. When Ray finished the translation, the strange man again spoke.

"Those that now stand before you are of the Imperial Guard of King Moton IX, Monarch of the Nation of Cantor. I am Gyzull, their Captain. His Highness is aware of your plight and wishes to speak with you. He sends his Imperial Guard to convey his wishes and to offer safe passage to the Palace."

Ray dutifully translated these words for Hanshee before turning to the captain with a question of his own.

"How do we know you speak truth?" Ray asked, surprised by his own boldness in addressing the man.

"Your caution is understandable," said Gyzull, "considering how your master has been trailed every step of the way from Stronghold to Gunjunson. Even as you entered our walls, there were eyes directed toward you, eyes that may have followed you to this inn, just as we did."

"Come with us now," Gyzull continued, "willingly, and speak with our Monarch. If His Majesties words do not move you, we will bring you back here this very night. Of this you have the word of King Moton, as it was given to me."

As was proven by his words, the captain knew more about them than they had thought. His message held the ring of sincerity and Ray repeated all that had been said to Hanshee, who had been studying Gyzull as he spoke to Ray.

"It seems we have little choice," said Hanshee, after hearing the words translated.

"I know it sounds naïve," said Ray, "but I feel this man, and the word of his king, can be trusted."

"As do I," said Hanshee. "Though they think me important, my duty is to protect you. That would be difficult should we come to blows here and now. Let us follow them, even as we followed the Pith. There are schemes at work here that may yet be revealed to us. It may be that his king can aid us in ways we do not yet know."

"My master says that we will go with you on the word of your king that we may return here this night should we feel the need," Ray said to Gyzull.

Hearing this, Gyzull extended his arm back toward one of his men and two hooded robes were draped across it. These he extended to Hanshee.

"Tell your master that it would aid in our stealth if you both were to don one of our robes and move as one with us, giving further confusion to any prying eyes."

Ray explained the plan to Hanshee and they quickly shed their own robes to don those offered, pulling the hoods over their faces. To the casual observer, they appeared indistinguishable from those that surrounded them. The imperial guardsmen then formed up around them so that Hanshee and Raymond stood in the center of a ring of protection.

A signal – a shrill series of whistles – was launched into the night and three heartbeats later a reply from the direction of the inner city was heard. At this reply, the gathered guardsmen broke into a trot that took them out of the stable yard and onto the cobblestone streets of Gunjunson. The pace they set was easy for Hanshee and Raymond and the group of twelve hooded men – fourteen counting themselves – moved swiftly through the night. They made for a ghostly sight as they traversed the darkness in gray hooded robes that appeared to shimmer when caught in the intermittent torchlight. To onlookers who still roamed the streets at this hour, it was as if a procession of spirits floated almost noiselessly through the night.

As they moved, Raymond noted that a care was taken to stay to streets less traveled. Any well lighted area was avoided, and the procession seemed to take a mazelike course through the backstreets of Gunjunson. Eventually they found themselves striding parallel to high inner walls that were much more formidable looking than any but the outer walls of the city. These walls curved gently to their right and led to what appeared to be a small guard station situated in a most out-of-the-way location. Though small, it appeared heavily guarded, and the company of soldiers stationed there smartly saluted as the robed runners passed through the gate.

Into a short tunnel they ran, eventually spilling out into an open space identifiable by the barnlike buildings, and the scent, as the Royal Stables of Gunjunson. Here they came to a halt.

Looking around, Ray noticed that none of the Imperial Guardsmen appeared to be winded despite running over quite a good distance. He was proud to note his own breathing was calm and regular and it occurred to him that, despite his recent injury and recovery, he might now be in the best shape of his life.

Several of the guardsmen now separated from the group, moving off on their own for reasons unknown to Hanshee and Ray. A core of six guardsmen continued to encircle the pair, leading them toward a door on the far end of the stable yard. Passing through this portal, they entered a dark hallway lit only sporadically with small torches. This hallway went straight for about eighty feet, with other hallways and doorways intersecting at random intervals. At the end of the hall, they came upon a spiral staircase. Ray lifted his gaze to judge its height and saw that the circular column of stairs eventually disappeared into darkness.

Each guardsman bent near the foot of the stairs and arose with a small torch which they lit from the last torch on the wall that served to illuminate the lower steps of the staircase. Once all torches were lit, the guardsmen arranged themselves with three in front of their guest and three behind. Then, as one, they began to ascend the stairs at a vigorous trot. To Ray it was like running the stadium steps when preparing for football season, only not as intense. Up they went, passing doors that seemed to be evenly spaced along the staircase. Raymond lost count of the number of doors they passed and by now was beginning to labor for breath.

It was at this point that the leader stopped beside a dark door hung on heavy hinges. Producing a key from inside his robe, the guardsman worked the large lock until an audible click was heard. He then braced himself with his foot against the stone wall and heaved the heavy door open. Motioning the others through, he was the last to enter, immediately turning and pulling the door closed behind him, working the lock with the key until he was sure it was secure.

Now the group traversed another dark hallway, this one much narrower than the last. Here it would be difficult for two men to walk abreast and two going in opposite directions would turn sideways so that each could pass comfortably. This hallway was not nearly as long as the last and soon they stood before another heavy wooden door, the twin to the door at the other end of this passage.

No key was produced to unlock this door, rather a series of knocks were done in such a way that Raymond could not quite catch the cadence. When this was complete, the door swung inward and the group stepped through into a well-lit medium sized chamber.

The hoods were now pulled back and,, in the bright lights, the features of the guards were revealed. Though there were one or two with darker complexions, most had skin of a lighter hue than the pith. Their hair, cut short and pulled away from their faces, varied from a dark brown to almost blond. Aside from the slight differences in skin tone and variations in hair color, the similarities between the guardsmen were surprising. They were all roughly of the same height, with the same powerful build, as if conforming to a mold of what an Imperial Guardsman should be. All sported full beards, all trimmed to approximately the same length.

Now the robes were collected and the guardsmen could be seen in their daily attire. They wore matching shirts and breaches, the latter being the first such seen by Ray in a city, of the same blue as was worn by the soldiers on the road. Covering their torsos were leather tunics bearing an unusual crest worked into the chest. Light but sturdy boots adorned their feet.

Their weaponry varied from man to man, with most choosing a short sword attached by scabbard to their waist. Two wore long handled light axes in place of the swords and two others carried crossbows and bolts on their backs. All carried knives of varying lengths and edges, differing according to personal preferences. One guardsman wore a length of chain around his waist. Ray wondered at the purpose of this embellishment. As he pondered this, the six guardsmen formed up before a large and heavy chair that could be accurately described as a small throne. The six were all turned to face Hanshee and Ray and, as if by a prearranged signal, they all grasped the hilts of their weapons of choice and eyed Hanshee.

"Acolyte," it was Gyzull speaking again, "tell your master that you and he must now surrender your weapons."

Suddenly there was a palpable tension in the chamber, accentuated when Ray, taken aback by the request, hesitated to translate for Hanshee. Always perceptive, Hanshee had noted the formation and stances that the guardsmen assumed. He waited patiently for Ray to relay their message but already had a good idea of what it would entail. For some reason Ray continued to hesitate, perhaps perceiving the obvious readiness of the Imperial Guardsmen as a threat and not wanting Hanshee to disarm himself.

Another heartbeat passed without Ray uttering a word and the guardsmen could be seen tightening their grips on the hilts of their weapons. Then a gruff and animated voice cut the tension.

"They may keep whatever weapons they have, as long as they stay sheathed."

King Moton strode without pomp into the room and quickly ascended to the miniature throne. He was a man of medium height and stocky build, but his movements seemed nimble and quick. His head, swiveling freely on his thick neck, and his darting eyes, spoke of a man always in motion, who saw all and missed nothing.

"As you speak, your Highness," Gyzull said in a clipped voice and instantly the hands of the guardsmen were dropped to their sides, their once threatening demeanor completely changed as they now stood at attention for their Sovereign.

"Spread your men about Gyzull" King Moton said, "so that I may gaze upon the cause of such turmoil in the Kingdom of Pith."

No order was necessary as the guardsmen moved aside leaving an open space of about fifteen feet between his Majesty and his two guests.

The King had an expressive face and he put it through its paces as he examined Hanshee, weapons and all. He gave much less attention to his evaluation of Ray, even though he carried a weapon on his back; the sword of the assassin that he had killed. Apparently, they were well informed as to which of the two was at the center of the recent upheaval in their neighboring kingdom.

Having now taken the time to eye each of the strangers, King Moton again spoke up.

"I have been told that the acolyte speaks our language?" the King said as he looked directly at Ray.

"This is true M'lord," said Gyzull.

"Then let him speak up, man!" Moton bellowed, still locking an expectant gaze on Ray.

Raymond was again caught off guard and it took him a moment to realize that the King was awaiting his response. After conspicuously clearing his throat, Ray found his voice.

"I am able to speak you tongue, your Highness, and will faithfully interpret for my master all that is said here."

"Good," said the King, "for I now have some questions for your master. Have a care that your translation be as true as you promise. Much will be determined by the answers I receive this night."

Here the king paused, to let the weight of his words sink in so that Ray understood the gravity of the situation. Once satisfied, King Moton leaned forward in his chair and locked eyes with Hanshee even as he spoke to Ray.

"By what name are the two of you called? Moton asked.

Having now assumed a role with which he had become quite comfortable, Ray was quick to respond.

"My master is called Hanshee. I am known as Raymond."

"And from what lands do you come?" the King continued.

"My master comes from lands far to the west, beyond the mountains you refer to as the Blue Towers," Ray said. "I came to this place from lands far to the east, from a land called America." Raymond felt that a degree of truth was warranted here. Since the place Hanshee found him had been uninhabited, he did not think naming it would affect this situation for good or ill.

"Now, acolyte," King Moton again spoke, leaning even further from his seat and using his eyes to bear down on the continence of Hanshee, "ask your master this: 'are you Usaid risen'?"

Ray noted the weight King Moton's demeanor added to this question. Taking a deep breath, he turned to Hanshee and, after explaining the conversation that had already taken place, asked the question put forward by the King.

Hanshee listened to the question and then looked off into space as he considered what was being asked and how he should respond. After a moment his eyes sought those of the King.

"Usaid was a powerful man in the long-ago history of my people, the 'People of the Earth'," Hanshee began. "He was a High Priest of the ancient clan of Pith, when the Pith still held lands on the plains west of the Great Mountains. The 'waah' of Usaid was great! He was the first...and the only...to succeed in uniting the fiercely independent clans into a single mighty force. But as great as Usaid was, he was also greatly flawed. These flaws led to the downfall of his clan, a clan that was defeated in battle by their brethren and cast out from the ancient lands of the People of the Earth."

"As I have walked these lands east of the Great Mountains," Hanshee continued, "I have come to learn many things. Usaid once proclaimed himself ordained by The One Spirit as the 'father of a great nation'. I now know that those ancient words were not folly, for he can truly be named the father of your rival to the east, the nation of Pith."

"Usaid was a great and powerful High Priest, but Usaid died long, long ago. I am not Usaid."

Ray translated as Hanshee spoke; doing his best to confer all the reverence, the glory, the shame, and the truth that Hanshee's words contained. When Ray finished, King Moton leaned back in his chair, his eyes still locked with those of Hanshee.

"Acolyte!" the king barked. "Ask your master if he walks in the *spirit* of Usaid."

Ray did as he was requested and watched as Hanshee's expression turn to stone.

With fire blazing in his eyes Hanshee allowed his voice to rise so that all in the room could bear witness to his words.

"I am Hanshee of Clan Dula! I am Maiyochi!"

With his last word Hanshee struck his chest for emphasis.

Though none but Ray understood his words, all present recognized them as a rebuke of Usaid. When Ray spat out the same declaration in as close to the same forceful manner Hanshee had used, to include the striking of his chest, all their thoughts were confirmed.

Now the room was silent as the King continued to evaluate the man standing before him, not yet willing to release his gaze. After a time, the King was able let down his guard somewhat and broke the silence with one more question.

"Acolyte, ask your master if he knows of the upheaval he has caused in the eastern nations, simply with his presence."

Ray dutifully asked, and relayed Hanshee's response.

"Again, I say that I have learned many things in my travels among the eastern lands. I have learned that man has spread himself far beyond boundaries thought insurmountable by my people but, no matter how far man spreads, treachery and intrigue dog his steps. I have learned of fledgling cities such as Aggipoor, far to the southeast, and great kingdoms such as Cantor. I have learned that the 'clan of the jackal', once banished in disgrace, has risen to become a powerful nation. I have been offered favors for no reason that I can discern, only to find that the favors conceal the schemes of they who offered. And I have endured attempt after attempt on my life, again, for reasons that I cannot discern."

"Though I know not of what turmoil you speak, that I should be its cause is no longer a surprise to me."

The king took in all that Hanshee had to say with a knowing nod of his head. He had now received the answers he had sought and they had lain to rest many of his pressing concerns. He appeared more relaxed, and this was reflected in how he now addressed Ray.

"Raymond," the King said, "your master has answered each question that I posed, and I hear the ring of truth in his words. I will now attempt to enlighten your master as to the reason the two of you were summoned tonight."

Now King Moton IX recounted, in surprising detail, all that had happened to Hanshee and Ray since their capture in the forest of the southern Ursal Mountains. His explanation may have missed a point here or there, but it provided much insight into the Royal House of Pith and the Temple, insight that had eluded Ray and Hanshee even as they had been housed there as guests.

Ray dutifully explained everything to Hanshee, exactly as it was explained to him, and he watched the subtle changes in Hanshee's expression as he folded this new information into what he already knew, and what he thought he knew. Arguably, the most important information that the King shared was a succinct description of the Fourth Prophesy and the plans that Ammon IV had set into motion upon the revelation of Hanshee's arrival. This filled many gaps in their knowledge and made clearer the reasons behind the recent attempts on their lives.

King Moton had been studying both Ray and Hanshee as he revealed what he had come to learn over the last several months. He was now sure that much of what he said had been unknown to these two. The king was fascinated by the changes in expression, which told of how they were fitting this new information into their own theories about why they seemed so valuable to both the Temple of The One Spirit and the Throne of Pith, and why someone, or maybe several someone's, had made regular attempts on their lives.

It was a complicated explanation but the king did his best to condense it. When he had finished, Hanshee and Ray spoke animatedly between themselves in Hanshee's native tongue. After this short discussion Ray again turned to the king.

"Your Majesty," Raymond began, "it is not that my master doubts you, but he asks how you have come into so much information from a neighbor whom you name your enemy?"

King Moton actually chuckled upon hearing this question.

"Tell your master," he said, "that I have spies in every capital of every nation and every city-state east of the Blue Towers. I even have spies in the tribes that inhabit the northern wastes! And I am equally sure that every nation has at least one spy in my court."

"I was made aware of your master not long after you arrived at the Citadel. The turmoil you have caused has made for nights of entertaining reading and much pondering on what was to happen next. But the changes that your presence portends may tear apart this entire region…and your master's homeland as well."

"Now you know why King Ammon so desperately needs your presence in the Citadel, and why someone else wants you dead. I suspect that the group commissioned to pursue you contains elements of both. For that reason, I am willing to offer you sanctuary… a *temporary* sanctuary… within the walls of my palace."

After Raymond relayed the King's response and offer of sanctuary to Hanshee, they engaged in another animated conversation. Both agreed that King Moton had spoken truly, or what he believed to be true, but for them to accept it on its face would be folly. They needed time to digest all that they had learned; time to 'separate the wheat from the chaff'.

"My master agrees to your offer of temporary sanctuary," Ray told the King. "However, there is an additional concern. There is a child, a boy, who travels with us and now sleeps in our chambers at the Golden Lantern Inn."

The King turned to Gyzull.

"Captain," he said, "take however many men you deem necessary and bring the boy, and all their belongings, back to the Palace. Tell the innkeeper he may keep their livestock, and give him three pieces of gold for his trouble."

Captain Gyzull bowed his compliance. "It will be done, M'lord."

Turning back to Ray, King Moton asked, "Will that be sufficient to set your master at ease?"

Ray spoke quickly to Hanshee before assuring the monarch that his generosity was indeed sufficient.

CHAPTER 29

Lucius stood by the open window across from the door. From here he had an unencumbered view of the entire room.

As he leaned against the sill, he wondered on how he had arrived at this place at this moment. Blocking out the drama that surrounded him, he let his mind drift back to the time, right after dusk, when he first spied the Harbinger and his acolyte entering the city.

He had been standing just inside the doorway of a tavern, in a place chosen to give him a good view of the city gates while keeping him concealed. From this vantage point, he first thought he saw the three, two men and a boy, in line to be accosted by the city guard. Leaving his post and idling closer, Lucius had his suspicions confirmed. While the three were held up by the guards, he had quickly gone to fetch Fevor, the younger of the two brothers who had hired on with Captain Hendric as trackers. He found Fevor where he had left him: at a corner table of the same tavern, still nursing his first flagon of ale.

Other than his native wine, Fever had yet to develop a taste for spirits.

Lucius slid into the chair beside the young tracker and nonchalantly broke the news.

"They are here," he said in a matter-of-fact voice, causing Fevor to almost choke on his ale.

"Wha... (cough, cough)... you mean... (cough!)... them we follow? Here, in the city?" Fevor began to rise from his chair.

Lucius grabbed him by his arm and held him steady, half in and half out of his seat.

"You cannot rush outside now!" Lucius said. "They may see you!"

"Oh," Fevor said as he eased back into his seat, never considering that if they had ever seen him, it was from the opposite side of the ravine. From that distance, he was simply one of many, his features unrecognizable.

"This is what we will do," Lucius spoke quickly, before the tracker had time to think. "I will ease out the front door and follow them to wherever they plan to bed tonight. Give me some time before you slip out. Then get to your horse and ride for the others. If you ride hard, you may catch them before they make camp. You can then lead them in come morning. I will wait for you near the gate. Once we are all together, we can fall upon the murderous escapees and drag them in chains back to Stronghold. Only then can we claim our share of the chest of gold that awaits us!"

Lucius had thrown in the part about the gold to further confuse and convince the tracker. It had brought an instant smile to Fevor's face, as well as a nod of agreement. After wishing Fevor luck, Lucius slipped back out of the tavern and fell in behind the Harbinger, following from a safe distance.

The trio had moved slowly and deliberately through the strange city and Lucius had no trouble following them, nor in staying concealed from their eyes. He had been well trained, in stealth and other disciplines, by his father who had disappeared before he reached manhood. Lucius was cautious and careful, taking few risks and staying abreast of the Harbingers movements right up to the time when they chose this old inn to bed down.

Lucius waited patiently while they ate their meal. He had entered the inn while they tended their horses, and now sat at a dark corner table across the room. When they finished, he watched them steer the youth, staggering from exhaustion and overeating, up the stairs to the third floor. He could hear their movements on the creaking planks even from the ground floor, and so had a good idea about what room they took. Once that was determined, he left to put his real plan into motion.

While watching the gate, Lucius had also watched the people. Many were visitors to the city, here for what the citizenry referred to as 'the counting'. But this many people in one place is what certain others call *opportunity*. If one knew what to look for it was not too difficult to pick out those, like himself, who were watching and waiting. It was in this way that he identified the first of his recruits.

He had waited until the man made a move, in this case it was to rob a certain reveler who had paid his taxes and was using the excess to finance his pleasure. Bidding Fevor to stay put, Lucius had followed the man and caught him in the act. Rather than intervene, he let the man know that he had seen him and enjoyed how he had brutalized and robbed his victim. Lucius made it a point not to ask for a name and the thief did not offer one. Even so, an understanding was reached that a payment, much greater than that which the thief had just collected, could be had if he were available later in the night: and even more for him if he were to pull together a few more willing toughs.

That is how it had started.

Now certain of where the trio would lay their heads, Lucius left the inn to collect his man and any others he could provide. He found three of them in the same tavern where he had identified the first recruit. Although there was some initial reluctance, they followed him to the Golden Lantern. There Lucius explained what was required: two killings, plain and simple. As each man agreed, Lucius placed in his hand a gold coin, promising that more gold would be found among the belongings of the men they were about to kill. As the gold was distributed, Lucius watched their faces and saw their initial caution turn into greed.

They waited only an hour more before the stable hand left for the night and the innkeeper blew out the lights. Then, using the stealth and skills he had counted on so many times in the past, Lucius quietly snuck through a window and unlocked the door for his companions. Together, they subdued the old innkeeper and his wife, tying them down to their beds without making any undue sounds or revealing their faces. Then, as quietly as they could, they made their way up the stairs to the third floor and the second room on the right.

The way the floor boards creaked, they thought it most fortunate that no alarm was raised. When they made it to the door, and placed an ear against it, the sounds coming from within spoke only of sound sleep.

His three companions wanted to crash through the door and rush those inside, trusting they would be groggy and disoriented, thus easy targets for a quick kill. Lucius had other ideas.

Placing his shoulder against the door, he applied steady pressure until it separated from its frame. At this point Lucius paused, listening carefully for any noise that would alert them that a sleeper was now awake. Hearing none, he continued pressing. All four men were surprised when the ancient and heavy door swung open noiselessly on its newly oiled hinges.

With Lucius leading, the killers carefully made their way into the bedchamber. They had been inside the darkened inn for some time now and their vision had long since acclimated. They had no problem making out the three beds but, as they crept closer, they could also make out that only one of the three was in use.

Lucius crept closer to the figure sleeping heavily in the small bed, a cot really, and cursed under his breath.

"Damn," he whispered flatly. "It's the child."

"What?" one of his accomplices hissed in response.

"The child!" Lucius said in a slightly louder and irritated whisper. "It's the child that travels with the two men."

By this time the other three had gathered around him to see for themselves the source of his disappointment. One of them used an ember from the smoldering fire to light a lamp, which he held above the bed as they all examined the child that slept there.

Lucius's first recruited suddenly wheeled to face him.

"They're not here!" he said in a voice now unconcerned with detection. "Where is the gold?"

"It could still be in this bedchamber," one of the others said.

"Search this place," the first recruit said as he glared at Lucius.

Lucius appeared unconcerned under the watchful eye of the man. He had long experience manipulating these types and knew that the wrong reaction now would only serve to undercut his authority.

"Start with the beds," Lucius interjected as he turned and began taking one of the beds apart.

Soon both beds had been searched, as had the chests and the corners of the room. Every inch of the floor had been paced in an effort to reveal loose boards where a treasure could be hidden. Now the men had wandered back to encircle the child still sleeping in the cot.

"This child may know where the gold is," the first thug said, "or where the other two have gone."

Before Lucius could respond, the man clamped his large hand around Kellen's neck and snatched the boy to a standing position on the bed. The still exhausted boy was so sleepy that this violent motion did not bring him fully awake, and only the grip the thug maintained on his neck kept him from collapsing onto the blanket. That changed when the man brought a viscous forehand slap across the child's face. Instantly Kellen's eyes went wide with surprise. He had a moment to wonder what was happening, and to take in the scowling face of this tormenter, before the powerful hand was reversed in a backhand slap. The child's body went limp as the vice-like grip released his neck and he fell back to the bed, still too stunned to cry out.

Now the man reached down and flipped Kellen onto his stomach before taking hold of his left arm and twisting until it had attained an unnatural position behind his upper back. This brought a reaction and Kellen let out a screech that would have awoken the inn had any others been boarded there. As it was, the scream was heard only by those present, until it was muffled when the thug gripped the back of the child's head and shoved his face into the pillow. There it remained while Kellen thrashed violently, trying to relieve the pain in his arm as well as move his head to a position where he could catch his breath.

The thug now pushed his entire weight into the boy and spat a question.

"Where are your companions, boy? Tell me now!"

Lucius had been taken by surprise at the ferociousness of the attack on the child and his eyes darted around, eventually coming to rest on the faces of the other two men. They looked on with anticipation as the brute continued to question the boy and Lucius knew he would only forfeit any control he still had if he spoke up against this now.

The thug lifted Kellen from the pillow as he again questioned the boy, this time giving him enough room to respond.

While trying to catch his breath, the boy screamed, "I... (gasp!)...I don't know where... they are!

"Dammit boy, don't toy with me!" the thug said as he twisted the arm even higher. "You travel with two men! Where did they go? When will they return?"

Kellen responded with a blood curdling scream of pain and the vicious thug thrust his face back into the pillow.

"Where is the gold, boy?" he spat. "Where did they hide it?" The nameless thug emphasized the urgency of this last question by giving the child's arm and additional twist, and everyone in the room heard the 'crack' that followed.

Kellen was screaming and sobbing even as he struggled to breath. When his face was again lifted from the pillow, his words came out in a rush.

"Chezza has it!" the boy wailed. "Chezza has the gold!"

"I knew it," the thug shouted in triumph. "I knew he'd talk! Pull that chair closer!" he yelled to one of his comrades, who rushed to obey. When the chair was placed in the center of the room the thug, still holding the boy's damaged arm and hair, lifted Kellen from the bed and slammed him into the seat.

"Cut some strips from the blanket," the thug ordered, and the same accomplice rushed to comply. Once this was done the thug continued to hold Kellen down while his partner tied the boy to the chair by his wrists and ankles.

Squatting down in front of the chair, the thug spoke with a strange satisfaction in his voice.

"Listen, boy... you're going to answer whatever I ask you, right?"

He punctuated his question with another hard open hand blow to Kellen's face. The slap twisted Kellen's head to the side and, when it again came forward, a torrent of vomit launched from his open mouth. The stream of vomit struck the violent thug squatting before the chair in his chest and ran down the front of his shirt.

Startled, the thug looked down at his moist, smelly shirt. Then, with a snarl of anger, he erupted on the child, slapping him repeatedly with all of his strength.

Lucius wanted to step in and stop the torment of the boy. He had spun the lie about the travelers having gold to pique the interest of his recruits. He knew there was no gold in the room. But now the boy had complicated things. Under the torture administered by this... animal... he had begun babbling about gold that wasn't there!

Lucius recognized the name of Chezza, the old stable master that they found dead. The boy had worked for Chezza and must have known about the same chest of gold that the pursuit party had found and hidden. The boy would say anything at this point to stop the pain and once he had told the whole story, these three would be heading east on the Cantor Road.

Without conscious thought Lucius had retreated to a spot before the window across from the closed door. He knew he couldn't leave the room but he wanted to be as far away from the savagery as he could get. From this spot he looked about him and saw that the treatment of the boy had finally awoken something in one of the other recruits. He had mimicked Lucius, retreating to a place in front of the second window. The other recruit, he who had aided the thug by bringing the chair and cutting the blanket into strips, continued to look on in fascination and greed as the thug tormented the boy.

As for the nameless thug, there was a look in his eyes that Lucius had rarely seen, and then only in times of war. He inflicted pain on a child... A Child! ...with what could only be described as perverse delight.

Along with being a thief and a murderer, this man was also a sadist.

Lucius continued to hold himself at a distance as the man landed slap after slap on Kellen's swollen and bloody face. He had yet to ask another question about the gold, having lost himself in his anger and the stimulation he received from causing the boy pain. Finally, after one more powerful blow, the boy's face fell forward onto his chest. He had been slapped unconscious.

"He might even be dead," thought Lucius.

The thug was not satisfied.

"You won't pass out on me boy!" he hissed before turning toward the fireplace.

Striding over, he grasped the end of a poker that had been resting within the flames. The hot iron burned his hand, causing him to drop it and reach for a cloth to wrap around its end before again lifting the poker. Pulling it from the flames, he smiled in satisfaction as he noted that the tip bore a feint red glow.

As the thug turned back to the child, Lucius had finally seen enough. Stealthily his hand slid inside his tunic to the hilt of a blade he kept hidden there. Closing his grip tightly about it, he prepared to move forward and put an end to this madness.

Then Lucius paused.

Was that a creaking he had heard? He strained his hearing, consciously blocking out the footfalls of the thug as he approached the boy with the red-hot poker.

There it was again!

Lucius swiveled his eyes toward the door an instant before it exploded inward! As he continued to look, a man... *it must be a man...* in a hooded robe moved swiftly through the portal, crouching low, with a foot and a half of razor-sharp iron in each hand.

Hearing the door burst open, the sadistic thug, now consumed with bloodlust, turned to face the hooded death; the red-hot poker held high and an insane relish in his eyes. So focused was he on the oncoming attacker that he did not see the second hooded figure standing in the doorway, raising a crossbow.

The bolt caught the sadist just under his chin, tearing through tissue, muscle, and bone until the iron head protruded from the base of his skull. He was dead before his corpse hit the floor.

Lucius processed this as quickly as it unfolded.

He noted that the first hooded aggressor never broke stride as he moved past the falling corpse to engage the thug who had helped him subdue the child, even as the archer fixed his stare on Lucius while loading another bolt.

Lucius turned and threw himself out of the window, the bolt imbedding itself in the sill as his body cleared the opening. He tucked into a ball before striking the roof of the stable eight feet below. Gathering himself after the impact, he turned to his left and darted towards the nearest shadow, even as he heard another heavy impact onto the stable roof.

Once in the shadows he turned, just in time to see the third recruit. He had thrown himself from the other window and was now scurrying up the roof toward its peak. Just before he reached it Lucius saw a hooded head thrust through the window he himself had used.

The archer reached the window just in time to see the last recruit shimmy over the crest of the stable roof and out of sight. He then looked to his left, into the shadow where Lucius crouched motionless. Seeing nothing but darkness, he turned briefly to the right, scanning the roof in that direction. Still seeing nothing, the archer tuned back toward Lucius and spent long moments staring into the heart of the shadow.

Lucius did not dare take a breath.

Finally, the hooded head pulled back from the window. Lucius could now take a breath, but he remained motionless in the shadow. How long he crouched there, he did not know. He only moved when he heard the door to the room close and, after continuing to listen, heard no more movement within the inn.

Careful to remain noiseless himself, Lucius now moved toward the crest of the stable roof. Reaching the crest, he turned to look through the window and into the room he had so recently escaped. The chair, now empty, still stood in the center of the room. It looked that at least one of his dead partners was draped face up across a bed. There was nothing else for him to see.

In the blink of an eye Lucius disappeared behind the crest of the roof. Soon he had lowered himself down the stone wall, marking the edge of the property of the Golden Lantern, and disappeared into the night.

CHAPTER 30

Raymond was awakened by Hanshee well before dawn.

Their quarters were located in a part of the palace well away from prying eyes. When he regained full consciousness, he noted that Hanshee, as usual, had made a bed on the floor with blankets from the unused bed opposite his own. The next thing he noticed was the Imperial Guard standing stiffly just inside the door. Raymond cast a questioning glance at Hanshee and the look he received in return was all he needed to hurry and dress.

While dressing he asked the Guardsman why they were being awakened.

"There is something that your master must see," was the reply.

Now, with additional concerns brought about by the secrecy, Ray hurried to don a robe and he and Hanshee quickly followed the guard a short way down the corridor to a room similar to that which they shared.

In this room there was but one bed placed against the far wall. Stretched out upon it was the body of a child. As Ray moved closer his apprehension grew. He knew who he was looking at, but the bruised and battered face that greeted him from the bed was unrecognizable, even by gender.

Turning first to Hanshee, whose stoic demeanor revealed nothing, Ray faced the guard and asked him, "Is this Kellen, the boy who was sleeping at the inn?"

"When we arrived, he was being tortured," the guard said. "There were four of them. Two escaped."

Raymond could feel Hanshee's eyes on him and so quickly translated the words of the guard.

"Who were the dead," Hanshee asked Ray, who then repeated the question to the guard.

"The two dead were citizens of Cantor," Gyzull said as he strode into the room. "The boy has been severely beaten. The Kings Physician has examined him. He is not expected to live."

This pronouncement brought Raymond up short and he turned back to Kellen, looking carefully at his chest. The boy was covered by a blanket from his neck down but, if Raymond looked closely, he could see the slightest rise and fall of the cloth. Kellen was still breathing! He still lived!

Hanshee had noticed this before Ray and now asked what Gyzull had said. Mentally kicking himself for forgetting to translate for Hanshee, Ray quickly passed on the information about the attackers. Then he told Hanshee that, according to the Royal Physician, Kellen was not expected to live.

"I must have my pouch," Hanshee said, as he turned to hurry back to their quarters.

Taken by surprise, the guard who stood just inside the doorway moved forward to stop Hanshee with an open hand to his chest. Hanshee never broke stride as he gripped the meat of the palm, below the little finger, twisted, and bent the wrist upward. The wrist lock instantly bent the guard over, his straightened arm and painfully bent wrist now held away from his body at an awkward angle. While taking his next stride, Hanshee twisted the wrist further and pushed, sending the guard staggering across the room where he was halted only by crashing head first into the stone wall. Before he could collapse to the floor, Hanshee had vanished.

"My master is a skilled healer," Ray hurriedly explained to Gyzull. "He is simply going to retrieve his pouch, from which he can mix his potions."

Gyzull had been caught completely off guard by the brief but decisive conflict, and he looked questioningly at his man still lying on the floor. He then looked to the door through which Hanshee had passed and finally at Ray. In an obvious effort not to feel impotent, he said curtly, "This will be permitted."

Though the situation was grave, Ray still had to suppress a smile. Then, anticipating Hanshee's needs, he requested that hot and cold water and many clean cloths be brought to the room. Gyzull looked expectantly to the guardsman who was just now rising from the floor. The man nodded his understanding and, holding his wrist in the opposite hand, hurried from the room.

"He was very effective in our assault on the torturers this night," Gyzull said absently, as he pondered how easily the highly trained Imperial Guardsman and been 'discarded' by a wandering priest.

Hanshee soon returned with his pouch of herbs and medicines and, not long after, a different guardsman arrived with a pot of water just off the boil, accompanied by an urn filled with cool water. Behind him was the first guardsman who now had several clean cloths draped over the forearm above his injured wrist.

Without formality Hanshee went about his task, first examining the stricken child from head to toe before turning to his bag. As he worked, he spoke to Ray.

"The boy has been beaten about the head and face," Hanshee said. "He may be bleeding on the inside. I must slow down his heart to slow down the bleeding."

He was now measuring different powders and dried plants that he carried in his pouch. When he was sure his measurements were correct, he produced from his pouch the equivalent of a mortar and pestle, which he used to thoroughly blend the different ingredients before adding hot water. He then gently lifted Kellen's head and shoulders and used a bamboo tube to feed small amounts of the compound into his mouth, pausing when necessary to induce swallowing. Once he had fed the child the entire potion, he used the mortar and pestle again, this time to grind out ingredients for a salve made by adding a small amount of hot water and mixing the compound into a paste. After cleaning the child's many cuts and bruises, Hanshee generously applied the salve before bandaging the wounds.

Sometime during this process, the Royal Physician had made his way into the room. Word had been passed to him that the wandering priest fancied himself a healer and was working on the child that he himself had written off. Apparently, he had been present almost from the beginning and had followed closely everything that Hanshee had done. He found himself appreciative of the sound technique, and intrigued by the different compounds that were being mixed before his eyes.

At one point he sought to interrupt Hanshee with a pointed question only to be told by Gyzull, who was also intrigued, that the priest did not understand their tongue.

Since the king's physician appeared to be impressed, Ray offered him an olive branch, of sorts.

"Physician, if you wish I will ask my master to speak with you *after* he is done. If he agrees, I will faithfully translate your queries as well as his responses."

"That would be greatly appreciated," the physician said. "I have many questions concerning the compounds that he uses. Though he may not look the part, it appears your master may indeed be a healer. Let us hope that the lad recovers."

Hanshee continued to work on Kellen until well after sunrise. When he finally stepped away, the child's breathing was noticeably stronger. Bandages concealed his facial injuries so it would not be known if there was progress there until they were changed. Hanshee had also found the dislocated left shoulder, an injury of which the royal physician had been unaware. He had reset the joint and prepared a sling for when the child regained consciousness.

Afterward, though tired, Hanshee consented to speak with the physician. Many questions were answered and many techniques were shared. The two would have been sharing information late into the day had Ray not tired. After again checking Kellen, he and Hanshee sought, and finally found, what remained of their night's sleep.

CHAPTER 31

The sun was halfway down from its peak toward the horizon when Raymond finally arose from his bed. As usual, Hanshee was already up. He was sitting on a chair at a table, neither of which had been there when Ray had fallen asleep. Now there was a table and two chairs, and Hanshee smiled as he sat in a chair and ladled steaming hot stew from a stewpot into a bowl.

Ray swung his legs over the bed and sat up, thinking that this adjustment would somehow clear his head and cause the scene before him to change. He was right, for now that he was sitting Ray could see the tray of bread and cheeses that sat to one side of the stewpot. To its other side sat an urn and two goblets. There was also a second bowl.

Suddenly the aroma of the food struck Ray and he realized he was famished.

Rising from his bed he took two steps toward the table before Hanshee's raised hand brought him to a halt. The warrior motioned toward a corner of the room where there now stood a high table on which sat a large urn filled with cold water, a large bowl, and several dry cloths.

The message was clear. Hanshee had now *become* his mother.

With a smile and a shake of his head, Ray headed to the corner to see to his personal hygiene. Feeling clean and refreshed, he then joined Hanshee at the table.

"When did this get here," he asked, making a motion with his chin to encompass everything new in the room.

"Two guards arrived shortly before you awoke," Hanshee replied.

By now Ray had picked up the ladle and was stirring the stew in its pot. Suddenly, he froze and looked across the pot to catch Hanshee's eye.

Hanshee read his mind and, without hearing a question, spoke.

"The guard now outside our door insisted on tasting everything before leaving," Hanshee said. "He still stands."

Ray chuckled as he dipped the ladle into the pot and filled his bowl. Grabbing a spoon and a chunk of bread, he began to dig in. It was good stew... not as good as Ole Jed's, but worth getting out of bed for.

While they ate, Hanshee informed Ray that he had already gone to care for Kellen. The boy was awake. The wounds to his head and face were healing quickly though he could not yet talk. Hanshee had changed his bandages and given him another dose of medicine which he knew would sedate the boy for the next few hours. Before Kellen fell off, Hanshee took the time to secure his arm in the sling. It held the arm in place so that it would not be reinjured while healing.

Ray was impressed with Kellen's progress.

"You could teach the Kings physician a few things" he said to Hanshee. "And it looks like you're improving," he joked. "As I recall, you cared for me twice and both times I was unconscious for days before I had the strength to rise, or to even move."

"That was different," Hanshee said.

How so? Ray asked, stuffing a piece of bread dripping with gravy into his mouth.

"Both times, you were dead," said Hanshee matter-of-factly.

Raymond froze in mid chew, his mouth open and his eyes wide in astonishment.

****

Not long after they had finished their meal, a squad of Imperial Guardsmen approached the door. It seemed the king required another meeting.

The two were led to the same room where they met with the king the previous night, though now they entered by a different door. King Moton was already present and seated on his 'throne'. Gyzull and several other guardsmen were present. When they entered, the King greeted them warmly and had a guardsman prepare goblets of hot spiced wine for them. Then two chairs were brought forward and Raymond and Hanshee were seated. In a surprise move the King had his chair brought down so that he could sit at eye level with his guests. After sampling the wine, the King opened the discussion.

"I have been informed of the events of late last night," His Highness began. "It is unfortunate that my country could breed an animal capable of torturing a child. By his death we are all enriched."

Raymond raised his goblet in agreement before explaining to Hanshee what the King had said.

"And I have been told the child has you to thank for his life," the King continued, nodding toward Hanshee. Ray translated and Hanshee nodded to King Moton his acceptance of the compliment.

"Unfortunately, the events of last night, and this morning, have opened many eyes to this part of the palace. We are off limits here to the rest of the staff and nobility that freely wander my halls. You've probably noticed that there are no servants here. Imperial guardsmen have seen to all of your needs."

Both Raymond and Hanshee had noticed this, commenting on it while finishing their meal. Ray translated the king's words and then Moton IX continued.

"The nation of Pith is our enemy. I doubt that will ever change. Still, Cantor cannot allow itself to be seen harboring two personages as volatile as you; the Harbinger of the Fourth Prophesy and his acolyte. For the moment your presence here is known only to myself and a few select guards. Fewer still know who you are and your significance to our rivals to the east. With the injury to the boy came much unwelcomed attention. Now many eyes are focused on these quarters.

Here the king paused and let Ray translate, continuing to maintain his silence as the pair discussed and digested all that had been said up to now. When both sets of eyes returned to him, King Moton resumed.

"What I am saying, as you may have already guessed, is that your sanctuary here is to be more limited than I intended. Plans have been made for you to leave this night."

The king was correct in that Raymond and Hanshee were expecting a pronouncement of that nature. When Ray translated, Hanshee was quick with a question.

"My master asks what will happen to the child, Kellen?" Raymond asked of the king.

"I have spoken to my physician and he will take over the child's care," Moton said. "He is prepared to assume full credit for the miraculous recovery, provided your master will leave a portion of his wondrous potions and instructions on how to administer them."

Ray explained all to Hanshee, who nodded in agreement with the plan. Then Raymond asked a question of his own.

"Your Highness, your hospitality is greatly appreciated. But we wonder what will happen to the boy once he is healed? I ask this because we do not know his family. The boy once worked at a stable in Pith and has proven to be gifted with horses. He has a great affection for them. In truth, it was his tutelage that enabled us to ride from Stronghold to Cantor, as we had no prior experience on horseback."

King Moton took a moment to consider what Raymond was asking.

"Raymond," the King said, "if the boy is as gifted as you say, I am sure we can find work for him in my stables, once he is healed."

"That would make my master very happy, Your Highness," Ray smiled his appreciation before turning to inform Hanshee of this new boon offered by the king.

Upon hearing the king's offer, Hanshee stood and extended his hand to King Moton. Moton looked at the extended hand questioningly as every guardsman in the room took at least one step toward their sovereign. Ray was quick to intercede.

"It is a custom in my land, Your Highness," Ray said. "When two men can reach an accommodation, it is our custom to shake hands. My master offers you his hand in respect and friendship."

"I see," said the King, waving his guardsmen back as he stood. Then he mimicked Hanshee, who took the extended hand and began shaking it vigorously before releasing it. The King first examined his hand as if it were something new. Then he looked up at Hanshee, and both men laughed.

That wasn't as corny as I thought it would be, thought Ray.

CHAPTER 32

As promised, Lucius was waiting on horseback near the gate when the pursuit party arrived in the afternoon.

Hendric had called a halt well before they had to join the line of people wishing to enter the city. Now Lucius moved forward to meet with his current captain. Though both were military men, it was understood that they would dispense with salutes, formal greetings, and mention of rank whenever there were others about.

"Hail Hendric," Lucius said as he steered his horse beside the captain. He let his eyes move over the others in the party, surprised at the toll the road seemed to have taken on them.

"Good news, I am told?" said Hendric. "Fevor says that you have the location of our quarry and we have only to silently breach the city in order to take them alive."

"That was the case, M'lord, until the early morning hours." Lucius said, and watched as Hendric's eyes hardened in his face.

"What happened?"

"As I watched, a group of men attacked the inn where the Harbin... the escapees had bedded," Lucius said. "They were clothed in gray robes, with hoods to hide their faces. The way they moved marked them as military trained," he concluded.

"And what did they do?" Hendric asked impatiently. "Why would the military attack an inn?"

"I believe it was for the escapees," Lucius replied. "It was an out of the way inn, with no other boarders. Still two men were killed. I investigated after they left and the escapees were gone. The two dead men were not those we seek."

"So… you believe they took the escapees?" Hendric asked.

"I'm sure of it, M'lord," said Lucius. "But I have the situation in hand. I have asked about, and expect that soon someone will come to me with the information we need. I would ask that you and the men find a place to wait. Maybe let them partake of the tents," he gestured toward the tent city from which many inviting sounds and aromas still called, "as a reward and a distraction while I gather information. When I have what we need, I will inform you, and we can then plan our next move."

Hendric now looked at Lucius with undisguised doubt.

"What makes you think you can penetrate the secrets of this city," he asked, "a foreign city, the capital of the primary rival of Pith?"

"Did Commander Galin not tell you, M'lord?" Lucius replied. "This is what I do."

****

That evening Lucius again roamed the city of Gunjunson, just as he had done that morning, seeking the places he thought best to stake out for information. At each one he found men who could be bought. Taverns, brothels, and the local gathering places of the rough and lawless were his first choices. He also staked out the various gates of the city, sometimes slipping a coin to a nearby vagrant and promising more if a tally was kept of the comings and goings this night. It was in this way he learned about 'the Robes'.

It turned out there were several men who could attest to seeing them pass in the night. They were always on foot yet, somehow, they were upon you before you were aware, and gone before you could react. Stealth and speed were their stock in trade and those who had witnessed their passing likened them to spirits moving through the night. But, though several had seen them pass, it turned out that none could bare witness to seeing them do more.

Of course, there were stories; many that passed for truth. Most were about men and groups of men who were found dead, or had disappeared without the slightest clue as to where or why. They had been troublesome in one way or another, or secretive. Either way the story ended the same every time; The Robes were seen passing through the area, and somewhere close by tragedy struck. These vague rumors were the most that anyone would attest to. This meant that Lucius was in a very exclusive club: those who had actually seen the Robes in action… and lived. He was one of only two men that he knew of.

Piecing the stories together only served to confirm his earlier suspicion that these Robes were military men. They appeared to be highly trained, extremely secretive, and empowered to act with impunity. Since they worked within the city, Lucius deduced that they had to be attached in some way to the Palace. This made the Palace the most likely place for the Harbinger to be.

Lucius knew that this information would be useless to Hendric. There was no proof of it being true. It was all the speculation of one man, based on the fabulous tales of killers and thieves, grifters and ne'er do wells. Only by an assault on the Palace could his theory even be tested. That sounded too much like suicide, especially if the Robes really were based there.

This was the dilemma Lucius faced the following evening as he sat at a corner table in a decrepit inn near the South Gate of Gunjunson. It was here that he was approached by a man who looked, and smelled, like a common beggar.

Lucius was not in the mood to deal with the likes of this man and was prepared to raise his voice and his hand to chase him away. Then something about the man clicked in his mind and he remembered a vagrant who had staked out the South Gate and had promised to keep a count of any strange entrances or exits. On a hunch Lucius kicked out a chair for him.

"Thank you, milord," the vagrant said as he took the proffered seat.

Lucius instantly regretted his action as the pungent odor emanating from the vagrant made its way to his side of the table.

"Do you remember me, milord?" the vagrant spoke up. "You gave me a silver coin on last evening, and promised me more if I were to keep you a count."

"You were at the South Gate," Lucius said as proof that he remembered.

"That's right milord, the South gate. It is usually much busier than it is now. It's 'the counting', it is. There is so much commotion at the East Gate due to the counting, and everyone wants to see the tents and partake of the music and food and the whole of it. There is almost no one using the South Gate this time of year, and surely none as generous as you milord."

"Do you have something to tell me?" Lucius asked flatly, not having the patience to deal with what sounded like a demented mind.

"Oh, I do, milord, I do!" The vagrant now looked around as if concerned about someone listening. Even though no one was near, he still leaned over the table until he had covered half the distance to Lucius' face.

The smell intensified.

"As I was saying, milord, no one enters by the South Gate during the counting... but late last night someone left."

Lucius was only slightly interested.

"Who was it," he asked absently.

"Oh, it was more than one milord. It was..." the vagrant now went to his fingers and slowly worked his way from one hand to the other… "six!" He held up six fingers in triumph. "Six men on horseback wearing ghostly robes."

"What did you say?" Lucius interjected, now sitting upright, his full attention focused only on the smelly stranger.

"Six men… well… I could not tell if they were men. They wore robes with hoods and I could not see the faces underneath…"

"We will call them men," Lucius said quickly. "Tell me what else you saw."

"The six men…he, he…yesss… rode from the South Gate," the vagrant continued, "and started down the South Road, but then they turned off to the west and to the road that leads to the river.

"The Manchess River?" Lucius asked. "Are you sure?"

"Oh, yes, milord. I have been to the river often. Sometimes, when they are loading the barges, some grain will spill out. And sometimes the river men are more generous than those in the city," the vagrant said.

Now Lucius leaned in and attempted to lock eyes with the vagrant, who only glanced at his face before turning away.

"Look at me," Lucius commanded and the vagrant again met his eyes only for a moment, before letting his gaze drop, then wander around the nearly empty room.

Lucius was on his feet now, leaning over the table into the face of the vagrant. He smelled nothing now, so focused was he on pulling information from the man. Reaching out and grabbing him by the shoulders, Lucius was about to shake him violently. Then he remembered, and still holding him by the shoulders, spoke to him.

"Last evening, I promised you coin for good information. Do you remember that?" Lucius asked. "Do you want the coin… a *gold* coin?"

Now the man found the courage to meet Lucius' eyes. Now he was focused.

"Tell me," Lucius asked slowly, "about the river."

"The river men use the river," the vagrant said. "They load the barges that float down to Rayine. Then they take them apart, and horses pull them back up."

Lucius' mind was spinning. Maybe this information was important. It had the feel of something he needed to know. But there had to be more!

"What else can you tell me?" Lucius asked, almost shaking the man. "For the gold... what else can you tell me?"

Then the vagrant smiled.

"Now I remember!" he said. "Six rode to the river, but only four returned!"

EPILOGUE

As soon as the horses had clambered onto the barge, Raymond and Hanshee unpacked their gear, removed the saddles, and secured the reins. Then they settled down to get what sleep they could. They had been told that, considering the distance and stops along the way, the barge should sail for three nights, counting tonight, before it reached Wroughtmire, the capital of Rayine. They had been told that they would not see its spires until well after sunrise on the third day. Since they would not be leaving the barge for two days, and three nights, sleeping seemed the best way to pass the time. They would have to trust that the money and threats would keep the river men honest, and themselves safe.

It had seemed a well thought out plan.

They were still being pursued; the events at the Golden Lantern made that clear. No one believed that four men had randomly broken into an almost empty inn, tied up the inn keeper and his wife, stolen nothing, and tortured a child.

They were definitely still being pursued.

So it only made sense that the roads leading in and out of the city were being watched.

The South Gate Road ran south-southeast, intersecting the Merchant Way after about two leagues. Enough men could easily watch both roads, both gates, and also search the city. A limited group would have to use their numbers more wisely.

Men stationed at the crossroads of the South Road and Merchant Way could effectively cover a southern escape, making that the logical move.

But by taking the barge downriver, the crossroads would be bypassed, allowing Raymond and Hanshee to disembark at the Wroughtmire pier. From there they could continue south on the Merchant Way before turning west and following what remained of the Plateau Trail, the path of the ancient Pith, to the southern gap in the Blue Towers. By the time their pursuers discovered the ruse, if ever, Ray and Hanshee should have a lead almost impossible to overcome.

That was the plan King Moton had laid out to them and it appeared to be a good plan. The next several moons would most likely require all of their strength, all of their guile, and all of their heart just to survive. But tonight, and hopefully for the next two nights, they were secure.

That is why Raymond and Hanshee slept soundly as the barge drifted down the river, under a clear night sky filled with twinkling stars and a bright half-moon.

THE END OF BOOK III

ABOUT THE AUTHOR

Phillip L. Johnson was always a bookworm. A military brat, he did most of his growing up in Columbia, South Carolina, attending Columbia High School and graduating from The University of South Carolina School of Business.

He enjoys the outdoors and wildlife, hits the gym regularly, and relaxes with film noir, good music of any genre, good food, good drink, and the company of family and friends.

After a not entirely misspent youth, he settled into a career, married, raised a family, and eventually retired from the world of nine-to-five. Now, along with his many other interests, he has the time to indulge in what he considers the most extended fun he's ever had: writing stories of excitement and adventure.

CHECK OUT WHERE THE SERIES BEGAN!

AWAKENING
The Maiyochi Chronicles

"A REAL TALE OF HEROIC ADVENTURE..."
—JILL HAND, AUTHOR OF *WHITE OAKS*

PHILLIP L. JOHNSON

NOTE FROM PHILLIP L. JOHNSON

Word-of-mouth is crucial for any author to succeed. If you enjoyed *The Maiyochi Chronicles: The Road to Cantor*, please leave a review online—anywhere you are able. Even if it's just a sentence or two. It would make all the difference and would be very much appreciated.

Thanks!
Phillip L. Johnson

We hope you enjoyed reading this title from:

BLACK ROSE
writing™

www.blackrosewriting.com

Subscribe to our mailing list – *The Rosevine* – and receive **FREE** books, daily deals, and stay current with news about upcoming releases and our hottest authors.
Scan the QR code below to sign up.

Already a subscriber? Please accept a sincere thank you for being a fan of Black Rose Writing authors.

View other Black Rose Writing titles at www.blackrosewriting.com/books and use promo code **PRINT** to receive a **20% discount** when purchasing.